Awards for Cayla Kluver's debut book, *Legacy*

- Bronze medalist in the 2008 Moonbeam Children's Book Awards for Young Adult Fiction

- Finalist in two categories in the National Best Books Awards 2008, sponsored by *USA Book News*

- First-place winner (Reviewer's Choice) in the Reader Views Literary Awards 2008 for Young Adult Fiction

- Young Voices Foundation book of the month for January 2009

PRAISE FOR CAYLA KLUVER

"*Allegiance* is a beautiful continuance of the fantasy that began with *Legacy*."
—*San Francisco Book Review*

"Anyone who says teens can't write should meet 16-year-old Cayla Kluver.... Kluver's writing is impressive, fluid and focuses heavily on social customs and deep, complex characters; the skill of the writing and the resulting story make *Legacy* one book that any fantasy fan should pick up at the earliest opportunity."
—*Cleveland Literature Examiner*

"I recommend you get this book in your hands as soon as possible."
—*Teen Trend* magazine on *Legacy*

"Alera's sensitivity and willfulness will win readers over who will sympathize as her choices dwindle. A looming war, characters with intriguingly hidden pasts, and a sad endi̶n̶g̶ ̶s̶e̶t̶ ̶t̶h̶i̶n̶g̶s̶ ̶u̶p̶ nicely for a sequel."

"A thoroughly enter̶t̶a̶i̶n̶i̶n̶g̶ of promise,
fo̶

D1166422

"With likeable characters and v̶i̶v̶i̶d̶ ̶d̶e̶t̶ails, this is an engrossing story for young adults.... Kluver's grasp of language, dialogue and character development shows that she is as promising as her heroine."
—*Renaissance Magazine* on *Legacy*

Books by Cayla Kluver
from Harlequin TEEN

The Legacy Trilogy

(in reading order)

Legacy
Allegiance
Sacrifice

CAYLA KLUVER

SACRIFICE

HARLEQUIN®
entertain, enrich, inspire™

Recycling programs
for this product may
not exist in your area.

ISBN-13: 978-0-373-21044-2

SACRIFICE

www.HarlequinTEEN.com

Printed in U.S.A.

For Mom, as always: may you live long and prosper.

Every word on these pages is also dedicated to
my walking inspirations: Robyn, Stacey, Stacey^2, Jo, Melissa,
Carolyn, Renee and Tori. I'm so blessed to have you all in my life.

MAPS

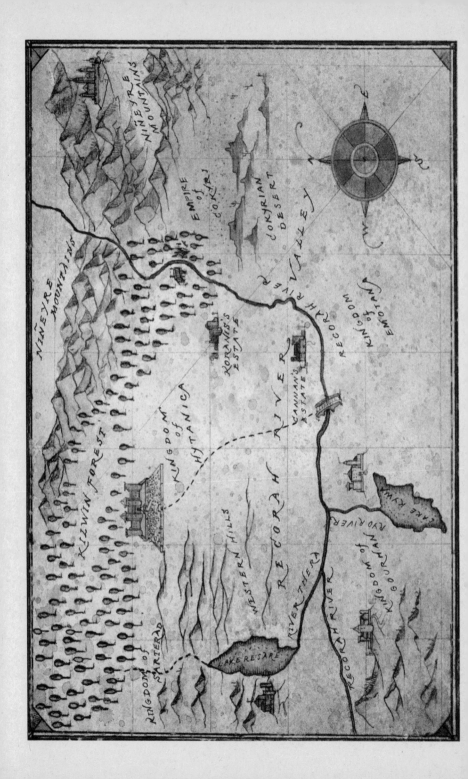

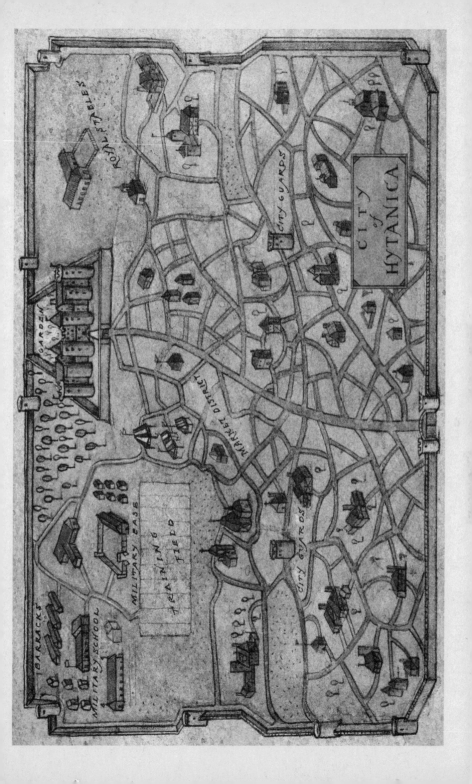

PROLOGUE

THE CAPTAIN OF THE GUARD INSTINCTIVELY glanced behind, scanning the palace's third-floor corridor for enemies who might be monitoring him. In truth, there was no reason for anyone to fear subversive activity from the Hytanicans, not this soon after the takeover. But the Cokyrians were long on suspicion and short on trust. Thus, Cannan took careful note of the Cokyrian soldier at the end of the hall, one of the many fouling his kingdom, before pushing open the sickroom door.

As expected, the room had only one occupant. Having stubbornly evaded death more times than could be counted, it was only fitting that London would be sitting up in bed, a mere day after he had roused, pulling on his leather jerkin. The deputy captain had been unconscious for two and a half weeks following the torture he'd endured at the hands of the Overlord; it had only been the High Priestess's strange healing abilities that had kept him from death. Cannan's stomach tightened at that notion—if it was the last thing he did, he would see them out of her debt.

London reached for his boots, wincing as he pulled one on, and the captain strode toward him, letting the door shut.

"Is that wise?" Cannan asked, concerned.

"I'm done being idle." London pulled on his other boot and fastened the buckles, then his indigo eyes found his captain. "I assume you are, as well."

Cannan nodded. Through the window on the far wall, he could see the remains of his homeland—buildings crumbled, the city wall in ruins, streets upturned, Cokyrian flags flying high to lay claim to its newest province. And that was just the outer layer. Beneath, there were families in shreds, bleeding where the deaths of loved ones had left wounds so deep they would eternally fester. Cannan, his son and the family his murdered brother had left behind were bleeding. Hytanica had nothing left to give and, therefore, nothing else to lose.

For months, their kingdom had been under siege, their people living in terror. They had been overrun by the Cokyrians; the Overlord, in his brutality and malevolence, had slaughtered their military leaders like cattle before meeting his own end. They had struggled against hopelessness, hiding in the mountains to help their people, and at present had come to this, living under the enemy's rule. Here, now—this was not the time for the fight to end. Now was when the fight would begin. This was the time to regain what had been lost.

Bringing his attention back to the present, the captain said, "I have thoughts."

Coming to his feet, London met his commanding officer's dark gaze. "I have a plan."

ALERA

CHAPTER 1

FACE-TO-FACE

I INHALED DEEPLY, HELD MY BREATH, THEN released it in a *whoosh,* repeating the process thrice over to quell my anxiety, with a predictable lack of success. Looking to the door at my left, which led into the corridor, I imagined my guests entering and realized for the thousandth time the danger, stupidity and yet necessity of what I was doing. I was creating an explosive situation and, like lightning striking dry grass, I didn't know if I would get sparks or a wildfire.

"The time?" I asked, throat dry.

"They aren't late, if that's what you mean."

London was leaning against the wall behind me, having been reassigned as my personal bodyguard, a duty he took most seriously. Although I had been named Grand Provost of the Hytanican Province by the High Priestess, London did not trust that the Cokyrians would respect that decision, and felt I was in greater need of protection than ever before.

After much thought, I'd chosen what had been the King's Drawing Room for this meeting, believing it to be the most neutral ground. Memories and pain lurked in almost every corner of the Palace of Hytanica—which had been redubbed the Bastion by the Cokyrians—but this room was nondescript and held no particular significance, unlike the Hall of Kings, where the thrones of our royalty had been removed along with the portraits of rulers past; unlike the strategy room where we had planned our last defenses; unlike the offices that had formerly been Steldor's as King, Cannan's as the Captain of the Guard and Galen's as Sergeant at Arms.

This would be the first time since the occupation that the most influential men of my kingdom would come face-to-face with Narian, the Commander of the Cokyrian Forces. These were the men who had delivered me to safety during the attack and who had proved their valor again and again while we'd grappled for leverage from our hiding place in the caves of the Niñeyre Mountains. And Narian was the man I loved, who had operated under duress, for the Overlord had held my sister's life in his hands; he had bargained with the warlord, done all he could to save our troops and our people, but still wounds were raw among my fellows. Cannan's beloved brother Baelic had been tortured to death by the Overlord merely for his relation to the captain. London and Halias, deputy captains in the Elite Guard and bodyguards to my sister and me, had suffered "more than they would ever say," by the warlord's own claim; and Destari, another faithful deputy captain, had been slain before London's eyes. I could not blame my friends for their bitterness, nor deny my own, though mine was not directed at Narian.

At long last, the door I had been watching opened and the Hytanican men entered: Cannan and Steldor, so alike with their formidable builds, dark eyes and nearly black hair, although Steldor's features were otherwise those of his beautiful mother; Galen, slightly lighter in coloring than his best friend, his generally more forgiving nature eradicated by the war; and Halias, whose twinkling blue eyes seemed harder and whose sandy hair was cut short, physical signs of the loss of his easygoing manner.

All bowed before me, to my chagrin referring to me as Queen Alera, before sharing nods with London that bespoke of the respect the men held for each other.

"You should not call me Queen," I reminded them, keeping my volume low, always conscious these days that someone might overhear. "I am Grand Provost now. I don't think we should flout the High Priestess on such a minor matter as titles."

"It is not a minor matter," Cannan briskly contradicted me. "You are a member of the royal family with a right to the throne—*our* Queen. The High Priestess will have no choice but to tolerate our insolence, for we will address you in no other way."

I bit my lip, exasperated but not knowing how to articulate it in light of their loyalty.

"Won't you sit, then?" I managed to say, gesturing toward several armchairs.

"No. We wouldn't want to offend our *delegate*."

It was Steldor who had spoken, his infamous temper sizzling as he referenced Narian, though it was not the same anger that I had come to know during our tumultuous marriage, which had ended when he'd sought an annulment from the church out of respect for my wishes. No, this anger was deeply rooted, born out of pain, oppression and the knowledge that the man he held at least partly responsible for Hytanica's destruction would join us at any moment.

Cannan glanced at his son, sympathy and an admonition in his gaze, then more civilly expressed the sentiment.

"We'll stand, at least until Narian arrives."

With no choice but to accept this decision, I continued to wait with them in awkward silence, my nervousness growing with each passing second, for I knew what Narian would say. I had called this meeting at his behest, both of us having recognized that the request needed to come from me if there were to be any chance of getting provincial rule off to a decent start.

It was not a sound but the stiffening of backs that told me Narian had arrived. I turned to face the door opposite the one the Hytanican men had used, the one that led into the Throne Room—or what had been the Throne Room—and saw him standing there. Like the others, he was several inches taller than me and well-muscled, though we all knew his power ranged beyond the physical. His deep blue eyes went briefly to me, then he appraised the former military men who, despite their stoicism, could not conceal their enmity, and quietly closed the door.

"Gentlemen," Narian said, the word a touch too well pronounced. "Grand Provost Alera."

The formality Narian maintained toward me in official capacities was essential. We had repaired our relationship, but the province was not ready to learn of it. And though the present company was knowledgeable of the affection between us, they were far from ready to accept it.

I nodded, although no one else issued a welcome. Narian, who was cool and controlled almost to a fault and had long ago given up hope of befriending these men, ignored their disrespect.

"I bring word from the High Priestess," he informed them in his subtle accent, stepping farther into the room, London also joining the group. "I suggest you seat yourselves. She has much to say."

When none of the men stirred, I moved to occupy an armchair, thinking they would follow my lead. They did not, and

I wondered if they would have seated themselves if the suggestion had not come from Narian.

Ignoring their effrontery once more, Narian proceeded to untie a leather cylinder from his belt, removing a scroll from within it. My heart pounded as though it alone were driving blood through everyone's veins. He unrolled the document and began to read.

"Upon this Twenty-second Day of May in the First Year of Cokyrian dominance over the Province of Hytanica, the following regulations are put into place, to be conveyed directly to Hytanica's upper tier—" Narian nodded to the men assembled, whom the proclamation indicated "—and posted throughout the city and countryside so that no citizen may avoid accountability by a plea of ignorance. The violation of any rule herein established will be punished severely, with bodily harm, imprisonment or execution.

"Regulation One. The possession of weapons of war by any Hytanican man, woman or child, other than the Grand Provost's bodyguard, is strictly prohibited. All such weapons must be surrendered immediately to Cokyrian forces. Permitted are farm implements, one ax per household for the chopping of wood, cutlery, tools for construction and daggers under six inches long by the blade."

Cannan motioned to Steldor and Galen, both of whom met his gaze in a silent challenge before simultaneously reaching into their right boot shafts and withdrawing daggers that contravened this law. Each flipped his knife around to catch the blade before extending it to Narian, who confiscated the weapons with a cold stare they gladly returned. After laying the daggers on the table beside the chair in which I sat, Narian again unfurled the parchment.

"Regulation Two. Cokyri will maintain complete control over access in and out of the city. Cokyrian soldiers will man the gate and may subject any passers to search and seizure with or without cause.

"Three. The borders of the Hytanican Province will be guarded by Cokyrian soldiers during and after the construction of the Province Wall. No citizen may cross the border without explicit permission from the Commander of the Cokyrian Forces within the province, such permission to be evidenced by the seal of the High Priestess."

I looked at the ring on Narian's right hand, knowing that London would also recognize it as the Overlord's, for he had stolen it while a prisoner and had worn it for seventeen years. The twin to the ring resided on the hand of the High Priestess; thus Narian had the ability to provide her seal.

"Four. The Hytanican Province will maintain no military force of its own. The former military base will belong exclusively to Cokyrian soldiers, who alone will be the peacekeeping force within the city and throughout the countryside. The military school will continue in a strictly academic capacity, for the intellectual betterment of the province's youth, both male and female.

"Five. Foreign trade will recommence following the completion of the Province Wall in order to accelerate the recovery of the province's economy. However, all tradesmen will be searched and those carrying impermissible items will be turned away.

"Six. Hunting parties will register with the Cokyrian Weaponry Officer in order to receive permission and appropriate arms. At the conclusion of the hunt, all weapons shall be returned to Cokyrian control."

My eyes roved over the men, knowing how offended they had to be by these constraints, but I could detect no reaction beyond the seething resentment of the younger pair. Cannan's gaze did not falter, and his face remained impassive. Halias, relying on habit to rein in his sentiments, stood at attention with his hands clasped behind his back, staring somewhere past his captain, Narian not even in his line of sight. But London's aspect perplexed me, for he looked resigned, yet I had never known him to bow to authority.

"Seven. Harvested crops will be divided with twenty percent delivered to Cokyri and eighty percent remaining within the province. Special Cokyrian envoys will be in charge of coordinating the planting and farming effort.

"And Eight. A tax will be imposed on trade and businesses in the amount of ten percent of earnings, in accordance with rules to be established by the Cokyrian tax collector."

The ensuing silence was thick, the Hytanicans no doubt having been ordered by the captain not to respond. The High Priestess might have declared that Hytanica no longer had a military, but these men still had a chain of command.

"The people revere you and will follow your example," Narian concluded, rolling up the parchment and looking at each man in turn. "If you abide by these laws, this province can prosper. The Hytanican people can know peace."

"We can live comfortable half lives, you mean," Steldor retorted. He had changed so much since his brush with death, but when angered, he still had difficulty controlling his tongue.

"For now, comfort is more than you have the right to expect. You are a conquered people, and the High Priestess is being exceptionally generous."

Galen's hand fell on his friend's shoulder. Neither he nor Steldor had spared a glance for me throughout this meeting, perhaps because they knew where my convictions lay. I had been first among my people to see these regulations, and though they intimidated me, it was my responsibility to encourage cooperation between Hytanica and Cokyri. I had negotiated with the Overlord to allow my people to exit our conquered homeland, preferring a nomadic life to one of tyranny, and later had signed a treaty with the High Priestess to permit our return. But we were now a Cokyrian province, and that status brought restrictions. With time, limitations would be lessened and we would be granted more privileges. I had to make sure we survived this difficult stage to find a better one, for everyone's sake.

I came to my feet, intending to say something, but London interceded.

"Narian's right. Were the Overlord alive and in command, we would likely be enslaved."

I could have sworn gratitude graced Narian's countenance, for London was reminding the others that the eighteen-year-old had paved the way to the Overlord's destruction when he had challenged his master in the clearing to protect me. It had been the High Priestess, however, who had delivered the final blow, saving Narian's life by slitting her brother's throat when she had realized that his evil exceeded her control. The other men grudgingly accepted London's point and Narian moved on with the meeting.

"There is one more issue to address—the positions you men will hold in this new Hytanica. The High Priestess feels it would be unwise to leave you to your own devices."

This was spoken as a warning, and Narian let the words hang in the air for a moment before he went on.

"Each of you is hereby given certain duties. London has already taken up the role of Alera's bodyguard and will remain in that post. Cannan, you will operate from your old office in an advisory capacity to Alera while she learns to govern the province. As for the rest of you, the city is in dire need of repairs, and you will be assigned to that task, working with the Cokyrians who are managing the effort. Steldor, you are assigned to the southern section of the city, Galen to the west and Halias to the east. The north will remain under my jurisdiction."

I could sense indignation flaring within Steldor—his pride was enormous, while Galen was less easily offended; and Cannan, Halias and London had the presence of mind and the years under their belts to take what they were handed. None of them, however, was pleased with the current state of affairs, and I feared how long their subdued attitudes would last.

"Why not simply execute us?" Steldor asked, his jaw tight, no doubt thinking of his uncle Baelic's fate after Hytanica had surrendered.

"To appease the public," Narian snapped.

"Very well," Cannan said, holding up a hand to stifle his son. "I assume that's all?"

His words sounded like a dismissal rather than a question, a harsh reminder that there was no enjoyment to be found for him or his men in Narian's company. There was a tense pause, and I could feel an immense struggle for power beneath the surface.

"Yes. You are free to go."

Cannan looked to Steldor, Galen and Halias, tipping his head toward the exit at his back to indicate that they should depart. The three obeyed without a word, and when the door had closed, he once more addressed Narian.

"The High Priestess does not misjudge us. We could be dangerous to her." The captain scrutinized the young commander, and there was something strange in his expression, something hidden in his thoughts that I could not deduce. "But I think you know I have lost enough and have no desire to lose my son, as well. I will restrain Steldor and the others. They will cause you no strife."

Narian nodded his appreciation, and Cannan's gaze went

fleetingly to London, who had retaken his original position against the wall. After a bow to me, which was inappropriate if it indicated I was still Queen and a slight to Narian if it was deference to a leader, for he offered him no such show of respect, he disappeared into the corridor after his men.

"If you'll excuse me," Narian said to me, holding up the scroll. "I must see to the immediate distribution of these rules."

"Of course."

He picked up the daggers Steldor and Galen had relinquished and departed the way he had come, through the door into what was now known as the Hearing Hall, leaving me where I had started—alone with London in the Drawing Room.

"You certainly handled that meeting well," the former Elite Guard remarked with a cynical lift to one eyebrow.

"And what is that supposed to mean?" I bristled, not in the mood for subtlety or his teasing.

"Only that you did an excellent job of assembling everyone," he replied, ignoring my tone. "I'm just wondering if that's what we can look forward to from the Grand Provost in the future."

"And what would you want from the Grand Provost in the future?"

He laughed and pushed away from the wall.

"I know you, Alera, perhaps better than anyone. I've seen your courage, your resourcefulness. I know the leader you can become, the leader I believe you *want* to become. But what you need to understand is that you have to take hold of the reins right from the beginning. If you don't, by the time you feel ready, the reins will have slipped through your fingers and you'll be led by another."

"You mean by Narian."

He shrugged and ran a hand through his unruly silver hair.

"Was there nothing in the regulations that struck you as overly severe? You must have seen them before this meeting. Was there nothing you might have wanted to alter?"

I stared at him, finally understanding his point.

"Take hold of the reins," he repeated, opening the door into the Hearing Hall so that I could cross its expanse to reach my office, formerly the King's study. As I walked past him, he added with his signature smirk, "In Cokyri, women can wear the breeches."

When evening came, I returned to my rooms, which had for generations been the quarters of the King and Queen, dismissing London before I entered. Hytanica no longer had a King and Queen, but the High Priestess had permitted me to occupy this part of the second floor out of respect for tradition. Although the furnishings had survived the Cokyrian occupation with little damage, I spent most of my time in my bedroom, for the parlor and the bedroom that had been Steldor's felt haunted. In truth, they were haunted by memories, both from my childhood and my marriage. Since I'd taken up residence, I had not even entered the room that had been the King's, and it felt to me that the closed door led to nothing.

Every so often, I would force myself to sit in the parlor, not retreating so hastily to sleep. I would try to read, but the worries and responsibilities that cluttered my mind interfered with my concentration. Tonight I had prepared for bed, donning a nightgown and robe, then had gone to sit upon the leather sofa, trying my best to feel comfortable and at home in a palace overrun with Cokyrian soldiers.

It wasn't long before Kitten, the pet Steldor had given me after my sister had been abducted, jumped up beside me. The black-and-gray tabby cat settled in contentedly, oblivious to the issues that troubled me. I stroked his back, thinking about Miranna, who had been held in Cokyri for months, to be rescued eventually by London. Two weeks ago, she had married Temerson, the boy she had been courting prior to the abduction, but she was still far from her effervescent former self. I saw her frequently, for she and Temerson resided in the palace on the third floor, in the same wing as my parents. But Temerson would before long purchase a house with the money he had inherited from his father, one of the officers slain by the Overlord. While it was not customary for royalty to leave the palace, the Palace of Hytanica as we had known it no longer existed. Moving out of the Bastion would be good for Miranna—we lived too close to the enemy here, too close to remembrance and fear.

Hearing a noise from my bedroom, I glanced toward its open door, but not in alarm, for it was an indication that Narian had come. I watched him slip through the window, his lack of stealth due to no form of clumsiness—the first time he had snuck into my quarters was when I had been Crown Princess, and he had given me a dreadful scare; he was simply making certain not to do it again. It was strange to have relapsed into the pattern of that long-ago clandestine relationship, but precautions were necessary. It was too soon for my people or the Cokyrians to learn of our connection. Although Narian and I trusted each other, the High Priestess's suspicions about us had weakened her trust in him, and my people saw him as the enemy. If not for the fact that he was ideally suited to the position he held, for he understood both cultures, I doubted she would have left him in charge. It was ironic that we had for months hidden our relationship from my father and now were keeping secrets from the woman who had raised Narian.

I stood and went to meet him, his face lit only by the moonlight filtering between the drapes he had left parted.

"I've missed you," he said softly, for he did not work out

of the Bastion, and our separate duties did not often bring us together, nor did they allow us much privacy.

He stepped closer to me, bringing his lips to mine, and I ran my fingers through his thick blond hair. One of his hands slid behind my neck, the other trailing down my back to rest on my hips, and a thrill tickled my spine. When our lips reluctantly parted, we rested our foreheads together, our breathing falling into the same rhythm.

After a moment of comfortable silence, I asked, "Do you think they took it well? Cannan and the others, I mean."

I wanted desperately to believe no more lives would be lost. I prayed the men would recognize that this was the way to safeguard our people.

"They took it as well as can be expected," he answered with a shrug, then his tone grew puzzled. "London, especially."

I studied his face, noting the slight crease in his brow. "What is it?"

"Nothing," he responded, removing his weapons belt and laying it on the table next to the bed before reclining on the mattress against a stack of pillows.

I lay down beside him, nestling against his shoulder, his arm around me. Although our positions were terribly improper by Hytanican standards, the faith I had in Narian made it all seem innocuous. He would never take advantage of me, nor pressure me for anything I was not ready to give. I waited, knowing he would tell me what was bothering him in his own time.

"It's just that London's reputation belies a willingness to admit defeat, and I find his complaisance…disconcerting."

"Well, we've already *been* defeated," I pointed out. "He can't deny it or fight it. And he may well see the same opportunity to direct Hytanica's future that we do. The High Priestess did not have to name me Grand Provost, after all.

Had she put one of her shield maidens in this position, our straits would be much worse."

Narian continued to think, his posture unchanged. He'd always had misgivings when it came to London; my bodyguard had been the one to uncover the legend that had foretold of Narian's conquest of Hytanica and had also been the one to discover our relationship and endeavor to keep us apart. And it had been London who had improved our negotiating position with the Overlord toward the end of the war, for he had developed and executed the plan to abduct the High Priestess. There were thus plenty of reasons to be apprehensive when it came to the former deputy captain. Remembering the most significant outcome of my tendency to let my mind overrule my heart—London's dismissal from the military—I forced myself to banish what doubts I might have harbored about my bodyguard.

Narian rolled onto his side to gaze down at me, his intense blue eyes finding mine of dark brown. He kissed me deeply, his body coming into light contact with mine, and all the feelings I had fought against with Steldor came achingly to the surface. With a sigh that revealed his own yearning, he shifted away, propping his head up with his hand.

"I've been thinking about changing my center of operations to the Bastion for some time now," he confessed. "The High Priestess's rules are an attempt to move the province forward, despite their restrictiveness. Setting up here would help the Hytanican people to see me as a leader and not just a conqueror."

"You would live here?" I asked, my eyes wide, knowing how much easier that would make it for us to spend time together. At the moment, Narian worked out of the building in the city that had belonged to the Master at Arms, who had

been in charge of the City Guard, and it was difficult for him
to break away to see me.

"Perhaps on the third floor, or in your old quarters in the
other wing here on the second."

"How soon?"

"Without delay." He reached out to touch my cheek with
the backs of his fingers. I took his hand and held it there, warm
against my face. "The High Priestess won't question it. She
has impressed upon me the need to keep careful watch over
Cannan and London, in particular."

"Is that why you don't trust them?" I asked, assuming a position similar to his. "Because she doesn't?"

"It would be unreasonable to trust them at this point."

I took umbrage at his words, for it sounded like he still
viewed the men as his enemies. All I wanted was for such per-
ceptions, such preconceived notions of people-versus-people,
man-versus-man, to be gone, along with the prospect of further warfare.

"I thought it was your goal, like mine, to bring these countries together," I accused, letting his hand drop to the mattress between us.

He knew I was annoyed; unlike him, I lacked the ability,
and the need, to close off my emotions. I could already feel
him pulling back behind that detached facade.

"Alera, that *is* my goal. But we have to be realistic. For
some, our ideal is the worst end imaginable. And the nature
of these men pushes them in that direction. If it helps, I found
Cannan to be genuine. That doesn't mean we can let our guard
down, but I would trust him sooner than condemn him."

I couldn't even bring myself to resent that he was right. I
hated the idea that my aspirations might be different from the
people alongside whom I had lived and worked, the people
who had saved my life and whose lives I had saved. I didn't

want to lose that camaraderie. I couldn't, *wouldn't*. There were ways to fix things, to allay Narian's concerns. I would just have to make certain that none of those concerns came to fruition.

Our conversation drifted off, and it wasn't long before I extinguished the lantern. We kissed once more, then I curled up beside him, my back to his chest, his arm encircling my waist. In Steldor's company, especially during our marriage, I had been tense and wary, but with Narian, I was at such ease that I fell into sleep more readily than when I lay alone. He was strength and safety; fire and desire; comfort and happiness. In short, he was the man I loved.

CHAPTER 2

THE WEIGHT
OF SORROW

"I DON'T CARE!" I STORMED, NOT MINDING WHO heard, almost hoping everyone—my siblings, the servants, the entire kingdom—might.

Across the parlor from me, my mother put the heel of her palm to her brow. With the stress I was putting on her, she looked almost fevered, her skin pale and glistening, her eyes marked by circles that could be attributed to consecutive nights with little sleep. I imagined it was difficult enough to rest in a cold and empty bed, and the nightmares my younger brother had been having ever since Papa's death did nothing to ease matters.

"A lady does not shout, Shaselle!" Mother admonished, ironically raising her volume to match mine. "Cannan will be here in a few hours—it's time you made yourself presentable."

As she said this, a strand of her light brown hair came free of its bun, joining the other frazzled pieces that surrounded her face. Normally she was so tidy, and it was disconcerting to see her this way, in a simple skirt and blouse that were clean only because the maid was attentive. Sympathy swelled inside me, combating my anger, but as usual the latter won out.

"No," I muttered, my feet shoulder width apart, my hands on my hips. "I said I don't care. I don't care what's proper, what's respectable, what's *feminine*. I won't sit here in a pretty gown while you and Uncle decide into whose hands to thrust me."

My mother sat wearily on the sofa, but her voice was still forceful when she spoke, her critical eyes boring into me.

"I've had all I can take. You are a young woman and need someone to support you now that your father is dead. It's time to dispense with these inappropriate activities, or no decent man will desire you as a wife. No more horseback riding, no more playing about, no more *breeches*." She gestured to my current attire. "Your childhood is over, Shaselle. This is life—*accept it*."

I cast about the room, desperation and hatred clawing at me—hatred of her, of this place and its painful memories, of the *life* she was advocating. She didn't understand. She never had. Papa's decision to let me ride and dress like a boy from time to time was the only subject on which Mother had ever challenged him during their marriage, and they had argued about it more times than I could recall.

"Everything that he was to me you would take away." I heard the choke in my voice before I felt the hot tears running down my cheeks. "Everything he wanted for me means *nothing* to you!"

"Please listen," she said more sympathetically, coming to her feet and smoothing the skirt that did not need smoothing. "As painful as this is for you to hear, your father *spoiled* you. He indulged you, promising me always that he would find you a husband who would indulge you as he did. But Baelic will never be able to make good on that promise. I'm the one who is left to cope with the task of finding a man of stature to marry you."

She took a breath to try to banish the quaver from her voice, for her own pain at her husband's death was not far beneath the surface. "It's too late for blame, so the least you can do for me is to go and *put on a dress*."

Trying in vain to control my tears, I tipped my head forward, hiding behind a curtain of hair.

"No," I repeated. "I don't want any of this."

"Shaselle."

I knew without looking that she was coming closer, reaching out to comfort me. I sniffed and wiped my shirtsleeve across my eyes, turning my back to her before she could do so, for I did not want to succumb to her touch. Embarrassed by my emotional display, I rushed from the parlor to the entryway, rammed out the front door, then sprinted when I hit the open air, not wanting her to follow. The path beckoned, and the street beyond.

Everywhere was evidence of the battles our men had fought, along with evidence of the Cokyrian victory—at intervals along the rubble-lined street enemy flags fluttered in the gentle spring breeze, and enemy soldiers patrolled the neighborhoods. Even in this wealthy residential area, which lay to the west of the main thoroughfare, crumbled pieces of stone from homes, splintered wooden beams, remains of furniture and other household items, and abandoned children's toys were relegated to the ditches by the reconstruction crews, and ash from Cokyrian fires soaked multiple times with rain made a vile-smelling, mudlike substance that slickened the walk. We were more fortunate than most, for my family's home had sustained little damage in comparison to the other houses in the area and had been among the first repaired, at Galen's insistence, for he had been assigned to the reconstruction work in this section of the city.

In truth, the crews were making good progress. The streets

became visibly cleaner by the day, and dwellings that had slouched under the force of Cokyri's domination gradually came upright with the hard work of Hytanican and enemy folk alike. I could hear workers calling to one another as they hauled materials up to second floors using ladder-and-pulley systems, the sound competing with those of straining horses, the thud of hammers and the grating of stone against stone.

Where the problem lay was in looting—possessions and supplies would be stolen from homes and businesses by those who yet had no shelter. While the Cokyrian peacekeeping force did all they could to keep order, it was heartrending to think that our fellow Hytanicans might pose more of a threat to us than the soldiers who had invaded our homeland. Desperation could overtake good people. People who didn't deserve what fate had handed them.

I stopped at the end of the street, realizing that to go farther might be unsafe. There were pockets of the city, including my family's neighborhood, that were, all things considered, calm—as peaceful as Hytanica got these days. Other places, in particular the wide thoroughfare that ran north and south, cutting the city in half, were rife with small rebellions—rebellions that Cokyrian soldiers brutally subdued.

By this time, the afternoon sun had dried my tears, although the hole inside of me seemed to have grown. No matter what I did, that horrible, sickening emptiness in my gut expanded each moment I lived without my father. I tried to shut my mind, not wanting to think of it, of the manner of his death at the Overlord's hands, a death I had been forced to witness, the cruelty of which had stranded me.

Leaning against the side of a building adjacent to the roadway, I sank down, not wanting to go home. Here, where there was noise and activity, it was easy to pretend things were different. My father's ghost didn't wander these streets like it did the halls of our home. But I would soon have to return and comply with my mother's wishes, for it would not do to rile Cannan, my father's brother.

I had always known I would marry, and had not been resistant to or afraid of the prospect, but that had been when Papa was alive to make sure my husband would be a kind, tolerant, high-spirited man who would not deny me that which I truly loved—riding horses. Now, with the choice of suitors narrowed by war casualties and the more traditional mindset of my mother, the prospect of wifehood was terrifying, along with the knowledge that in embracing it, I would have to let go of the best way I knew to remember my father. At that, the anger boiled back, and with it, inexplicably, a fresh surge of tears.

A small amount of ash-mud splattered toward me as a horse-drawn wagon went by, leaving dribbles on my clothing, and I came to my feet, sending some dirt flying after it with the toe of my boot before starting home. When our manor house, with its second-story gallery that served as the reception room where my father had loved to host parties, came into view, I veered toward the back of the property. No one would see me, and I needed additional time to compose myself. Without thought, I walked toward the barn where I had spent hours—days cumulatively—with Papa, learning about horses and tack and the proper care for both.

The moment I stepped inside the sturdy stone structure, I was met with a devastating and powerful rush of nostalgia. The smell of leather and hay was the smell of my childhood, of everything I had lost. It was all so *wrong,* the idea that Papa would never again step out of that tack room carrying his saddle, getting ready to take me and my brother out riding, the ridiculous concept that *he* would never ride again.

I walked up to the first stall on the left, which housed a

dark bay mare named Briar, the horse my father had always called his baby. Every time he approached her, she had perked up her ears and rumbled a greeting deep in her chest. I put my hands atop the door, and she came close to let me stroke her face, but made no sound. Even she knew the world was amiss. I glanced down the row of stalls, which housed my petite sorrel mare and my brother's gelding, as well as Alcander, our best beginner horse, the one Queen Alera had occasionally ridden, and heavily exhaled. Would I ever ride again?

At the touch of a hand upon my back, I jumped, not having heard anyone come in. At first, the familiar features, the hair so dark it could have been black, the deep brown eyes and the muscular build of a military man sent a jolt through my being. Then I realized it was my uncle standing beside me and not the brother he resembled so distinctly.

It was impossible to disguise my condition—I was an exhausted, puffy-eyed, miserable mess, and I hated to have the captain see me like this. I blubbered some nonsense about needing to leave and tried to step past him, but he caught my elbow and pulled me into strong arms that felt so painfully similar to my father's. Too tired and weak to resist him, I crumpled against his chest, surprised to find after a while that I was gripping his shirt like a child.

He held me for a long time, until I eased myself away, my eyes on the wooden floor. I didn't want to look at him, mortified by the state in which he had found me, and having no idea what he must be thinking. It was to be expected, after all, that when the head of the family came to discuss marriage plans for his niece, the young woman in question would be polite enough to show up.

"Don't be ashamed, Shaselle," Cannan said, with more understanding than I deserved. "This family has endured a tragedy."

His straightforward approach had unnerved me at times over the years, particularly when I'd gotten into trouble alongside Steldor and Galen, but this time I appreciated it immeasurably. He wasn't angry with me.

"You know your mother is frantic," he resumed.

It wasn't a question, just a reminder, for he was aware that I had a functioning brain. Of course my mother was worried—who wouldn't be with our kingdom in disarray? Nonetheless, due to some horrid fault in my conscience, I didn't feel guilty.

"Uncle, please," I implored, raising my hazel eyes to his face. "Can all of this not wait?"

"All of what?"

"The marriage," I said more meekly. "It's too soon. I can't… I'm not ready. You understand, don't you?"

He was nodding. That was good. He looked around the barn for a moment as though he were remembering his younger brother, then his eyes came to rest once more on me, a decision lying in their depths.

"Shaselle, your mother is coping the best way she knows how—by refusing to let herself dwell on the past. She's moving on. To you it may feel premature, but it's what she needs to do."

"I know," I murmured, putting a hand over my mouth in disbelief of the number of times sadness could overwhelm me in a single day. And my mother would be feeling the same, having lost her husband of twenty years. It didn't seem fair, how tremendous sorrow was—no one stood a chance against its weight.

"But are my needs so unimportant?" I finally asked, in spite of the remorse that had at last wormed its way into my gut.

"No, and I will give you time, as much as I can. But your mother is being practical. Dahnath is already betrothed, and at eighteen, it's time for you to find a husband, as well. This is how things would have progressed were your father alive."

Despite the reasonableness of his words, I shook my head. "You don't understand. Papa was going to find me a husband who would appreciate me, *all* of me."

"I will do everything within my means to see that your father's standards are met." Cannan waited, but I did not acknowledge him, wanting even further assurance. "Shaselle?"

I took a shaky breath. "Do you swear?"

My uncle's eyebrows drew together in response to this unladylike demand, but I wanted an answer, and to hell with being a lady anyway.

"I swear that I will try." His response was safe, but still reassuring, for at what did the Captain of the Guard fail? Even our defeat by Cokyri had not been complete, for it had resulted in a treaty and our return to our homeland.

He walked with me to the house, where I could see my mother gazing at us through the parlor window. She came into the entryway to greet us, her face awash with relief at my safe return. I hung my head and walked past, no doubt seeming disrespectful when all I really wanted was to retreat. She knew better than to take offense, but I nonetheless heard Cannan tell her to leave me be. I climbed the stairs and turned left toward my bedroom, listening to their footsteps enter the parlor, where presumably they would discuss my situation.

I closed the door of my sanctuary and leaned against it, releasing my breath. More than anything, I craved solitude of late, and this was one of the few places where I could find it. I gazed past my bed through the double window on the opposite wall, wishing I could fly as free as the birds twittering in the trees. With a sigh, I crossed to the dressing table, pulling the pins from my straight, light brown hair and letting it tumble almost to my waist.

After a sponge bath, I donned a simple blue dinner gown, black garb for mourners having fallen out of practice since the war. If every person who had suffered a loss were to dress in accordance with custom, the city's occupants would appear to have withered just like the scorched lands beyond the walls. Aggrieved was everyone's state of being; it was understood.

I left my room, my elder sister, Dahnath, auburn-haired and beautiful like all the women on my father's side, joining me in the hallway. To my relief, she said nothing, although I was sure she knew of my flight from the house. Her nature was to be soft-spoken and studious, but she readily found fault with me for my candor and volatility, and for the fact that I didn't do much to control it. Papa had always joked that I should have been a boy, but on some level my family believed it, and it wasn't difficult to tell whether or not they approved.

Mother had called my younger siblings to dinner, and they were gathered around the large mahogany table when Dahnath and I entered the dining room. It was apparent that we had walked in on the end of an uncomfortable exchange, for our mother stood beside our father's vacant chair, her eyes upon Cannan.

"Won't you please?" she said, her voice beseeching.

Following a moment of atypical uncertainty, the captain acquiesced, coming forward to lay his hand atop the chair's back and nodding once. My uncle's words about Mother and her need to move on swam in my head as we all took our seats, Cannan settling into Papa's place. Incredibly, I didn't resent this, perhaps because the empty chair was too stark a reminder of our loss; perhaps because my father and Cannan had not only been brothers, but best friends; perhaps because it felt like I had a little bit of Papa back.

The kitchen staff entered with platters of savory food, serving Cannan and my mother first, then the children: Dahnath and me; Tulara, who was dark like Cannan and Papa, and at sixteen, easily the prettiest and most feminine of the girls; Lesette, who at fourteen had not yet lost all of her baby fat, her rounded cheeks framed by wavy medium brown hair; Ganya, who had been sickly since birth and was still too fragile for her thirteen years, but whose chocolate hair and delicate beauty drew approving glances; and Celdrid, who in looks and disposition was my father's double and who had taken Papa's death, if possible, harder than the rest of us. At eleven years of age, he had worshipped his father and, as the only son and youngest child, had been given an acceptable amount of special treatment. He had always been a cheerful, energetic, exceptionally adorable boy, but in the aftermath of Papa's death, he had become morose, speaking little and sleeping less. Like the rest of us, he had been forced to the military field where the Overlord had methodically murdered all of Hytanica's military officers, taking extra time with my father for his resemblance to the captain, who had escaped his hands. Although my mother had attempted to shield Celdrid's eyes from what was happening, the tortured screams of the dying men could not be shut out.

Conversation throughout the meal was spare, largely because there were few pleasant matters to discuss. Cannan also seemed more interested in observing than in talking. We had, after all, become his responsibility. He would safeguard Celdrid's inheritance, arrange marriages for each of his nieces when the time came and provide for my mother throughout her life. My uncle, as with all things, took his duties seriously, and was watching for signs that any among us was ailing more than circumstances warranted.

We were about twenty minutes into our dining when my brother pushed his plate away, the food upon it barely touched. He slumped forward, putting his elbows on the table and drop-

ping his face into his hands. His manners and appetite had
been sorely lacking of late, along with the rest of the personality we loved, but none among us could stand to reproach
him, not when he was so melancholy.

"Celdrid?" Mother asked, sounding disquieted but not surprised.

He shook his head, fingers enmeshed in his dark hair, eyes
still on the tabletop.

"I'm not hungry," he said, the words barely audible.

"You have to eat, Celdrid," Mother insisted, while Cannan watched with a minute crease in his brow.

My brother's moan would have been a "no" had he been
in a mood to articulate. His elbow slipped off the edge of the
table, and he barely caught himself in time to avoid a hard
knock on the forehead.

"I want what Papa's having," he mumbled, no longer making sense.

With a tiny, diffident smile for Cannan, my mother slid
back her chair and stood. "Excuse me everyone."

She walked around the table to the end where Celdrid sat,
touching his cheek and putting her arm around him to coax
him out of his seat.

"All right, love," she said softly, assisting him from the
room, for his legs didn't want to work.

The door swung shut behind them, and an awkward silence
ensued. I peeked at my sisters, none of us knowing where to
look or what to say, or even if we should continue eating.

"He hasn't been sleeping well," I supplied at last, picking
at the napkin in my lap. "He'll eat later."

Cannan said nothing. When my mother returned, there
was even less conversation than before, and I wondered how
we were all measuring up in the captain's eyes.

That night, after my uncle had departed and the house was

quiet, I lay on my bed atop the covers, my room illuminated only by the gray moonlight sifting through the window. I didn't feel like sleeping, and for the first time in my life, I examined that window, contemplating how I might escape this room, this house, this life. It was big enough for me to fit through, and I could reach the large branch that brushed the side of the house; from there, I could make my way down the trunk of the oak tree to the ground. Other than the fact that I would cause my mother worry, I might be doing everyone a favor. Then, right on time, I heard whimpering through my closed door, which shortly turned to crying, and I realized how wrong I was that my family would be better off without me.

I rolled out of bed and went down the hall to my brother's room, the door to which was ajar. My mother was waking Celdrid and pulling him into her arms, though she was barely able to keep her own eyes open. At first he pushed at her, gasping for air between sobs, but then he melted against her, his lips forming the word *Papa* again and again. I came up behind them and laid a hand on my mother's shoulder, silently offering to take over. She needed the rest, and on some level it didn't matter who held Celdrid, for it would never be the person he wanted.

CHAPTER 3

DISTURBANCES

COME MORNING, NARIAN WAS GONE. ON THE nights when we were together, he would rouse before me, both by disposition and because he needed to depart before he might be missed—or worse, discovered with me in his arms. I awoke to the sun dancing across my body and the scarcely disturbed bed coverings, Narian having kept me warm throughout the night. There was also a steady but muffled sound that I couldn't identify.

I dressed in a simple gown. In this reforming Hytanica, I could have worn breeches, but had I done so, I would have been seen as aligning myself with the enemy. My people were being asked to accept a Hytanican woman in a position of authority, a first in the history of our kingdom; the least I could do was keep faith with the rest of our way of life.

The sound had heightened, my apprehension along with it, and I hastily brushed my dark brown hair, which had regrown to just above my shoulders since I had cut it during our time in hiding in the cave. Ready for the day, I stepped from the parlor into the corridor, only to find that London was not at his post.

By the time I reached the Grand Staircase, the noise had amplified twice over, and my brow furrowed with legitimate concern, for I had a burgeoning belief as to its source. I quickly descended to the first floor, the troubled mutterings of the Cokyrian guards in the Grand Entry Hall adding credence to my theory, then pushed on to the Captain of the Guard's office. Before I could knock, London pulled the door open, about to leave. We stopped face-to-face, neither of us having expected to encounter the other, then my bodyguard moved aside to permit me to enter.

Cannan's office looked almost unchanged, its furnishings dark and imposing, much like the man himself. There were bookcases filled with pristinely kept volumes on strategy, armaments, falconry, hunting, politics and the like; a single, padded armchair that provided the only comfortable seating for a guest; a large map of the Recorah River Valley that identified our neighboring Kingdoms of Gourhan and Emotana to the south and Sarterad to the west, as well as the Cokyrian Desert to our east; and a clean, uncluttered desk behind which the captain sat and before which were placed several straight-backed wooden chairs that I still thought of as interrogation chairs. The only items missing were the glass-fronted weapons cabinets that had lined one wall, and the captain's private collection of arms.

I had barely crossed the threshold when Cannan stood and approached. Forgoing pleasantries, he solemnly asked, "Are you prepared to address your public?"

"Yes—I mean, I can if necessary," I clumsily answered, wringing my hands, for he had just confirmed my fears about the genesis of the noise.

"Our citizens are assembling outside the gates of the palace. Throughout the city, the High Priestess's mandate is being ripped down, tossed into the streets, burned. The people are angry and need to know they are heard—*you* have to convince them of that before we have a riot on our hands. If things get out of control, I don't know what the Cokyrians will do, only that it will be bloody. Now, come with me."

He ushered me from his office and we retraced my steps to the second floor. We picked up followers as we proceeded, primarily Cokyrian soldiers stationed within the Bastion, but as Cannan guided me toward the Royal Ballroom in the East Wing, I also saw my father, mother, sister and Temerson coming down the corridor.

We crossed the ballroom to stop before the balcony doors where London awaited us, a band of perhaps twenty at our heels. Cannan gripped my upper arms, turning me to face him.

"Do you know what to say?" he asked, and I wondered if he would tell me if I said *no*. My mind was spinning, frantic to find words that could calm an infuriated populace.

I swallowed, glancing at the faces of the people who formed an arc behind us—at my sister's fine-boned features, which were beautiful even when alarmed; at Temerson, who had settled a comforting arm around her waist; at my father, who was rubbing his hands together in agitation, while his eyes, dark like mine, flitted as quickly as a hummingbird's wings to assess the situation; and at my serene mother, whose blue eyes were focused encouragingly on me, while one hand absentmindedly smoothed her honey-blond hair into place.

I forced my attention back to the captain, whose grim expression told me he was trying to determine if I were ready in any sense of the word to deal with the mayhem. In truth, there was no way to prepare, no time. Apprehensively playing with the waistband of my gown, I took a shaky breath and nodded.

London pushed the doors outward, and he and Cannan ushered me through them. The soldiers who had followed us gravitated closer, filling the doorway at our backs; only my family members were bold enough to step with me into the open air.

The spring day was unusually still and therefore also unusually warm. For what must have been a thousand yards beyond the walled courtyard of the Bastion, all I could see were people, and I momentarily felt faint. Those closest to the gate had climbed its iron bars halfway to its peak, while others shoved their hands and petitions through it, only to be hit back with the hilts of Cokyrian swords. All, however, were crying out. Angry shouts resounded, battling each other above the general din, and at times, their speakers fought, as well. The citizenry was screaming for justice, for rebellion, but quieted to listen when I came into view.

"I hear your cries," I shouted, only to receive a slight nudge from London telling me to raise my volume. I cleared my throat, then shed the last vestiges of my useless indecision and filled my lungs with air. "I hear your cries," I repeated, slowly and distinctly. "I feel your frustration. You are my friends, my family, my people and to see you in this pain is…is agonizing."

I paused, considering what direction I should take, knowing how important my words would be, and the positive or adverse effects they could have. My thoughts at last came into order, and I pressed on.

"You want the best for this land and its people. You want peace and happiness, and stability for your families. This is not the way to that end. Return to your homes, let your tempers ease."

A swell of muttering greeted my plea, eroding my confidence. I glanced at London, who nodded reassuringly, and doggedly continued.

"We are a strong people. But we must demonstrate that strength by adapting to the demands placed upon us. That is the path that will lead us to security and greater freedom."

I could see shock and confusion on the faces of my countrymen, the single mind of a body of people working to understand my lack of outrage at Cokyri's oppressiveness. But it was their desire to understand that encouraged me to speak once more.

"I promise you, our fate is not out of our hands. But for now, this is the course we must take. I implore all of you to trust my judgment, and the judgment of those here with me. We have not led you astray thus far, and I swear to you, we will not do so now. Please, disband and return to your families."

There were continued mutterings and occasional shouts, but the furious yelling did not resume and the people started to disperse, some with acceptance and grace, others spitting on the ground or in the faces of the Cokyrian guards on the other side of the gates. Cannan's hand fell lightly on my shoulder, and he inclined his head respectfully before conducting me and my family inside.

The Cokyrians who had followed us were still in the ballroom, with one addition. While I had been speaking, Narian had arrived and was standing a few feet from his troops, his keen eyes resting on me. My father, taking note of this, stepped in front of me to block his line of sight, clasping my hands between his own in a congratulatory gesture. When I next looked, Narian had ordered his soldiers back to their posts and was departing, his back to me.

The kingdom—the *province*—was in a state of unrest for the remainder of the day, but those of us who lived within the Bastion could not ignore our duties. While Cannan revisited his office to settle paperwork, I returned to my study to review plans for construction of housing for displaced villagers and other homeless within the city. London walked with me, eyes straight ahead, unintentionally making it difficult for me to pose my question—or perhaps what made it difficult was my fear of the answer.

"London, I couldn't tell if..."

He cocked an eyebrow, suggesting he already knew what was on my mind, and I breathed more easily.

"Did I say the right things? I feel that I did, but our people could see me as patronizing, arrogant. I'm a woman. Hytanica doesn't want me for its leader. What if I...made things worse?"

"If you think yourself capable of making things *worse* in this kingdom, you're giving yourself an awful lot of credit," London replied, then his demeanor became serious. "Alera, you've always had the people's hearts, and they don't doubt your intentions. But if you want their confidence, you have to prove yourself. I think you took a sizeable step in that direction this morning."

I blushed at his praise. Encouraged, I voiced my other concern. "And you—you believe in what I'm trying to do, don't you?"

London's hands dropped to the hilts of his double blades, and I couldn't tell if I was seeing indecision or a desire to take a moment to get the words right.

"The path you have chosen is one that will protect your people. The welfare of the people has always been of the utmost importance to me."

While London's declaration could have been reassuring, it gave me pause, particularly in light of the things Narian had said to me.

"Narian doesn't trust you, London," I told him a bit pointedly. If he supported my goals, it should bother him that he was under suspicion.

He shrugged, unperturbed. "Who *does* Narian trust?"

"He's quite *willing* to trust any of you. You have to give him a reason to do so, as Cannan has done."

London stopped with his hand on the door to my quarters, turning to me with a slight smile. "I meant no offense, Your Highness."

He stepped inside ahead of me, checking for intruders and, for what felt like the thousandth time, I couldn't tell if he had been honest or irreverent. Feeling wholly unsatisfied with our conversation, I pressed him further.

"It seems you have reservations—about me, as well as Narian."

"I don't have reservations about *you,* but I know the Cokyrians, and I cannot blindly trust that your efforts to preserve our way of life will be successful."

I frowned, feeling we were going in circles. London crossed his arms over his chest, studying me, the intensity of his gaze disconcerting.

"What you must understand, Alera, is that Cokyri respects strength and despises weakness. If we are seen as beaten—not just conquered—they will tighten their grip, become even more oppressive. They are wolves—we cannot be viewed as sheep. If that happens, they will obliterate us, and we will lose our identity. At the same time, they will not tolerate any insolence from us, just as a master will not suffer disrespect from his servants."

London's indigo eyes sparked, accentuating the fervency of his tone, yet I could not seem to grasp the import of his words.

"I don't understand, London. What further danger do you see from Cokyri?"

"The High Priestess is a strong but practical ruler. What she wants is the bounty of our land, not the sweat of our brow. If she can have the first without taking the second, she will. And that's the primary difference between Nantilam and the Overlord. He would have asserted his full power and enslaved our people, setting some to task here and sending others to

Cokyri. She does not see the necessity of that. But if we prove troublesome, her patience will be taxed, and she will take that step. That's why your appointment as Grand Provost is such a pivotal one. The High Priestess did not have to put you or any other Hytanican in a position of influence within the province—the fact that she did gives us a voice. But push too hard and she will remove you, replacing you with someone whose only goal will be to dominate us."

"So if we are either too compliant or too unruly, the Cokyrians will overrun us, replacing our way of life with their own?"

He nodded. "I do not envy your position."

"So what am I to do?" Now that I was fully aware of the significance of my role, I was terrified. I could neither afford to sail into a storm nor languish in stagnant water. But I had no charts or compass to guide me.

"Be involved in decisions that will affect your people. Raise our concerns, fight for us on important issues and make concessions on lesser ones—use both your head and your heart."

I nodded, and he came to stand in front of me, his visage softening.

"You have good instincts, Alera—trust them."

He bowed, then strode out the door, leaving me with more to think about than the construction of housing.

After a quick lunch in the second-floor dining room, I descended the spiral staircase at the rear of the Bastion, at one time reserved for the private use of the royal family, and entered the King's Drawing Room, where Miranna and Temerson waited. It had become Miranna's habit, following my first request, to attend and assist me in receiving petitions from the people, for the process was both difficult and, at times, heartbreaking. Children sought shelter; men whose homes had been destroyed pled fare for their families; widows came one after another, begging coins and comfort, having been left destitute in the wake of their husbands' deaths. Sometimes their eyes were empty, their bodies hollow of food and feeling. Sometimes they could not control their weeping. And when I wanted to weep with them, Miranna would lay her petite and graceful hand upon my arm and offer solace in my stead.

London rejoined me, and the four of us went into the Hearing Hall—the Throne Room with no thrones—where Miranna and I sat in the carved wooden chairs that had been placed at its head. In a few minutes, the antechamber doors would open and citizens would one at a time be permitted to address me. After a brief exchange of words with Temerson, London, came to stand beside me, while my sister's cinnamon-haired husband departed. I nodded to my bodyguard and he signaled to the Cokyrian sentries at the opposite end of the hall that they should permit the first of the petitioners who waited in the antechamber to enter.

On this day, many men came forth with demands that forced me to reiterate what I had said on the balcony: I would endorse no revolt; I would *condone* no revolt. This was the sound course. Despite how tiresome it became, I retained my patience, and slowly the number of comers with the same agenda diminished. This made room for the mourners, and by the time the doors closed at evening, I was exhausted— and feeling guilty about my exhaustion when circumstances offered those who suffered no reprieve.

I went to my quarters and ate, then prepared for bed. Too tired to sit in the parlor and try to read, I crawled under my covers, leaving a lantern burning in the hope that Narian would come. At some point, I dozed off, only to rouse with my head upon his chest and his arms around me. I peered up at him and he gently kissed me.

"Shhh," he murmured. "Go back to sleep."

I yawned, then reached up to touch his sun-streaked hair. "Tell me about your day."

"As you wish," he said, turning onto his side to look at me. "I've directed my officers to prepare for our move to the Bastion, but I still need to decide on an appropriate location for us. I was thinking of the strategy room—it's convenient to both your study and Cannan's office, and large enough to be partitioned into a private office for me, with plenty of space left for my staff."

"That's a good idea. It would be nice to have you close by, and you wouldn't be displacing anyone."

"As for Rava, I think it would be best to give her the office that was formerly used by the Sergeant at Arms. It currently stands empty."

I stiffened at the mention of Narian's second-in-command, a sharp, bronze-haired woman who was but six or seven years older than were we. I had taken an instant dislike to her, based primarily on her overbearing attitude, for I knew little else about her. Sensing my change in temperament, Narian gave a soft laugh.

"She has to make the move, Alera, but I prefer a little distance between the two of us."

I nodded and we went on to discuss the events of my day. When I yawned for the third time in less than a minute, he brought his lips to mine in a kiss that lingered an especially long time, revealing a desire within that my body reciprocated, and I was glad he was lying on top of the bed coverings rather than beneath them with me. I knew not how hot our passion would flare, or if I would have the strength to resist him. As it was, I simply tucked myself into his embrace, and he held me, accepting though he might not understand.

It was too much to have hoped that my impromptu speech would have settled affairs in the province. With a society in turmoil, a confused and railing populace and an overwhelming hunger for relief in any form, what happened the following week was in principle inevitable, and in reality the worst I could have imagined.

My morning schedule saw me first in Cannan's office, conferring with my advisor, but our meeting was interrupted within minutes by Narian, who entered without knocking and whose eyes were colder than I had seen them in a long time.

"I thought you intended to control them," he stated, walking toward the captain's desk and standing directly beside the chair in which I sat.

He slammed a lengthy piece of parchment down on the wood surface, an unusual amount of tension in his movements. I glanced toward the open door and caught sight of Rava. She stood with one hand resting against the frame, her calculating eyes evaluating the scene while she awaited orders.

Cannan's gaze went to the parchment, but he did not reach for it, scanning its contents from a distance. Then he looked at Narian, unruffled.

"I can think of a dozen or more men capable of this."

"But you *know* who is responsible."

Cannan sat back, assessing his opposition. "I don't know with certainty any more than you do. In the absence of definitive proof of guilt on behalf of my son and his friends, I suggest you and your fellows develop a sense of humor." Then the captain's tone changed, becoming more forbidding. "I can prevent an uprising, Narian. This, you'll have to get used to."

Not wanting to be in the dark, I snatched up the parchment in question. My mouth opened in shock and dismay as I silently read its contents, the men waiting for me to finish.

On this Thirtieth Day of May in the First Year of Cokyrian dominance over the Province of Hytanica, the following regulations shall be put into practice in order to assist our gracious Grand Provost in her ef-

fort to welcome Cokyri into our lands—and to help ensure the enemy does not bungle the first victory it has managed in over a century.

Regulation One. All Hytanican citizens must be willing to provide aid to aimlessly wandering Cokyrian soldiers who cannot on their honor grasp that the road leading back to the city is the very same road that led them away.

Regulation Two. It is strongly recommended that farmers hide their livestock, lest the men of our host empire become confused and attempt to mate with them.

Regulation Three. As per negotiated arrangements, crops grown on Hytanican soil will be divided with fifty percent belonging to Cokyri, and seventy-five percent remaining with the citizens of the province; Hytanicans will be bound by law to wait patiently while the Cokyrians attempt to sort the baffling deficiency in their calculations.

Regulation Four. The Cokyrian envoys assigned to manage the planting and farming effort will also require Hytanican patience while they slowly but surely learn what is a crop and what is a weed, as well as left from right.

Regulation Five. Though the Province Wall is a Cokyrian endeavor, it would be polite and understanding of Hytanicans to remind the enemy of the correct side on which to be standing when the final stone is laid, so no unfortunates may find themselves trapped outside with no way in.

Regulation Six. When at long last foreign trade is allowed to resume, Hytanicans should strive to empathize with the reluctance of neighboring kingdoms to enter our lands, for Cokyri's stench is sure to deter even the migrating birds.

Regulation Seven. For what little trade and business we do manage in spite of the odor, the imposed ten percent tax may be paid in coins, sweets or shiny objects.

Regulation Eight. It is regrettably prohibited for Hytanicans to throw jeers at Cokyrian soldiers, for fear that any man harried may cry, and the women may spit.

Regulation Nine. In case of an encounter with Cokyrian dignitaries, the boy-invader and the honorable High Priestess included, let it be known that the proper way in which to greet them is with an ass-backward bow.

My hands were trembling out of anger and distress by the time I reached the end. When I finally raised my eyes to his, Narian answered my unspoken question.

"These have replaced the High Priestess's laws everywhere they were posted."

He turned from me to address Cannan. "The regulations as they were intended still stand, and will be enforced whether or not the people are aware of them. Inform any who *might* have had a hand in mocking the High Priestess's rules that their game is putting their countrymen at greater risk."

Cannan remained silent in face of the order, and Narian did not wait for a reply. With a quick, respectful nod toward me, he departed, Rava at his heels, and the office door closed resoundingly behind them.

I stared at the parchment I still held, unable to keep it from shaking, and my vision blurred. It was foolish to be hurt, for this blow was not aimed at me, but yet the insolence of the document stung.

"Steldor and Galen did this?" I demanded.

"So it would seem."

"Why?" My throat and jaw were tight. "Why would they do this, undermine my authority? They've taken what I'm trying to do and ground it underfoot. The Cokyrians will be furious. They'll bear down harder than ever." I whisked the moisture from my eyes, taking deep breaths to calm myself. "How can they think this will help?"

Cannan sighed and leaned forward, assuming a more fatherly posture.

"They're allowing the people to dissent. They're showing

that we can still laugh and, most of all, that we haven't been forgotten. I don't approve of the method, either, Alera, but what they've done may not be all bad."

I forced myself to nod, struggling to control my raging emotions. The hard work had scarcely begun, I knew that, but to see what I had accomplished tampered with and ridiculed was painful, even with Cannan's assurance that it could be taken in a positive light. Then London's words about being neither too cooperative nor too defiant returned to me. Perhaps this was what my bodyguard had meant—opposition, but on an isolated scale.

"You're right," I finally said. "This might not be all bad, provided it doesn't escalate."

"I agree. I will, however, talk with them."

"Thank you," I murmured, and he rose to see me to the door. As I crossed the Hearing Hall toward my study, I debated whether I should be the one to talk to Steldor, all the time knowing he would probably deny any involvement if I broached the topic. No, he was far more likely to listen to his father. When had he *ever* been open to listening to me on matters affecting the kingdom?

It was a mere day after the disturbance caused by the revised rules that Narian made the move to the Bastion, claiming it as his new center of operations. The chain of command that began with him and Rava was completed by six others, all but one of whom was female. Narian took over what had been the strategy room, while Rava laid ownership to Galen's old office, which was separated from Cannan's only by the antechamber on the south side of the Hearing Hall.

Tension was to be expected, but was not excessive over the next few weeks—with Steldor and Galen out in the city, all in my inner circle wanted things to go smoothly. Of course,

some wary and unpleasant glances were thrown by both Hytanicans and Cokyrians, but everyone for the most part co-
existed peacefully.

Rava, despite her competence and practicality, was the only
one who worried me. To have been chosen as Narian's second,
she had to be among the High Priestess's elite, and it showed
in her lofty attitude toward my people, even the ones who
worked alongside me. The women she found deplorable and
weak, with their dresses and subservient manners; the men she
found inferior for their entitled attitudes and Hytanican blood.

Her potential to create a problem became apparent when
a middle-age maid accidentally brushed against Cannan as
she hurried through the Grand Entry Hall toward the service
areas of the Bastion.

"Oh, excuse me, Captain!" she exclaimed.

Rava, who had been consulting with me and the former
Hytanican military leader, extended a hand faster than my
eyes could follow, snatching the maid's arm and yanking her
around with such astonishing strength that she nearly dropped
the oddly shaped bundle she was carrying. While Rava's pale
blue eyes scrutinized her captive's fleshy face, the maid's expression escalated from alarm to panic, and I shifted uncomfortably, uncertain what the woman's transgression had been.
Having reduced the servant to the status of a frightened rab-
bit, Rava shifted her gaze to Cannan.

"He is no captain," she spat, still addressing the woman,
but the disgust in her voice meant for the object of her contempt. "Not anymore."

Cannan did not react, other than to meet Rava's eyes with
an equally intense glare of his own, and the maid looked uncertainly between the two of them, shifting as Rava's grip bruised
her forearm. Only I, standing at his side, saw Cannan's jaw
clench before he redirected his attention to the poor woman.

"She's right," he said, succinct and gruff.

"Of course, sir," the maid replied in a quaky whisper, adding with a glance at Rava, "Ma'am, sir, Commander."

Rava thrust her away, finding her of no further interest now that she had made her point, and the woman hastened away, clutching her package as though it were her life. Out of the corner of my eye, I saw Narian at the foot of the Grand Staircase, one hand on the hilt of his light, thin-bladed Cokyrian sword and the other on the railing, watching his second-in-command with a detached but clearly displeased countenance.

In order to give my family—my parents, Miranna and Temerson—privacy on the third floor, Narian had decided upon my old second-floor quarters for his residence. There was the added benefit to this arrangement of less ground to cover in sneaking through the corridors to reach my rooms, although he continued to regularly use my window for an entrance. Long ago, he had discovered how to climb over the palace roof to visit me, and I could only assume this remained his habit. I didn't complain, knowing that the method reduced our risk of being caught.

We were sitting upon my bed, facing each other, when I voiced my fears about the altercation in the Grand Entry.

"I can't control whether Rava shows respect to my people or not, but the approach she demonstrated today is bound to stir up resentment, and we have enough of that already. And I can't help but worry that she might pose a bigger problem for us, for what we're trying to do, than we realize."

Narian pondered my words, the fingers of his right hand rubbing the wrist that had been broken by the Overlord during the fight over my life. The warlord's training had instilled in Narian such control that he had no noticeable mannerisms, nor did he fidget, and this simple, inattentive action told me his level of comfort with me equaled mine with him.

"Rava?" he said, weighing the possibility. "She's no diplomat, I'll grant you that. But she wants what the High Priestess wants. I think she knows her bounds and won't cross them. In any case, she's under my orders—I can control her if need be."

"And are you so sure of what the High Priestess wants?"

"Until Hytanica attacked Cokyri a century ago and started the war, what Cokyri wanted was crops and knowledge about irrigation and soil. And we were willing to trade to acquire those things."

I bristled at the way he characterized the beginning of the war. In reality, Hytanica's Crown Prince had been sent to negotiate the treaty to which Narian had alluded, and Cokyri had executed him over some insult he had paid their ruler. Nonetheless, I held my tongue, not wanting to divert our discussion.

"Over time, winning the war became a matter of pride, for Cokyri does not back down. But now that is over, and from the High Priestess's point of view, Hytanica has been put in its place. Her focus is once more on our need for crops and knowledge, and she sees little else to gain from this land— we are a mountain people, not valley dwellers, and ours is a wealthy empire in its own right.

"Unlike the Overlord, the High Priestess will obtain what Cokyri needs in the most efficient manner possible, shedding as little Cokyrian blood as possible. If she can walk over your people, she will. If not, she will abide the Hytanican way of life up to the point where it disrupts her goals. All Cokyrians stationed here know this, including Rava. And they know that the High Priestess is not forgiving when someone under her command steps out of line. Rava will not disobey."

"London said something to the same effect the other day—

that the High Priestess won't interfere in our way of life, provided we are neither too compliant nor too disorderly."

"London?" Narian's eyes narrowed, and I tried not to take offense over the misgivings he continued to harbor about my bodyguard. "Sometimes I think he knows too much about the Cokyrian way of life."

"We happened to be talking about my role as Grand Provost."

"I suggest that you take what London says with skepticism. He may have his own agenda."

"That may be true of all of us. Still, I asked for London's opinion and he gave it. He's not pushing me in any particular direction. I trust him, Narian, whether you do or not."

He nodded, but did not address the issue further. Knowing he considered the matter settled, I changed the subject.

"Does it bother you?"

"Hmm?"

I motioned to his hands. "Your wrist. You haven't left it alone. It's the one that was broken, isn't it?"

He ceased rubbing, dropping his right hand to his leg and flexing the other to prove his coming point.

"No, it doesn't bother me. It's just...a habit, I guess."

An amused smile lit my face at the measure of surprise in his voice. The only habits he'd developed under the Overlord's control were his need to be armed or, at the very least, not far from his weapons at all times, and to scan every room he entered for exits and enemies. Even if it were just around me, seeing him break free of some aspect of that monster's tyranny was gratifying, and I leaned forward to kiss him full on the mouth. His response was ardent, eager and we lay down together, having no further use for conversation.

CHAPTER 4

BACK TO LIFE

THE SCREAM ECHOED THROUGHOUT THE HOUSE and, I speculated, well into the street.

"Celdrid!" my mother cried, struggling with my irate brother.

I hastened into the entryway, pushing my hair, which was still damp from my bath, out of my face. I stopped with a hand on the banister of the staircase to listen.

"No! I don't want to wear that *silly* doublet!"

I smoothed the skirt of my blush-pink gown, thinking I could relate to his sentiments about dress clothes. It was unlike him, though—Celdrid had always enjoyed special occasions. He'd been a charmer just like Papa, and had known that the cuter he looked, the more likely adults were to fawn over him. But this was beyond objection—he wouldn't let Mother anywhere near him with the clothes in question.

"It's not *silly*," my mother pleaded, trying to calm him. "It's not even overly fancy. I just want you to look nice for your uncle and Steldor when they arrive."

"It doesn't matter how I look."

I could hardly believe how belligerently he was behaving. I

heard my older sister come into the house behind me—she'd been out with Lord Drael, her betrothed, but had returned shortly before our relatives were to arrive. Like me, her attention was captured by the argument taking place upstairs.

"Is Celdrid—" Dahnath's question was cut off by the sound of something shattering.

"Leave me alone!"

"Darling, just—"

"*Don't* call me darling!"

Dahnath and I exchanged a glance, both of us thinking the struggle might be getting out of control and silently deciding I should be the one to intercede. Celdrid felt closer to me because I had been closer to Papa.

I hurried up the stairs, but as I went down the hall toward my brother's room, he sprinted past me in a half-buttoned white shirt and a pair of breeches. My mother followed, clutching the doublet she had been trying to get him to wear, one hand pressed against her forehead.

"Celdrid!" I called, dashing after him, striving to catch him before he fled the house. By the time I reached the bottom of the stairs, he was at the door, having dodged around Dahnath.

"Come back here!" she snapped, adding to the pandemonium.

He flung open the door, about to escape, only to be caught around the waist by Steldor.

"Slow down, soldier!" our startled cousin exclaimed, holding on tight.

Celdrid squirmed and fought until Steldor took hold of his upper arm and pulled him around. Forced to look the cousin he revered in the eye, my brother's boldness evaporated, and he stared uncomfortably at the floor. Steldor knelt down, then glanced up at Cannan as if unsure what to do.

"Let me go…please," Celdrid mumbled.

"And where is it you plan to go?" Steldor asked, a hint of amusement in his voice.

"I don't…I don't know." My brother sniffed, his anger giving way to the sadness that had brought it on in the first place.

Standing up, Steldor tousled the boy's dark hair. "Let's just stay here. I have something for you anyway."

Celdrid shifted his weight from foot to foot for a few moments before nodding.

"Good day, Uncle," Dahnath cheerfully greeted Cannan, regaining her senses before I did and unintentionally making me seem rude.

"Good day, Dahnath. Shaselle." Cannan nodded to each of us, and I flashed a brilliant smile, hoping to redeem myself.

Ever since Uncle and I had talked in the barn, I had been trying—honestly trying—to behave more sensibly. I had not raised my voice to my mother in nearly three weeks, hadn't said so much as a disrespectful word, even though she and Cannan had arranged for a suitor to join us at dinner tonight. I had hoped being more sympathetic and understanding might make life easier for me, too, but thus far it hadn't helped.

Mother appeared at the second-floor landing, having taken a moment to straighten up after her struggle with Celdrid, and some of the tension left her body when she saw that he was still within the house.

"Cannan, Steldor, I'm so glad you're here," she said a bit breathlessly, coming to join us. "Although I'm sorry you had to witness the end of that dispute."

"No apology necessary," the former Captain of the Guard responded, sparing a glance for Celdrid to let him know he was not in trouble. "Steldor," he then prompted.

"I'll take care of him," Steldor told my mother, motioning to Celdrid's haphazard dress, and he deftly ushered my brother past us and up the stairs.

My mother touched a hand to her temple. "I just don't know what to do with him, Cannan."

I examined her worried face, astonished at how forthcoming she was about her feelings. She needed to confide in someone, and the head of the family was the obvious choice, but she didn't generally speak so candidly in front of her children. Was this another sign that we older girls were to shoulder more responsibility?

"Do your best," the captain said simply. "Steldor and Galen will spend time with him, and I'll do everything I can. There's no easy remedy."

"I'm afraid that's the only truth in this house."

Her words were slightly embittered, and my sister and I looked anywhere but at her and my uncle.

"Come, Lania," Cannan said, breaking the silence. "I have some financial matters to discuss with you."

Money was not a topic generally discussed with Hytanican women, but Mother wanted to know our situation, and Cannan was willing to oblige. We were nowhere near short of funds, but without a working male in the home, it was essential to take note of our expenditures.

Cannan and Mother adjourned to the parlor, and Dahnath and I were joined by Steldor and a fully dressed Celdrid. The four of us went out into the hot but breezy late June weather, Dahnath and Steldor settling on a bench in a shaded area of our yard and Celdrid and me on the grass.

"I'm keeping an eye on you, so you best behave," Steldor teased my brother with a wink, and the corners of Celdrid's mouth turned up. Even when everything was hopeless, my twenty-two-year-old cousin could strike a spark.

I had always worshipped Steldor and his best friend, Galen. As a young girl, I'd followed them around whether they'd wanted me to or not—climbed trees with them, raced horses with them, gotten into trouble with them. When I'd grown older, their conversations had been more fascinating than those of my mother, sisters or any other members of the nobility, and I had loved to listen, despite the razzing I would sometimes receive from them for being neither a typical girl nor a boy.

Since the war, my admiration for Steldor had increased all the more. He was bold, fearless and answered to no one. And despite our kingdom's loss of independence, he still bucked Cokyri's authority, for every Hytanican knew what he and Galen had done. There was little doubt that they had been the ones behind the *revised* regulations, which now had everyone reading the High Priestess's rules with surreptitious smirks. Even my serious and sensible uncle couldn't keep Steldor from invigorating his countrymen—and I knew Cannan would have tried, both to protect his son and because he was working with Queen Alera. But Steldor had no interest in being protected, a sentiment to which I could relate.

Dahnath, Celdrid and I spent a pleasant hour in Steldor's company, though we could all tell when the youngest among us began to grow jaded with the conversation. My brother was hard to entertain of late—he couldn't stay content with anything for very long.

"I have an idea, Celdrid," Steldor said, after exchanging subtle glances with Dahnath and me.

The eleven-year-old looked up from the blades of grass he was plucking, but didn't respond.

"Why don't we leave your sisters here and go see what I brought for you?"

At this, my brother perked up. "Where is it? I mean, you didn't have to bring anything for me, but since you did…"

"It's in the barn." Steldor laughed, tipping his head in the direction of the outbuilding. I understood what he was doing—it was probable that Cannan had put him up to it.

Celdrid hadn't wanted anything to do with horses or the barn since Papa's death. A good first step would be to help him overcome that instinctive, self-protective aversion.

Celdrid hesitated, chewing on his bottom lip as he glanced to the building in question. "Can you bring it over here?"

"Well, I *could*," Steldor drawled. "But I thought the point was to be rid of the girls."

He motioned to Dahnath and me, and my sister hit him lightly on the arm.

"Whatever you do, Celdrid, don't grow up to be like him," Dahnath joked, and Celdrid grinned.

"Besides, your present's a secret," Steldor added. "No one but me knows what it is."

Eyes growing wide, Celdrid asked, "Not even Uncle Cannan?"

"Not even him."

Steldor stood and offered a hand to my brother, then in a single motion swung the boy up and onto his back. The two of them moved away from us, and Dahnath and I went back indoors, she to assist the younger girls with their grooming while I freshened up in anticipation of my suitor's arrival. I also needed to check how much dirt I'd collected on the back of my dress.

Although no change of clothes was required, I did have to sit in poor temper as Dahnath and Mother attempted to style my hair, which had been a mistake to leave damp and loose after my bath. Over the course of the humid day, it had expanded and grown fuzzy, and now resembled a horse's tail.

"I have to check on the other girls," Mother said. She had sent my siblings to help our cook with dinner preparations, and none of us particularly trusted their skills or attention spans. This left Dahnath to fight the battle alone. At long last, she redampened my tresses, pulling the strands into a single plait down my back. My straight hair would be wavy—tomorrow.

By this time, Steldor and Celdrid had returned to the house and everyone was ready for our guest to join us. He arrived precisely on time, at six o'clock. My family stood courteously behind our chairs at the dining table while Cannan answered the door. He led the young man into the room and Steldor went to greet him, saying something about it being a pleasure to meet; which meant my cousin didn't know him; which meant he wasn't in Steldor's rowdy group of friends; which was a disappointment to me, but probably a good thing over-all—and would definitely be a good thing in my mother's eyes.

"Lord Taether, the lady of the house, Lady Lania," Cannan said, beginning the introductions. "Her son, Lord Celdrid, and her eldest daughters, Lady Dahnath and Lady Shaselle."

As was customary, the younger girls required no introduc-tion and would say little during the meal. I stepped back to make myself known and curtseyed.

At once, Lord Taether approached and took my hand, of-fering a bow.

"An honor to meet you, my lady."

"And you…my lord."

For some reason it was difficult to form the proper words. Deep inside, I could feel myself pulling frantically away from him. He hadn't done anything to provoke such a reaction from me, but still I didn't want to be anywhere near him. I forced myself to breathe, working hard to admit he was rela-tively attractive. Curly chocolate hair met his dark eyebrows, beneath which were two perfectly fine blue eyes. His nose wasn't truly as big as it looked upon first glance, and his soft pink lips were well-shaped. But there wasn't even a tiny part of me that wanted to kiss them.

We stood awkwardly for a moment, then Cannan indicated to the servant who waited by the kitchen doors that we were ready to be served. We all took our seats, Lord Taether politely pulling my chair out before settling in next to me. The meal began with delicious vegetable soup, served in our best dishes with our very best cutlery, then progressed to wild boar, provided by Cannan and difficult to come by in these times. Of course, for those living on the streets, the biscuits we commonly ate with tea would have been a luxury.

"So, Shaselle, tell me," Lord Taether said unexpectedly, having spent his time thus far conversing with—and trying to impress—Cannan and Steldor. "What are your hobbies?"

"Well, I..." I looked at my plate, scrunching the linen napkin in my lap. "I don't...I don't really have any."

My answer was decisive. I didn't want to lie and say stitchery—he'd probably want me to mend his socks. And I couldn't tell the truth and say horseback riding.

Cannan's eyebrows lifted slightly at my response and Mother glanced at me with pursed lips, but Taether chuckled. He was being good-humored about this at least.

"Come, there must be some particularly pleasurable way in which you spend your time. Perhaps we could arrange another day to do what you most enjoy."

Again, that strange urge to be far, far away from him seized me. "Actually, I enjoy eating. I like dinner. We should just have dinner."

Cannan cleared his throat in an understated manner, but Mother breathed my name with a distinct lack of subtlety.

"All right," Taether said, maintaining politeness despite his confusion. "Well then, I shall hope to be graced with your company at dinner on another occasion."

I nodded, the only sound I could produce a noncommittal "Mmm-hmm."

What was wrong with me? I was being purposefully boorish and he didn't deserve it, but God help me, I wanted him to dislike me so I wouldn't have to see him again.

Both Taether and I glanced around the table, not quite comfortable looking at each other anymore, and my interest was captured by Steldor, for he was up to something. He had folded the corners of his napkin—our best dinner lace—to make something of a pouch, and was pointing between it and his plate of food with a devilish twinkle in his eye.

Cannan had started up a conversation with my mother about the household, oblivious to his son's actions. I cocked my head, thoroughly bewildered, then followed Steldor's gaze to Celdrid, who was trying not to grin as he snuck bits of gravy-soaked meat into his napkin.

With my brother awaiting the next instruction, Steldor moved his napkin to rest alongside Lesette's plate, quickly and discreetly snatching hers so that his became its replacement. Celdrid mimicked him motion for motion, placing his soiled linen beside Ganya's place setting, his cheeks flushed with excitement.

It was a few minutes at most before Ganya picked up the cloth to dab her mouth. She gave a small shriek, dropped it on her plate, and stared at her gravy-slimed hand, a perfect match to her gravy-slimed chin, her pallid cheeks blossoming like red roses. Celdrid shook with the giggles, bringing smiles to his other sisters' faces for no reason other than the relief we felt that he could still make such a sound.

"Ganya, what in heaven's name…" Mother began, trailing off at sight of the mess and her youngest daughter's flustered expression.

"I—I don't know, Mother, I…" she stuttered, as Dahnath quickly handed her another napkin. "I didn't do this!"

"Just keep your voice down."

Ganya seemed to shrink in her chair, then Mother fixed her eyes on her son—it was obvious the boy had done something, for he was laughing much too hard.

"Celdrid?"

"I haven't a clue, Mama," he answered, sobering a bit at her warning tone. "Maybe I used the wrong napkin?"

Steldor winked at him from across the table.

"Yes, I'm sure that's what happened," Mother charitably replied. "Ganya, it's all right, dear. You are excused to wash your hands."

None among us wanted to reprimand Celdrid, especially not when he was laughing for the first time in what honestly felt like years. Then something unpredictable occurred.

"I can tell you what happened." It was Taether, sounding quite appalled. "Young Celdrid thought he would play a trick and obviously believes he can get away with it by lying. I saw the whole thing."

Though all eyes had been on my suitor, they now shifted to my brother, who was staring at the tabletop, his lower lip trembling.

"It's all right, Celdrid," Steldor interceded with a smirk. "Beg pardon, Ganya—I put him up to it. It may not be an appropriate thing to teach him, but it sure is fun."

I could see amusement in the captain's eyes, and Celdrid giggled again. Taether, however, set down his fork, implying he had lost his appetite. Shenanigans did not seem to suit his tastes. A discomfited silence reigned until Cannan suggested to my mother that she have the servants bring out dessert, and we slipped back into a table manner that bore some resemblance to sanity.

Following the meal, we had wine in the parlor, then I was expected to spend additional time with Taether. He approached me to suggest a walk in the evening air, and I agreed out of courtesy, excusing myself to retrieve a shawl from my bedroom. It wasn't long after I reached the second floor that

I heard footsteps behind me, and I hastened to close my door, hoping she would be deterred. She was not.

"Shaselle, you have been rude to Lord Taether all evening," Mother said in a dangerous whisper, entering my room without knocking.

I bit my tongue, for this would not be a good time for an argument, then turned to my wardrobe to retrieve the wrap.

"I thought you had become more receptive to the idea of marriage," she continued.

"I'm not receptive to it. I just wanted to stop being a problem, but evidently I can't. There's something wrong with me."

She contemplated me for a long moment, then went to sit on my bed, her face pale.

"You've never been a problem," she said, her tone gentler. "Not to me. I know I've been hard on you since your father's death, but…I haven't been myself. For a time, I wanted to die with him, but that is in the past. You and the other children are my reason to live, my happiness. I hope you can forgive me for how I've treated you."

I stayed in place, the shawl clutched in my hands, feeling ashamed, like the terrible daughter I was. How could I have wanted her to be remorseful? How could I have tried to make her so with my harsh remarks?

"I'm sorry, too," I mumbled, closing the wardrobe. "I'll be polite to him."

I hurried downstairs, Mother coming more slowly after me, in all likelihood cringing. She was dignified and refined; I was clumsy and loud. If I'd been thinking, I would have taken my time—Taether wouldn't keep me out late, and every second I was apart from him was one less second I'd have to spend with him. But that was not an appropriate attitude. Those thoughts stemmed from the same side of me that wanted Mother to be impossibly strong; it was the same side that wanted Cannan to trade places with his dead brother so I could have my papa again; it was the same side that wanted Steldor to lead a rebellion that would take back our kingdom. It was the side that served no good.

Taking a deep breath, I shook off that wicked part of me and decided that for the rest of the evening, I would be a lady. I would show Taether that I could be pleasant—I had been well-raised and did have the ability to be charming company. I would focus on the future, and seriously consider whether I could wed this man.

By the end of our walk, the answer was an unequivocal no. Steldor's and Celdrid's conduct at the dinner table had irked Taether and released something within him that I doubted Cannan had ever seen; if he had, my uncle would never have envisioned me with the man. It was as though our positions had reversed—just when I began to put on a show, he stopped acting.

"Your posture would put a queen to shame," he said at one point during our walk. Although I found the compliment a bit strange, I demurely inclined my head, accepting it as my mother would have wanted.

"Your strides, however, are far too long to befit a lady."

Caught between confusion, offense and amusement, my feelings settled on the latter when Dahnath, who was our chaperone, smothered a laugh. My elder sister thought me appallingly boyish, so if she found his assessment absurd, then there was no basis for it.

"I merely wish to keep up with you, my lord," I said with some measure of grace.

"But it is *my* duty to attend to *you*. You must let me be the gentleman I am."

"Very well, we will walk at a slower pace." I consciously took smaller steps, trying to ignore my prickling resentment that he was giving me an etiquette lesson. While it was within the bounds of Hytanican society for men to correct the women for whom they were responsible—sisters, daughters, nieces and those whom they courted—whatever flaw it was in my nature that made me hot-tempered also made me unwilling to take criticism of the kind he was proffering.

"You were avoiding my questions at dinner," he went on, putting his hand over mine where it lay on his arm. "Please be open with me about yourself. I want to know you, not a volume on good manners."

Despite the irony in this invitation, given the exchange we'd just had, I obliged.

"I enjoy reading."

"And what do you read?"

I thought for a moment. He professed to want to know the real me.

"Poetry, and stories. I especially love to read about horses."

"Horses?"

"Yes, I find horses fascinating. They're powerful and beautiful animals, so full of life."

We walked on in silence while he digested this piece of information.

"Do you ride?" he asked, sounding stunned, but I couldn't tell if he was judging me or if the conversation had merely taken a turn he had not anticipated.

"Yes, sometimes," I said, deciding to be honest. "My father taught me. It isn't an activity I'd like to give up."

He gave a breathy laugh, patted my hand and directed me around to return to the house. I had thought our stroll would take us farther across the property, but I wasn't going to object to an early end to our time together.

"Let's walk at my pace, shall we?" Taether suggested, and I agreed, knowing what he really meant.

★ ★ ★

When all the guests had gone, Mother herded the younger children upstairs to see them ready for bed. I went to my room to don my nightdress, then returned to the first floor, walking into the kitchen where warm tea was likely to be found, for it was my mother's favorite drink. After pouring some of it into an old mug, I carried it to the parlor, my limbs feeling strangely heavy.

I tucked my legs beneath me in a padded armchair and sipped the tea, which was by now tepid and not very appealing. The evening's events, though I wished I could laugh them off, were troubling me. Maybe Mother was right that no decent man would want me as a wife if I did not change. Tears seared my eyes, and I let myself fall prey to juvenile thoughts. *I don't want to be a wife.*

I heard feet shuffling across the rug and turned my face away to hide my misery, hoping it wasn't Dahnath or Mother. I didn't want to discuss the evening or my behavior with either of them.

"Shaselle?"

I came about, surprised by the small voice. "Celdrid, what are you doing up?"

He stumbled over to me, wearing a long, loose-fitted cotton sleep shirt. His dark hair was sticking up in the back the way it always did in the morning, which meant he'd crawled out of bed; perhaps he was not even fully awake.

"Ganya said she wasn't feeling well so Mama's with her. She's not paying any attention to me."

"That doesn't mean you should disobey her," I said out of principle, recognizing my own hypocrisy.

He shrugged and sat cross-legged on the floor in front of me. "What's wrong?"

Just like Papa, my brother was astute. And just being asked the question was enough to bring back the tightness in my throat.

"Nothing's wrong," I said, trying to reassure him. "I'm just tired—perhaps a little sad."

"You don't get sad unless something's wrong."

Simple logic—it was so innocent I couldn't resist it.

"I walk too fast!" I squeaked, unable to hold back tears any longer.

There was a pause, then Celdrid started laughing. "Lord Taether couldn't keep up?"

"No, that's not it—he couldn't stand me. I don't meet the standards for a lady. Walking with me is like having a clomping, ugly ox for company."

"A clomping, ugly ox that walks too fast?"

I rolled my eyes at his amusement. "You're just a little horror, you know that? You'd better go back to bed before Mother comes looking for you."

He stood, then hesitated, something more on his mind.

"If he didn't like you, Shaselle, it's probably because you could've beaten him in a fight any day. Besides, someone who tattles at the dinner table doesn't deserve to be part of this family."

Whether intentional or not, Celdrid succeeded in making me laugh. I didn't doubt his sincerity, but it was clear that a day in his impressive cousin's company had improved his mood. And a return of some of his precociousness was enough to lift my spirits.

"Tell me something. Just what did Steldor give you today?"

"A sword—a sword Papa gave to him when he was four years old and Uncle Cannan had been gone for a long time. Papa told him it would help him remember to be brave, and to remember that he had Papa to watch out for him." Celdrid's lip trembled, then he smiled and finished. "Steldor said it will help me remember to be brave, and that he and Galen and Uncle Cannan are all watching out for me now."

"Good night, Celdrid," I said, giving him a hug, then he turned and left the room.

I stared after him for a moment, mulling over the things he had said. Then I realized he was right. No one worth my time would have tattled on a sad little boy.

CHAPTER 5

LOVE AND LONGING

NARIAN WAS ONCE MORE MAKING PREPARATIONS for a journey to Cokyri; as official liaison, he frequently traveled between the mother empire and the province. Knowing that the trip was long and arduous, I didn't expect him to come to me that night, and I didn't bother to light a lantern when I adjourned to my bedroom. Instead, I relied on memory and moonlight to guide me to my dressing table.

I unpinned my dark brown hair—it was not yet long enough to tie back, but letting it merely hang was impractical—and reached behind to tug at the laces of my dress. They were difficult to loosen without the aid of my personal maid, Sahdienne, who had been among those servants rehired for the sake of the economy. I sighed in frustration and stood, about to send for her when I felt warm hands rest on my waist from behind. My irritation dispersed as I closed my eyes and tilted my head back against a sturdy chest, breathing in his presence. Narian had come.

He swept my hair off my neck, his fingers giving me pleasant chills, then took over what I had been attempting. My dress rustled to the floor, leaving me standing in my chemise, and he sweetly and tenderly kissed my neck and shoulders. He pushed my shift down my arms, his mouth following, and I leaned against him, my legs weak, keenly attuned to every brush of his lips against my flushed skin.

My heart beat faster, and I twisted to face him, kissing him deeply, hardly aware that he had begun to walk backward, leading me toward the bed. We fell together upon the mattress, not entirely gracefully, but neither of us thinking about form. He rolled on top of me, his breath quickening along with mine, and it was only when he took hold of my bunched up chemise that my brain snapped into action. I placed my hands on his shoulders and shook my head, and he flopped flat on his back beside me with a groan.

After a moment to regain his composure, he propped himself up on his elbow to look down at me, desire still lurking in his mesmerizing eyes.

"Alera? Are you…all right?"

"Narian, we can't do this." I was more than a little shocked at the both of us.

His brow furrowed, and he ran a hand through his disheveled hair. He took a breath and opened his mouth, then stopped, apparently unable to decide exactly what he wanted to say.

"Why not?"

"Because," I said, pushing myself upright. "We're not married!"

He sat up as well and lit the lantern on my bedside table. I pulled my chemise back onto my shoulders and wrapped my arms around my legs while I waited for his reaction.

"And marriage, that's…important to you…for this," he surmised, trying to work out the basis for my objection.

"Yes," I told him fervently. "Isn't it to you?"

He glanced at the bedclothes, as though he anticipated an unpleasant reaction to what he would say.

"Well, no. We don't have marriage in Cokyri."

My eyebrows shot upward. "You don't have…marriage? Well then, how do you…I mean, where…where do your children come from?"

"We just choose a partner," he said, ignoring the absurdity of my question. "A woman chooses a man, and if he accepts, he is marked with a tattoo around his forearm. The tattoo is a great honor—men in Cokyri are proud to bear it."

"What about the church?"

He shrugged, no longer worrying about how I might react. "Cokyri has no official religion. Some people seek the High Priestess's approval to be bound, but they come to her of their own accord. Again, it is a choice."

"So…in order to be with me, all you would need is a tattoo?" I spoke tentatively, trying to absorb and understand his words.

"Only to signify that I am yours and no one else's. If that is what we both want."

His closing statement, though subtle, sought confirmation, his steel-blue eyes filled with love and longing.

"I choose you," I said, leaning toward him, and his mouth met mine with such ardor that my senses reeled all over again. He lay down with me on top of him, and it took all my strength of will to pull away.

"But we have to be married."

He studied me, concluding that I truly believed in what I said.

"Then let's go get married."

"Now?" I blurted, eyes wide.

"Is now a problem?"

"The banns need to be published six weeks in advance of the wedding!"

"Banns?" He rolled me sideways off him so that we lay facing each other, his voice dubious.

"The banns announce our betrothal," I elaborated, hoping not to dampen his enthusiasm or his readiness to tolerate Hytanican tradition. "They give time for anyone who might have an objection to our union to come forward."

I recognized the problem even as the words left my mouth, but he was first to say it.

"And when the entire province objects, what then?" He pushed himself into a sitting position, then took my hands and gently pulled me up beside him. "Alera, how important is this custom to you?"

I peered out the window at the stars while I gave the matter serious thought, pondering Narian's way of life and if I could reconcile myself to it. I wanted to, but part of me was afraid of it—of going against the doctrines I had been raised to follow. I believed strongly in my kingdom's religion. I also knew I had to uphold the traditions my people valued if they were to believe in me and accept me as their leader. If I were to switch now to Cokyrian custom, their trust would be betrayed.

"It's very important," I ultimately answered, not looking at him.

"Don't be embarrassed," he said, cupping my chin to raise my eyes to his. "I wouldn't deserve you if I didn't respect your beliefs."

He gave me a light kiss, signifying that things were resolved between us, although the real problem remained.

"I don't know when the people will accept you, but I cannot go behind their backs. It may be a long wait."

Narian's expression was resigned. "So we wait."

His attitude lifted my spirits, and a splendid idea struck me. "Our priests are sworn to keep confidences—we could be betrothed."

"And betrothal—it doesn't involve banns or ceremonies or parades in this kingdom?" He was teasing me, assuring me he was fine with my decision.

"No." I laughed. "Just an exchange of rings. I'll wear mine around my neck."

"I'll wear mine on my hand where I should. My soldiers will be oblivious." He smirked, then added, "And it will confirm your countrymen's suspicions that I am ignorant."

I gazed into his eyes, at the love that shone within them, and laid my head upon his chest, content, for now, to have him hold me.

Narian would be in Cokyri for several days. He would report to the High Priestess on the state of the province and discuss with her such incidents as Steldor and Galen's revised regulations. He would also present to her a proposal I had prepared concerning the military school. Under the High Priestess's regulations, the school now served a strictly academic capacity, for the education of both males and females. Given this change, it no longer made sense in my mind for it to be a boarding school—parents would want their daughters to help at home and the buildings were at too great a distance for many children to travel on a daily basis. As a result, I had developed a proposal for four schools, to be situated in the different sections of the city. The plan was reasonable, practical and affordable—all valued by the Cokyrians—so I was confident she would approve. I didn't know what other business was generally addressed during these visits, or much about Narian's relationship with Nantilam, except that she was the closest thing to a mother he had ever known. And he always returned to Hytanica well-rested.

During Narian's absence, I arranged to dine one evening with my parents, sister and brother-in-law in the royal family's dining room on the second floor. This was a simple pleasure that I was often denied, for my duties as Grand Provost could not be confined to specific hours of the day. But Miranna had recently turned eighteen, and though my nineteenth birthday had been lost in the midst of the efforts to organize the province, I wanted to mark every one of her milestones.

"Alera, what an honor it is to have you join us," the former King declared upon my entry. "We see far too little of you these days."

My father's greeting was more formal than it once would have been, indicative of the deference he now displayed toward me. My relationship with him had been tumultuous the past couple of years—he had pressured me into marriage to Steldor, been disappointed in my conduct as Queen, turned cold when I had asserted my superior status and been grateful when I had negotiated with the Overlord to save his and my mother's lives. Still, in all my dreams of the future, I could never have foreseen the outcome of our relationship—but neither could I have foreseen the position I now held.

"How is the work on the Bastion coming?" I asked my father after the meal had been served.

"It is difficult, but we're making steady progress."

He glanced at Temerson, who was also working with the Cokyrians on the rebuilding project, and I had the impression he was seeking assistance.

"The Cokyrian officers are very knowledgeable, but their approaches are, at times, different from ours," Temerson supplied, the confidence in his voice belying the shy young man he had been. "We would like to restore the structure to its original grandeur—they're more interested in it being functional."

"I could talk to Narian about the project," I volunteered, seeing the opportunity to put in a good word for the man I loved. "I'm certain he would support what you want to do."

"No," my father sharply responded. "It's important that we deal with the Cokyrians on our own."

I nodded, a bit confused by his reaction. Was he uncomfortable with the topic? Or was his reaction due to the mention of Narian?

"What King Adrik means is that we can't rely on Narian if we hope to earn the respect of the officers with whom we work," Temerson clarified.

I nodded, for his explanation seemed plausible; and yet there was an undercurrent of tension that suggested they weren't telling me everything.

"And how are you handling the stress of your new position?" my ever-elegant mother asked, filling the strained silence that had fallen.

"It's a challenge, but I have Cannan to guide me, and Narian is quite willing to listen to my ideas." Despite a stiffening of backs, I persisted. "He wants to see our kingdom joined with his country in as peaceful a manner as possible."

My mention of Narian resulted in another momentary shutdown of conversation, then my mother finished her thought.

"Just be sure to take care of yourself. You look tired, and the mantle of leadership is a heavy one."

Another discomfited pause ensued, for she had highlighted a further change my people were being asked to accept—unlike in Cokyri, women had not been permitted to rule in an independent Hytanica. But responsibility wasn't weighing me down; expectation was tearing me apart. In order to retain my position as Grand Provost, I had to prove worthy of the

High Priestess's confidence; at the same time, I had to establish credibility with my people as a ruler. I could not afford to disappoint either side; yet I did not know if it were possible to satisfy both.

To everyone's relief, the conversation moved on to more mundane matters. But despite the casual nature of the discussion, Miranna didn't say a word. Her cheeks had regained their rosiness, and her curly, strawberry blond hair tumbled once more upon her back, but the extent of her emotional recovery was not so easily gauged. She and Mother spent much time together, for the former Queen had also endured unmentionable cruelty at the hands of the Cokyrians when the Overlord overran the palace. But despite their similar experiences, it was Miranna about whom we all worried.

After dinner, we excused ourselves to go our separate ways, and I invited my sister to accompany me to my quarters. Although we tried not to leave her unattended, there were inevitably times when she was on her own, and I had a partial solution in mind.

Temerson stayed in the corridor, at ease keeping company with London, while Miranna came with me into my parlor. Even this early in the evening, there was weariness in her face and in her stance, and I bade her to sit on the sofa. Then I *clucked* with my tongue.

"Kitten!" I called, raising the pitch of my voice.

The lanky, easygoing tabby cat poked his head out of my bedroom, arching to stretch his back before coming to me at an ever increasing pace. I picked him up, feeling the vibration of his purr, then carried him to my sister.

"Here, Mira," I said, placing the hopelessly trusting cat into her arms and giving him a scratch behind the ears. "I want you to have him, for now. He's a good companion. He was to me while…while you were gone."

I smiled sadly, for however sensitively I had made mention of her ordeal, she had withdrawn from me, not wanting to remember it. Something in her deportment, perhaps the way she shifted her body weight away from me, spoke as loudly as anything she could have said.

"Thank you, Alera," she murmured, nuzzling her cheek into the cat's soft fur. She stood, Kitten lounging in one arm, and leaned forward to give me a half hug.

"Good night," she said, then left without another word.

Taken aback by her abrupt departure, I hesitated for a few moments, then went to open the door. I rested a hand upon the frame, staring down the corridor after her and Temerson as though I might glean some revelation from the invisible trail of my sister's passing. London was leaning against the wall with his arms crossed upon his chest, his perceptive indigo eyes fixed on me.

"How is she?" he asked, then he cocked an eyebrow. "I assume you *gave* her the cat."

I motioned for him to come into the parlor, in part to discuss my sister, but largely because I didn't want to be alone.

He lit a few more lanterns before taking up his usual position against a wall, this time by the hearth. I sat on the sofa where Miranna had been, not at all uncomfortable that he remained on his feet. It was, and had always been, his duty to stay on alert.

"I still don't know what happened to Mira," I said, staring unseeingly at the rich and intricate rug beneath my feet, my chest seeming to squeeze my heart. "Maybe she's spoken to Temerson or my mother, but neither has said a word to me about her condition. I hate to think she's locked everything up inside."

I looked at London, remembering the story the High Priestess had told me about his ten-month imprisonment in Cokyri nearly twenty years ago. No one in this kingdom other than me knew the full extent of what he had endured—he had repressed those memories and never shared them with anyone, but Miranna did not have his constitution. London could survive with those horrors buried inside, but I feared they might get the better of my sweet sister.

"She won't speak until she's ready," he gently said. "And there isn't anything you can do to change that."

As usual, he had read my thoughts, and I waited for him to go on, but when he did, he spoke more generally than I expected. "You, Temerson and your mother and father are doing the right things. Be there. Don't let her feel alone."

I nodded, and London moved toward the door. I was keeping him from his leisure time.

A rattling from my bedroom caused me to jump, and I sprang to my feet, my thoughts flying to Narian and the potential repercussions of an encounter between him and London. In the next instant, I remembered that Narian was in Cokyri, but it was too late, for my bodyguard was eyeing me curiously.

"You know the wind can't get us in here," he wryly commented.

My cheeks pinked, affirming his suspicion. He shrugged in the direction of my bedroom door, drumming his fingers against his biceps. "Thinking of someone?"

"I… No," I said haltingly, and my blush deepened. I had never been able to lie to London.

"Narian released me from Cokyri," he reminded me, and I had the impression he had given the Cokyrian commander much thought. "He saved Miranna, and he saved your life. And I know you are in love with him. Because of all these things, I cannot begrudge you a relationship with him."

His word choice was careful, as it often was, and I realized he was keeping his personal opinion—his preference over my closeness with Narian—to himself, and that spoke volumes.

Caught between thankfulness and the slight offense I often felt when the topic of Narian came up with any of my countrymen, I asked a delicately pointed question.

"Are you ungrateful?"

"Not at all. I am extremely grateful to him. But there remain many issues on which Narian and I will always disagree. And many ways in which we might be obstacles to one another."

My skin prickled with unease at his words; then I opted not to wonder in silence.

"London, are you planning something?" I hated how my wary tone seemed to pit us against each other, but he laughed.

"If I were, what would you do?"

"I would beg of you to stop." I anxiously played with the folds of my skirt, for I did not view this as a laughing matter. "London—"

"Don't fear, Alera."

London definitely knew his way around words, for he had neglected to tell me there was nothing *to* fear. But there was nowhere else I could take this conversation, and so I sat back down, deciding to pursue *his* personal life for a change, something I rarely did.

"Tell me—how is Tanda? Have the two of you reconciled?"

His eyebrows shot up at my prying. London and Lady Tanda, Temerson's mother, had been betrothed in their youth, shortly before he was taken prisoner by the Cokyrians. As he was believed to be dead, she had married another. Her husband had been one of the military officers executed by the Overlord, a tragedy that had strangely opened the door for old love to be rekindled.

"Lady Tanda and I are...well," he replied.

"You were not at Miranna and Temerson's wedding," I went on, knowing I was treading into thorny territory. "Was it because of Tanda that you were absent? I know Mira wished you could have been there, and I'd hate to think you stayed away out of awkwardness, or—"

"I assure you," London interrupted with a smile at my persistence. "Lady Tanda and I are well. I was sorry to miss Miranna's wedding, but it was business that kept me away."

"I see." I considered him, then nodded, accepting his explanation. The wedding *had* been mere weeks after he had regained consciousness following the Overlord's torture. In addition to coming to terms with the suffering he had endured, he would have been behind the rest of us in evaluating the city and our circumstances. And he would have been dealing with the loss of his friends and peers in the military, which included his best friend, Destari.

I came to my feet and walked with him to the door. He turned to give me a slight bow, and I blurted one concluding thought.

"You should take more leisure time, London. Things have settled down considerably in the Bastion over the last couple of months. I can do without a bodyguard at times."

He shrugged, then noted cheekily, "I can see you're quite eager to play matchmaker."

"Just think about it, please?"

"I'll keep it in mind. I promise."

We bid each other good-night, and I retired to my bedroom, my mind still on London. I wanted him to have a chance to truly reconnect with Tanda. He had always seemed untouchable to me, able to handle anything, but during our experiences when we were in hiding, I had come to see in every person around me both their incredible strength and their humanity.

I crawled into bed and extinguished my lantern, knowing
I did not want London to be alone; knowing I did not want
to be alone; missing Narian so much that my chest felt hollow, and yet it ached unrelentingly.

When Narian returned the following afternoon, he brought
rings from Cokyri, knowing we could not go to a jeweler in
Hytanica, and we decided to meet that evening in the Royal
Chapel located on the first floor in the East Wing. I arrived
before him, having dismissed London for the day, and told
the priest what I desired.

"I would like you to perform a betrothal ceremony."

"Of course, Your Highness, a betrothal is always a happy
event. But when? And between whom?"

"Right now. My intended will be joining us shortly."

Before I could say anything more, Narian entered the
chapel, and the priest's aged face registered shock, then dis-
approval. I stared at the clergyman, my jaw tight, daring him
to refuse me. When he did not speak, I turned to Narian.

"Do you have the rings?"

He reached into a pouch on his belt, then placed the pair
of rings in my hand. I gasped, for their splendor was match-
less—gold bands with rubies, emeralds, sapphires and diamonds inset around them.

"These are beautiful," I murmured, beginning to lose hold
of my emotions.

I held the rings out to the priest, who reluctantly accepted
them, his reservations evident.

"Proceed," I edgily commanded. "And remain silent on
the matter."

The priest looked askance at me, then he conducted the
simple ceremony in which both Narian and I pledged before

God that we would wed. We sealed our vows with a kiss in the near darkness, for only a single candle lit our secret rite.

Narian said nothing as we walked down the corridor from the chapel, but I could sense his dismay at the priest's attitude toward him. He was accustomed to the way people received him, but familiarity did not erase the hurt it caused.

We climbed the stairs to the second floor, then parted ways, and I wasn't certain he would come visit me in my quarters. He would be exhausted from travel, after all, and the ceremony was of less significance to him than it was to me. I went to bed, joy at the step we had taken mixed with sadness that people didn't really know him, didn't know his heart. I silently railed at the unfairness of the world, eventually falling asleep, feeling almost lost in the large four-poster bed. But when I woke in the morning, he was beside me, dozing with his arm draped across my waist. His thick blond hair fell over his forehead, and I pushed it back, tracing a finger along his handsome cheekbone. I rarely saw him like this, so peaceful, so vulnerable. I also knew that I was the only one who ever did. He breathed softly and steadily, all guards down, and had not the duties of the day called to us both, I would have been content to stay with him like this forever.

SHASELLE

CHAPTER 6

A TERRIFYING
SORT OF SYMPATHY

MORNING BROKE CHAOTICALLY, AND I TOSSED caution aside to investigate the noise coming from the street. It didn't take long to determine what was causing the commotion—word traveled fast, through Cokyrians and Hytanicans alike, when waves were being made. Every enemy soldier's face darkened at the news that the pranksters were at it again, just as our people's spirits lightened at the mere thought of what Steldor and Galen might have come up with this time.

I hurried onto the thoroughfare, rushing north with countless others toward the training field, which had been vacant since the abolition of our military force. I fought through the boisterous crowd and saw that the bowl-shaped field was certainly not vacant anymore, its new occupant a rather unsightly scarecrow dressed in a Cokyrian uniform, framed against the tranquil green of summer grass.

I gazed down the hill, ignoring the shoving and jostling of the people around me, brimming with pride. This was the work of *my* cousin. Only he and his friends would have had the nerve to do something like this.

Cokyrians were preventing Hytanicans from descending

the slope, pushing us back like cattle and trying to make us disband. When one of the soldiers passed close to me, I spat on his boots, jumping back so the blunt end of the sword he thrust at me ticked my temple and nothing more. I grinned at him, then tensed as someone put their hands on my shoulders from behind.

"It makes you wonder, doesn't it?" the person said in a lazily irreverent tone that I knew well. "Whatever befell the poor soldier who *lost* his uniform to that creature?"

Before I could turn around, Steldor tugged me backward through the crowd, out of harm's way. Releasing me, he strode toward the thoroughfare, forcing me to jog in order to keep pace with him.

"How did you manage it?" I breathlessly asked, scrutinizing his handsome profile. He stood several inches taller than me, and it was difficult to look at him, keep up and dodge people all at once. Quite the opposite, the throng parted for him, his height and build such that he could not pass notice, and his recent actions earning him a few hardy pats on the back.

"You really shouldn't be out here, Shaselle," he responded, sidestepping my actual question. He glanced at me, and despite his next words, there was bemusement in his dark brown eyes. "And you certainly shouldn't be spitting on Cokyrian boots."

"You laugh in their faces—why shouldn't I spit on their boots?" I countered, earning a smirk and a shrug.

"Perhaps…because home is a better place for you?"

Despite the tease in his voice, there was seriousness behind what he said.

"You agree with your father then?" I concluded, shoving my hands into the pockets of the breeches I had again donned, my humor waning. I had never worn trousers this regularly before, but I felt a need to wear them now, despite the fact that they were standard attire for Cokyrian women. To me, they represented horseback riding and time with my father, memories to which I desperately clung.

"I have to, although I don't suppose you're too thrilled about any of it."

Now it was my turn to shrug, though a tiny spark of…I didn't know what—optimism, relief—ignited within me at the ease with which he recognized my feelings. He wanted to help. At least, some part of me latched onto the belief that he wanted to help.

"Uncle discussed it with me," I forced myself to say. "It makes sense, the marriage and all."

"But…" Steldor flourished a hand in front of him, illustrating the drawn-out word.

"But I hate it. More than anything, I hate it. Lord Taether made me see that."

Steldor nodded, leading me aside as we reached the main roadway to lean against the cool stone wall of a shaded shop, observing the passersby instead of fighting through them.

"I'm sorry. For everything, I mean—not just this." He turned to me with regret, sympathy and traces of his own hurt upon his face.

I knew how important Papa had been to Steldor. As a four-year-old, after the kidnapping and murder of his baby brother at the hands of the Cokyrians, Steldor had been sent to live with his aunt and uncle for six months. The connection he'd developed with my father had lasted through his wild teenage years, during which time our home had represented an escape for him. While Steldor had a strong, inimitable bond with his own father, mine had been a close friend and confidant, not only for him, but for Cannan, as well. Rather glibly, Papa had pointed out on more than one occasion that there were two sides to every story, and he was guaranteed to hear them both. Steldor had to be feeling the same pain I was.

"I'm sorry, too," I said brusquely, trying to shake off the automatic constriction of my throat. I wanted to cry in front of Steldor even less than I had wanted to cry in front of Cannan in the barn. I took advantage of the pause to begin a new vein of conversation.

"Steldor, maybe you could try to deter your father, you know, from making arrangements for me so soon. Would another year or two really matter?"

He responded with a dry laugh. "Deter my father? Shaselle, trying to deter my father once he's made up his mind is like yelling *whoa* at a stampede of wild horses."

"Doesn't stop you," I muttered, crossing my arms with a huff.

Again that cynical chuckle. "I assure you, it does."

"No, it doesn't." I pushed off the rough stone to stare at him. Annoyance came to me ever more quickly these days, and now the disagreeable temperament my mother and older sister condemned was emerging. I pointed back up the road. "Explain that scarecrow to me, if you're so obedient! I know your father was upset with you after you posted your rules, but you went ahead anyway, *without* his blessing."

Steldor clamped a hand over my mouth, the other holding the back of my neck, then he leaned close to hiss, "I'd prefer if my involvement in both of those incidents remained undisclosed."

My cheeks burned, and I pushed his hands away. "Sorry. That was stupid. But isn't there anything you can do? You have the captain's ear."

"What I have is his attention," he corrected, having accepted my apology and brushed aside our tense exchange. "Not intentionally, mind you, but I'll be keeping it over the next few weeks. He'll probably be distracted from you anyway."

"You're planning another stunt?"

He winked. "Would you expect anything less of Galen and me?"

"Can I help you?"

The up-and-down nature of our conversation persisted, and he shook his head vehemently.

"This is dangerous, what we've been doing. We laugh, but these aren't games. If we're caught, we'll be arrested. There's a reason my father disapproves, in spite of his own ambitions." He let his rebuff hang in the hot air while I again felt color rising in my cheeks. "Just go home, Shaselle. Put on a dress. Be a lady, and stay out of trouble. Understand?"

"I hate them, too, you know," I said, his dismissal and the humiliation that came with it rankling me. "It's not just *your* homeland that the Cokyrians have sullied—it's my homeland, too. And those bastards killed my father."

"And bitches," he added, catching me off guard. "Wouldn't want to forget the women."

I didn't know how to respond, so I gaped at him foolishly until he stepped onto the cobblestone of the thoroughfare.

"Come on. Let me take you home."

We walked in silence back to the western residential area where I lived, though he stopped at the beginning of my street to let me traverse the rest of the distance by myself.

"I shouldn't be seen around here. Not where Galen's as-signed—the Cokyrians are trying to keep us apart to avoid plots big *and* small, and will be suspicious if we're seen in the same area."

I nodded and turned to go, but he grabbed my arm.

"I know how you feel, Shaselle. I know you want to do something, and it's not even that I don't think you could. I just can't let you be involved, for the sake of your safety. And mine," he added as an afterthought. "My father would kill me if I let you help and you came to harm. Just please, let this go, and I swear I'll do my best to influence him on your marriage issue."

Now that I was thinking rationally, offering my assistance had been absurd—I had no special skills aside from horseback riding, and certainly no military training, so accepting Steldor's offered compromise was not difficult.

I left my cousin at the crossroads and meandered homeward. I took my time since, to some degree, I dreaded arriving, and it took me longer than it normally would have to notice the increased number of Cokyrian soldiers on my street.

I lengthened my stride, suddenly wanting to be home, but nothing could have prepared me for what I would find when I arrived. Everyone was outside, near the barn, Mother's arms coming down over Celdrid's shoulders to restrain him, while Dahnath stood with the younger girls gathered around her. I rushed forward, and Galen stepped out of the stone building. When he saw me, a terrifying sort of sympathy rushed into his face.

"I'm sorry," he said.

I didn't need to ponder the reason for his apology, for three Cokyrians, a man and two women, all dressed in black, appeared behind him. The first woman held a scroll, while the second woman and the man each led a horse. One was my father's prized stallion; the other was Papa's beloved young mare, Briar, whom he had raised from a filly and trained himself. The mere thought of these filthy Cokyrians laying a hand on any of my father's mounts was enough to make me sick.

"Take them," the officer with the scroll commanded. She had bronze hair, pale blue eyes and freckles across her thin nose—a nose I wanted to break.

"No!" I snarled, jumping forward to reclaim those invaluable animals. They belonged to Papa; I couldn't lose them, I couldn't let them go. He had loved them, and I could see him and hear his voice when I watched them, and at no other time. But Galen caught me about the waist, using his entire body to hold me back. I kicked and hit at him while the Cokyrians led my father's favorite horses away.

"Stop!" I screamed, not even sounding like myself, desperation and rage leaving me hoarse and raspy. *"No!"*

"Shaselle, there's nothing we can do!" Galen said, raising his voice to counter my shrieks. "The Cokyrians lost mounts during the fighting, and the High Priestess has authorized the taking of our best stock to supply their military. Baelic's are the very best."

I melted against him, devoid of strength, my breathing quick and shallow. Then I looked past his shoulder and saw the bronze-haired officer standing there, tapping the scroll against the open palm of her other hand.

"I will make you sorry, I swear to God," I vowed.

She appraised me for a moment, unimpressed.

"Her Grace the High Priestess thanks you for your cooperation," she informed us, the haughty inflection of her voice grating on my nerves. She strode past me, but reached out to tug a strand of my hair, letting me know I was nothing more than a little girl.

CHAPTER 7

AN UNUSUAL MORNING

STELDOR AND GALEN HAD STRUCK AGAIN, ONLY this time even I had to laugh at their antics. Besides, it would have been difficult to mar my mood following the betrothal ceremony. Narian and I were bound together, and however secretly it had been done, it was, in my mind, the most significant event of my life. We would never be separated again.

My first appointment this day was, as always, with Cannan. I stepped into the corridor outside my quarters, happily fingering the ring that hung on a chain around my neck, and almost bumped into London. He had taken my advice about spending more time away from the Bastion and so was less frequently waiting for me when I started my day.

"You startled me," I said with a nervous laugh, hastily dropping the betrothal band. My hand hung inelegantly in the air for a moment, and heat raced to my face and ears. London considered me for a moment, then boldly reached out to pick up the ring and examine it.

"This is nice," he remarked as I stood completely still. "Different."

"I...b-bought it," I stammered. "Yesterday. While you were away."

He raised an eyebrow to remind me he wasn't daft, but thankfully didn't question my lie.

"We'd better be going, Your Highness. Cannan is waiting for you in his office."

Feeling self-conscious, I led the way through the hallway and down the Grand Staircase, but we were intercepted before we reached our destination.

"London, I need a word."

I turned around to find Halias with a hand on my bodyguard's shoulder. He looked tired, but there was strength of will in his light blue eyes and, I knew, a distinct purpose for him to be in the Bastion.

"Of course," London said, his attitude sobering.

Halias gave me a respectful nod, and London motioned me toward the captain's office, then the two former deputy captains strode off. I tucked my betrothal ring into the neckline of my dress so no one else would see it and stood indecisively in place, musing that I had sunk quite low on everyone's priority list. Then a new concern blossomed. London knew the ring's significance, I had no doubt. Could that fact have ramifications? Would he share what he had learned with anyone else? He wouldn't want my relationship with Narian to become widely known, for such news would upset the citizenry. But if he told anyone, the word might spread. Someone might overhear. Deciding Cannan could wait a few minutes longer, I hurried back up the double staircase on the off-chance Narian might still be in his quarters.

I went straight down the corridor into the West Wing, proceeding toward my old rooms, but slowed when I heard voices ahead. I darted into the small dining room where my family took its meals and held my breath, having stumbled upon Rava and Narian in heated debate. I doubted either of them had noticed me, so I dared to stay and listen.

"Orders come through *me*."

"Orders come from the High Priestess, and both you and I are tasked with carrying them out," Rava rebutted. "If you were not so insecure in your command, you would be pleased that I took care of a problem in your stead."

"You *created* a problem, Rava. Alera and I are trying to placate these people—"

"Alera, Alera. All I ever hear from you is *Alera*."

"She is essential to our goals, is she not?"

Narian had grown defensive, and I prayed that Rava would not be able to detect the subtle change in his tone. He was usually adept at hiding his feelings, but the topic had caught him off guard. I couldn't fathom what would come of Rava discovering our relationship, nor did I care to find out.

"She is," Rava granted, dropping the issue, and I was relieved she did not know him as well as I did.

"Then let's come to it," Narian pressed. "We follow the High Priestess's orders, but how and when those orders are carried out is my responsibility. Through angering these people by stealing their horses, you destroyed any progress *I* may have made toward quieting their rebellions. And if you carry out an order without my knowledge again, I will see you dismissed."

There was a tense pause, then Rava's equally tight voice gave response.

"Do you really think you could, Narian? Have me dismissed? How have you served the High Priestess other than as a weapon and a problem?"

"I will not let you ruin what we have started, Rava."

I heard a door shut and Rava's light footsteps coming in my direction, and I stepped to the side of the doorway, flattening my back against the wall, not wanting to be detected.

She passed the room in which I hid, oblivious to my presence, and continued down the corridor toward the Grand Staircase.

I waited a moment longer, then followed after her. A rush of warm air from the opening and closing of the front doors hit me upon reaching the second floor landing of the staircase, and I peered over the railing to see her step outside, perhaps to regroup after her confrontation with her commander. Regardless, I wasn't sorry to see her go. Then Cannan emerged from his office, glancing around, and I realized that he was looking for me. Deciding my worries about London would have to wait until later, I descended to meet the captain at the bottom of the stairs.

"You seem flustered, Your Majesty. Has something happened?"

"No, not really. It's just been an unusual morning."

"I see. Well, let's move into my office and gain some privacy."

I nodded and we walked through the antechamber to access Cannan's office along the east side of the Hearing Hall. As usual, he settled into the chair behind his desk, while I sat facing him, although I had of late been using the padded armchair. It made me feel more like we were working together and less like I was under scrutiny.

"Do you want to tell me about your unusual morning or get right to work?" Cannan asked, wasting no time on small talk.

I reviewed the past half hour in my mind, and decided there was something upon which he could shed light.

"There is one thing. When London and I were on our way here, we came upon Halias. He wanted to speak with London, and they went off together. Only I found Halias's manner troubling—he was tired and grave, not at all himself. Which makes me think his business with London was rather important. Yet I'm not aware of any issues affecting the province that would bring them together. Do you know what they might be doing?"

Cannan moved his chair forward, resting his forearms upon the surface of his desk. "You sound suspicious, Alera. Do you not trust them?"

I could feel my neck and cheeks turning scarlet. "No—no, that's not it. I would trust them with my life, but I worry that they may stir up trouble, like Steldor and Galen."

"I see. Remember that these are seasoned Elite Guards, hardly the type to play pranks."

"Of course, I didn't mean to imply." I was becoming more and more out of sorts, and wished I had not raised the topic.

"But to answer your question, I don't know of any official business that involves the two of them. And Halias, like the rest of us, has had little to smile about of late. On the other hand, he and London are friends, and it's possible Halias sought him out for something as simple as a hunting trip. Since London is your bodyguard, he'd have to come to the Bastion to do so. Hunting is one of the few pursuits the men are allowed that lets them retain some dignity."

"What do you mean?"

"Our military, the Palace Guards and the City Guards have all been disbanded. Our prized horses and other possessions have been seized by the Cokyrians. We're not allowed to carry weapons of any sort, our persons and our homes are randomly searched, and we cannot move freely in and out of the city. We're being turned into tradesmen or field hands, with no ability to protect ourselves or our loved ones. When we hunt, we at least can breathe the fresh air, move through the forest and the foothills, provide meat for our families and teach our sons something about weaponry."

I nodded, for the first time understanding the demoralizing effect of the High Priestess's regulations. As Cannan saw it, the restrictions went to the heart of our way of life, while I had viewed them as removing a few privileges. I had never before considered that the rules affected our men to a much greater extent than they did our women.

"Is there anything else, Alera?" Cannan asked.

"No, nothing other than our usual business."

I tried to smile, wanting to move on to a different topic. But as Cannan sorted through some papers on his desk, I realized I needed to take hold of the reins, as London had suggested, before the tension the men were feeling became unbearable.

CHAPTER 8

HYTANICAN COLORS

I WASN'T A HELPLESS LITTLE GIRL. AND IF STELDOR and Galen could do it, so could I. Perhaps something on a smaller scale, and a little less likely to rile the authorities; more of a practical joke, really. It would have to be simple, for I had no military training. These thoughts chased round and round in my head over the next couple of days. They did not, however, point me in a particular direction. In order to prove I wasn't a helpless little girl, in order to get back at the Cokyrians, I needed an idea. I needed a plan of action.

Inspiration came to me in a strange fashion. My mother was helping our maid dye some muslin fabric blue in order to make day dresses for my younger sisters. All that was involved was soaking the cloth in the watery dye until it penetrated the fabric; the longer the muslin soaked, the deeper blue became its color. The dye also colored the sticks the women used to stir and flip the fabric so that all fibers would be exposed; and if you weren't careful, it colored your hands. As I watched the process, it slowly dawned on me that the blue in its deeper shade was the same blue of our Hytanican flag, a blue that I longed to see waving in the breeze, displayed on our military uniforms and blanketing our horses. And that was when my scheme took form. If the dye could color not only fabric, but sticks and hands, could it dye hair? And, in particular, could it dye horse hair?

I waited until my mother and our maid had left the fabric soaking in a tub, then dipped a mug into the liquid and carefully carried it outside. I walked with it to the barn, setting it down next to Alcander's stall, for his coloring was better suited to my purposes than that of my own mare or Celdrid's gelding. He turned to look at me, and I patted him on the neck, then plucked several strands of his cream-colored mane. Kneeling down, I placed the hair into the mug to determine if it would soak up the dye and, if so, how long it might take. After waiting impatiently for fifteen minutes, I checked the strands, pleased to see they were indeed turning blue. To turn a dark enough blue would take a while, however, for the hair of a horse's mane and tail was quite coarse. Would the hair of the coat work better? I grabbed a grooming brush and entered Alcander's stall, then lifted one of his hind feet to brush his white sock and fetlock hair. Feeling I had enough fuzz on the brush, I tried my experiment again. This time the effect was more dramatic, and it didn't take as long for the color to grab hold. I smiled, for what I had in mind could definitely work. The dye would be easy to obtain and transport, I was comfortable around horses, and I knew my way around the military base. The biggest problem was that the work could take an hour or more; but at least it would be a quiet process.

Over the course of the next two days, I surreptitiously collected and stored some of the dye, thinking I would need at least a bucketful. I also left the house at every possible opportunity, walking toward the military base, then surveying it from a safe distance, taking particular note of activity around the stables. My father had been the cavalry officer, so I was familiar with the layout of the barns, having visited them many times while he was alive. But I needed to know when guards were posted, how many were posted, and were the buildings ever left unguarded.

As I expected, there was a lot of activity around the stables until late evening. But after all the horses that had been ridden during the day were returned and the animals had been fed, lights went out, the doors were locked and all was quiet. No guards in sight.

The military base itself was a different matter—there were always guards on patrol. But they only passed in the vicinity of the stables once every half hour; and the barns could be approached from the blind side—the side that faced the apple orchard which separated the military base and the palace. While many of the trees were scorched, they would still provide good cover.

My basic thoughts in order, I waited for an evening with adequate cloud cover, then put my plan into effect. After tying my hair back, I snuck downstairs and out the back door, then hurried to the barn, where I had stored the blue dye. Just before I went inside, I rubbed my hands in the dirt, then smeared some of it across my cheeks and forehead, hoping it would make me less visible. Entering the tack room, I picked up the bucket and grabbed several cloths that would normally be used for cleaning tack. Suddenly struck by the danger of what I was about to do, I hesitated, wondering if I should forget the whole idea. Was the prank I had in mind worth the risk? What would happen to me if I were caught? Then I pictured the Cokyrians leading away my father's horses and hate rose inside me, giving me the courage to act and the confidence that I would succeed.

I walked toward the palace, hugging the sides of buildings so as not to draw attention, then waited in the shadows of the apple trees until the guard had passed on her rounds, giving me an initial half hour. With a deep breath, I covered my light brown tresses with my hood and hurried forward, not giving myself a chance to change my mind. Bypassing the stallion barn, the foaling barn and the training barn, I moved to the main building that housed the working horses.

I arrived safely enough, ready to face my first challenge—getting into the building itself. But time spent on these premises had taught me that the bottom half of the double swinging doors did not have a separate lock and was the least secure. I pushed on it with my shoulder until it swung inward, then ducked beneath, carrying the bucket of dye with me. I stood, letting my eyes adjust to the dimmer lighting, then approached the first stall. While the horse had a dark mane and tail, it had two white stockings, easy enough to work with. I soaked two rags in the dye and entered the stall, offering some oats that I carried in a pouch on my belt. As these were well-trained military horses, I simply ran a hand down a hind leg, then wrapped the damp cloth around the white sock above the hoof, repeating the action on one of the forelegs. I then left the stall to select another appropriate animal.

A little farther down the aisle stood a white horse, and a thrill passed through me at my good fortune. I carried my bucket of dye over, grabbed a nearby brush and entered the stall. As the mare munched the oats, I dipped the brush into the dye, working it into her mane and tail, leaving them wet enough that water ran down her neck and the back of her legs. I stepped back to admire my handiwork, and grinned. This was fun, this was sweet and these Cokyrian horses were going to look magnificent in Hytanican blue.

I returned to the first horse and retrieved my wraps, then moved down the line. Deciding I would have to work faster, I focused on white stockings and white manes, letting the dye set as long as I could. A sound at the barn door told me a half hour had passed, and I ducked down inside a stall, praying the sentry would not come too far down the aisle. To my relief, she raised a lamp and gave a cursory glance around, then departed, once more locking the door. I now had another half hour.

My bucket rapidly emptied, covering six, then seven horses. I hadn't known for sure how many mounts I would be able to "beautify," and was extremely pleased with my number count. I was almost done, and things had been quiet other than for the occasional horse's snort or stamp of a hoof.

I swished the remaining liquid in my bucket, thinking I had enough for one more animal, then spotted a beautiful gray gelding on the opposite side of the aisle. I entered his stall, talking softly and extending a handful of oats. He snorted them off my hand, apparently not interested, which should have been my first clue.

Thinking the gelding was perhaps a bit skittish, I laid a hand on his hindquarters, intending to give him some time to get used to me. Before I even knew what was happening, he whirled to face me, his ears pinned back against his head. I froze, then he reared, slamming his forelegs down while I scampered to the side. My second clue that I had not made a good choice.

The horse spun, kicking out at me, his hooves crashing like thunder against the wood. With no way to defend myself, I grabbed the bucket with the remaining dye and tossed it at the loco gelding, as much landing on me as on him. Desperate to escape, I yanked on the stall door and stumbled through it as more kicks resounded. Faint with relief, I fell onto my hands and knees, panting heavily, my arms quivering, only to hear a sound like the clearing of a throat.

I stared at the floor and saw four black boots, then I felt the flat end of a sword against my chin, lifting my head until my eyes met those of two unamused Cokyrian guards. My heart dropped to my stomach, for in all my planning, I had not considered how to explain myself if I were caught.

"Well, well, what have we here," said a female voice.

"Looks like a rather scruffy Hytanican to me. Or perhaps it is a Hytanican pony, given her position." This speaker was male, so the woman was no doubt his superior.

"No, I think she has finally learned her place, down in the dirt at our feet."

Despite how scared I was, resentment was pushing at my very skin, seeping through my pores.

"If you think you can handle the girl," jested the woman, "I'll take a gander and see what she was doing here."

She walked up and down the aisle, peering in the stalls on each side, occasionally holding her lantern closer to one of the horses to get a better view. I remained on my knees, although I was now sitting upright, sweat trickling down my neck as my mind whirred to find a means of escape. Would they let me go if I vomited? That was a feat I was quite certain I could pull off, for it felt like I had been hit by the plague. But it was too late for that, for the woman had already seen some of my masterful work. It wasn't long before she returned, each of her footsteps resounding in my head.

"Well, it appears we have a prankster in our clutches. She has made quite a mess of several of our horses. Rava will be extremely displeased with her and highly satisfied with us."

"On your feet," ordered the man, and I hastily complied, wishing I had never had such a foolish idea, for then I never would have attempted it, and I never would have ended up on my knees in the dirt in front of two Cokyrians. The woman yanked me around to bind my hands behind my back, and I winced as the rope cut into my wrists.

"This is going to be entertaining," she said, and my legs shook so violently that I doubted I would be able to walk. Steldor and Galen were brave, they were daring, and they could handle fear. I had none of those qualities. Panic hit me in waves at thought of the treatment I might receive from my captors. It was entirely possible I would never again see the light of day.

CHAPTER 9

POWER STRUGGLES

I ENDED AFTERNOON AUDIENCES EARLIER THAN usual and walked into the King's Drawing Room, intending to pass through it and seek out Miranna. She had not joined me in the Hearing Hall as had become her habit over the past few months, and I worried that she might not be well. I did not have to go far to check on her, however, for I nearly bumped into her when I entered the corridor. She squeaked in alarm and clasped the hand of her best friend, Semari, who was standing beside her.

"Alera," Miranna gasped, a blush rising in her cheeks. "You startled me!"

"I think we startled each other," I responded with a laugh, then I greeted Semari, immediately understanding what had been more important to my sister than listening to the petitions of our people.

"What plans do you two have?" I asked, glad to see Miranna was socializing.

"We thought we would take tea in the garden," Semari answered, her voice and demeanor telling me she had grown up considerably since I had last seen her. She would soon turn seventeen—had her father begun to consider suitors for her?

Miranna reached out with her other hand so that she held mine in addition to her friend's.

"Join us, won't you? It will be like old times."

"I was actually looking for you, so of course I'll join you."

With a brilliant smile, Miranna led us through the doors that opened onto the garden at the rear of the Bastion.

The midafternoon weather was warm, sunny and altogether delightful. We walked along one of the paths toward the fountain situated at the garden's center, where the servants had prepared a table, complete with a steaming pot of tea. We seated ourselves around it, and Miranna, our hostess, poured the amber liquid into three cups. Pleasantries were exchanged, then the conversation turned to what I had inferred might be on Semari's mind—her marriage prospects.

"It hasn't been easy," she revealed. "With the war, there are twice as many eligible young women as there are men to marry them. Papa has suitors in mind for me to meet, but I honestly don't know what to expect."

I frowned, for it seemed unlikely that a girl of Semari's breeding would have difficulty enticing a husband, even given the tough times. Her father, Baron Koranis, was a rich man; she would bring a large dowry to a marriage.

"Surely you exaggerate. A young woman with a background like yours will always draw good marriage prospects."

Semari shrugged. "Well, there is the *other* factor. Half of them are afraid of me."

I glanced between my sister and her friend, now thoroughly baffled. "Why in the world would men be afraid of you?"

"Well, they all know Narian is my brother and, I suppose, that taints my blood. Or perhaps they worry he'll, I don't know, come after us."

"They think Narian will come after you?" I repeated in disbelief. "What is he, a mon—" I stopped, and all three of us looked down.

"I'm sorry," I breathed, distractedly fingering the betrothal ring around my neck.

"Where did you get such a beautiful necklace?" Miranna exclaimed, grasping for a change in conversation, and my unease doubled.

"I purchased it," I began, knowing there would be no stopping my sister once her curiosity was engaged. In desperation, I knocked the back of my hand against my teacup, spilling the liquid over the tablecloth and onto Semari's lap. She sprang to her feet, followed by Miranna and me.

"I am so sorry," I fussed, firmly tucking the ring inside my dress while Miranna dabbed at her friend's skirt.

"No, it's quite all right," Semari graciously replied. "It's only a small amount, hardly a stain at all."

We once more took our seats, and my sister struggled to restart a polite conversation, but my spirits never did recover. Perhaps people would always believe Narian evil. That thought made me more depressed than angry, for I knew so much better.

Finished with our tea, we walked through the heavy oak doors and back into the Bastion; at the same moment, Narian emerged from the stairwell of the spiral staircase, and I felt that our discussion had been prophetic. We all halted, and it seemed that we had gone back in time to the fateful day when brother and sister had first met—Semari and Narian were staring at one another as they had then, their faces so strikingly similar that the resemblance had been the impetus for Narian's identification as a Hytanican. But their expressions, then as now, were opposite—Semari seemed inclined to hop behind Miranna and hide, while Narian had shut down so completely that not even I could conceive of what he was thinking.

"Good day," he finally said with a nod of his head.

Semari's mouth flickered into a smile, and she gave a small curtsey. Narian's gaze went to me, but I did not know what he wished me to do or say. Without another word, he walked away from us toward the front of the Bastion.

"I didn't know he'd be here," Semari whispered, and Miranna laid a hand on her arm. I didn't respond, too dismayed for words.

After parting from Miranna and Semari, I spent time in my study, then returned to my quarters for a light dinner. With great effort, I exiled the melancholy that had lingered in the aftermath of my conversation with my sister and her friend, for it did no good to dwell on things that were outside my control. And no matter how I felt about his situation, Narian had reconciled himself a long time ago to his relationship, or lack thereof, with his family, just as he had accepted the way Cannan, Steldor, London and the rest would always regard him.

I changed into my nightgown and propped myself against my pillows with a book, hoping Narian would come to visit me. It wasn't long before he dropped with ease through my window, and I smiled, laying the novel aside. He removed his sword belt and came to sit on the edge of the bed, more subdued than usual, then drew one knee up against his chest, his body turned away from me.

"How are you?" I asked, his demonstrative posture suggesting that he had either reached a new level of comfort with me or was particularly upset. While I hoped for the former, experience told me it was more likely the latter.

"I'm fine," he said, those two words confirming that he was troubled.

"It appears something is on your mind," I noted, trying to make this easy for him, if he did want to talk.

My words had some effect on him, for he stood and faced me, although he simultaneously crossed his arms in a posture to block me out.

"Do you think it's…?" He trailed off, shaking his head. "Never mind."

He again sat on the bed, facing me this time, an indication he had come to a decision with which he was content.

"What is it?" I encouraged, taking his hand.

"It's not important."

"I think it is."

"Alera, if I'm saying it's not important, it's not. Trust me."

"Trust *me*." There was a pause during which we stared into each other's eyes, testing to see who would relent. "You can tell me whatever it is, Narian. You can tell me anything."

He exhaled—almost a laugh—and broke eye contact. "I know that, but it's not as easy as you make it sound."

"Neither is it as hard as you make it sound." I reached up to run a hand through his hair. "Just say it. I promise I'll keep it secret from the proper authorities."

Although I was joking with him, the reason for his reluctance was no laughing matter. The Overlord had tried to train Narian not to feel; he'd succeeded in teaching him not to reveal his feelings. I waited, praying he would for once abandon that godforsaken instinct.

"Do you think it's too late for…for my family? Enough has happened to make it too late. I mean, I've done enough."

"You'll never stop taking the blame for everything, will you?" I asked, trying to keep the frustration from my voice.

"I'm just looking at it from their perspective, Alera."

"I know."

I sighed, realizing he wanted that family, wanted a mother

and father and siblings, despite how much effort he put into convincing me that I was all he needed.

"I've seen you with your family," he said, luring me away from the conclusion I had drawn. "Those connections are of importance in Hytanica, and whatever I can do to gain acceptance here is in our best interests. But perhaps it's too late for that."

He had no idea that I could see the boy in his deep blue eyes; that I knew how he was truly feeling. I played along, not wanting him to shut down.

"No, it's not too late," I said, sounding more certain than I felt, and his face subtly brightened. "I don't know about your father—about Koranis." I corrected how I referred to the Baron, endeavoring to keep emotional connection to this discussion at a minimum, for that was what Narian was trying to do. "But Alantonya. While you were in the mountains, missing, I spoke to her. She was worried about you. She wanted you to come back, and prayed you were safe. I don't think she has ever stopped loving you."

Though he hardly moved, I could feel him pull back from the conversation, almost as though someone had blown out a candle and left me in the dark.

"Narian?" I said in confusion, but he was unreadable.

"She never loved me."

The comment was so perfunctory it jarred me, and it took me a few moments to realize that, to his mind, it was easier to believe he'd never been loved than to consider that he might have been loved and lost it.

I woke early the next morning, though not early enough to see Narian off. He'd had a restless night, his mind undoubtedly on the things I'd said. I wished that I'd done a better job of advising him—he wouldn't know how to forge a connection with his family, and I didn't think it likely he would revisit the topic after the way last night's conversation had ended. I was left perplexed, fretful and with the distinct feeling that there was nothing else I could do.

I dressed and left for the captain's office, even though it was earlier than I usually met with him, for I needed to occupy my thoughts. Cannan was standing in the entryway, speaking with a Cokyrian guard, as I came down the Grand Staircase, but he waved the woman away when he heard my approach. We were about to proceed to his office when the front doors swung open and Steldor strode in, his face etched with worry.

My former husband's gaze went to Cannan, not acknowledging me in any way. This alone told me something was wrong, for he tended to be either overly polite around me or overly familiar. Ignoring me was not his style. He strode close to his father, wary of speaking in the presence of the Cokyrian sentries posted on either side of the doors.

"I have to tell you something," Steldor muttered, his voice urgent.

"My office."

"There's no time." Steldor grasped Cannan's jerkin at the shoulder, momentarily losing control of his volume. With a mighty effort, he dropped his voice, then elaborated. "Shaselle's been arrested. I don't know what they'll do to her, except that they will try to blame her for everything…every prank that's been played. You have to—"

Cannan shirked off his son's hand and strode toward the front doors without a word.

"What will you do?" Steldor called after him.

"I don't know."

"I'm coming with you."

At this, Cannan whipped around. "You'll stay here. Lost tempers won't help anything."

"I won't lose my temper."

"And if you would only do what I ask, we might not be in this situation."

The former military leader departed, leaving his son standing in place, jaw clenched. After a moment, Steldor followed, and I found myself alone at the base of the staircase, trying to comprehend what I had heard. Shaselle? Arrested? My hands shook as I thought of what the Cokyrians might do to her. In the current state of unrest, they meted out punishment like a baker kneaded his dough—thoroughly, forcefully and daily.

Ignoring the Cokyrian guards' suspicious looks, I flew up the Grand Staircase, hoping Narian would still be in his quarters. What *could* Cannan do? He had no authority in the Province of Hytanica, no way to affect Cokyrian forms of justice, nor did I. If they felt like executing Shaselle, they would. That poor family had lost too much already.

Without care for decorum or protocol, I rushed through the door into Narian's parlor to find him near the hearth, strapping a dagger and sheath to his forearm. He stared at me in alarm, and I gasped for breath, then blurted out what I had overheard.

"You must help," I pleaded. He strode past me heading into the corridor, and I called after him. "Wait, I'll go with you!"

He stopped and faced me, his brow furrowed.

"No, Alera, you can't. The High Priestess gave us two realms of responsibility. Yours is here, in the Bastion, seeing to the welfare of the Hytanican citizens. Mine is to command the peacekeeping forces and enforce her rules. This is my business, not yours. My effectiveness may even be hampered if you come with me."

I nodded and watched him depart, leaving me with hope but no concrete idea of what he intended to do.

SHASELLE

CHAPTER 10

NOT GOOD AT ALL

I HAD EVALUATED THE SITUATION FROM EVERY angle, and there was no other conclusion to draw than that I was in serious trouble. The room in which I sat was furnished with a wooden table in its center, with but one barred window to let in light. I was on one side, my hands shackled to the legs of my chair, and across from me were two Cokyrian women, their faces set and their intent clearly to glean information from me.

No, this was not good at all.

My shirt and breeches were splattered with blue dye, my hands stained—there was no disguising my guilt, and the wenches knew it.

"You think you're a smart little girl, don't you?" said the first one, a short-haired brunette. "A smart little girl playing a funny game. *We* don't play games."

"Wasn't it a game to you, murdering our military leaders?" I retorted, bolder than I should have been, and in a flash the second soldier's palm met my cheek, nearly knocking me over. For a moment, I felt numb, dazed, then my cheek flamed and

I could almost feel my lip begin to swell. So far, my vengeance was not panning out according to plan.

"You've been sly up 'til now," the brunette went on in a snarl. "Why so foolish last night? Emotions finally get the best of you?"

I kept my mouth shut, horrified that the stunt I had attempted had led them to assume I was responsible for them all.

The brunette snatched my chin and forced me to look at her, squeezing so hard I thought my jaw would break.

"Listen when I'm talking to you, child."

I quivered, fighting the bile rising in my throat. I was a stupid, stupid girl. And now I was going to pay for it.

"Please," I said with difficulty, her grip on my face inhibiting my speech.

"Please?" The woman laughed, releasing me and shoving me so hard my spine cracked against the chair, and a small cry escaped from me. "You break into our stables, dye our horses' tails and hooves the color of your defeated kingdom, get caught, and now are foolish enough to beg? You may go to your silly heaven when you die, but until then I'll see that you're in hell for what you've done."

I was terrified and nauseated, scrambling to find a way out of my straits. There was none. I was at their mercy, and mercy was something the slaughter of our officers had shown they didn't understand.

"I didn't do those other things," I said, sniffling though I wished I could stop and be brave like Steldor would have been. The opening and closing of the door barely caught my notice, for it was only another Cokyrian, probably to take me to the stocks or the dungeon.

"Yes, you did," the brunette insisted, leaning close and staring into my hazel eyes. "Confess, and you will be executed for your crimes. Fail to do so and your punishment will be far worse."

I was on the verge of saying goodbye to my pride in favor of openly weeping and groveling when the soldier who had entered, a man not much older than me, spoke up.

"She bungled this attempt so miserably that you know she couldn't be responsible for the rest. I understand it's not your field, but try to have some compassion, Corza. You've got her scared to death."

The brunette froze, displeased. Without looking at the newest arrival, she said, "What are you doing here, Saadi?"

"Rava wants her lashed, then brought back here to see if her tongue has loosened enough to reveal the identities of the true culprits. I'm to see to her punishment."

Corza's lips pursed, irked that this young officer was interfering with her tactics. But she stood regardless.

"Take her."

The man walked over to me and released me from the chair, his light blue eyes assessing me. He yanked me to my feet, but I didn't fight him, despite how frightened I was by the idea of a lashing—I could survive a lashing. In my experience, very few people survived execution.

He took me past the two women who had been interrogating me and out the door into a hallway. When we passed through a second door, I recognized the main room of the City Guards' headquarters, where the Master at Arms had been in charge prior to the Cokyrian takeover. Now it crawled with enemies, with one exception—my uncle Cannan was there, demanding to see me.

He abandoned the enemy officer he had been addressing the moment he noticed me, and came to block our progress.

"Shaselle, are you all right?" he asked, voice low and rumbling, like a gathering storm.

I nodded, my heart beating unevenly as it battled the hope that he could somehow save me—even Cannan had little clout in these times. Saadi spoke before I did.

"She is to be lashed, eight times for the eight horses she damaged. We will send for you when she is released."

"She's just a girl, not a soldier and certainly not a warrior," my uncle argued. "She was angry, she was foolish, she wanted to act. Surely you, and your superiors, can have sympathy for that."

"I have respect for it, in fact."

"Then you want something else from her."

"Our business and intentions are confidential, as I'm sure yours were when you were Captain of the Guard."

"Tell me what you want, and I will provide it."

Saadi relinquished his hold on me and crossed his arms, considering my uncle. He was several inches taller than me, though he wasn't particularly brawny, but Cannan still had the stature to glare down on him.

"We can make a deal," Saadi said. "Turn in whoever is responsible for ridiculing Her Grace the High Priestess's regulations and for the assault of a Cokyrian soldier in order to create that disgusting scarecrow. Do that and I will release her without punishment."

"Are you in a position to do so?"

Saadi nodded once, without elaboration.

"Very well. I am the party responsible. Let her go and take me into custody."

My jaw dropped and some idiotic protest rose to my lips, to be drowned out by another male voice.

"You are accounted for, Cannan. Do not arrest him—he is lying."

Saadi, Cannan and I looked around to see Commander Narian, the infamous boy-invader, striding over to us. Hatred rose within me at the sight of him. He had been at the Overlord's side when my father and the others had been lined up for slaughter, and he hadn't done a thing to stop it.

"Commander," Saadi greeted him, but this was ignored by Narian, who instead issued orders.

"There's nothing to be gained by this. Free her."

"Rava will be displeased," Saadi warned. "The High Priestess will be displeased."

"The longer you argue, the more displeased *I* will be. How do you think the Hytanicans will react to our making an example of a young woman? Release her. I will report the matter to the High Priestess."

This time when my Cokyrian captor glanced at me, I dared to look back, noticing his bronze hair and the freckles that danced across his nose. I shifted self-consciously, unable to believe that I was thinking of my appearance. Damn Cokyrians and their damn freckles.

Saadi took my hands and unshackled me, and I examined the unusual lock that had held me. It was made of several small metal wheels, completely unlike the locks we had in Hytanica. When the wheels had been turned to display the proper characters, the cuffs fell off and I was free.

For a moment. With a swift nod to Saadi and Narian, Cannan grasped my wrist none too gently and pulled me through the door, out onto the busy thoroughfare. He did not slow down to speak to me or to accommodate the length of my legs, nor did he stop until someone shouted his name.

"Cannan!"

Narian was behind us, pushing through the milling crowd, and my uncle awaited him impatiently.

"I appreciate what you did," Cannan said when the enemy commander reached us. "But don't expect me to thank you for it."

Normally the former captain would not have been so cold, but anger at me was seeping into his attitude.

"I didn't come after you for thanks. I came to warn you. Keep her out of trouble, keep Steldor and Galen out of trouble, make certain nothing can be traced back to you. I can appease the High Priestess for now, but the moment I can no longer do so, you will all be dead."

My mind and body froze as I attempted to comprehend Narian's words. Were we really such a danger in the High Priestess's eyes? Could I have gotten my uncle and cousin killed with my rash actions?

"I know." That was all Cannan said, but his hold on my wrist became more painful.

Narian nodded, and the men locked eyes for a moment, then Cannan once more headed off with me in tow.

"Uncle…" I tried to talk, but he did not halt, nor was he in a mood to listen; neither did he address me until we were approaching the path to my house.

"Go to the stable and wait for me there," he ordered. "I must speak with your mother."

He let go of me and I stumbled in the direction of the barn, which still housed three horses but nonetheless felt dreary and hollow without my father's prized mounts. I went inside, humiliation making my stomach swirl, tiredness causing my temples to hurt, and fear of my uncle's wrath urging me toward the back window. If I ran away, maybe I would never have to face him. I could live on the streets or sneak over the Cokyrian Wall and actually *be* at liberty. But in reality, I would never make it if I ran.

Tears filled my eyes, and I kicked a bucket that was half-full of grain, sending it soaring into the door of Briar's vacant stall, its contents scattering across the floor. At the same moment, I heard the barn door open, and pivoted to face Cannan, the fight inside of me once more burning.

The captain's face was inscrutable, but his eyes bored into me, almost physically painful in their intensity. When he spoke, his tone was severe enough to make a hundred soldiers cower, but I refused to do so.

"If you ever step out of your place again, I will have you betrothed within a week to a man who will keep you, and keep you well."

"Let him try," I retorted, maintaining some distance between us, though I was fairly certain he would not strike me.

"There is far more at stake here than your well-being, Shaselle. I can't fathom what you were thinking."

I tugged at my hair and almost wailed in frustration. "I was thinking that I'm not useless! I was thinking that my father is dead and no one is doing a thing to avenge him. I was *thinking* that Steldor is the only one brave enough to stand up to the Cokyrians, and it's still *not good enough*. So I *thought,* what the hell do I have to lose?"

"Your life!" Cannan barked. He stepped closer, looming over me, and my resolve faded. Cowering seemed like a good idea, after all.

"Do you know what it did to your mother to have you disappear like that? To have Steldor tell her what had happened, and that we were powerless to intervene? You're lucky Narian was feeling charitable, because we *are* powerless. You would have been severely and painfully lashed, perhaps worse, if not for him."

"I know, Uncle, and I'm sorry. But what do you want me to do? Sit around and wait for my life to end in some other way? What's my alternative to risking my neck? Being a plump, miserable housewife?"

"Being what you were raised to be."

"That's *not* how my father raised me. You don't have the right to make me into someone he didn't want me to be."

Cannan exhaled, closed his eyes and pinched the bridge of his nose, reining in his anger in favor of understanding.

"Shaselle, your father never wanted you to be a *man*. He didn't want you to fight wars or put yourself in danger. From now on, you need to stay out of this. It's not where you belong."

I met his eyes, but didn't respond.

"Do you understand me, girl?" His voice was sharp and crisp, regaining some of its earlier fervor.

"I understand," I replied, suddenly meek.

"Good. Now return to the house and accept your mother's punishment. I have detailed the situation, and she is not happy, to say the least."

"Yes, Uncle." I walked past him, then stopped and turned around. "And thank you for coming to help me."

He gave a curt nod and I walked up the path to my front door, glad to enter into the warmth of the house, despite the looming lecture I would receive.

CHAPTER 11

AN IMPOSSIBLE CHOICE

THE HOURS PASSED, BUT NEITHER NARIAN NOR
Cannan returned to the Bastion. I tried to ignore my anxiety
over Shaselle and go about my day as usual, but after answering correspondence and attending a few meetings, I could
stand the wait no longer. Narian might not be in his office,
but there was a good chance that Rava was in hers.

With a determined set to my chin, I left my study and
crossed the Hearing Hall to the former office of the Sergeant
at Arms, which Rava now occupied. The door stood open,
but it was not Narian's second-in-command who was inside.
It was an officer closer to me in age whom I saw with some
frequency around the Bastion, one of the few among the command hierarchy who was male.

"Excuse me," I said as I stepped over the threshold. "I wish
to speak to Rava."

He looked up from a stack of parchments, his light blue
eyes judging me.

"She is not here."

Instead of pressing him for Rava's whereabouts, I decided
to press him for the information I sought. From what I knew,

he held significant rank and it was obvious from his presence in Rava's office that he worked with her.

"Your name?"

"Saadi, at your service."

"Very well. A young Hytanican woman, eighteen years of age, was arrested, either early this morning or last night. I want to know what happened to her."

"Many Hytanicans are arrested, Grand Provost."

"That may be, but I am inquiring about only one."

"And why do you seek the information?"

I stared at him, irritated that he was evading my question. He would not act thus with Narian or any other Cokyrian superior. Narian's contention—that such matters were his business and not mine—rang in my ears, along with his belief that his effectiveness might be hampered by my presence. Did Narian come across as weak if he consulted with me? Or were there things from which he sheltered me? In any case, either I had authority or I did not, and it was time to find out which it was. Straightening my posture, I met Saadi's eyes and took the same no-nonsense approach the commander employed.

"The young woman. What is her status?"

Saadi dropped the parchments upon the desktop and stepped closer, telling me I had at last gained his full attention.

"If you are referring to Cannan's niece, she has been released upon Commander Narian's orders."

"With or without punishment?"

"The commander overrode Rava's orders that she be lashed."

My heart pounded, for I could not imagine what Shaselle could have done to merit such a harsh consequence, but my gaze did not waver.

"For what offense?"

"Perhaps you should take that up with the commander."

"For what offense?" I repeated, taking a step toward him. My place within the chain of command was clearly at issue with this officer, and I wondered if I had weakened my position by dealing with issues through the commander.

"An act of petty vandalism," he disclosed.

I considered Saadi carefully as I digested this information. There was something more going on here.

"And how many lashes would she have been given had Rava's original order been carried out?"

"Eight."

While I tried not to show it, I cringed inside. Eight lashes for an act of petty vandalism? Even for the Cokyrians, this seemed excessive.

"And would she have then been released?"

"Not immediately."

Once more exasperation rose within me at the officer's evasiveness—trying to obtain information from him was more taxing than hearing petitions from the people. And then it hit me. Saadi was treating me much as Steldor had during our marriage. The function of the Queen in the former Kingdom of Hytanica was to supervise the household, plan and execute the social events, and raise the children. She played no part in the actual governing of the kingdom. I was not about to let myself be shuffled aside in the same manner in my position of Grand Provost.

"You will tell me everything you know about the matter," I boldly stated, praying he would obey, for I did not know what I would do if he flouted me. "And you will do so now."

To my surprise, Saadi dropped his hands to his sides, almost as if coming to attention. While his initial instincts might have been to avoid me, he was used to taking orders from a woman.

"She would have been lashed and then questioned to obtain information about others involved in acts of vandalism.

More particularly, those who mocked the High Priestess's original regulations and those who staged the scarecrow at the military field."

"Questioned?"

"Interrogated. Forcefully. Until we obtained the information we wanted."

I felt faint at the thought of what Shaselle might have endured, and at what she might have revealed, whether she knew for certain of her cousin's involvement or not. But now was not the time to show weakness.

"And is such a punishment, such an approach, typical in dealing with a Hytanican citizen?"

"Yes."

My head spun, for his answer was appalling, the thought of how my people were being treated was sickening, and the idea that this was not my business was insulting. Then anger rose. In Narian's own words, my realm was to oversee the welfare of the Hytanican citizens. And this struck me as pretty central to their welfare.

"Is there anything else, Grand Provost?"

Saadi was studying me, almost warily, and I wondered how much of my emotional turmoil could be read upon my face.

"Yes, there is. Beginning tomorrow morning, you will provide me with a report of all arrests made the previous day, all punishments carried out with an identification of their associated crimes, and all interrogations conducted."

"I'll have to check with my superiors first."

My temper and patience snapped. "I *am* one of your superiors. You will provide me with the information I desire beginning tomorrow morning or I will inform *my* superior, the High Priestess, of your insolence."

"Yes, of course. My apologies."

"Then see that it is done."

I turned on my heel and stalked back toward my study, my legs beginning to weaken halfway across the Hearing Hall. By the time I entered my office, I was shaking and sank upon my sofa, trying to compose myself for the afternoon audiences I would soon have to hold.

But how could I have ignored such a fundamental facet of my own position? Cokyrian justice had a most immediate effect on the welfare of my people, just as immediate as their housing, their schools and their livelihoods. And how had I let myself be taken out of the chain of command? It was clear I relied too much on Narian in dealing with the Cokyrians who inhabited the Bastion, making it easy for them to see him as the one in charge, bypassing me. And it was my own fault. I had done my best to avoid direct contact with Cokyrian officers, whether due to my own newness with command or some personal aversion to associating with *them*. Was I just as narrow-minded and prejudiced in dealing with the Cokyrians as they were in dealing with my people?

I took several deep breaths to calm my racing pulse and my nerves. Now that the problem had been identified, it could be solved. It was time I sought out my own issues rather than waiting to be asked for my input; it was time *Grand Provost* became more than just a title. Thoughts in place, I stood to reenter the Hearing Hall to begin receiving petitions from my people.

Miranna had again failed to join me for the latter part of my day, and I closed my doors early, despite the guilt that came with shutting out the needy. Feeling at loose ends and desperate for some companionship, I went to the dining room on the second floor where I hoped my family might be found. Platters of food had already been placed upon the table, telling me I had arrived a few minutes late, but I was greeted cordially nonetheless. I considered my sister carefully, for it had been just over a year since her abduction, but she seemed to have passed that anniversary with no ill effects. Shifting my focus from her, I made an effort to follow the dinner conversation, which had turned to the reconstruction work on the Bastion.

"Are things still progressing well?" I asked, innocuously enough.

"Just fine," Temerson answered, unfortunately at the same time my father blurted, "We have shortages of—"

They stopped and stared at each other, my father's face turning ruddy.

"Are you still having difficulty working with the Cokyrians?" I pressed, confused.

For an instant, neither answered, then Temerson pasted on a smile.

"Not at all. King Adrik only meant that the work is far from finished."

I frowned. "Have there been other complications?"

"No! No, no, of course not," my father blustered, waving his hand in the air like he was swatting at a fly. "We're moving at a steady pace, but there really aren't enough people involved to ensure a timely finish."

He was dodging around some aspect of the topic, though I couldn't guess what it might be.

"I'm sure we could arrange for some more workers," I volunteered.

My father's gaze went back to Temerson with a strange, pleading expression, and my confusion grew. I glanced at my mother, who had been unusually quiet all evening, but her eyes were directed to the tabletop.

"We truly don't need them," my sister's husband told me emphatically. "We know the men can't be spared, and as your father said, we're making steady progress."

I dropped the subject despite the intrigue it now held, choosing to trust Temerson's and my father's motivations. Besides, I could get information on the status of the reconstruction from other sources.

After dinner, I went with Miranna to her third-floor quarters, where Kitten was lounging on the sofa, not such a kitten anymore. We sat across from each other, the cat beside me, and by my sister's relaxed mood, I could tell that time was at last healing her wounds.

"Temerson and Father didn't mean to act so strangely, Alera," she said, tossing her curly hair over her shoulder. "They *have* been terribly busy, day and night."

"Night?" I repeated, wondering what work the two of them could be doing at such late hours.

Miranna shrugged. "All I know is they've been slaving away. I do miss him, though—Temerson, I mean. He's changed so much from when we first met."

Two years ago, Temerson had escorted my sister on a picnic my father had arranged for Steldor and me. She had become smitten with the timid sixteen-year-old almost immediately, though it had taken him months to say more than a few words to her. But since his father's death, Temerson had indeed changed, just as Narian had since our original introduction.

"Your mind has wandered, Alera," Miranna said with a sparkle in her eyes. "Are you thinking about someone?"

I stared at her in bewilderment and she laughed. "I know you and Narian have been seeing one another."

"How could you possibly know?"

"As usual, you have no idea what love has done to the two of you. You're lions who look at each other and become lambs. It's obvious!"

My eyebrows peaked, my worries about the discovery of

our relationship increasing dramatically. If Miranna could tell, who else might?

"How is Mother?" I inquired, changing the subject. "She didn't seem herself tonight."

Miranna twirled a piece of hair around her fingers. "Really? I guess I didn't notice."

Rather than try to clarify my instinct that our mother had been reluctant to meet my eyes, I waved off the topic. We chatted for a bit longer, but I couldn't shake the impression that something was wrong. At last I said good-night and stepped into the corridor, startled to find London waiting for me.

"I was told you were here," he said, by way of explanation.

"It's late, and you're off duty," I pointed out, bewildered. "I'm sure I can make it to my quarters unharmed."

"Nonetheless, I'll accompany you."

There was no humor in his tone, no desire to engage me, and my apprehension grew. When we arrived at my quarters, he followed me into the parlor, and I wondered why everyone was behaving so strangely tonight, for despite how well London and I knew each other, he would normally have waited for an invitation before entering.

"London, what are you—"

He cut me off, closing the door. "Alera, you must know that this war is far from over."

"What are you talking about?"

He considered me for a moment, then approached to lay his hands on my shoulders, gazing into my uneasy brown eyes.

"I realize that since Narian came into our lives, you and I have not always been on the best of terms. You have not always agreed with me, and you have not always trusted me. But I beg of you to do so now."

I took a deep breath to steady my nerves, for his intensity was disconcerting.

"Please, London. Just tell me what's going on."

"I know that you and Narian are betrothed," he said, confirming my suspicion. "This increases the difficulty of your position, but it is imperative that you do as I say."

He released me and untied a small pouch from his belt, then took my hand, pressing it into my palm.

"Pour this into a goblet of wine and give it to Narian when he comes to you tonight."

"Why?" I choked, feeling faint.

"Because he is the only one who can stop us. And because you are the only one he won't suspect. Please, Alera, you must do this for me. For Hytanica."

"But what are you going to do?" I demanded. "What exactly is it I'm doing for Hytanica?"

He strode to the window, gazing out at the last streaks of light cast by the setting sun before turning around, his face in shadow.

"Tonight, we will take back our kingdom. Halias and his men are positioned to take care of the Cokyrian sentries on the city wall. Once that's done, we'll lock down the gate." His voice was calm, but forceful. "We're ready for them, Alera—do you realize we outnumber them? We've been planning this for months, but Narian can thwart us. The magic the Overlord taught him is too great. He is unnaturally strong, as quiet as the mist, can conjure fire, cause pain with a wave of his hand and has an array of potions at his disposal. You are our only hope of success."

I bridled at his assumption that our goals were the same.

"Why would I do this?" I angrily demanded. "People will die. *My* people, Narian's people. You're setting them up to die, and for what? An attempt that will fail! Let me talk to Narian, negotiate for more freedoms. I love Hytanica as much as you do, but this is *foolish*—no, this is *reckless*."

"This is going to happen. Just think of how many people will die if Narian is unleashed."

"Narian is not a monster."

"Narian is a weapon."

We glared at each other until it seemed time had stopped altogether, then London stepped toward me. "Sides aren't easy to pick. But you know which one needs you the most."

"And what if Narian doesn't come to me tonight? What then?"

"He will."

With that, London departed, the click of the door sounding like a death sentence, and panic hit me with surprising force. My hands shook, and my thoughts crashed together, making it impossible for me to concentrate on any particular aspect of the situation. I thought of Narian, who could arrive within the hour. If I remained in this state, he would see through me in an instant and I would have no chance of doing what London wanted. I needed to calm myself and think this through. I sat down and closed my eyes, deliberately slowing my breathing, hoping to also slow my racing blood.

If I did as London had directed, there would be bloodshed. The tremulous peace Narian and I had established would be eradicated. On the other hand, the only way to stop London and the others would be to tell Narian what I knew—which would also lead to bloodshed. I walked to the mantel, the path suddenly quite clear. If it were possible to reclaim Hytanica... how could I oppose such an end? I poured wine from a jug into two chalices, thankful London had at least given me the option of protecting the man I loved from the fray.

I heard a noise from my bedroom and jumped, almost knocking over the goblet intended for Narian, and spilling some of the sleep-inducing drug London had given me. I brushed it over the mantel's edge and into the barren fireplace where it would not be seen, reminding myself to behave normally.

"Are you all right?" Narian had entered the parlor and was scrutinizing me from across the room.

"Of course," I said, forcing a cheerful tone.

His eyes darted around the room's perimeter. "You just... look pale."

"There's hardly any light. So how can you tell—am I glowing?"

He smiled, relaxing a little.

"Sit down and have some wine with me," I invited, moving to the sofa. He joined me, and I offered him the tainted drink, which he accepted with a puzzled expression.

"You're shaking, Alera."

"I'm cold."

"It's quite warm."

"But the evening temperatures drop quickly now that summer's sultriness has passed. The wine helps." I took a sip from my goblet, deliberately stilling my hand.

"So would a quilt," he pointed out. "You detest wine."

I laughed uncomfortably, trying not to recoil at the flavor of the drink.

Narian was taking his time. Did he suspect there was something wrong? He knew there was something wrong with me, yes, but perhaps the wine smelled off and it had alerted him. London *had* given me an abundance of the herb, whatever it was, and I had used it all.

Narian let go of his reservations and lifted the goblet to his lips, and nausea hit me full force. London believed Narian to be nothing more than a dangerous weapon, one that would fight against us, and he was right that I was the only one around whom Narian would lower his guard. Would

London, thinking of the greater good, be willing to use me to poison and *kill* his enemy?

"Stop!" I cried, reaching out to grab the goblet and spilling wine all over the rug. Narian leaped to his feet, tensed for a fight, and I burst into tears.

"Alera, what is it?" he asked, not sympathetic, but demanding and urgent.

I was gasping, unable to catch my breath and feeling like I might vomit.

"It's London. He asked me to drug you. He said I had to do it, for Hytanica."

"Where is he?"

"I don't know. He left. He said their plan was to kill the sentries on the wall and close the city. I'm sorry, I'm so sorry."

I wasn't sure to whom I was apologizing, or even for what exactly, but the guilt was close to unbearable. I put my hands over my face, my heart splintering at the thought of every one of the night's possible outcomes.

Narian ran to the door, and I summoned the strength to follow him. We flew down the Grand Staircase, where he snapped orders to the Cokyrian guards at the doors.

"Rouse Rava and alert the soldiers on duty to monitor the city walls. There is a rebel party waiting to strike and I want them caught, *now*. Bring them here alive."

The guards left to carry out his instructions, and Narian turned to me.

"Alera, I will do everything I can to protect the people you care about, you know that. But I will not be focused unless I know you are safe. Please, stay here."

I nodded, despite my desire to do anything *except* stay put, and he kissed me deeply right in the middle of the Grand Entry Hall, without a care for secrecy.

"Be safe," I murmured, watching him go. For a moment, I

stood indecisively in place, then went into the Hearing Hall, not wanting to return to my quarters.

It was late and at first silent, but after a while I became aware of vague noises—shuffling sounds and occasionally what I could have sworn were muffled voices. They seemed to be coming from one of the rooms at the other end of the hall. I drew near to the dungeon door and eased it open, for I was not aware that we were keeping any prisoners in the Bastion. Voices floated up to me from the narrow, dank stairwell.

"That's the last of them," said a young man who sounded unsettlingly like Temerson. "They're in Steldor's and Galen's hands now."

"The men in the villages are armed. My crew has met every hunting party and seen them fitted, and continues to do so." This time it was London who had spoken—his voice I knew well. "There's no more to be done right now."

"Except wait." Was it my father? "Are you quite certain we're not under suspicion? That Alera doesn't—"

"Alera will have done exactly what I expected. That's all that's important."

I took umbrage at London's tone—he spoke of me like a servant who had been given orders. Without thinking, I backed up, scuffing my shoes against the stone floor.

"Quiet!" I heard someone hiss, and they all fell silent. I hesitated, knowing my presence had been detected, then opened the door and felt my way down the dark staircase, making sure they heard my approach. As I neared the bottom, I called out to them, not wanting to have my throat slit.

"London, is that you?"

The blood was pounding in my temples as I stepped into the main area, off of which corridors led to individual dungeon cells. A torch on the wall opposite me was lit, and the faces of the men standing in front of it were in shadow. One

of them walked forward, and I knew from the familiar build
and gait that it was my bodyguard.

"Alera, what are you doing here?"

"I should be asking you that," I retorted, and he put a finger to his lips, telling me to keep my voice down.

We stared at each other for a moment, then fear of who
was involved in this takeover plot, of who might be killed,
took hold.

"I told Narian," I blurted. "You must abandon this now,
before it goes any further. He doesn't know names, so it's not
too late."

"It is too late," London disagreed, placing a hand on my
arm. "At least for Halias and his men. They are already in
place, and I must join them."

"No," I breathed. "Can't you stop them?"

He shook his head, then looked at the two men behind him.
"But your father and Temerson don't have to come with me.
Their part in this does not need to be known."

"And what part have they played?"

London sighed and ran a hand through his silver hair. "They
have helped me smuggle in weapons from outside. We can't
fight without weapons."

I nodded, certain things falling into place for me. London
had probably not been spending time with Tanda. I had, unwittingly, made it possible for him to be gone but not missed,
permitting him to go out through the escape tunnel to acquire
weapons, most likely from neighboring kingdoms. My father
and Temerson had been helping to move those weapons into
the hands of the rebels during the night.

"Go, Alera," London urged. "Go back to your quarters
and forget what you know. King Adrik and Temerson will
follow, but I must join the others. Whether or not we will

be successful remains to be seen, but your loved ones will be safe regardless."

"Not all of them," I choked out, the thought that he might die making it difficult to breathe.

"I will be careful."

"I'm sorry, London."

He gave me a slight smile. "You did what you thought was for the best. I must do the same. Now, please go."

I made some sound of acquiescence and London lifted the torch from its bracket, shining its light into the stairway as I climbed up. I glanced back one last time before I reentered the Hearing Hall, wondering if I would see him again—alive.

I closed the door to the dungeon behind me and hurried across the hall, exiting through the King's Drawing Room to reach the second floor by means of the spiral staircase. From there, I hurried past the library and on to my quarters. I entered the parlor and threw myself down on the sofa, trying not to think, trying not to feel. Things had been put in motion that I could not stop, could not affect, and every outcome I foresaw was filled with blood and death and regret.

CHAPTER 12

BRAVE MEN

I KNEW SOMETHING WAS WRONG THE MOMENT I woke. Mother's expression was pained at breakfast, and the noise from the street was louder than it should have been—most of the work in this part of the city had been completed during the summer. Dahnath and I exchanged glances, wondering what had happened during the night, while our younger siblings chatted obliviously, but I saw in my older sister's gaze a warning not to ask. It was not our place to know unless Mother saw fit to tell us.

The shouts from outside grew louder, until they penetrated even the sensibilities of the children, quelling their talk.

"Mama?" Celdrid said, alarm creeping into his face.

"We're staying indoors today," Mother said, her voice flat. "It's not safe—"

My heart exploded and I ducked as the dining room window shattered, spraying glass across the table's surface. Lesette and Tulara screamed; Ganya burst into tears; Dahnath's chair toppled, followed by a crash, for she had fallen to the floor with Celdrid in her arms. Mother sprang to her feet, drawing all eyes to her.

"Everyone, upstairs," she ordered, her voice strained with fear. She began to pull the younger girls to their feet, gathering them around her to head for the staircase.

I emerged from beneath the table, my eyes taking in both the stone that had caused the damage and the smear of blood across the tablecloth that told me someone had been hurt.

"It's okay, baby," Dahnath soothed, trying not to touch Celdrid's injured hand.

"Get some bandages and alcohol," Mother urgently directed me, and I hurried into the kitchen to grab the necessary supplies.

I wasted no time in joining my family in our parents' bedroom, where the younger girls were huddled together on the bed. Dahnath was sitting at the dressing table, holding Celdrid in her lap while Mother examined his injury, but even from the distance at which I stood, I could see the shards of glass protruding from his palm.

"Mother, what's going on?" I demanded. Celdrid whimpered as she began to pluck out the shards, tears drowning his cheeks, and I cringed.

"Nothing that concerns us! We live in a dangerous time, Shaselle. Our only responsibility is to keep ourselves safe."

"Safe from what?" I persisted, earning a glare from Dahnath. Mother held out her hand. "Alcohol, please."

I was still clasping the medical supplies and hastened forward to bring them to her. She looked plaintively at me, and I dampened a cloth with the alcohol for her use.

Celdrid sobbed, then tried to fight Mother and Dahnath off, remembering the pain of alcohol cleansing from previous injuries. I knew it myself.

"Shaselle, help us!" Dahnath exclaimed, and I took the bandage from Mother, wrapping it around my brother's hand while they clasped him tight. He kicked at me, getting me once in the ribs, then collapsed against his oldest sister, and I poured more of the offending substance through the fabric and into his wound.

Celdrid's breathing was uneven, but he had exhausted himself, and Mother knelt to take him into her arms, kissing him on top of his head. He curled up against her, needing her comfort, and she whispered further instructions to Dahnath and me.

"Go back downstairs and get my sewing materials, but stay away from the doors and windows."

I nodded, fighting nausea, for I knew what she intended to do, then left with my sister to creep down the stairs.

"Something did happen," I whispered to her as we reached the landing.

"Yes, but we don't need to figure it out right now." She likewise kept her volume down, although with the noise outside, I doubted anyone could have heard us.

"You just don't *want* to know." I sounded more accusatory than I had intended, and Dahnath's nostrils flared in indignation.

"You're right, Shaselle. I don't want to know. I want to stay safe. I want to keep Celdrid, Ganya, Lesette and Tulara safe. I want to survive this. Do you think knowing would make that any easier?"

I could have argued, but opted to keep my mouth shut. Her anger dissipated, just like Mother's always did—she tended to remember that others had feelings. I could never quite grasp that concept when my temper flared.

"I want you to be safe, too, Shaselle," she added, reaching out to touch my hair.

An abrupt pounding on the front door forestalled my response. My sister and I stood still, staring at each other, panic washing the color from our faces. Who wanted inside?

"Go back upstairs," Dahnath muttered. "I'll get what Mother needs."

"But—"

"Just *go*."

I nodded once, my breathing short and shallow, and Dahnath disappeared through the archway to our right. I hesitated, slightly embarrassed that she was either braver than I was or more responsible. The pounding on the door resumed, and even though I knew I should obey her, I stepped forward and threw it open. A man stood on the front stoop, his eyes wild.

"Sign a petition for release of the prisoners!" he yelled in my face, turning to make the same plea to the others crowding around him. "Free the prisoners!"

I snatched the document he was waving, seeing names scribbled in haphazard fashion up and down its length.

"What's this for?" I shouted, fighting the general din.

"The brave men who will be executed for trying to reclaim our kingdom!"

The parchment slipped from my fingers to be caught up by someone else before the wind could take it. The sky was overcast, seeming more so every moment, but before I could press for additional information, the man pushed his way back toward the street, calling for signatures.

"Shaselle, close the door!"

It was Dahnath, standing with supplies in hand. She tugged me away and locked the door without waiting for me to act.

"What do you think you're doing?" she scolded.

"There have been arrests. I think there will be executions for some sort of revolt."

"Who? Who has been arrested?" Dahnath demanded, her anger replaced by dread.

"I don't know!"

We stared at one another, sharing an unspoken fear. Our

family consisted of strong, indomitable military men. Whoever was behind this, it was almost guaranteed that Steldor,
Galen or the captain was involved—if not all three. And Drael,
Dahnath's betrothed, had fought in the war and was as loyal
to Hytanica as were the rest of the men. It was possible he had
joined the fray, as well.

We returned to the bedroom and assisted Mother while she
stitched Celdrid's hand. He moaned and tried several times to
pull away, but I held him fast against my chest.

"Be brave," Dahnath murmured, stroking his hair to calm
him. "It's almost over, almost done."

Finished, Mother splashed more alcohol over the sutures,
then again tied a cloth bandage over the wound.

"Now don't fuss with it," she reproved, pulling Celdrid
into her arms.

Neither my older sister nor I said a word about what we had
learned, afraid of Mother's reaction and of what she might tell
us. Was it bliss or torture to be in the dark when the fate of
our loved ones might already have been determined?

Hour by hour, the day wore on, and we tried to entertain the younger children with word games and rhymes.
This became easier as our street gradually quieted, although
I supposed that activity on the thoroughfare and around the
Bastion remained out of control. After helping Dahnath to raid
the kitchen for bread, cheese and fruit, I went to one of the
second-story windows and watched Cokyrian soldiers sweeping through the neighborhood, subduing the small pockets
of citizens who had no means to organize without the proper
guidance. By my guess, the proper guidance was locked away.

We were quite relieved when Galen came later in the day
to tell us that the captain, Steldor and Drael were not among
those arrested, granting us some measure of peace. My mood
was darkened, however, by Mother's news that she and Can-

nan had, prior to the failed revolt, arranged for another suitor to come to dinner, and that she saw no need to cancel the invitation. Her drive to maintain normalcy, especially given the renewed unrest, was that of a carriage horse wearing blinders—focused straight ahead, unable to see what was really going on around her. I grimaced, but said nothing, thinking that the occasion two days hence would at least give me a chance to find out what had happened in the uprising.

The day of the dinner threatened rain, and I had the nerve to be thankful, for it meant I would not have to go on a walk with our guest. The servants had by this time cleaned up the shattered remains of the broken window, and Mother had drawn the drapes to hide its condition and block out the nippy fall air, for there would be a long wait to obtain a new pane of glass.

In midafternoon, Dahnath undertook the not-so-simple task of trying to make me gorgeous. She was naturally attractive, for she took after Papa's side of the family, with her auburn hair, dark eyes, slender figure and perfect features, while I was stocky, with chipmunk cheeks and long, flat brown hair. My hazel eyes, a match to my mother's, were my one and only beauty.

Dressed in my favorite color, lavender, which Dahnath thought darling and Mother dubbed becoming, I once again sat nervously at the dinner table with my family, having given my solemn promise that I would be on my best behavior. My newest suitor had come with his father, which meant he was younger than the last—perhaps eighteen years of age. I could feel the older man's eyes on me throughout the meal, judging me, even while he conversed with Cannan, with whom he was quite comfortable. I thought it likely he had been in the military before our forces had been disbanded.

The young man whom my uncle considered a marriage prospect didn't look at me much, or say much, or seem to have much going on in his head at all. Perhaps I was being overly critical tonight—part of my irritation stemmed from not yet knowing the fates of the men who had been arrested—but still I resented him, despite his dark hair, sparkling green eyes and upturned nose. I scoffed internally, for how could I *not* resent someone who was prettier than me?

"Lady Shaselle, I must say, that gown is quite distinctive," Lord Landru, the father, complimented, and I wondered vaguely who I was succeeding in attracting. I shot a scowl in Dahnath's direction, feeling she should have been more honest with me about the dress. No one could quite bring themselves to say I looked lovely this evening. Descriptors like *darling, becoming* and *distinctive* sounded like praise one might give to a toddler who had picked her own wardrobe.

"Thank you, sir," I murmured, less politely than I should have, and Mother's discontent loomed like another presence in the room.

As dinner ended, rain began to fall outside, and I could tell Mother was relieved when the captain invited our guests to move to the parlor. She would have been mortified if water had trickled into the dining room through the broken window while our company was present, although the movement of the drapes in the wind had probably revealed our secret by now.

The customary wine was served once we were situated, a splash in tiny glasses for my youngest siblings before they were sent to bed, and generously filled goblets for the rest of us. I wanted to keep company with my immediate family, but Cannan, who was still speaking to my suitor's father, motioned for me to join them. It was only when I drew near that I realized the boy was there also, for he was smaller than the older men and as silent as a mouse.

"Perhaps you would converse with us," Cannan suggested, the slightest bit of pressure in his tone, an indication that my behavior was not meeting his standards.

"I'm pleased to be asked," I replied, giving a small curtsey in hopes of appeasing my uncle, for I didn't want to risk his wrath.

"Young Lord Grayden excelled in military school," the captain informed me. "I was telling our guests about our family's military history, and of Baelic's love for horses."

I looked Grayden up and down, wondering how someone with his slight build could excel at anything that required strength and coordination, but kept such thoughts to myself.

"Papa did love horses," I confirmed.

"I thought you might be pleased to know that Grayden has an interest in training them," Cannan added.

"How wonderful," I said, and this time my smile was sincere. When no one responded, I realized they were waiting for me to say something else. Not wanting to repeat my disastrous experience with Lord Taether, I kept my mouth closed, no doubt coming across as a bit thick in the head.

There was an awkward pause, then the young man's father finished the rest of his wine.

"Shaselle, perhaps you would refill Lord Landru's goblet," my uncle said.

I nodded, knowing I should have made this offer without prompting. I was, after all, well-schooled in social graces; there were just times when I didn't want to use them. As I proceeded with the task, walking toward the small refreshment table, I overheard Lord Landru's remarks to Cannan.

"Your niece is a hardy girl. Does she cook?"

"She has the knowledge any wife should, but has relied primarily on servants throughout her life."

"Good. If this marriage goes forward, I'll be sure to hire a cook who'll watch what that one eats."

"Father!" Grayden reproached.

I forced my legs onward, having no desire to hear more. Cannan would want to defend me, but I could not expect him to do so—Landru and Grayden had come here to evaluate me, and had the right to ask questions and raise concerns. Nonetheless, the anger and humiliation Landru's comments generated made my cheeks burn. How could I return to face him, knowing what he thought of me?

I sniffed once as I refilled the wineglasses, making up my mind that the opinions of our guests didn't matter. None of this mattered. It couldn't, or I would be a complete and utter failure. My resentment built and gained strength; at the same time, the wine I had consumed defeated my better sense, and an irresistible desire to retaliate took hold. That rude old Lord Landru needed to be shown how it felt to be disgraced.

Forcing a cheerful countenance, I sashayed back to the group of men, staring straight at Lord Landru as I offered him a fresh goblet of red wine.

"Here you are—"

The toe of my slipper caught on the rug and I pitched forward in a most unfortunate manner, the wine flying from its glass, splattering across Landru's gold and ivory dress coat. He swore in a most ungentlemanly way, and my mother rushed over with a cloth to dab at his expensive clothing.

"You clumsy girl!" he sputtered. "Look what you've done!"

"Oh, my! I'm so sorry, my lord!" I apologized, my voice coated with sarcasm. "As hardy as I am, it's just impossible to catch myself when I trip."

Silence reigned and I could almost see the comprehension as it came to Cannan, Landru and Grayden. Then Landru surveyed me with undisguised contempt.

"Come, Grayden, we're leaving. I'm sorry, Captain, but your niece is intolerable."

"As are you, my lord," Cannan replied, catching everyone by surprise. "I'll walk you out."

The three men left the parlor, but Grayden grinned over his shoulder at me, green eyes shining.

When Cannan returned, his gaze fell on me, and mine went to the floor. It was ironic that I had been worried about angering him before. Now I had intentionally spilled wine on one of his acquaintances, an offense deserving of punishment if for no other reason than my loss of temper. He approached me, his visage somber, though that in and of itself was not unusual. My anxiety grew while I waited for him to speak, wondering if eight lashes at the hands of the Cokyrians might not be better than what was about to rain down on me. To my astonishment, he took my hands in his.

"I'm sorry for Lord Landru's conduct tonight. You should not have had to endure his criticism."

"I shouldn't have spilled wine on him," I admitted, glancing past my uncle to my sister and mother, who still looked appalled.

"I remember a proud, loyal, fun-loving younger brother of mine who would have done the same."

I stared at him, feeling stupid for wanting to cry. "Thank you," I tried to say, but I ended up mouthing the words, for my throat was too tight for sound to emerge.

I was allowed to go to bed without reprimand from Mother or Dahnath, one blessing to add to the list I was required by God to count. But when I lay in bed, there were certain thoughts I could not banish from my mind.

I was ugly. I was fat. Cannan had said I should not have had to endure Landru's criticism, but he hadn't denied the truth of his assessments. Simply put, I was a burden to hand off to someone else, to the someone who would be my husband. And I was guilty of sabotaging every attempt to find a man willing to undertake that responsibility. If there were a lower being in the world, I dared anyone to introduce me.

And, at the end, the worst part of it was that I was a misfit. I was not a boy, but neither was I a proper girl. Nothing and no one could change that. And only a proper girl could attract and hold a noble young man. I curled up on my side, one thought continuously circulating: staying in this house, allowing myself to be presented to suitors with whom I was ill-suited, no longer made sense.

The pain I felt at these conclusions was physical—strange, since I knew it was all in my mind—and I struggled out of bed and to my double window, gauging it as a means of escape. Concluding that the tree branch that brushed against the house just within my reach would be strong enough to support my weight, I retreated to my wardrobe. Grabbing a canvas sack that I had used when riding with Papa, I packed a few shirts and pairs of breeches, then hastily penned a note to my mother.

> *Dear Mother. Please don't worry about me, but I need to get away for a while, to think things through. I don't believe I am a good candidate for marriage, and I need to figure out my place in life. I'll be careful. Love, Shaselle.*

I set the note on my pillow and swung a cloak over my shoulders, then hoisted myself through the window, struggling out onto the limb. I took a few deep breaths, then picked my way from tree branch to tree branch, scratching my arms and hands on the oak's harsh bark. I grimaced but didn't make a sound, hoping no one inside would hear the scraping of boots that accompanied my drop to the ground.

Once I had landed, I brushed the dirt from my raw hands, feeling quite accomplished. I inhaled deeply, taking one last look at my home, and walked into the night without any idea how long I would be gone.

CHAPTER 13

EXECUTE THEM ALL

HALIAS AND HIS MEN WERE IN THE DUNGEON. The High Priestess had been informed of the situation and could arrive this very evening, depending on how fast she traveled. Every Hytanican feared, and every Cokyrian hoped, that the offenders would be executed.

I had spent the afternoon in and around the Hearing Hall, although there had been little demand for audiences this day. Cannan was gone, and London had not returned to duty, a blessing for which I was extremely grateful. Even if no one else knew of my bodyguard's involvement in the revolt attempt, I did, and through me, so did Narian. I didn't know if I could face London, much less what I would say to him. It was because of me that most of his remaining brothers-in-arms were in prison. The remorse I felt was crushing.

I was about to return to my quarters when the Hearing Hall doors opened and Cannan entered. He halted when he saw me and I hastened toward him.

"I thought you'd left for the day," I remarked, and he motioned me toward his office.

"I had—I needed to take care of some other business, but my thoughts have remained here."

He held the door open for me, and we sat across from each other, he behind his desk and me before it like a pupil about to receive a lecture.

"The news has traveled fast," he informed me. "Especially your role in this—the information is well distributed in the Bastion. For better or worse, you have aligned yourself with Narian in the eyes of Hytanicans and Cokyrians alike."

I nodded, the feeble hope that my involvement had not become known dashed. Then guilt washed over me, for my personal situation was hardly of significance now.

"Will they be put to death?" I rasped, uttering the fear that made my skin turn cold. "Halias and the rest?"

Halias had been my sister's bodyguard since she had been an infant, and I hated to think of the effect his execution would have on her. The men who had been arrested with Halias were former foot soldiers in the Hytanican army—men with families who depended on them. Each man who had died that night, each man who had been taken prisoner, had fought bravely for what he believed in, and I had the blood of every one of them on my hands.

"That will be decided by the High Priestess," Cannan told me, but something in his stoic face betrayed his own belief. I swallowed, my mouth tasting foul.

"A noble person believes in a cause, and sees it through to the end," he went on, leaning toward me. "That is what you are doing, Alera."

"And you believe in my cause, do you?" I bitterly asked.

"I was not involved in last night's incident."

"Thank you for that," I murmured, feeling a bit reprimanded. "And I'm sorry. They are your men."

"They were. But these are different times, and men do what they must."

I pondered his words, staring at my clasped hands, not daring to look at him again. He was so calm, so resigned. How could he accept this? Was it just an act to ease my guilt? Truly he must abhor me. Whatever the case, I could abide it no longer and hastily departed. I climbed the Grand Staircase to the second floor, noticing through the windows that the sun was setting, streaks of pink and orange painting the gray-blue sky. Coming to a decision, I quickened my pace and knocked on Narian's door.

I was lucky to find him in his quarters—he was unendingly busy, especially now that the High Priestess was coming, and could have been anywhere. After a glance in both directions down the hall, he ushered me into what had, for many years, been my parlor. Given the considerable time we had stolen together in these quarters when I had been Crown Princess, his presence didn't seem strange to me.

"You shouldn't be here, Alera. What is it?"

"If I'm disturbing you—" I said, taken aback by his attitude, for he was closed off, unreadable, frustrating. Was he angry with me? He had forgiven me for my actions on the night of the revolt, hadn't he? When I had been put to the ultimate test, I had confessed everything to him. And he, more than anyone else I knew, understood walking a dagger's edge.

"What is it you need?" he asked once more.

My eyebrows drew together, but I forged ahead. "We can't let them die. The High Priestess will execute Halias and the others if we don't stop her. I can't be responsible for that."

Narian sighed, his blue eyes devoid of sympathy. "The only ones responsible for what happens now are those locked in the dungeon. The High Priestess's regulations were clear about how this sort of behavior would be handled, and those regulations must be upheld."

"This sort of behavior?" I repeated, shocked. "You remember what the Overlord did to Halias, to the people of this kingdom. Don't you think *mercy* might make a stronger impression on these men, on my people, than more slaughter?"

"What do you expect me to do? This isn't my decision. Do I want to execute them? No. But I see the sense in it. These matters have to be handled with your head, not your heart. I learned that much—"

"From your *master?*"

"Just trust me," he said, words clipped.

Before I could argue further, there was a rapping on his door.

"Go," he urged, shoving me toward his bedroom. "Stay in there, stay quiet and keep the door closed."

Narian turned his back to me, and though I hid, I neglected his final instruction and left the door slightly ajar. As I peeked out, the parlor door opened, though he had not answered it, and the High Priestess entered, stepping past the Cokyrian shield maiden who had accompanied her. Nantilam nodded to the woman, who stepped into the corridor to wait, closing the door behind her.

Narian stood tensely with his hands behind his back, observing the leader of his homeland, who was also the closest resemblance to a parent he'd had during his childhood.

The High Priestess studied him, then said, "Relax, Narian. You look like you expect a rebuke when you've done well."

I saw Narian's hands tighten into fists, then release as he forced some of the rigidity from his body.

"You wanted to speak with me?" He was calm, collected, betraying none of his feelings.

"I knew it was only a matter of time before those men organized. I should not have let you persuade me from executing them at the start."

She rested one of her hands on the hilt of the sword at her hip, her vibrantly green eyes hard and dangerous. Her flaming hair was drawn back, and she was dressed in the typical black garb of the Cokyrians.

"No harm was done, however," she continued. "Tell me, who was captured?"

"Halias, among those you know."

"Anyone else of import?"

"No."

"Have those incarcerated put to death."

"I expected to do so."

I bit my lip, tears stinging my eyes. If I had just let Narian drink the wine…but then he might be dead, along with countless others, for any battle was a breeding ground for casualties. For the thousandth time, my mind raged against the prison of circumstance. There had been no course open to me that would not have left a trail of bodies.

"And London—was he not part of this?"

"He was."

"Then he will return to Cokyri with me, and this time he will remain there. I won't have him getting in the way again."

Now Narian imparted news I had not heard.

"London is gone. I've had troops scouring the city and countryside for him. He won't be found."

The High Priestess let out an exasperated laugh. "I should have known. But the others—they are all accounted for?"

"The others?" Narian sounded confused, and I knew he was playing at being naive.

"The boy King, his father, the rest from the cave." There was a testiness to the Cokyrian leader's tone that revealed she was aware of his pretense.

"Yes," Narian replied after a moment, hesitant about something.

The High Priestess noticed and looked at him with what was very near to sympathy.

"Whether or not they participated in the attack, Narian, you know they all had a hand in the plot. I want them executed. Once they're gone, the Hytanicans will have no leaders to inspire them."

"The *deaths* of these men will inspire the province to riot. Considering all aspects, I don't think killing them when their crimes are unproven would be wise."

I suddenly understood why Narian had tried to placate me with regard to the deaths of Halias and his men—he had known what the High Priestess would want, and what was within his ability to negotiate. I put my hand across my mouth to stifle any sound, for I wanted to cry out. Instead, I prayed Narian would be successful.

"I have decided," the High Priestess pronounced, her tone unassailable. "It is your duty to see my commands carried out. Send your soldiers to arrest Cannan, Steldor, Galen, King Adrik, that boy Princess Miranna married and anyone else you believe to have been involved. Have them executed before noon tomorrow—make an example of it for the people."

She swiveled on her heel to stride out the door, but Narian stopped her, his tone sharp.

"Alera will never forgive you. She is on our side for now, but if you do this, you will lose her."

The High Priestess turned around to face him, her eyes flashing, and I pulled back farther within Narian's bedroom, worried she would catch me.

"I do not need Alera," she snapped. "You mean that Alera will never forgive *you*."

"I *mean* that it would be in our best interests not to enrage our only solid connection to the Hytanican people. As liaison, it is my duty to speak for both sides and keep the peace."

"Enough games, Narian!" The Cokyrian ruler was angry. "Rava is not blind, nor is she without purpose in her position."

"So she's spying on me?"

"Even you have not been sure of your loyalties."

"I grow more uncertain by the moment."

Both the High Priestess and I recognized the veiled threat. She frowned and stepped closer to him, meeting his eyes and letting go of some of her pride in an effort to be fair instead.

"If our plans for the province succeed, you won't have to choose. I apologize—you know the state of affairs here better than I do, and I should trust your judgment."

"Thank you," Narian said, suspicion lacing his words. "Then you will only execute those men who were captured on the night of the rebellion?"

The High Priestess nodded once. "As you recommend."

She laid a hand on his shoulder, her thumb momentarily tracing his jaw. He turned his face slightly away, closing his eyes, but not in enjoyment of the contact.

"From now on, jurisdiction is yours in this province, Narian," she said, not deterred by his response to her touch. "I will no longer second-guess you. I don't want you to lose faith in our goals. Tell me now if you have."

He shook his head, his manner unusually subdued. "I haven't."

"Then I will see you in the morning. Sleep well."

The High Priestess departed, but I waited to be certain she was truly gone. Narian faced me as I stepped back into the parlor, and his eyes found mine, an apology within them, for he knew people I loved would still be dying. Without a word, I walked to him and put my arms around his waist, leaning into him. He held me, understanding both my gratitude and incredible sorrow.

At my request, Narian took Miranna and me to see Halias, who had been my sister's bodyguard for the better part of eighteen years. Temerson came along with the three of us to offer comfort—saying goodbye would not be easy.

Temerson clasped Miranna's hand as Narian led us down the dungeon stairwell, so small and dark it was near suffocating. The main area below had doors on every wall, each leading to a corridor lined with cells. Narian took us through the eastern door, dismissing the Cokyrian guards within the inner passageway so that we could have privacy from their ears and stares, and showed us to a cell midway down, behind the bars of which Halias and three others lay on cots. The rest of the cells incarcerated about thirty more men, all of whom would meet their deaths in the morning.

Halias looked up at our approach and rose to kneel at the bars, hooking his fingers through them. Miranna mirrored his position, grasping his hand, her upper lip trembling.

"Don't be sad," he murmured to her, brushing back her curly locks with his free hand. "It's all right."

"How can you say that?" she whispered, tears flowing freely. "You're going to die and there's nothing right about it." Miranna closed her eyes, pressing her delicate face against his large palm. "How can I bear losing you?"

"Listen to me," Halias said gently. "When the Overlord came, I escaped death. Now I'm going where I belong, with Destari and the rest of those men."

"Don't say that. You don't belong in a grave. Those other men were murdered—they deserved life. *You* deserve life."

"I'm sorry. But it is a noble death, Miranna. I'm not afraid. I'm doing this for you, and for all of Hytanica. How can that be a cause for sadness?"

"Because…" Miranna gave a small gasp in an attempt to control her weeping. "Because I love you."

"It is because I love you that I can face tomorrow without regret."

They sat together for what seemed like hours, until Miranna fell asleep, exhausted from sadness and tears. Temerson lifted her, cradling her against his chest.

"Thank you," Halias said softly to me and to Narian. "If you hadn't brought her, I don't know how much strength I would have."

Narian nodded, and I whispered my own "I'm sorry." There were no other words that could convey what I was feeling. Bravery like his was rare, and somehow made it that much harder to meet his gaze.

Temerson had carried Miranna toward the door, and stepped through it when he saw Narian and I walking toward him. Bars rattled and men shouted as we passed the other cells.

"Cokyrian! Boy! Bring us our loved ones, our families! Or would it be too much to learn our names? *Cokyrian!*"

Narian walked with his eyes straight ahead, his face inscrutable, but I could not ignore the pleas of the other prisoners. I stopped at the end of the corridor and turned to face them.

"I will get a list of your names and send for your families. You will all be given a chance to say goodbye."

Murmured thanks greeted my words, and Narian held the door behind me open, inviting my exit.

"That is not the Cokyrian way," he said as I stepped past him. "Condemned men are not given privileges."

"We are not in Cokyri," I reminded him. "And this is the Hytanican way."

Narian escorted me across the main room of the dungeon and up the stairs, but did not continue with me into the Hearing Hall.

"I will see to the matter of the prisoners' families," he said, then to my surprise, he bowed. "On your behalf."

When the sun rose, I went as Grand Provost to the training field at the military base to show respect for those who were about to die, though I did not know how I could stand to be a witness. Cannan accompanied me to where we would watch from the hillside, along with Narian and the High Priestess, both composed and emotionless.

The Cokyrian leader had, of course, brought her shield maidens—six in total, counting Rava. All were armed and dressed in black, formidable and fierce, almost eager for the executions to begin. I had not heard from or seen my sister and Temerson, but knew the young man would be keeping her from watching this horror.

Gallows had been erected before us, around which a closed circle of Cokyrians held the ends of their sheathed swords in either hand to create a barrier against the countless protesting citizens of Hytanica, and a ring of Cokyrian archers stood to the north, ready to rain arrows down upon them if things got out of hand. My people screamed and swore revenge, and I was not sure which sickened me more—seeing their anger and pain, or the gratefulness I felt that their noise would drown out the sounds of death that were to come.

The condemned men were walked up the stairs four at a time, hoods were placed over their heads, and nooses were put around their necks. Most were frightened; a few cried or pleaded or prayed. Halias refused the hood, staring stoically off in the direction of the Bastion—the palace—with the forest rising beyond, as though he wanted to be viewing the land of the kingdom he loved until the very last second. I closed my eyes whenever the trap doors dropped, aware only of the outcry of my people and the wailing of new widows and fatherless children, sounds that faded once it was finally done.

SHASELLE

CHAPTER 14

ON THE STREETS

I SPENT A MISERABLE NIGHT ON THE SOUTH SIDE of the city, dozing in the ruins of an assembly hall—likely at one time a church—that had just enough walls remaining to block the wind. Cold and miserable, I continually debated whether I should give up and go home, but stayed put in the end, frightened of the city at night and believing it would be safer to remain where I was.

I rose with the sun, having slept little, and gathered my hair into a single plait down my back. It already felt coarse and dirty, and I longed for a place where I could wash. Knowing the ruins wouldn't provide such luxury, I went out into the streets, where I easily learned details of the rebellion my mother had tried to hide from us—it was all anyone talked about. That and the upcoming executions.

A distant hum emanated from the northwestern side of the city, protesters at the military base. Any stragglers who had been avoiding the scene now answered its morbid call, myself included, though my pace slowed as I reached the Market District. The occasional Hytanican—never a Cokyrian—darted up or down the street, but for the most part, the area was deserted. The entire kingdom had gone to the training field, but I could not.

Not after having watched my father die.

The Overlord stretched out his hand, ready to kill yet another nameless, faceless Hytanican officer, only to pause.

"Surely not the captain?" he said mockingly.

"No," the boy-invader corrected. "This is not him."

"Yet—" the Overlord sneered "—the resemblance is unmistakable."

Turning toward the terrified crowd, the warlord called, "Perhaps, if the captain is here, he will come forward to save the life—well, the dignity—of his…cousin? Nephew?"

"His brother."

When the Overlord came about in feigned surprise, Papa defiantly met his gaze.

"I hope your brother is out there, in the crowd, to hear you scream and watch you cry, pup."

The hand stretched out once more—

I closed my eyes and pressed my palms against my temples in an effort to crush the memory within my skull. No, I would not relive that. Moving to the side of the road, I sat and wrapped my arms around my knees, shaking from the cool morning air and from the past.

I had no concept of how long I remained there, except that eventually, I could not ignore the rumbling of my stomach. This forced me to acknowledge another problem I had created for myself—I hadn't brought any money.

I looked around, realizing that even if I'd had money, no shops were open; I doubted they would open at all today, in honor of those who were dying. Weighing my options, I got to my feet. My family would not be at the execution field, so if I went home, I would have to answer to them. I would have to explain my stupidity, my impulsiveness and worst of all, how I couldn't stand to be in that house anymore. And then Cannan would come, and more suitors, until I was married off, a housewife. With a sigh, I pulled up the hood of my cloak, hunger overpowering my conscience.

Fresh Fruit and Wine was painted across the front of the stand I chose. I wouldn't take much, just enough to fill my belly—no one would miss a few apples.

I went around the back, knowing I would find a door for the owner's use, and also that the rear entry would decrease my likelihood of being caught. It was locked, but with a few good kicks, I managed to take the handle off, and the door swung inward.

Glancing about, I slipped inside. I felt my way around the small, dimly lit space, and found stacked crates along one wall, along with a pry bar for opening them. Inside were bottles of the advertised wine. Thinking it couldn't hurt, I snatched one, settling it in the bottom of my canvas bag.

Toward the front of the store were open boxes of fruit, and I tossed several apples inside my sack, adding some dates, finally stuffing a handful of berries into my mouth. Swallowing my guilt along with the fruit, I departed, although my conscience twinged at my inability to close the door behind me—with no handle, it swung and creaked in the wind. I hadn't taken much, but the open door might attract a real thief.

I stepped into the street, breathing more easily and feeling strangely capable. I hadn't been caught. Intending to wander back to the ruins where I had slept, I took a couple of bites of an apple, then stopped outside the butcher's shop. If I could start a fire, I could have meat.

My first attempt at stealing had gone smoothly, and I really hadn't done any harm. I could take just a little venison, maybe pork—no one would even notice its absence.

The butcher's shop was not a stand like the fruit vendor's,

but a solid, stone building, which presented a greater challenge. Nonetheless, I opted to try my original method of kicking at the back door. It didn't open quickly like the last one had, but I was tenacious, kicking it again and again, smack on the handle. I quit, panting, having had no success.

"Good lock," I muttered, frustrated but almost enjoying the challenge.

A prickling sensation ran up my neck, telling me to take what I had and go, but I ignored it like a bothersome insect, walking to the side of the building instead, where I spotted a window just large enough to accommodate me. It was higher than I could reach, but had no pane—just cloth hanging over the opening.

I tried jumping for the sill, and managed to grab on with my fingers. My boots scraped vainly against the stone of the wall and I fell, landing uncomfortably on my rear. Scanning the area, I saw a good-size stone and dragged it under the window, hoping even a few inches might make the difference.

I wiped dirt from my hands onto my breeches, stepped onto the stone and tried the leap again, this time gaining enough of a hold that I could hoist myself up. But with nothing to stop my momentum, I tumbled gracelessly through the window, knocking against some shelves stacked with boxes. Miraculously, nothing toppled along with me, although I did make more noise than I would have liked. I cringed and inched forward, praying no one would look through the window to investigate.

It was when I reached the main area that I realized the only people who had neglected to attend the execution were me—and the butcher. He was not a friendly man, at least not to people breaking into his store.

"What the bloody—" he exclaimed when he saw me, then

he gestured toward the back door. "Was that you making all that racket, you Cokyrian bitch?"

Given my attire, I could understand his mistake.

"I—I'm not Cokyrian," I stammered, too afraid to move, hoping the burly, hairy man wouldn't kill me here and now. "And—and I'm sorry. I mean, I shouldn't have…"

He didn't seem to hear.

"Thought you'd steal from me, did you?" he snarled, taking large, heavy steps toward me. "You've taken this kingdom, my son, my whole life from me, and you still haven't had your fill?"

"Did you hear? I'm not Cokyrian!" I was shouting, but he ignored my words. Picking up a meat tenderizer from the counter, he continued to approach me, pace steady and menacing.

There would be no escaping in the manner I had entered— I couldn't climb fast enough. Taking my chances, I darted for the back door, praying I would be able to unlock it. Just as I reached it, the butcher's beefy, sweaty hand closed around my upper arm, and I cried out.

"I'm sorry, I'm sorry! Please let me go, please!"

"I'll let you go once I'm good and done with you."

I tried to scream, but he pushed his mouth against mine, forcing my lips apart. I struggled desperately, vainly, but he grabbed a handful of my hair and made me look at him.

"It's because of you my wife is dead. Your fires took our house. And my son died in the fighting!"

His scent, the scent of blood and flies and perspiration, was overwhelming, and I gagged as his hold on my hair tightened.

"Let me *go!*" I cried, kicking at him, but he grabbed my leg.

"Stop fighting, whore," he growled. "I'm going to show you a woman's place."

He had set the meat tenderizer on a stack of boxes beside

the door against which he was shoving me, and I reached for it. Catching my movement, he snatched my hand, putting it together with my other and pinning them both above my head.

"I'm...the captain's...niece!" I screamed in one final attempt to bring him to his right mind, then I brought my knee up hard, connecting with his groin.

He released me, hunching over. Taking advantage of the moment, I wrapped my fingers around the handle of the tenderizer and swung it at his head. The crack was satisfying, and he lurched away from me, not hit hard enough to be knocked unconscious. I turned and flipped the latch on the door, then pulled hard on the handle, stumbling over the threshold into the fresh air. I would have fallen in the dirt for the second time that day except that someone standing outside caught me. Terrified that my escape was being thwarted, I struck out at whoever it was, feeling a sharp pain when my fist connected with the person's jaw.

"*Empress,* you hit hard!" a male voice exclaimed, then he captured my arms and trapped them behind my back. By the strange expletive he had used, I knew him to be Cokyrian— my luck was golden. "What's going on here?"

The butcher staggered into the doorway, squinting in the sunlight.

"Your girl's a thief," he muttered at sight of the man who held me, sparing a glower for me as though warning me to be quiet. I ground my teeth and looked away, intending to do just that.

Now that I had stopped struggling, the Cokyrian soldier released me, and I considered whether or not to run. Then I saw who had been restraining me—Saadi, the man with whom Narian and my uncle had dealt after my failed prank. There would be no point in running if he remembered who I was.

"My girl?" Saadi repeated, his pale blue eyes calculating.

"She is no Cokyrian. Besides, I would expect you to show any comrade of mine more respect than that."

"My apologies," the butcher forced himself to say, and rage filled me at his newly respectful attitude. "She broke into my store and I assumed from her clothing... I also assume you'll see her punished for her crime."

"You were about to punish her yourself, weren't you?"

Saadi scrutinized me, noting the red marks around my wrists and perhaps the beginnings of the bruises I would have across my mouth.

"In Cokyri, you would be killed for what you did to her—what you *tried* to do."

"It's good we're not in Cokyri then," the butcher sneered.

Saadi's jaw clenched, and he seemed to be fighting a deep urge to pummel the merchant who stood before him.

"I should take you to join the men at the gallows."

"I would welcome it."

"I can see why," Saadi coldly retorted, with a subtle look up and down at the heavyset man. "But I'm afraid the lack of your business might dampen the economy in the province, and that is something my sister would frown upon. She'll be disappointed, though—she does so enjoy seeing men like you hang."

"And I enjoy seeing women in skirts as God intended."

Another strained moment passed, then Saadi laughed. "Perhaps if your God had paid less attention to clothing and more to abilities, you and your kind wouldn't be in this position right now."

The butcher shifted uncomfortably, and Saadi quickly dispensed with him. "If you want me to arrest her for thievery, I'll also arrest you for assault. So I would advise that you go back to your meat and your customers, may they be few."

The man did not need to be told twice. He slammed the door in our faces, and I could hear the lock click into place. It was then that I noticed the canvas bag at Saadi's feet. He must have seen flight in my eyes, for he started running at almost the same moment I did. He caught me before I passed the next shop, snatching my upper arm just as the butcher had. I cried out, hoping he would think me in pain and let me go, but he did not, cocking an eyebrow and strengthening his grip.

"I take it you're responsible for this?" he said, hauling the bag of fruit, which he had slung over his shoulder, up to eye level with his other hand.

I kept my mouth shut.

"Despite the fact that you're breaking the law, you're lucky. The evidence you left at your previous site of conquest sent me on a search for you."

"Lucky, because you did a lot of saving," I scoffed.

Releasing me, he smoothed his bronze hair forward, but it stuck up at the center of his hairline, which I suspected was the opposite of his intention.

"I was getting there."

He was mumbling, disagreeable, an attitude I did not expect. Why was he bothering to make conversation with a Hytanican criminal? And why did he keep smoothing that stupid hair of his?

"I haven't done anything," I said, inching backward in preparation for my grand escape, the details of which I was sure would come to me at any moment. Motioning to the bag, I lied again. "That's not mine."

"Yes, it is."

"No, it isn't."

"But it is."

"*No,* it isn't."

"You know, the more you deny it, the more likely I am to arrest you."

I stared wide-eyed at him. "You weren't planning to?"

"No, it doesn't look like you've caused any real harm—a couple of coins in payment for the broken lock should resolve the problem. I have a feeling if I arrested you, you wouldn't make it out this time, not with what your uncle and cousin are guilty of."

"Bravery?"

"Corza spends an hour terrifying you and I get a confession after a few minutes."

Shocked and annoyed, I exclaimed, "I didn't confess anything!"

Saadi smirked. "Nothing I'm going to share. Women and men shouldn't be killed for bravery."

"I suppose you condone the pranks and riots then?" I challenged. He was unbelievable—making things up to manipulate me.

"I don't condone them," he said more seriously. "I have a different idea of what bravery is."

"What—complaisance?"

"In a sense. Acceptance, resiliency. How strong must one be to throw a temper tantrum?"

"Is that what you'd call this? You and your people storm our homeland, take us all prisoner and any form of resistance is a *temper tantrum* in your eyes?"

He pondered this for a moment, his freckled nose crinkling. "Yes."

I threw up my hands, not sure exactly what was going on or why I was still here with my enemy, but not willing to let this go.

"How do you justify that?"

"Well, for a century, our takeover of your kingdom has been inevitable. You should have acclimated yourselves to the idea by now."

"You're right. This is our fault, really. We've never been superb at preparation here in Hytanica."

Saadi shrugged, and I thought for one stunned moment that he had taken my statements to be sincere. Then his expression changed, and he looked at me with what appeared to be sympathy, perhaps even regret.

"I do understand it, Shaselle. Being second tier, overrun, overlooked. Not having influence."

It disturbed me that he not only remembered my relation to Cannan and Steldor, but also my name. Yet I did not flee.

"You have to take what you're handed and make what you can of it," he finished. "That's the sorry truth."

"I plan to make them pay," I snarled, hating his words and how similar they were to the message Queen Alera had been trying to send for weeks.

"*Them?* What about me?"

"Stop it!" I stamped my foot, not even sure what was upsetting me. "You killed my father!"

"And you want revenge. Naturally. Just like the butcher in there. But the problem is, Shaselle, revenge isn't a very satisfying goal. It eats away at you, destroys you from the inside out. You end up bitter and empty just like that butcher. And that's not a pretty sight."

"What is wrong with you? You think you know everything about me! You don't. Stay out of my way and out of my business."

I spun on my heel and began to stride away, but he called me back.

"Don't you want this?"

I turned to see that he was still holding my canvas bag filled with fruit. I breathed in and out heavily, my stomach complaining, my pride aching just as much.

"So far, it's been *you* who's getting in *my* way." He chuckled. "If you don't like it, let that uncle of yours catch up with you."

I warily returned to him to reclaim my bag, but he held it away from me for a moment longer.

"There is the matter of the damages for the door," he said, and my heart sank, for lack of money was what had gotten me into this mess in the first place. But before I could speak, he added, "I'll cover the cost for now. But you'll owe me."

Annoyed that I would be in his debt, I snatched my bag from his hand, then sprinted in the other direction, his laughter nipping at my heels.

I survived the rest of that day on fruit and a sip or two of wine. As I wandered the city streets, dodging Cokyrian soldiers who cast dubious glances at any Hytanican who seemed out of place, I realized with a sinking heart that living like this was really not feasible. Should I resign myself to going home? Or try to find work? I knew how to take care of horses, muck their stalls—I even knew how to break them. But I doubted any Hytanican would hire a girl to be a stable hand, and there wasn't the slightest chance I'd consider working for the Cokyrians.

I grimaced, knowing that my best option aside from giving up on independence was to offer my sewing skills to one of the tailors in the city, one who didn't know me and therefore wouldn't return me to my family. The dressmakers couldn't afford to pay much wage, but they wouldn't turn me away, and though I hated the chore, my mother had taught me well. Shivering but thankful I at least had a plan, I curled up in the corner of the church ruins that provided the most shelter, snugged my cloak about my body and went to sleep, using a balled-up pair of breeches for a pillow.

I woke with the sunrise and tucked my canvas bag in a crevice among some fallen stones, hoping no one would find it, and grabbed the last apple for breakfast. Then I hiked through the city, noticing a distinct lack of activity in the southern district, where Steldor usually oversaw construction. There was always something odd in this kingdom.

It was when I turned north along the thoroughfare that I saw why the streets felt dead—everyone was congregating yet again. If there was one thing the people of Hytanica were eager to do, it was assemble. This time, the people were streaming en masse toward the palace, but my height and my distance from the point of interest made it impossible for me to determine the reason. Frustrated, I worked my way to the edge of the thoroughfare and climbed atop a rain barrel in order to gain a better vantage point.

Atop the palace, on the foremost center of the roof, a broad blue-and-gold Hytanican flag waved boldly in the wind, the silk refracting the sunlight like some divine beacon of strength. Beside it stood the man who had planted it, his hand upon its staff, but I was too far away to see his face. I dropped to the ground and fought through the crowd, jostled and shoved about, but perfectly willing to shove back.

"Steldor," I heard those around me excitedly proclaiming. "King Steldor!"

My blood pounded when I squirmed through to the courtyard gates, able at last to determine the identity of the man on the roof. My cousin stood by the banner he held, magnificent and defiant and brave.

People were now emerging from the palace to see what was causing the commotion—the Queen, the Cokyrian commander, the female officer who had stolen my father's horses and my uncle. I darted to the side, out of Cannan's line of vision, and they came to a stop opposite me. The captain stiffened and I distinctly heard him breathe, "Goddamn it,

Steldor," when he recognized his daring and independent son, his son who obeyed no one. Queen Alera put a hand over her mouth, the bronze-haired officer tensed and curled her lip and Narian's countenance hardened—despite the aid he had given me, I doubted he had a heart inside him at all.

Cokyrians milled now that their superiors had arrived, but Steldor was unmoving, unrelenting, unapologetic—proud to be found guilty of this crime after the executions of the previous morn. This was in memoriam of those who had been killed trying to reclaim our kingdom, and I knew this idea had been Steldor's alone, for Galen was not with him.

Someone brushed past me to reach the palace gates, a few others following in his wake, and I recognized Saadi as he and his comrades were permitted entrance to the courtyard.

"You took your time," the female Cokyrian officer said to him. "Did you oversleep, boy?"

"Orders, Rava," Saadi testily reminded her, and blood ran to my face at the resemblance between the two of them. *This* was the sister to whom he kept referring. I forced my eyes back to Steldor, not understanding why I felt so angry and embarrassed over what I had just learned.

"Get him down," Rava snarled. "Arrest him and take that flag to my office. Then I—*Narian* and I—will decide what to do with him."

Glares were exchanged between the Cokyrian commander and the petite woman I could only assume was his second, but unlike in my case, Narian did not speak up to override her directives. Was he truly going to let her decide how my cousin would be punished?

Saadi went forward while others hurried to fetch ladders and ropes. As the enemy soldiers climbed up to him, Steldor called out to his people.

"Remember this flag!" he shouted, pounding the staff

against the roof. "Remember all who have died for it—don't let them have died in vain. This is *our kingdom!*"

Shouts went up from the Hytanican crowd, and they began to chant my cousin's name.

"Steldor the King! Steldor the King! Steldor the King!"

The Cokyrians reached him and he put up his hands, allowing them to shackle him without a fight. If anything, the voice of the people grew louder.

I beamed, proud of my relation to him, at least until I noticed Cannan's posture. He was rigid, motionless, but it wasn't anger I detected in his stance—he was afraid.

CHAPTER 15

THE HIGH PRIESTESS HAD LEFT HYTANICA THE afternoon of execution day, and as Steldor was brought to us by an arguable legion of Cokyrian soldiers, hands cuffed behind his back, I was thankful for that fact. Despite what Nantilam had promised Narian about trusting his judgment, I believed Steldor's actions would have enraged her beyond the point of reason.

"Steldor the King! Steldor the King!"

The people on the opposite side of the gates continued to chant, their admiration for my former husband jarringly apparent. Steldor did not acknowledge them, staring instead at me in a challenge to my attitude of cooperation.

Narian motioned us forward, and our party reentered the Bastion to stand in the Grand Entry Hall, Steldor and his captors in tow.

"Saadi." Rava prompted the man who was holding the rolled-up Hytanican flag, and he went into her office to store it, for no reason apparent to me. Looking at Steldor, she issued further orders. "Take him to the dungeon and await my word."

I stared at Narian, incredulous he was allowing her to take

control, then realized it would do no good to reprimand Rava here, not when his own orders would have been the same. Still, his intense eyes sent her a deadly warning.

Steldor gave us an impudent nod before he was led through the antechamber doors into the Hearing Hall, off of which was the entrance to the dungeon. All except Cannan watched him go—the captain had not once met his son's gaze.

The moment we were left to debate his punishment, Rava snapped, "Execute him."

"No," Cannan growled, and for an instant it seemed he might have let his emotions get the better of him. I was mistaken, however, for he followed up with sound logic. "Steldor has just made himself the people's hero."

In substantiation of his point, cries of "Steldor the King!" rang in the brief silence.

"You barely prevented a full-scale revolt with your latest executions," the captain continued. "Another death and you will *create* one."

Rava scoffed. "Your love for your boy is sweet, Cannan. Why don't you profess it and beg for him instead of trying to convince us your helpless people can work miracles?"

"Believe what you want," Cannan said, cold, dangerous fury emanating from him. He had endured enough of her condescension. "In time, you will understand that I do not make empty threats."

"It's a threat you're making, is it?" Rava crossed her arms, unsuccessfully trying to ridicule him.

"Yes," Cannan answered, without a beat of hesitation.

A soundless struggle between them culminated in Rava unexpectedly taking a step back from the former military leader, although neither showed a sign of breaking eye contact. Narian finally put an end to their confrontation.

"Enough, Rava. You're dismissed."

Rava blinked at her commander, astonished, then her muscles tensed in anger.

"You are dismissed," Narian repeated, his steely tone more deafening than any protest Rava could have mustered. She exhaled heavily, making an ignominious exit into her office just as Saadi stepped back out. Grasping the front of his shirt, she tugged him inside after her, slamming the door behind them.

Cannan did not waste a moment before he addressed Narian, his manner controlled, but intense, concentrated.

"What will you do?"

Narian was thinking, and it wasn't hard to guess what was going through his mind. Steldor's offense was one that would merit death under an unforgiving government, but he did not want to be that government. And he did not want to hurt me. I had no notion of his personal feelings toward Steldor, though I could not imagine they were overly positive, but I knew they would be the last factor he would consider.

"Don't put him to death," I said unhelpfully, only making his decision more difficult.

"I have to be just, Alera," he told me, then he looked to Cannan. "He cannot go without punishment. You know this."

"I know."

Narian nodded. "He'll be lashed. Publicly. Six times with a rawhide whip."

"You've been merciful. My son asked to be punished. I feared only his death."

The two men locked eyes, and I sensed something change between them—the former captain gained understanding of the type of man my betrothed had become, and Narian gained understanding of a father-son relationship he had never experienced.

The courtyard was where it would be done, that very afternoon. I despised the location, not wanting to associate the regal and once beautiful grounds of my home with this type of torture. At the same time, I knew the location made sense to the Cokyrians—the iron gates would keep Hytanican citizens from interfering yet provide a perfect view.

Heralds were sent out to announce the event and, gruesome though it would be, the people came to watch. Narian, Cannan and I, along with several Cokyrian soldiers, congregated in the courtyard, the only ones witnessing the punishment without a barrier to contain us. My eyes fell on Galen outside the wall, staring fixedly at Cannan in a silent demand to know how this had happened, but the captain, though he surely noticed, paid no heed.

It was important for Narian to distance himself in the eyes of the public from such cruelty, so he would not be the one to administer Steldor's punishment. While this was a relief to me, for I did not want to see him perform such a brutal act, we all knew without confirmation that Rava would take his place.

We didn't have long to wait before Steldor was led out of the Bastion by two soldiers, preceded by Rava and a young woman carrying a box that was perhaps four feet long. They passed us, Steldor tall and unafraid, the Hytanican crowd immediately resuming its earlier chant. Rava stopped, turning around with a raised hand to bring her cohorts to a halt, and I hoped the support he was receiving would not somehow make his punishment worse.

Rava approached Steldor and removed a dagger from a sheath at her hip. With her left hand, she smoothed the collar of his white shirt, then yanked the fabric away from his chest, slicing through it in a single motion. Spying the silver wolf's head talisman that he always wore, she seized it, ripping it free of his neck.

"Whether for good luck or good fortune, you'll have no

need of this," she sneered, dropping the pendant into a pouch that hung from her belt.

"I'm sorry it's not strong enough to cover your stench," he icily replied, for the mixture inside the talisman was the source of his rich, masculine scent.

Rava stared at Steldor, then stalked around him to tear the remnants of his shirt from his back, trying without success to strip him of his pride. She perused his muscular torso, and when she faced him once more, her eyes came to rest on the scar beneath his rib cage—the one that marked the life-threatening wound given to him by a Cokyrian blade—and placed the tip of the dagger she still held against it.

"Only slightly marred." She traced the knife's point along the jagged white line, leaving a trail of red. "I'll see what I can do to change that."

She tucked the weapon back into its sheath and gave a nod to the soldiers who had brought Steldor out of the Bastion. As they tied his wrists with rope, she went to the woman who had brought the box and lifted its lid. With a satisfied chuckle, she removed a whip more fearsome than any I had ever seen, cradling it like a mother would an infant, and the gathered throng fell silent. It was indeed rawhide, but uncoiled it reached four feet in length before meeting a silver ring, on the other end of which another two feet of metal-studded leather waited to strike. I looked to Narian and Cannan, and knew by both of their expressions that this was not what they had expected. Indeed, Rava purposefully made eye contact with Narian, her demeanor haughty, before returning her attention to her prey.

"On your knees," Rava growled, dangling the whip in front of Steldor. He obeyed, his eyes never leaving her face, continuing to radiate strength and insolence.

"How can a flag be of consequence in a dead kingdom?" she taunted. "It is *cloth*. It is meaningless. And it can be burned."

She ticked a finger for one of the many soldiers around us to come forward, and I recognized Saadi. He extended our rolled Hytanican flag, and Rava took it, letting it unfurl until the end touched the ground. She held out her other hand and Saadi passed her a lit torch, which she touched to the banner of my homeland, letting flames consume it. The courtyard's white stone walkway would now and forever be scorched.

Steldor's upper lip lifted away from his teeth, but aside from this snarl, he showed no reaction.

"Tell me, does it seem worth it to you to suffer this punishment for a *rag?*"

"Without question," Steldor forcefully answered, and cheers rolled like thunder through the Hytanicans who had gathered to watch, sending chills down my spine.

Rava's lip curled into a sneer and she walked behind him, motioning to the Cokyrians holding the ropes to pull them tight, spreading his arms wide. With a swift and practiced motion, she raised the whip and brought it down hard upon his broad back, drawing blood with her first stroke, and gasps reverberated almost as loudly as had the cheers.

"Is it worth it?" she demanded.

"Yes," he managed to answer, gritting his teeth against the pain.

She struck him twice more, and though I could hardly bear it, I forced myself to watch, the muscles of my back spasming as each stroke landed.

"Is it worth it?"

"Yes!"

Once more she struck, and again, until the ragged flesh and sinew of Steldor's back was coated with blood—blood that flowed so heavily it ran down his sides. Women in the crowd now wept openly, while men cursed and shouted. I took in a shaky breath, knowing only one lash remained. Steldor would survive, and so would I. So would we all.

Rava brought the whip down on Steldor for the sixth time, and his head hung forward. Was he still conscious? Or were the ropes around his wrists the only things keeping him from collapsing? Evidently wondering the same, Rava approached him and reached down, grasping a handful of his nearly black hair to pull his head up. His eyes were open, but barely focused.

"Tell me, boy. Is it worth it?" she said in a near whisper.

He smiled, revealing teeth smeared with blood from biting his tongue to hold back screams.

"Yes."

Rage marred Rava's face at her inability to break him, and she brutally shoved his head down. Backing up, she uncoiled the whip that was supposed to have retired, and flayed him again, more viciously than before. Steldor cried out this time, the sound tearing at my heart, and when the soldiers dropped the ropes, he crumpled forward. Knowing he had to be in tremendous pain, I was thankful for the respite the darkness would provide. Silence now reigned around us—no voices, no movements, hardly any breathing. It felt like the world had temporarily been turned to stone.

Rava handed the whip to another soldier and stalked back toward the Bastion without a glance or word for anyone. She was cruel and heartless and arrogant, and hatred for her boiled within me as I watched the Cokyrians remove the ropes from Steldor's wrists. They hauled him up by his arms and dragged him inside, leaving a crimson trail on the white walk.

The rest of us followed, and I glanced at Cannan, who had managed more stoicism during the proceedings than had I. He had been witness to greater brutality during both wars with Cokyri, but I knew he would have willingly taken his son's punishment in his stead. After seeing him in the cave, holding and protecting Steldor when we'd all feared the King's death, I knew that beneath his strength and bravery, he ached.

Rava was nowhere to be seen when the Bastion doors closed behind us, and I could sense Narian's agitation. She had flouted him, both with the whip she had chosen to wield and with the extra lash she had administered, and her lack of respect for his authority was already far out of bounds. But after what the High Priestess had suggested—that Rava, a close confidante of hers, was keeping watch on him—what could be done to bring her into line?

I had learned from the reports Saadi had been providing me that it was customary for criminals to spend a night in the dungeon following their punishment, but Narian halted the Cokyrian soldiers who supported Steldor.

"I'll send for a doctor," he told Cannan. "Where would you like him taken?"

"My bunk, for now," the captain replied, meaning the room off his office where he was provided a bed. "I don't want him moved more than necessary."

Narian directed the soldiers holding Steldor to Cannan's office, none of us addressing Rava's conduct. Then he left, keeping his thoughts to himself though I desperately wanted to know what they were. I followed the captain, who dismissed the Cokyrian soldiers with a wave of his hand before stepping into the small room where Steldor had been laid facedown upon the cot.

I stood hesitantly in the doorway as Cannan knelt by his son. With a hand on Steldor's head, he inspected the hideous wounds crisscrossing the young man's back.

"Will he recover?" I asked, the blood enough to make me queasy despite all that I had seen during the Cokyrian siege.

"It's worse than I expected," Cannan answered, alluding to the whip Rava had used. "If you have the chance, thank

Narian for me. Steldor would not have fared well if he'd been thrown in a cell with these injuries."

"I'm assuming I'll need stitches?" said a tired but sardonic voice.

Not in the mood for Steldor's dry humor, Cannan instructed him to lie still, and I stumbled out of the room, covering my mouth in an attempt to keep my nausea in check. How could the Cokyrians be so cruel? But that wasn't quite right. The cruelty belonged to Rava. And it was time I did something about it.

I took several deep breaths to gather my nerve, and then strode to Rava's office to pound on the door, the drag of a chair across the stone floor confirming that someone was inside. It was but a moment later that Narian's second-in-command appeared before me, her face registering shock, then immense satisfaction.

"Grand Provost," she sneered. "What a pleasant surprise."

She stepped back to permit me to enter, and I walked forward, glancing around as she returned to her seat behind the desk. My back stiffened as I noticed a collection of weapons mounted on one wall—a collection that had formerly belonged to Cannan.

"What can I do for you on this fine day?" she asked.

As I had not come to exchange pleasantries, I immediately stated my business. "I would like a return of the prisoner's property."

Rava's brow furrowed, as though she did not know to what I referred, then a sly smile crept across her face.

"We have a lot of prisoners, Grand Provost, and they have—"

"I want Steldor's pendant," I bluntly interjected, not in the mood to play games.

She stood and slowly pulled the talisman from the pouch on her belt.

"This old thing?" she taunted, holding up the chain so that the silver wolf's head dangled in the air. "If this is the source of his power and protection, I'd say it's not working very well."

"Be that as it may, it belongs to him and I intend to return it."

I stepped forward and she abruptly tossed the pendant at my feet.

"Makes no difference to me," she said, walking around her desk. "Although it does seem to be a pretty poor substitute for a crown."

I bent to retrieve the talisman, which had been through many an ordeal with Steldor, realizing as I did so that she had managed to get me to assume a subservient posture—it looked like I was bowing down to her. I took a deep breath, reining in my frustration, and met her gaze.

"Is there anything else?" she asked, her smug expression wearing on my nerves.

"Yes. If you ever again lay an excessive lash upon the back of a Hytanican, you will feel it upon your back, as well."

This time Rava's initial surprise turned to anger, her blue eyes icing over. "Be careful, Grand Provost," she cautioned, closing the distance between us so that we stood face-to-face. "I don't react well to threats."

I stared at her, my heart thudding, then pushed further, unwilling to back down.

"The High Priestess is a great leader of a great empire. You and I both know that a great empire cannot be founded on deliberate disobedience. And a great leader will not be forgiving when someone under her command steps out of line. So I suggest you learn to count."

Holding Steldor's pendant against my heart, I turned and

left her office, feeling her glare burning into the back of my neck as I walked across the Hearing Hall toward my own study. I had once before safeguarded Steldor's talisman—when he had been fighting for his life during our time in hiding in the caves—and I was more than willing to do it again.

SHASELLE

CHAPTER 16

SACRIFICE

I MADE IT ANOTHER TWO DAYS BEFORE THE LACK of good food and a decent place to live got the best of me. The day of Steldor's lashing was the first one in which I had not heard whispers of Cannan searching for me, and when, at long last, I started using my head, I suspected he knew exactly where I was—and had people keeping track of me. Who wouldn't be willing to do the captain a favor, especially when his son had just made himself the people's champion? But at least my uncle wasn't forcing me to go home. He seemed to want me to come to that conclusion on my own.

The conclusion I had reached was that I needed to go *somewhere* other than the streets. I was still too afraid to approach Cannan, so I waited, wanting to talk to Steldor. I had not gone to see his punishment meted out, but knew he had spent a night in the palace afterward, and now was at Galen's manor house. It was not difficult to hear news of my cousin these days.

Galen and his wife, Tiersia, lived in the same section of the city in which my family dwelled, but thankfully his home was closer to the thoroughfare—I wouldn't have to pass my own to reach it. Upon his marriage almost a year ago, Galen had gained control of the money his father had left in Cannan's care—the Baron Miccard had died before Galen's fourth birthday—and the house he had purchased was magnificent, with vines growing up the sides, a blessed sign of renewal in our drab times.

Both eager and resigned, I went up to the door and rapped upon it. After a moment, the latch clicked and Tiersia herself stood in front of me.

"Shaselle." She said my name with relief, obviously aware that I had run away. "Come in."

She stepped aside, her skirts swishing the floor and her golden brown hair bouncing, and I caught a whiff of her scent—warm honeysuckle. Now that I considered it, most of the time I probably smelled like horse.

The afternoon sun that streamed through the windows set high above the door lit up the entryway in which Tiersia and I awkwardly stood. I didn't know what to say to her, a problem that was compounded by the fact that she and I had never before had a true conversation, for she was several years older than me.

"Are you hungry?" she asked, breaking the silence. "I could get you something to eat right now, or you could stay for dinner." She was soft-spoken and proper, but there was also warmth and concern in her eyes.

"Please don't fuss—I did come here without invitation."

"You're always welcome here." She was so kind, so willing to care for me, that I wanted to cry. I cast my eyes to the floor, no longer able to deny that I was, at my core, a pampered, wealthy, city girl who had no business being on her own.

"Thank you. But really, I don't need anything." I prayed she couldn't hear my belly's rumbling opinion on the matter. "Is Steldor here?"

She nodded. "Upstairs, in the guest room, although it's more of a sickroom at the moment. It will take him a while to heal. Galen is with him. When my lord comes down I will ask if your cousin is in form for visitors."

"All right, thank you."

To my left, I could see the foot of the stairway, and I fought the urge to dart past Tiersia and find Steldor on my own. Such behavior would be rude and likely pointless, for I would only run into Galen.

"Come with me, Shaselle, and I'll find you something to eat. You may as well put the time you'll be waiting to good use."

I smiled, for Tiersia would have her way; she would make a great mother when the time came. As if to provide further evidence of that, she led me into the kitchen and handed me a damp cloth. I wiped dirt off my face and hands, wondering how wretched I looked, then ran my hand down the plait that still captured most of my hair, recoiling at how stiff it felt.

Ignoring my appearance, Tiersia set bread and cheese on the table in front of me, and I could no longer hide that I was starving. I tried to eat with attention to manners, especially since she sat opposite me, daintily sipping tea like the lady she was. I realized with a blush that, if I had to marry, I wanted to be like her, with a handsome husband and gracious home. I loved horses and riding, and hated the thought of giving them up, but maybe my mother was right; maybe the time had come to put aside my childhood.

"Thank you," I again said, having cleared my plate without trouble.

"You're welcome." She ran her finger along the rim of her teacup, and I supposed she was having trouble coming up with a topic for conversation. With a wispy smile, she made an effort to engage me. "Tell me, how have you been?"

"I'm sure you're aware that I haven't...I haven't been home, so...I've been surviving." I stumbled over my words, not certain what she thought of me and my recalcitrant ways.

"We've all been worried about you."

"I'm sorry," I mumbled, examining my hands, glaringly aware of my broken nails and the dirt that had taken up residence beneath them.

She placed one of her hands over mine, and I met her sympathetic, soft green eyes.

"You're safe now, Shaselle, and that's what matters." It was clear that, to her mind at least, the past wasn't important.

Bold, unrestrained footsteps on the stairs announced Galen's descent, and he came in search of his wife. He poked his head around the doorway, seeming almost to hop back when he saw me.

"Shaselle!" he exclaimed. "Where did you come from?"

I knew how to handle Galen's forward, outgoing style much better than I did Tiersia's maternal, forgiving attitude. I was used to him, for I had spent almost as much time around him as I had around Steldor.

"I needed somewhere to go," I told him honestly. "And I was hoping to talk to Steldor."

Galen ran a hand through his wavy, medium brown hair. "I don't know, Shaselle. It's not pretty. His injuries are severe. He needs much rest in order to recover."

"I guessed they would be." I stood, waiting for his verdict. If I couldn't talk to my cousin, I would leave.

Galen studied me, knowing me well enough to infer my thoughts. At last he shrugged.

"Come with me then. At least Steldor will know you're safe."

"Dinner will be served at seven," Tiersia said, and Galen

gave her an appreciative kiss on the cheek before leading me from the room.

The second door on the left in the upstairs hallway marked the guest room where Steldor was staying, and Galen knocked to announce us before we went inside.

Steldor lay on the bed, chest to the mattress, medicine-soaked bandages covering his shirtless back. The wrappings, though fresh from his best friend's last visit, were dappled crimson and yellow from his body's efforts to cleanse the wounds, and I could see shadows of long lines of stitches crossing his skin.

"Steldor, Shaselle is here," Galen said.

My cousin lifted his head to squint at me.

"Where did you come from?"

"Outside," I answered dryly, recognizing on its second asking just how inane the question was.

Steldor was not amused.

"I'll leave you two alone," Galen said, backing out of the room.

When the door clicked shut, Steldor propped himself up on his elbows, wincing with the movement.

"I wanted to see you," I told him.

"Could have guessed, since you're here. Well, what have you been doing?"

I considered his inquiry, scratching the back of my head. "I got attacked by a butcher."

The incident was still on my mind, not one easily dismissed, and part of me wanted his reaction.

"A butcher?" he repeated, concerned. His eyes roved over me and he pronounced, "You appear to have survived."

"The same can be said of you."

"Thus far, anyway," he responded with a self-deprecating

chuckle. "You don't have to tell me how smart that flag stunt was. My father has covered that."

I quickly countered his sarcasm. "I thought it was brave."

"The captain thought it was daft. And, in the aftermath, I'm tempted to agree with him."

Steldor motioned vaguely to his injured back and I drew nearer, half out of morbid curiosity, half to prove that I wasn't afraid to look. For the first time, I noticed his damp hair and the sheen of sweat across his brow—he was fevered, and no doubt miserable.

"Why did you do it? I know it was to honor the men who died, but…but it's over now, isn't it? The revolt, our chance at freedom. The Cokyrians stopped it."

"Because we gave the Cokyrians something *to* stop."

I furrowed my brow, confused. "What do you mean?"

"Yes, what I did was to honor the men who died." Steldor laid his head back down on the pillow. "But it was also to show the people that we're *not* defeated."

"That's a bit optimistic, isn't it?"

Agitated that I wasn't catching his subtle hints, he propped himself up once more.

"Narian, the High Priestess—they know we're not the type to sit still and take what they hand us. They were expecting a rebellion, so we gave them one. Those men knew they were dying before any of this started."

Somehow the prospect of people willingly walking to their deaths made the executions of just a few days ago all the more horrifying. His revelation was so shocking that my stomach lurched, my hand flying to cover my mouth.

"Shaselle? Are you all right?"

"Yes. But—but I don't understand. Why would they do this, if they knew they were doomed?"

Steldor, realizing he had upset me, tried to clarify, his voice gentle. "For Hytanica. For the kingdom."

"But what did their deaths accomplish?" I demanded, near tears.

"I shouldn't have brought this up. Forget what I said."

"No, I can't. Please, you have to explain this to me." I was struggling to comprehend not just the sacrifices of these men, but of Steldor...and of my own father. Papa had proudly, defiantly, told the Overlord who he was, even though he knew it would make his suffering that much worse.

Relenting, Steldor motioned for me to come closer and took hold of one of my hands.

"Our enemy expected us to wage one more fight. Now, thanks to those men who gave their lives, the Cokyrians believe we have, and that we've been cowed. They're wrong."

What had flitted through my mind at his first hint now took hold. "You're planning something else."

"And we're going to succeed."

"But how? You don't have weapons, and the Cokyrians have forbidden Hytanicans even to assemble. How can you plot a rebellion?"

"Just trust me, Shaselle." He smirked. "Things are in place."

"It's not funny! I don't want to watch you die and not know—"

He released my hand, exhaling in aggravation. "This isn't why you came here. We've talked about it enough."

I shook my head. "No, we haven't."

"You already know far more than you should. Be content with that, and for God's sake, keep your mouth *shut* on the matter."

I bristled. "I wouldn't tell anyone. And if I know too much, what would be the harm in telling me the rest?"

"Because you'd want to be involved. And you can't be, because you wouldn't have survived what I just went through, the punishment I suffered. Everyone with a hand in this game is at risk for the same or worse." He paused, letting his words sink into my brain. "Now, tell me why you're here."

"Perhaps coming was a mistake," I huffed, starting for the door.

"Shaselle, come back," Steldor drawled, tired and somewhat apologetic. "I don't want you on the streets."

I turned and looked at him, my resolve slipping at the depth of feeling in his dark eyes. I scuffed the toe of my boot against the edge of the rug, my irritation dissipating.

"Where should I go?" I asked, knowing the answer that made sense, the one he would provide.

"Home."

I nodded, inexplicably sad, then walked out the door. My head was spinning, and yet it felt dull after all I had learned. Galen appeared at the first-floor landing, watching me descend the stairs. He had probably been listening for my footsteps, not wanting to lose me again.

"Everything well?" he inquired, and I wondered how he could so effectively pretend that all was normal.

"Steldor and I had a good talk."

"Glad to hear it. Tiersia told me that you ate earlier, but you're welcome to stay for dinner. Even if you're no longer hungry, we'd enjoy your company."

"I don't want to impose."

In truth, I was suddenly so exhausted that if I didn't leave soon, I wouldn't make it home tonight. And I needed to be home tonight. I'd been selfish and unfair to my family for long enough. Galen, like Steldor, thought the same.

"Then let me take you home."

"It's not a long walk—I can make it on my own."

"But I'd like to stretch my legs."

Smiling at his transparent desire to make certain I didn't wander off, I yielded. "If you insist. But won't you be late for dinner?"

"Dinner doesn't start without me," he joked. "It's impossible for me to be late."

He put a hand on my back to escort me to the front door, pausing to inform Tiersia of what he was doing.

The evening was brisk—cold enough to remind me that I'd left my cloak and canvas bag in the church ruins on the south side of the city, no doubt a welcome donation to one of Hytanica's street dwellers. Galen and I didn't talk much as we traversed the short distance to my home, but the closer we came to our destination, the more thankful I was that he was at my side. Especially once the manor house came into view, for my mother's anger seemed to radiate from it.

Galen escorted me all the way to the front door. I looked pleadingly at him before I opened it, and with an understanding nod, he followed me inside. The voices I could hear coming from the parlor quieted, and I could almost feel the curiosity in the air at who had entered. Swallowing hard, I moved into the hallway and into sight.

"Shaselle!" Mother cried, standing so abruptly that her sewing slipped from her lap onto the floor. My sisters and brother, all of whom were present, stared at me, faces mixed with shock and elation.

"You came back!" Celdrid hopped to his feet, trailing Mother, who had hastened to embrace me.

"Where in heaven's name have you been, girl?" She held me at arm's length, inspecting me. "What were you thinking, disappearing like that? You had me scared to death."

"She stayed with me," Galen unexpectedly supplied, and I glanced questioningly at him.

Mother stepped around me, and displeasure would have

been a charitable description of her emotion. Now I understood Galen's tactic—he was bringing her anger at my conduct down on him; he was also keeping from her the knowledge that I had been alone on the streets, vulnerable to butchers, the enemy and the cold.

"Galen, you had better not be lying to me."

I went over to my siblings, all of us wary of her harsh tone.

"I would never lie to you, Lania. You know me better than that."

"I know you well enough." She was considering him shrewdly. "You kept my daughter at your house for four days and didn't tell me? You didn't send her home?"

"You and Baelic never sent Steldor and me home when we showed up here," he said with a shrug and a surreptitious wink for me that did not pass Mother's notice. He and my cousin had been a bit wild during their teenage years, and had found a place to sleep at our house when they'd been too afraid to face Cannan.

Mother shook her head, trying to hide her affection for the young man behind a frown. "You're fortunate you have a charming smile, Galen."

"That's why I practice," he said with a slight bow. "If you'll excuse me, my wife is holding dinner."

He bade us farewell and departed, leaving me to stand awkwardly among my siblings, waiting to see what Mother would do next. She took a deep breath, smoothing her skirts.

"Off to bed with you—*all* of you."

Relieved, I rushed past her with my sisters and brother, who were probably thankful they didn't have to witness an argument. Reaching my bedroom, I washed off what seemed like twelve layers of dirt and put on a nightgown. Deciding my hair could wait until morning, I snuggled beneath my warm, soft covers, ready to fall asleep, thinking I could easily stay put for days. Before I could snuff out the lamp on my bedside table, there was a knock on the door.

"Come in," I called with trepidation.

Mother entered and I hurriedly pulled the bedclothes up to my chin, afraid of what she might say. She sat down beside me and took hold of the quilts, easing them from my grasp, her expression sad rather than angry.

"You're not in trouble, Shaselle. I wanted to tell you how happy I am that you're home where you belong. I missed you, and I was terribly worried that something might have happened to you."

Her hazel eyes glistened with the light from the flame, and she tenderly brushed stray strands of hair away from my face.

"My darling child," she whispered, leaning down to kiss me on the forehead. "I love you beyond measure. Sleep well."

She stood and went to the door, prepared to leave without a word from me.

"Mama? I love you, too."

"Good night," she said, her tone brighter, then she departed, closing the door behind her.

I lay quietly in the dim light, one arm above my head, thinking for once that I had done the right thing. Home was not a terrible place, despite the memories of Papa. Home was where I was loved, and maybe the memories weren't such a bad thing.

Despite how tired I was, I left my lantern burning while my mind wandered back to my conversation with Steldor. Apparently he and whoever else was involved—definitely Galen, possibly my uncle, the men who had been executed and certainly London, who had not been seen in the city since the failed revolt attempt—had barely begun. Steldor had sounded confident. But what could they do?

I rolled onto my side, becoming more restless as I racked

my brain for an answer. They could not assemble, so had to be using some furtive form of communication, one the Cokyrians wouldn't detect. But this raised an additional question: how long had this plan been in place? It had to have predated the posting of the High Priestess's regulations because our remaining military leaders had been separated since that time, which put its origin almost simultaneous with the formation of the province. If I was right, I had underestimated these men right along with the enemy.

That still left the subject of arms. All the plotting in the world couldn't change the fact that Cokyri had disarmed our citizenry. The men involved in the failed revolt had managed to retain and hide some weapons, but those were now in Cokyrian hands. Steldor had made it sound like the coming rebellion would be on a much larger scale. How and where could they have hidden enough weapons to arm an entire kingdom?

I curled up tighter. The weapons could have been smuggled in from outside—perhaps from the surrounding kingdoms? Sarterad, Gourhan and Emotana might have been alarmed enough at Cokyri's new proximity to lend us aid, in spite of the neutrality all three had maintained during the war. Hytanica alone had incited Cokyri's wrath, and the other kingdoms had preferred to keep it that way, but I suspected they felt differently now that the warrior empire had a foothold in the valley.

If the other kingdoms had supplied armaments, and they had been smuggled into the city, where were they stored? I struggled against my inability to fit the pieces together. Then it struck me. Steldor, Galen and Halias had been put in charge of the reconstruction. What if the weapons were hidden inside the structures, built right into the walls?

I got out of bed, snatching up the lantern and tiptoeing into the hall, not wanting to draw anyone's notice. When I reached the first floor, however, I threw caution aside and scurried into the eastern wing. This side of the house had amassed the most damage during the siege, and intuition told me where I would find the weapons, if indeed there was a cache.

The door to my father's study swung open silently, thanks to new hinges. The entire office had been decimated, but Galen had painstakingly restored it, carefully putting the few things that had survived back in their rightful places. Papa's desk had been destroyed, but it had been replaced with an almost identical one; other than the fact that the scent of my father—and the feel of years of joy—could never be returned, all was as it should be.

Except for one bookcase. I hadn't noticed because no one entered this room anymore, but Galen would have known where the replacement case belonged—on the inside wall, adjacent to the door. Now it was on an outside wall. My heart thudding, I curiously approached it.

Setting the lantern on the floor, I took hold of the bookcase and pulled, but it would not shift. Odd—it had always been freestanding, but was now anchored to the wall. My excitement mounting, I grabbed armfuls of books, haphazardly strewing them on the floor. The back of the case was solid wood, but I pushed between the shelves, trying to make something budge. Nothing yielded. I paused, listening for movement from upstairs, then stuck my head and shoulders into each and every section to knock softly on the backing. With a tiny, exhilarated laugh, I realized the bottom section was hollow.

Determination revived, I shoved with all my weight against the wood, kicking over some of the volumes piled behind me as I grappled for leverage. My hands slipped, and my shoulder hit the left side, earning a groan—not from me, but from the bookcase. The right edge shifted toward me, just enough for me to fit my fingers behind and force it open.

The gap I had created was large enough for me to squirm through, and I found myself sitting on the dirt floor of a small room behind the wall. It was partially below ground, cool, but not drafty; in fact, it was difficult to breathe in the small, dark, dusty space. I leaned back through the opening in the bookcase and grabbed the lantern. When I could at last see what the room contained, I grinned.

Before me were stacked weapons of every sort—daggers, long-knives, swords, bows and arrows, lances, whips—legions and legions of glorious weapons.

CHAPTER 17

MARTYRS
AND SAINTS

I HAD DEPARTED WHEN THE DOCTOR CAME TO Cannan's office to minister to Steldor, and I heard word the following morning that Cannan was removing his son from the Bastion, a decision I thought wise. The number of Cokyrians within the structure had substantially increased since the attempted revolt, and with Rava literally across the hall from where Steldor lay, I worried for his safety. He had not made friends for himself among the enemy officers by his actions. Nor had he endeared himself to me.

Although I tried to understand his motivations, I was frustrated with him, especially since his actions had only led to his own pain. I had seen many sides of Steldor during our brief and difficult marriage and was familiar with his bravery, his pride and his tendency to follow his instincts despite what anyone else had to say, but I was through abiding his perniciousness. And the more I thought about his conduct, the more convinced I became that his insolence was as much directed at me as at the Cokyrians.

I continued to ask Cannan about Steldor's condition over the next several days, learning as I did so that the captain had not refrained from sharing his opinion on the incident with his son, but Steldor had yet to hear from me. Perhaps it was presumptuous, but I believed I might be able to make an impression on him when others could not.

I rose with the sun the next morning, well before my customary meeting time with Cannan. Believing this afforded me sufficient opportunity, I dressed and sent word to have a horse prepared for me, a decision that would see me in breeches for the first time in months.

With the hood of my cloak obscuring my face, I rode to the western residential area of the city, the clacking of my mount's hooves on the stone streets one of the few sounds in the early morning air. The sky was still gray and the ground was moist with morning dew as I pulled my horse to a halt in front of Galen's manor house and dismounted. I looped the leathers around the hitching post and walked to the door, which was opened by a servant upon my knock.

"Queen Alera," she said, unusually collected, her poise leaving no doubt in my mind that she had been attending royalty. Most people stuttered and stumbled over their words in my presence, but not this young woman.

She curtseyed, then stepped aside, ushering me into the foyer.

"The lord of the house is not at home, Your Majesty," she informed me. "Is there anything I can do for you?"

"I actually came to see Lord Steldor, if you would escort me to his room."

Now she seemed intrigued, for the reasons behind the annulment of my marriage to the former King had been kept quiet. I could read on her face her desire to eavesdrop.

"Certainly, although I don't know if His Majesty has risen."

"He has," I said without thought. Not once during our

marriage had I woken before him, and I doubted his sleep patterns had changed.

With a puzzled glance, she led me up the stairs and into a hallway, stopping before the second door. She knocked on my behalf, and gave another small curtsey when Steldor's voice invited entry.

I opened the door, waiting for her to return to the first floor before entering, catching her regretful glance that she could not dally. Steldor was sitting up on the bed across the room, his legs swung over the side, pulling a shirt carefully over his head.

"Should you be doing that so soon?" I asked, for it had only been a week since the lashing.

The garment fell over his muscular chest, and he ran a hand through his dark hair. He came to his feet with the hint of a wince.

"Making sure I'm cared for is no longer your worry. I'm not certain it ever was."

His mood was a bit dark, and I wondered if I should have given him more time to recover before paying him this visit.

"Perhaps what you need is someone to keep you from coming to harm in the first place."

He smirked, turning his back to me to idly straighten his bed coverings. "What is it—did you come here to coddle me or lecture me?"

"Both, I suppose." I was frowning, amazed at how swiftly we had fallen into our old patterns. "I've come to talk—and to give you this."

He swiveled to face me as I removed his silver wolf's head talisman from the pocket of my cloak.

"I never expected to see that again," he said, sounding awed. "Did you face the bitch yourself or get it from Narian?"

I smiled at his word choice. "I approached Rava myself—

I've been known to face down a bitch or two." He stepped forward to take the pendant from my hand and immediately slipped the chain over his head.

"Thank you. I feel better already."

"If you don't mind my asking, what is the significance of the talisman? When I reclaimed it from Rava, she remarked that it might provide power and protection, and that started me thinking about its purpose."

He chuckled ruefully. "I hate to admit it, but Rava's right. The wolf brings strength and protection. Depending on the mix of herbs and flowers put inside the talisman, other properties can be added, such as health and healing. The captain gave the pendant to me when I was four, following the death of Terek, at the time I was sent to live with Baelic and Lania. He didn't want me to think he'd abandoned me or that I was in danger. It was originally his, and his father's before him. I've worn it ever since."

"Then I'm very glad I was able to secure its return."

His eyes met mine, and the color rose in my cheeks, for I was still affected to some degree by his handsome features and soldier's build.

"I suppose that concludes the coddling," he finally said, crossing his arms and watching me expectantly.

"Yes, I suppose it does."

"Then let the lecture begin." He spread his hands, giving me a slight nod.

"You were part of that revolt," I accused.

"Yes."

I hesitated, his honesty taking my words away, and he sat stiffly on the edge of the bed, his back obviously ailing him.

"Why can't you trust what I'm doing, Steldor? Why can't you share my goals?"

"You're asking me to trust *Narian,*" he said with a condescending laugh.

"That's the reason? Because you can't stand being on his side?"

Steldor rolled his eyes. "This had nothing to do with *him,* and everything to do with our freedom. We fought too hard and lost too many good men to let this kingdom perish without one more battle. Now the battle's been waged. Just be satisfied with that."

He was bitter, and in many ways, I didn't blame him. But this was my chance to impress reality upon him.

"Will *you* be satisfied with that? I've been advising you, advising *everyone* on the course that makes the most sense for our people. If you had listened to me, not tried to undercut my efforts, you wouldn't be hurt right now, London wouldn't be hiding in the mountains and Halias and his men wouldn't be dead."

He glared at me, his anger beginning to simmer, which only increased my fervor.

"Look at you." I gestured toward him, for he could not disguise his pain, nor hide the fever that brought beads of sweat to his forehead. "You did this to yourself, Steldor. You punished yourself with your actions, but nothing else was accomplished. You just wanted to be a martyr."

"What's wrong with that?" he shot back. "You want to be a saint! You want to be the one who brings peace to these people. You're the one who brought *war,* Alera. You're the reason Narian didn't leave for good when he fled Hytanica. He loves you, and that's why——"

He stopped talking, unable to make himself complete that sentence.

"You're right about one thing," I whispered in the dead silence. "Narian loves me, but what you won't acknowledge is that he's the reason any of us still have our lives. He's the reason you weren't killed for that show you put on."

"Extend my thanks," he said, tone laden with sarcasm.

I threw up my hands. "This is pointless, us dancing around in circles. You still won't listen to anyone, let alone me. I may as well go."

"But you won't—you aren't yet ready to leave."

I didn't move, hating that he knew my threat had been empty, and he stood. He drew closer to me until I could feel the heat radiating from his body.

"Hytanica and Cokyri will always be different worlds, Alera. Before this is over, one of those worlds will be destroyed. We can't coexist like this."

"Not when people like you refuse to believe any different."

"At least I'm not hiding from the truth. You're so wrapped up in Narian that you can't see the situation for what it really is. Cokyri is a godless, brutal, warrior empire that despises the very way we live. Now that they are in power, they have no need to honor our traditions or tolerate our beliefs. Don't you see, it's not just the Kingdom of Hytanica that will no longer exist. It is our entire way of *life*."

I stared at him, shocked and confused. Narian and I had always been able to work through our differences, so I had assumed our countries could, as well. But he and I wanted to be together, we wanted to be joined. Our countries did not.

"Cokyri is interested only in obtaining certain things from us," I argued, although a bit of doubt now nagged at me. "As long as we follow their regulations, we can live in the manner we always have."

"Then I'd keep an eye on their regulations, Alera. They're already changing our educational system, what we are permitted to teach our sons. Religion will come next."

"Change isn't necessarily all bad."

"It is when it's forced down your throat. And in case you haven't noticed, the Cokyrians overseeing the work crews have not allowed us to rebuild our churches. They have been reconstructed, but for different, more *practical* purposes. The Cokyrians are quite enamored with practicality."

Not knowing what else to say, I turned to depart, only to feel his hand on my arm.

"It doesn't have to be like this, Alera. Between us, I mean."

He was looking at me with those dark, intense, fiery eyes—eyes that held love I had never reciprocated.

"Things are what they are, Steldor," I replied, decisive but desolate. "We're separated by too much. We always have been. Just please, give yourself time to get well."

Before he could stop me a second time, I stepped out the door, feeling the weight of frustration lifting from my shoulders with each step I took away from him. I had been foolish to think he and I could communicate in spite of our differing beliefs. Neither of us wanted to cause the other pain, but that was all we had ever been good at doing.

CHAPTER 18

INCORRIGIBLE

I'D CLOSED THE SECRET ENTRANCE TO THE weapons room to the best of my ability and replaced all the books on the shelves before leaving Papa's study in peace. Though my cleanup had not been perfect, I wasn't worried about someone else making the same discovery—I suspected I was the only person to have gone into that room in months.

I felt smug, however, at having taken a souvenir—Hytanica was a dangerous city, but rather than stay at home, I'd decided a sheathed knife strapped to my calf would be practical. Even though I knew it was silly, it also made me feel a part of something bigger. I could never tell Steldor, Cannan or Galen what I had found, but with a secret dagger, I felt like a member of their ranks.

My mother and siblings were quite observant of me over the next several days, though they consciously gave me space. It was strange, being treated so differently—in fact, the younger children were even bickering with less frequency. It was as though they all recognized that our less-than-ideal circumstances had driven one of us to the edge and were afraid of what another instance might bring.

When the walls finally closed in on me, I went to Mother for permission to go to the market. The simple fact that I was *asking* would put me in good favor, so I was hopeful of the result. And I had donned a traditional skirt, knowing it would please her. Even though I had thus created the perfect conditions, she hesitated, wanting to say no, but leery of holding on to me too tightly.

"Don't go alone," she at last said.

"I've been alone on the streets before," I unthinkingly argued, and her expression grew cautionary. "But I'll bring a friend."

I had no intention of honoring this promise, but it was the best I could do to repair the damage from my callous remark.

"Home for dinner," she relented.

It was midafternoon, which did not give me much time to enjoy my stolen freedom, but the fresh, crisp air was a blessing in and of itself. I meandered along the shop fronts lining the main street in the Market District, dodging the traffic of horses, wagons, soldiers and pedestrians, until the sound of frantic stamping and snorting drew my notice. I pushed through the crowd and into a deserted alley, where the owner of the nearby balm shop tied his horse. Indeed, someone's mount was there, still saddled, its reins tied so securely to a post that its desperate efforts to free its head were apt to break its neck.

"Whoa," I murmured, trying to calm the animal enough to set it loose, not wanting it to come to harm.

I gripped the reins, but the horse, its eyes wild with fear, snapped its head back, catching my hand in the leather strap, and I inhaled sharply from the sting. How long had the poor thing been out here? My senses on full alert, I glanced behind me at the busy street, weighing my options. Seeing no one, I hoisted up my skirt, and unsheathed the dagger I had kept.

The instant I cut the reins, the horse bolted past me, almost knocking me over. Its owner would not be happy, but at least the animal would live to see another day.

It wasn't until someone clamped an arm around my waist, seizing the knife, that I realized I was no longer alone. So much for having reliable senses.

"Well, aren't you just incorrigible?"

Imprisonment or execution was the punishment for bearing weapons in this new Hytanica. The dagger itself was a small loss, but I had to get away. I brought my elbow back, my mother's reluctance to let me leave the house flashing like lightning in my brain. If I were arrested, *killed,* she would never forgive herself, even though she would bear no fault.

"*Empress,* the bruises you've given me are too many to count!"

I whirled around, dismayed that I had not succeeded in getting the Cokyrian to release me, at the same time recognizing the voice and the curse. Saadi pushed me against the side of the shop, leaning in so close to me that I could feel his breath upon my cheek, and his pale blue eyes stared me into submission.

"I can't call you a horse thief for what you just did," he told me, glancing after the gelding. "At least, not a very good horse thief. But I *can,* and I *must,* bring you in for this little utensil of yours. Some niece of the captain you are."

"Are you going to take me to your *sister?*" I spat, and he grimaced, contemplating me for an instant before disregarding the barb. Gripping me by the upper arm, he hauled me toward the thoroughfare.

"Come on. To the Bastion."

Though my question about Rava appeared to have had its intended effect, I was numb with fear. What if he *did* take me to her? Rava had been the one to order me lashed for my failed prank, she'd been the one to inflict punishment upon Steldor. It seemed no one could exert control over her, a thought that made me ill.

The nearer we came to our destination, the more rapidly my heart beat, and by the time we reached the palace gates, I was again fighting Saadi.

"Let...me...go!" I howled, unexpectedly pulling out of his grasp, but one of the Cokyrian sentries caught me, laughing at my plight.

"Need some help, Saadi?" the burly man offered, shoving me back at my captor, who was rather slight in comparison to his comrade.

"No," Saadi grumbled and the sentry moved ahead to open the gates for us.

As we passed through, the large man called, "Rava is at the city headquarters, minding the peacekeeping force. If you were looking for her, that is."

"I wasn't." Even though my circumstances were inarguably bleak, a wave of relief washed over me. She, at least, would not be the one to show me the error of my ways.

We entered the austere palace—which as the Bastion lacked its former magnificence, the Cokyrians favoring practicality over beauty in the province—and Saadi asked the set of guards in the Grand Entry where he could find the commander.

"In there," one of the women said, pointing toward my uncle's office.

"Is he alone?" Saadi seemed reluctant to interrupt his superior's schedule.

"The former Captain of the Guard and the Grand Provost are with him."

My horizons kept getting darker and darker. The moment Cannan learned of my offense, he would set me drowning in woe.

Saadi studied me as though evaluating my worth, then opted to try his luck. He led me to the door and knocked. We didn't have long to wait before the captain called for us to enter.

Queen Alera and Cannan rose from their chairs as we came through the door, Commander Narian already on his feet. All eyes fell on me, and I bowed my head to examine the floor, combating the urge to run. Not only would I be caught if I tried to flee, adding to my humiliation, but success would gain me nothing. Cannan knew by now that I'd done something. If only I'd gotten away earlier.

"Report," Narian ordered, umbrage in his tone. He did not appreciate the lack of respect Saadi was displaying by coming straight to him.

Saadi pulled my dagger from somewhere on his belt, flipping it around to hand it to his commanding officer.

"I caught her with this illegal weapon on the street, sir. Considering the interest you took in her welfare last time, I thought it best this matter be brought directly to you."

"A good decision," Narian said, examining the knife. "Now return to your post."

Saadi gave a deferential nod to him and, to my surprise, a slight bow to Queen Alera before departing.

In the silence that briefly reigned, Cannan's gaze fell upon me, unwavering, unwelcoming and especially dark considering the reprimand he'd given me in the barn. I was in so much trouble.

"Where did you get this?" Narian asked, and my attention snapped from my uncle to the Cokyrian commander, who was brandishing my dagger. Which of them was the fiercer opponent? I didn't speak, afraid to find out, certain this was how a cornered animal felt.

"Shaselle, from whom did you obtain that weapon?" It was

Queen Alera addressing me now, her voice softer, kinder, but I hardly looked at her, for she was not where the problem lay.

When I still did not answer, Narian turned to Cannan. "You tell us then."

"I have no more knowledge than do you," the former captain said, not outwardly disturbed by the fact that my conduct had brought him under suspicion.

"I need to know how she came by this dagger," Narian said more forcefully, but I knew he was wasting his breath. Cannan was not about to be intimidated—certainly not by a young man of my age, regardless of whatever mythical powers he possessed. "These have been outlawed and removed from Hytanican hands. No young girl could wrangle one. Not unless she had access to some that were kept from my soldiers. Not unless she was the captain's niece."

"My answer remains the same," Cannan replied, unflappable as ever. "I suggest you stop accusing me."

A silent challenge passed between the powerful men, to be interrupted by the Queen, who spoke but one word—the Cokyrian commander's name. He looked to her more quickly than I would have believed possible, and his demeanor changed along with his focus, becoming softer, more cooperative.

"May I see the dagger?" she asked.

Without demanding a reason, he passed her the blade. Perhaps she had more influence than I thought.

She perused the weapon with a crease in her brow. "I think I recognize this."

"You do?" Narian sounded skeptical, while I was flabbergasted, and Cannan's eyebrows lifted ever so slightly.

"I believe this was Lord Baelic's. It must have been missed by the Cokyrians sweeping his home. A house of Hytanican women—they might not have been thorough." She paused and met my gaze. "This is your father's, is it not, Shaselle?"

I started nodding before I could even process what was happening. Was she mistaken? Did she actually believe the weapon had belonged to my papa? Or was she trying to help me? Whatever the case, I wasn't about to argue with her, seizing the excuse and hoping it would be good enough to save me, at least from Cokyrian punishment.

Narian scrutinized both me and the Queen with eyes so deeply blue I could not break away from them. I was glad he was no longer questioning me, for those eyes made me want to tell him everything. At the same time, those eyes revealed something to me. Was he in love with Alera?

"Is this true?" Narian asked, his question directed to Cannan.

My uncle shrugged. "I can't be certain, but the make of the blade would have met my brother's favor. He had a great many weapons—your soldiers could easily have missed one. I trust Alera's memory if she says she saw it on Baelic's person."

I held my breath in the tense interlude that followed. Alera looked earnestly at Narian, the Cokyrian commander considered, and my uncle maintained his facade of naïveté. He and Papa had shared a passion for weaponry—a common affliction among men in military families—and there was no chance he believed the blade in question had belonged to his brother, not when he'd been apprised of every dagger, bow and sword in my father's collection.

Narian stepped forward to retrieve the knife from Alera, then trained his attention once more on me.

"I warned you before to keep out of trouble. No one is invulnerable. Go, but I'm retaining your father's weapon."

He tucked the dagger into his belt and departed, leaving me quaking. My uncle was perhaps impervious to intimidation by the commander, but I was not.

The Queen watched him go with a strange expression,

then Cannan came toward me, taking my arm and escorting me from his office. We passed the guards in the Grand Entry and entered the courtyard, walking along the white stone path now infamously scorched from Rava's flag burning.

"I beg of you, Shaselle," he hissed when we reached the gates. "Go home and stay there. I cannot be worried about you now." He didn't sound angry, just agitated, so perhaps I would survive this, after all. "I'll come and discuss this with you later, but right now I need to know that you're home and safe."

"Yes, Uncle," I said, not sure what frightened me more—the prospect of an enraged Cannan, or this collected, apprehensive captain.

He escorted me through the gates before releasing me, then turned and strode back toward the palace. Confused and unnerved, I rubbed my upper arm where several people had roughly grabbed me today. I knew Cannan would have taken me home if he hadn't been concerned about affairs with Narian and the Queen. Unable to judge what damage I had done, I could only hope I hadn't somehow destroyed their plans, or put Narian back on their scent.

With these uneasy thoughts urging me onward, I hurried toward home, praying I would make it in time for dinner and thereby avoid having to answer to my mother. That was the only way my day could get worse. I was forced to adjust that conclusion, however, when I spotted Saadi loitering nearby. The moment he laid eyes on me, I knew he'd been waiting for me, and I groaned. Why couldn't he leave me alone?

"Shaselle!" he called, coming toward me.

I gritted my teeth, knowing I could not escape. The traffic on the thoroughfare had thinned, as was generally the case at this time of day, no longer providing the cover I needed to dart past him. He came abreast of me, but I didn't slow or acknowledge him.

"I'm glad I caught you," he said, and in my peripheral vision, I could see him smoothing that damn bronze hair forward, an impossible task, for as always it kinked upward at the midpoint of his hairline.

"Can't say the same."

"I didn't take you to my sister." He sounded like this small mercy should be eliciting gratitude from me.

"I realize that."

Saadi exhaled, baffled and exasperated. "How can you be angry with me?"

I halted and stared at him in disbelief. "I'm not! You're the Cokyrian soldier who arrested me when I broke the law. Our relationship ends there. It would be a waste of my time to be angry with you."

"That's it?" he said, eyebrows rising, and I was sure I detected disappointment. "I thought... I don't know. I thought you were angry with me before, for not having mentioned I'm Rava's brother. Weren't you?"

"No," I lied.

I still didn't understand why it upset me to know that this annoying tag-along was related to the woman I hated with such intensity that my insides burned. But there was no reason to complicate things by letting him know the truth.

"Well, I saved you today, didn't I? Just like I saved you before. You walked out of the Bastion free, without a scratch, and if any Cokyrian but me had caught you with that dagger, you might be drawn and quartered by now."

"You didn't save me from that butcher," I said irritably. "But you're right. About today, I mean." I could sense his satisfaction, which irritated me all the more. "So accept my thanks, but *stay* away from me. We're not friends, you know."

I was nearing my neighborhood and didn't want anyone

to see me with him. He stepped in front of me, forcing me to stop.

"We're not friends *yet*. But you've thought about it. And you just thanked me."

"Are you delusional?"

"No. You just said thank you to the faceless Cokyrian soldier who arrested you."

"Don't you ever stop?" I demanded, trying in vain to move around him.

"I haven't even started."

"What does *that* mean?"

There was silence as Saadi glanced up and down the street. "I want to know where you got that dagger. Or at least what story you told."

"Why don't you ask Commander Narian? The two of you seemed fairly close."

"Quit making jokes."

"I haven't made a single one."

"Well?"

"It was my father's," I said, clinging to the lie Queen Alera had provided, whether by mistake or not.

"Oh." This seemed to take Saadi aback.

"And now, because of you, I don't have it anymore." I knew I was pressing my luck, but I wanted to make him feel bad.

"I'm sorry," he muttered, seeming sincere enough.

Thinking I had maybe, finally, succeeded in getting him to leave me alone, I stepped around him.

"Shaselle?"

I stopped again, without the slightest idea why.

"Your father—what was he like?"

The question shocked me; I also wasn't sure I could answer it without crying. But Saadi appeared so genuinely interested that I couldn't disregard him.

"You have no right to ask me that," I answered out of principle. "But for your information, he was the strongest, bravest, kindest and best-humored man I ever knew. And none of it was because he took what was handed to him."

For the second time, I attempted a dramatic departure.

"Shaselle?"

"What now?" I incredulously exclaimed.

"Do you have plans tomorrow?"

"What?"

"I have a day off duty. We could—"

"No!" I shouted. "What *is* this? You expect me to spend a day with you, a Cokyrian—a Cokyrian I can't stand?"

"Yes," he affirmed, despite my outburst.

I laughed in disbelief. "I won't. This is ridiculous. *You're* ridiculous. Enjoy your time off duty with your own kind."

Turning, I sprinted down the street, and though he called after me yet again, I ignored him. As I neared my house, I glanced behind once or twice to assure myself he wasn't following. He was nowhere in sight.

I reached the security of my home just in time for dinner, and just in time to cut off Mother's growing displeasure—the first step in her progression to anger. I smiled at her, hurried to wash, and was a perfect lady throughout the meal. Afterward I retired to my room, picking a book from my shelf to occupy me until my eyes drooped. Instead of words on pages, however, I kept seeing Saadi's face—his clear blue eyes, that irritating hair, those freckles across his nose that made me lose willpower.

What if I had offended him earlier? He had only asked to spend time with me, and I had mocked him. But he was *Cokyrian*. It was ludicrous for him to be pursuing my company. It was dangerous for me to be in his. And that, I suddenly realized, was part of the reason I very much wanted to be with him. Saadi aggravated me, confused me, scared me, and yet I could no longer deny that he intrigued me in a way no one else ever had.

CHAPTER 19

CAUSE TO CELEBRATE

THE MORNING FOLLOWING SHASELLE'S ARREST and release, I descended the Grand Staircase to the entry hall below and was drawn toward the antechamber by raised voices. I entered to find one of my worst nightmares unfolding—Steldor and Narian were in heated argument, both seeming to have discounted where they were and who might overhear. They stood opposite one another across the room from me, Steldor likely having come from Cannan's office, while Narian had probably been passing through on his way to the Hearing Hall. I stared transfixed, not knowing what they were arguing about, but certain they would not appreciate my interference.

"What business have you in the Bastion?" my betrothed demanded.

"Business that is not yours, Cokyrian," Steldor spat.

Narian glowered at the former King. "Much as you might detest the thought, Steldor, I am no longer your enemy."

"These scars on my back argue differently."

"I was merciful in leaving you *alive*. You asked for execution and I ordered a lashing. If not for your ridiculous pride, you'd acknowledge that."

Steldor laughed mirthlessly. "I owe you *nothing* after all you've taken from me."

"Alera is not a possession," Narian astutely shot back.

"Alera hadn't entered my mind." The curl in Steldor's lip revealed the lie, and the hostility he exuded would have made most men run in the other direction. But Narian wasn't most men.

"And yet I see you around this Bastion, her home, more than any soldier or son need be. You yearn for any chance glimpse of her."

"I come to the *palace* on business, you mongrel pup."

"Then pray tell, what *business* is that?"

I stood miserably by, for it was apparent neither of them was aware of my presence. Still, the argument had come full circle, and I prayed it would soon be over.

"I don't have to tell you anything," Steldor seethed. "You are *not* my superior." His dark eyes glinted malevolently, a look he had once or twice directed at me during our unfortunate marriage.

"True enough. But you are nonetheless one of my subjects."

Steldor's fists clenched and unclenched at his sides, telling me how close he was to unleashing his hellish temper. Before I could intervene, he threw a right cross at Narian's chin, which the commander adroitly dodged, stepping back and raising his hands in a gesture of surrender.

"I suggest you walk away, Steldor," he said, unnervingly calm.

"I did so once," my former husband retorted. "I don't intend to do so again."

Narian perused his opponent, judging his strengths and weaknesses, then struck Steldor in the middle of his chest with the heel of his palm, sending him staggering backward. In a flash, a dagger appeared in Steldor's hand, and panic seized me. Would they spill each other's blood right here, right now?

"Stop!" I cried. "Both of you!"

They straightened warily at the sound of my voice, and I hurried to stand between them, so distraught my hands were shaking.

"I don't know what this is about," I beseeched, hoping Cannan would hear and lend assistance. "But please, for my sake, leave things be."

They glared at each other over the top of my head, then Steldor moved away, his eyes on Narian until he could place a hand on the door leading into the Grand Entry.

"Queen Alera," he pointedly acknowledged me. "I humbly honor your request."

With a disdainful smirk for Narian, he tossed the knife onto the floor, then exited, pulling the door firmly closed behind him. Narian crossed to snatch up the weapon, examining it carefully before showing it to me.

"Do you plan to tell me that you recognize *this* blade?" he asked, and I stared at him, dumbfounded. With a stiff nod, he strode through the same door Steldor had used, leaving me alone.

I hesitated, hoping he would return, but knowing he would not. Then I proceeded to my study, wondering how long it would take before he would seek me out. He was annoyed with Steldor, annoyed with himself and annoyed with me over Shaselle's dagger, but he also had a busy schedule. I was left with no choice but to wait for him to come back.

Though I had fallen in love with Narian a long time ago, I was continually learning more about him. I'd always been familiar with his principles and his personality, but it was the little things that made a human being. Little things like how he was not accustomed to sharing his space—had I not been forced to hide in his bedroom during his exchange with the High Priestess, I would not yet have seen it. There were other things, as well. He was nearly fluent in three languages in addition to our own; he absolutely could not sleep on his back; and he didn't know how to handle being irritated with me.

Had I lied for Shaselle? Yes. But he would have a difficult time confronting me about it. He never hesitated in handling issues with other people, but with me, he seemed to try his hardest to convince himself that there was nothing to handle.

It was late afternoon before he finally raised the matter. After holding audiences in the Hearing Hall, I had entered my office and was about ready to retire when there was a knock on the door. I knew it would be Narian, and that his countenance would be inscrutable. Indeed, when I granted him permission to enter, he was closed off, exactly as I hated him to be.

"I thought you would meet me in my quarters," I said, attempting to keep things light.

"I will. But I need to talk to you first." It was plain from the tone of his voice that he wasn't about to mix business with pleasure.

"Of course." I rose from my desk chair, straightening a few papers and avoiding eye contact with him, though I wasn't sure of the reason.

"The knife I took from Shaselle didn't belong to Baelic."

"Oh?" I looked up to meet his disconcerting eyes. If he wouldn't let me in, I wouldn't let him in.

"Alera, it was Sarteradan. You lied for her. Why?"

"And what of Steldor's dagger?" I asked, ignoring his inquiry.

"Hytanican. No doubt he managed to keep one of his own from my troops."

"What were you and he arguing about?"

"That's of no importance. But you needn't worry—I'm not

going to arrest him." He scrutinized me, and I squirmed like a bug under a magnifying glass. "What is important, Alera, is the question you're trying to avoid—why did you lie for Shaselle?"

I sighed, stepping around my desk. "She's a hurt and confused young woman."

"A hurt and confused young woman who got her hands on a weapon someone in her family planted. I needed to know *where* it was hidden."

I frowned, drawing significance from his use of the word *I* in place of *we*.

"How do you know Baelic didn't own a Sarteradan blade? How do you know this *wasn't* innocent? Are you so determined to suspect these men whose comrades you killed?"

"What did you say?" His tone was chilled.

"That's not what I meant," I said, appalled at my word choice. "That just…came out wrong. I know you saved the lives you could."

Narian's gaze was sharp, and my heart thudded as I prayed he would believe me. I spoke the truth—he was not a murderer.

"Do you know where the dagger came from, Alera?" he finally asked, ice hanging off his words. He sounded so accusatory that I bristled.

"Of course not."

"Do you know where London is?"

"No!" I exclaimed, in awe of the fact that he was interrogating me. "Narian, what is wrong with you? If I were aware of anything that might threaten our goals, I would tell you. If I knew London to be up to something, I wouldn't keep it a secret. But I'm happy to believe he's free and safe. Lord only knows he's suffered enough at Cokyrian hands. And I lied for

Shaselle because, no matter how she came across that weapon, none of those men would have armed her, and you know it."

He broke eye contact, stunned into silence, and his visage softened.

"You're right, I shouldn't have accused you. I'm sorry."

"Don't," I murmured, walking over to him. I swept his hair away from his face, and he closed his eyes at my touch. "Just hold me."

He obliged, wrapping me in his arms and his love, and I wished all disagreements could be so quickly forgotten.

Word came to the Bastion the following morning that, aside from a little cleanup, the five-month-long reconstruction effort that had been underway within the city was complete. For once, happiness was in the air. The time made by the work crews had been phenomenal—at least the Hytanicans and the Cokyrians had been able to cooperate with each other in some capacity.

In celebration, I decided to take the day and tour the city, wanting to see for myself that it had been returned to its former glory. The news was also a form of vindication for me, an affirmation that the path I had chosen for our people was the right one, after all. And if I was honest with myself, I needed to see what had been done with the churches, unwilling to blindly accept Steldor's version of the facts. Perhaps some of the churches had been reconstructed for a different purpose, but surely not all of them.

After discussing my plans with Cannan, I decided to invite my mother to accompany me. With her benevolent soul and her tender, graceful smile, there was not a member of the populace who had not fallen in love with her when she had married my father all those years ago. Her presence would further boost spirits, and her support would be a tremendous aid in changing attitudes about our circumstances once and for all.

I sought her out in the third-floor quarters she shared with my father. She was sitting on the sofa in her parlor when I entered, doing some handwork, and I was reminded of the embroidered handkerchiefs my sister and I used to award as part of the annual Harvest Festival. We would stitch a design of our choosing and present our handkerchiefs to the young men we desired as our escorts for the pretournament dinner. The festival, with its week-long faire and tournament, would attract vendors and contestants from throughout the Recorah River Valley and for miles beyond. Those days seemed so far away now, so innocent. Nothing was that simple anymore.

"Alera, what a pleasant surprise," my mother greeted me in her lyrical voice, sweeping her honey-blond hair over her shoulders. "It's been too long since we've talked. Please, come and sit."

Though my father could often be seen around the Bastion, my mother tended to keep to herself, with the exception of visits with Miranna and attendance at family dinners. In part because of this and in part due to my schedule as Grand Provost, she and I managed little private time together. I complied with her request, for I was in no great rush, sitting in an armchair opposite the sofa.

"Have you heard the good news?" I asked at once.

"What news is that?"

I was grinning, my cheeks flushed. "The hard work is finished and the city is standing again. Word came just an hour ago."

"Already? That is wonderful news. And it couldn't have come at a better time—there has been too much pain and death of late. I suppose you'll be going on a tour?"

Ever a teacher to her daughters, this was more a suggestion

than a question, in case I'd overlooked the importance of sharing this time with our people. To win their hearts, I needed to be a part of their lives in times of joy, not just sorrow.

"Yes. That's the reason I'm here, actually. I was hoping you would join me."

Her face brightened, and she lay her stitching on a side table. "I would be delighted. When do you wish to depart?"

"I've freed my schedule for the rest of the day, so we can leave as soon as it suits you."

"I'll only need to change clothes—something more celebratory would be appropriate."

Another reminder, although this one was much needed. My attire was suitable for my daily duties, but not ideal for a public appearance.

After agreeing to meet in an hour's time, I returned to my quarters, then sent for Sahdienne. Too exhilarated to wait for her, I entered my bedroom and threw wide my wardrobe, hunting for a gown to suit the occasion. I hesitated before coming to a decision, my hand clutched around the fabric of the garment I was considering. It was my most beautiful gown—the one Steldor had given me for my sister's seventeenth birthday party. In cream-and-gold fabric that matched my gold-and-pearl tiara, it was striking, with bell sleeves and a daringly cut neckline. It was the obvious choice—just as Steldor had been to be King.

Sahdienne arrived at that moment, pulling me from my muddled memories. She had always loved the particular gown I'd chosen and had been enamored with my husband's extraordinary taste. Now she eagerly assisted with my preparations, draping the beautiful gold-and-pearl necklace Steldor had given me to wear with the dress around my neck and styling my hair into an elegant roll at the back before fixing my tiara in place. With a quick curtsey, she departed and

I walked into the parlor where my mother was waiting for me. I had not been informed of her arrival and immediately began to apologize.

"I'm sorry to have kept you waiting, but…" I hesitated, for she was studying me with the strangest light in her blue eyes, and I wondered if I were overdressed. "Should I—? I mean, I can change into something else."

"No," she said, approaching me to smooth my dark hair. "You're perfect, dear. You've grown into such a beautiful woman."

I blushed, slightly embarrassed, but she candidly continued.

"Since you and Steldor parted ways, I've often wondered if you're lonely. No person has a whole heart until they find their match."

Though I had missed her often philosophical musings, her insights occasionally left me speechless. This was one of those times. In her own way, she was asking if I had another man in my life. Hytanica was changing, but not so drastically that the fundamental expectations for a member of the royal family would be altered. I would still be expected to bear an heir, although at nineteen, I was hardly running out of time.

I looked into my mother's compassionate eyes and suddenly wanted to tell her everything, wanted to share the love I had found with Narian and the joy I felt at our betrothal. But he and I had agreed not to tell anyone of that event and, though I knew she wanted me to be happy, I wasn't entirely certain how she would react to the news.

"What is it, darling?" she asked, seeing something of my internal conflict on my face.

Her voice was so gentle that my reservations fell away. She was my mother; I could trust her in all things.

"I'm not lonely," I divulged, excitement tickling my stomach. I had been forced for weeks to hide one of the most significant moments of my life, and only now did I realize how much I wanted to tell someone. "I'm…I'm betrothed."

Her eyes widened, then she took my hand and led me to the sofa to sit down beside her. In Hytanica, where arranged marriages were the norm, a young woman's parents often knew before she did that she was to be betrothed. This order of events was highly unusual.

"Whomever are you promised to, Alera? Tell me everything."

"Commander Narian." I held my breath, not knowing what she would do or say, watching her expression shift from astonishment to bewilderment to concern.

"You are in love with him?" she inquired, but it was too late to take my confession back.

"Yes, I am. And he is in love with me."

A few moments passed, then a gracious smile lit her face. Leaning toward me, she lightly placed her palms upon my cheeks.

"Congratulations, Alera."

Now it was my turn to be dumbfounded. "You're not upset?"

"How could I be upset that you're in love?" She very nearly laughed. "When I married your father, I was afraid. I know now that he is a good man, but that experience was never one I wanted for you. I don't know Narian, but I've come to realize he was never truly the enemy. He was in an impossible position, and yet he struggled to save as many lives as he could. But, more important, I know and trust you, Alera. If you love him, then I will love him, too."

I hugged her, then we both laughed at our emotional states, for my throat felt tight and her eyes were glistening with tears. We talked a bit longer, and she promised to keep my confidence, then we proceeded to the Grand Entry Hall where our escorts awaited us, courtesy of Cannan. What I did not anticipate, however, was that Narian would be there.

"Grand Provost," he said, offering a slight bow as he greeted us. "Lady Elissia."

I caught my mother's amused smile at the formality with which he addressed me. Narian also noticed, and a minute crinkle appeared in his brow.

"I thought I would accompany you into the city, with your permission, of course," he continued, addressing me. "To gain favor."

His words were so carefully chosen that I knew he was not speaking only of the *people's* favor.

"I would be pleased to have you join us," I replied, matching his manner, and our entourage departed.

The city was far from pristine—the streets were still dirty and despite the construction of several shelters, many people remained homeless, huddled into deserted buildings where they had been herded by Cokyrian soldiers. I suspected some of the churches were being used for this purpose, but was dismayed to see only one or two spires rising skyward. And work still needed to be done in the villages, for the Cokyrian priority in the countryside was to complete the Province Wall before winter. While farmhands worked the fields, they were under guard by Cokyrian soldiers, a constant reminder that they no longer had control over their own livelihoods. But still, shops in the Market District had reopened, the schools were ready for an influx of students following the harvest and there were fewer altercations between Hytanicans and Cokyrians.

The news that I would be inspecting the city had spread quickly, and men, women and children lined the streets, pleased with the successful rebuilding effort and glad for a break from the day's toil. We rode in carriages to each section of the city, then would disembark to walk some of the streets. Women would call to us and offer us flowers as we strolled along, while the men would respectfully bow their heads. We would nod and touch extended hands, occasionally tossing treats to the girls and boys. Although the sun was partially obscured by the light gray clouds of fall, and the air was chilly, nothing could dampen my spirits. There was hope again in the eyes of my people.

For part of the time, Narian walked next to me, but my mother's subtle glances in his direction eventually prompted him to drop behind and fall in step with Cannan. I smiled, for he was clearly puzzled by her, having little experience to fall back on.

As it turned out, it was a good thing Narian was not beside me when we reached the southern end of the city, for Steldor was among the crowd. I nodded to him, and he returned the gesture without averting his eyes. I recalled his argument with Narian in the antechamber, and even across the distance between us, I could feel the aching of his heart. It was terrible to know that I had the power to stop that ache, that what he craved was me. But I wasn't the only one who could ease that pain—he had the power to help himself, and I prayed he would move on and find someone with whom he could be truly happy.

We went in a wide loop, returning to the Bastion by late afternoon. Cannan dismissed the guards who had accompanied us, then adjourned to his office; Narian did likewise.

"Thank you so much for coming," I said to my mother. "It was right that you were there."

"I enjoyed myself very much, and would like to extend an invitation of my own. Would you join me in my quarters for tea?"

"Yes, thank you. That would be lovely, and warm." Her

cheeks were rosy from the day's activity, and mine were no doubt a match.

"Shall we say a half hour? And, Alera, please ask Narian to escort you."

My eyebrows rose dramatically.

"I don't know if that would be best," I hedged, for I had no idea how Narian would react to her invitation.

She drew me away from the Cokyrian sentries stationed by the door and dropped her volume. "Alera, if you're going to marry this man, he's going to be my son. I want to know him better."

"Yes, but...I don't know if he'd be comfortable. He's very reserved, and probably wouldn't say much."

"Then those are things I'll learn about him. It can't hurt to ask him, can it? If he prefers not to come, I'll accept his decision."

My mother was full of subtlety. She did not say that she would *understand* his decision, only that she would accept it. And her phrasing wasn't really chosen with Narian in mind—it was to let me know that this was important, and that I should do all I could to ensure he would be there.

"I'll do my best," I agreed, thinking that this would be the quietest tea I had ever attended.

Leaving my mother behind, I walked through the antechamber and across the Hearing Hall to reach Narian's headquarters, which was situated in the former strategy room between Cannan's office and mine. As always, there was much activity in the partitioned room; I also could not simply knock on the door to his private office, for a Cokyrian sentry prevented access to him without an appointment. In the end, I directed one of Narian's officers to inform him that I wished to speak with him about an "urgent provincial matter."

"Shall we go to your study?" Narian asked when he

emerged from his office, knowing full well I had no political matters to address.

"Yes, I think that would be best." I couldn't repress a smile, for his eyes sparkled with curiosity.

As soon as we had closed the door to my study, and before I could speak, Narian kissed me, catching me by surprise.

"I've wanted to do that all afternoon, Alera. I'm not particularly fond of the gowns Hytanican women wear, but I'm willing to make an exception for this one."

I laughed, my head spinning, and he took hold of my hands.

"Now, what's this about?"

"My mother has invited me to tea, and we would be pleased to have you join us."

Despite how casual I was trying to sound, Narian stiffened, and I could feel him pulling away. This wasn't going to be easy.

"You *both* would like me to join you?"

"Yes, she suggested it." I took a deep breath and made my confession. "She knows that we're betrothed, that we're in love."

I couldn't gauge his reaction from his face, but the fact that he released my hands suggested he was disturbed, piqued— not an encouraging sign. I waited, giving him a chance to straighten out his thoughts, then tried again.

"I know we agreed not to tell anyone—"

"Yes, we did," he snapped, walking over to my desk, not meeting my eyes. This was so uncharacteristic of him that I knew I had to proceed very carefully.

"Please listen. We agreed not to tell anyone, but she's my mother. She won't breathe a word."

"How can you be sure?"

I almost laughed, confused as to how he could question that. "Because she's my mother! She raised me, Narian. I've always been able to trust her. Just believe me."

I paused, expecting him to respond, but he did not. Instead he feigned interest in the papers lying atop my desk.

"Would you please look at me?" I gently prodded.

His eyes found mine, but they were steely, skeptical and almost defiant, as though I had challenged him.

"Narian," I murmured, hoping something in my voice would drive away whatever instinct had awakened. Again and again, I was forced to acknowledge the extent of the Overlord's reach; his shadow fell on Narian even now. It wasn't Narian's fault, though it was easy to become discouraged by it; eighteen years of someone's tyranny was not easy to overcome, and was impossible to forget.

"I'm sorry if this bothers you," I said, stepping closer to him. "But there's really no danger in her knowing."

"There *is* danger in her knowing." He walked past me to the hearth, increasing the distance between us. "There always is when the information itself is dangerous. You didn't have to tell her, Alera. I don't understand why you did."

I bridled, feeling like he was scolding me. "I'm not a fool. I would never knowingly put us or this kingdom at risk. Don't speak to me like you're the only one who understands the need for discretion. I made a decision that you obviously don't agree with, but that doesn't make it wrong."

We stared at each other, our postures stiff, neither of us breaking the hush that had fallen over the room.

"I didn't mean to imply," he finally muttered, without change in his expression.

I hesitated, unable to determine if he were being sarcastic or sincere. When he glanced to the floor, I knew it was the latter. He approached me, stopping a few feet away—just out of reach.

"But I don't understand it, Alera. I honestly don't."

I closed the remaining gap between us, not letting him

maintain either physical or emotional distance, then laid a
hand upon his chest, lightly scrunching the fabric of his shirt.

"Haven't you ever *wanted* to confide in someone?"

He didn't reply, disconcerted. He had, in fact, shared confidences with me, but it was always a struggle against his nature—against his training—to do so. After a few moments,
he nodded, still not understanding, but unwilling to prolong
the argument.

"Can I take that as agreement to accompany me to my
mother's tea?" I teased, bringing a slight smile to his face.
"Now that she knows about us, your willingness to come
would mean a great deal to her. When we are married, you
will, in her eyes, become her son."

He sighed, then nodded once more. By my guess, he was
perplexed and intrigued enough by this last notion to risk an
hour or two in the former Queen's presence.

We walked together across the Hearing Hall and through
the King's Drawing Room, then continued up the spiral staircase to my parent's quarters on the third floor. My mother was
waiting for us in the parlor, occupying an armchair across from
the sofa, intending to let Narian and I sit next to each other.

Once over the threshold, Narian began shooting me looks
that I found humorous, as though he regretted being pulled
into this and was wondering if he could fake illness to escape.
He could lead an army, face down the Overlord and challenge
the High Priestess, but apparently he had qualms about spending time with my kind and demure mother.

"Alera, Narian, I'm so glad you're here—both of you.
Please, have a seat." She motioned to the sofa and we complied.

"Good afternoon, Queen Elissia," Narian greeted her, deliberately choosing to address her according to Hytanican
custom, for he had a gentleman's manners. In fact, one of my

earliest impressions of him was that he was a chameleon, with a knack for having exactly the effect he wanted on people.

The low table between my mother's chair and the sofa held the tea service, and my mother filled the cups herself.

"I saw no need for a servant girl," she offered, but I suspected she was being cautious, not wanting to generate speculation or rumors about the reason Narian and I had joined her for tea. "Wasn't it a wonderful day today?"

All went smoothly for the first fifteen minutes—my mother was, after all, very adept at making people comfortable. She chatted, though not excessively, primarily with me. As I had predicted, Narian was silent and observant, letting me carry the conversation while he tried to get a feel for the woman across from us, not quite trusting that she was on our side. He was never rude, and never short with her; he simply hid himself behind good etiquette.

During a natural pause in conversation, my mother perused Narian and me, and her mood became contemplative.

"When was it that you fell in love?" she asked. "Was it right under our noses?"

"More or less," I said with a laugh, glancing at Narian. "We became friends when he first came to Hytanica. All those trips Miranna and I made to Baron Koranis's estate were really so I could see him."

Mother smiled and Narian glanced at me as if this were news to him. Then she picked up the thread of the conversation.

"I remember falling in love," she mused, and I wondered how far she would venture into her story, knowing it was not a wholly happy one. "I was fifteen, going through the very difficult experience of losing my family in a fire. I was brought to live in the palace, for I'd been betrothed for years to Andrius, Alera's uncle, who later died in the war before we could be married."

I realized she was not talking to me, and that, though he was still aloof, she had captured Narian's interest, for his deep blue eyes were resting attentively upon her.

"At the time, I was so lost and alone and frightened. And then Andrius and I grew close. With him, my life made sense again. I had something to hold on to, something to steady me. What was the worst time of my life became the best."

There was a pause, and she innocently met Narian's gaze. But her story was not innocent at all. If I could recognize the parallel she was drawing to his life in the aftermath of learning of his Hytanican heritage, then he surely could, as well. He didn't say a word, however, and she dropped the veiled attempt to connect with him before it became awkward, turning to me instead.

"I've told you before, Alera—Andrius lives on in you. I see him in you every day."

I smiled, tipping my head in acceptance of the compliment.

"And in *you*—" she said, once more turning to Narian, tapping a finger against her lips in thought "—I see Cannan."

She was lightly cajoling him, exactly as a parent would do. I couldn't imagine what was going on in his mind, but he was no longer eager to leave, his eyes never once flicking toward me or the door.

"What do you mean?" he asked.

"Cannan is strong and decisive. He seems unemotional, untouchable, but underneath he has more heart than most men taken together. And he could so easily have buried that compassion. In some ways, he would have hurt less throughout the years had he done so, but he would be half the man he is today."

I was remembering things Baelic had told me, vague things

about Cannan and their father. I had never considered that
my mother would have knowledge on the subject, although
I should have surmised it. She had grown up in the nobility
with the men of her generation, and Cannan had been one of
Crown Prince Andrius's best friends.

Seeing the curiosity on Narian's face, she went on, "It was
no secret that Baron Burvaul—Cannan's father—was a tyrant.
In their family, everyone wore smiles for fear of what Burvaul might do if they did not, and everything stayed behind
closed doors—except for bruises and broken bones, the vast
majority of which were bestowed on Cannan. At that time,
of course, Cannan could not fight his father, and so he fought
the world instead.

"But when he was eighteen and was sent into the field of
war, he changed. He gained perspective. And when Andrius
died and Cannan was called back to become Sergeant at Arms,
and later Captain of the Guard, he was more powerful than his
father, in position and character. He never abused that power,
but his victory lay in the fact that Burvaul could not bear the
reversal of control. He lived the rest of his life in fear of his
own son, who never punished him.

"I see that personality in you, Narian. Just like Cannan, you
will never become the man who controlled you."

"He didn't control me," Narian abruptly said.

"He didn't in the end, did he?" she agreed, taking a sip of
her tea. "Of course, the *real* question is about your mother.
What was she like?"

"You know my mother," Narian replied, his expression
strange. I'd never seen him this way before—he seemed
younger, less defensive. He was hesitant, but not guarded like
he had been upon entering the room. It was almost as if he
wanted to open up to her.

"I mean the woman who raised you. Your Cokyrian mother."

Narian was shaking his head, despite the change I had detected in him. "I didn't have a mother in Cokyri."

"You're far too well-mannered not to have had a mother growing up." Her blue eyes were twinkling, unthreatening. Again, she was teasing him, and although I expected him to simply sidestep her a third time, he did not.

"To the extent I had a mother, she was the High Priestess."

I looked incredulously back and forth between the two of them, for in half an hour, my mother had enticed Narian to divulge as much to her as I had gleaned in two years. Though I was now bursting to speak, I refrained, and she pressed him further.

"You're close to her then?" This was more a statement than a question.

"At one time we were very close. She cared for me, when I was young. I grew apart from her over time, and then, when I found out that I was born Hytanican..."

"Yes?"

"She lied to me. Had been lying for years—my entire life." He was not letting himself feel the words, but there was an ache underlying them.

I thought back to when Narian and I had first met—he had fascinated me, but I had never considered what he must have been enduring. At sixteen years of age, he'd run away, and not just from home, but from his country, into the land of his enemy. His anger and feelings of betrayal must have been overwhelming, and he had to have been scared, though he never showed it. And now my mother had him talking about it.

"The difficulty at this point," she said, nodding sympathetically, "is learning that you cannot judge the world by the actions of one person."

"Yes, I can," he responded, promptly enough that even my mother was surprised. "You can't object to me evaluating the world based on Alera's example."

She laughed, while I sat quietly by, feeling my face grow hot. Narian was not one to give compliments, though I knew he noticed many things. I glanced to him, highly appreciative of his words, and laid my hand upon his forearm.

"Quite right," my mother concurred, smiling at us both.

Narian and I left the parlor shortly thereafter in high spirits. The former Queen had been very accepting of him, and he had been remarkably forthcoming with her. Somehow, through common experience and maternal instinct, she had reached out to forge a connection with her future son-in-law.

We went to my quarters and Narian stayed in the parlor while I changed for dinner, although he would not accompany me to the meal—we may have had luck with my mother, but my father would not be so receptive to the news of our betrothal.

When I reemerged in simpler garb, he was in an armchair, contemplatively rubbing his once-broken wrist, his face growing progressively more troubled. I glanced around the room, wondering what could possibly have happened to change his temperament in the short time we had been apart.

"Narian? What is it?"

He shook his head, then ran a hand through his thick blond hair. "Your mother would make an excellent interrogator."

I couldn't help it—I laughed, harder than I had in a long time. "I hardly think she's the type!"

"Find it as funny as you like," he said with a smile. "But I don't know what I was telling her!"

"Well, do you regret it?" I asked, and he flashed through a myriad of emotions: confusion, deliberation, discomfort at having been so open with her, then, at last, acceptance.

"No," he said, with a touch of wonder. "I...I understand it now, I suppose—why you talk to her. Why you trust her. I wanted to trust her."

I walked over to him and sat in his lap, wrapping my arms around his neck. "I don't think I've ever said this before, but it's time I did. I'm in love with you, Narian."

"I love you, too," he said, the corners of his mouth flicking upward. The words weren't so difficult, after all.

CHAPTER 20

KEEP YOUR SILENCE

IT WAS DAYS BEFORE CANNAN CAME TO SEE ME. Perhaps he was trying to smooth things over, banish the crimp I had no doubt put in their plans. Perhaps he was busy with his usual duties—I knew he'd been with Queen Alera during her much-discussed tour of the city, though my family and I had stayed home, secluded and sheltered. For once I hadn't minded. I was scared.

When my uncle did come, it was at an odd time—after dinner, after nightfall. My mother hesitantly answered the door, ushering the patriarch of our family into the entryway.

"I apologize for calling on you at this late hour, Lania," he said, coming straight to the point. "But I would like Shaselle to come with me to the barn—I need to discuss something with her, related to the horses."

Without further explanation, the captain waited for a response. My siblings and I could hear them from the parlor, and I wondered if Mother would dare to question him. The outcome was predictable.

"Of course," she said. "I'll fetch her for you."

Mother came into the parlor, her brow puckered. "Shaselle, go with your uncle. The rest of you, off to bed."

Celdrid and Ganya groaned, but they nonetheless moped to the staircase with the rest of my siblings while I went to the front door. Before chasing her brood up the stairs, Mother cast a worried glance at Cannan, then tossed her shawl over my shoulders.

I went with the captain across the property and into the barn, trying to ignore the utter blackness of the night and the cold, whipping wind. I was too old to be frightened of such things. He closed the door behind us, blocking out some of the sound of the brewing storm, and lit a lantern that hung on a hook on the wall. Nervously, I approached Alcander's stall, reaching out to rub his silky neck.

"Everything seems fine," I said with a shiver, knowing perfectly well the horses had nothing to do with Cannan's reason for bringing me outside.

"I'm fairly certain where you got that dagger, Shaselle." Cannan walked toward me, pushing his cloak from his broad shoulders. "Why don't you tell me about it?"

I swallowed uneasily. "It—it was Papa's, remember?"

"No, it wasn't. Tell me how you came to have it."

I stared at him, afraid to answer, afraid to remain silent. He considered me, then laid his cloak around my shoulders. It was still warm from his body and enormously comforting.

"I don't intend to punish you, Shaselle. I'm trying to protect you. But I need to know the truth."

With a shaky breath, I confessed, "It was hidden in Papa's study."

"And were there others?"

"Yes. Many."

Cannan absorbed this, nodding his head.

"Sit down," he said, motioning to a stack of hay against the wall. I obeyed without a word, not sure what would happen now. He stood before me, dark, tall and grave, but not threatening. He had promised he would protect me; he wouldn't hurt me.

"You weren't supposed to find those weapons—no one was. Have you told anyone?"

I shook my head, my mouth so dry I wasn't certain I could form words.

"Is it possible anyone saw you with them?"

"No, I was alone. It was late at night."

"Did you disturb the rest of the armaments?"

"No. I left them in place and again covered the entrance."

"Good." Cannan noticeably relaxed in light of my answers. Maybe my mistake would not create problems for them, after all. "One last question. Can you keep silent on the issue?"

"Of course," I said, mortified that he might think otherwise.

"And can you stay out of it?"

The horses snuffed and pawed the ground in the quiet. I sat stupidly, my lips parted, not sure how to answer. Could I forget what I'd discovered and never wonder about it again? No. Cannan crossed his arms, guessing my thoughts.

"Then ask me what you want to know and I'll tell you."

"What?" I blurted, flabbergasted by what he was offering.

"I cannot risk you getting hurt, Shaselle, and your curiosity cannot disrupt what we have planned. If giving you information will keep you from disrupting things, I will do so."

"How are you doing it? Where are the weapons coming from? How are you getting them into the city?" Questions tumbled from my mouth, in no particular order, for my mind was in chaos.

Straightforward as ever, Cannan expounded. "When London regained consciousness in the spring, he and I recognized the need to move quickly if we were to establish a stash of weapons. As soon as he could travel, he left the city to entreat aid from the neighboring kingdoms. Men from Sarterad and Emotana began leaving weapons in the forest for us, and London's men took them into the palace through the escape tunnel we used to remove the royal family at the time of the Cokyrian siege. The Cokyrians, other than Narian, do not know of the tunnel's existence, and he has neither closed it nor been monitoring it. In the night, we used servants within the palace to move the armaments out in delivery boxes, whereupon they were taken to Steldor, Galen and Halias. Select Hytanicans on the work crews hid them inside the buildings during the reconstruction work. Everything has been put in place."

"What will you do now?"

"We wait."

I stood up and paced, agitated. "What are you waiting for?"

"The right time."

"To do what exactly? Tell me that."

"To take back our kingdom."

This was a non-answer, one that gave me no information I could not have deduced on my own.

"When, Uncle? I want to know when. I can—"

"You don't need to know when, Shaselle. You're not part of this."

He was watching me, arms still crossed, and I stopped pacing, pulling the cloak tighter around me.

"But I *could* be. I'm not just a curious child, Uncle, I can *do* things. I could help. If you would just tell me what to do, I wouldn't be a problem!"

The wind rattled the barn door, and Alcander whinnied, making me jump.

"You're scared of the wind, Shaselle," Cannan said, shaking his head. "You're a young woman, and this is dangerous.

This is a game you've not trained to play, a game you could never handle."

"That's not true," I argued, resentment bubbling inside me at his denigrating words.

"I'm sorry, but it is. If we're discovered, every one of us will be executed before we even have a chance to revolt. And if we do revolt, there's a very strong possibility we will die in the fighting, whether we're successful or not. In case you've forgotten, a number of good men have already died."

His words hit me hard, breaking through my bitterness. Forced to contemplate a hangman's noose, my zeal faded.

"I don't want any of you to die," I murmured, a tremble in my voice.

He shrugged. "We're not eager for that end, either. But someone has to take a stand. Someone has to speak for Hytanica before we let *her* die."

Exhausted and mentally battered, I asked, "What am I supposed to do?"

"I'll tell you." He was surprisingly sure; then again, Cannan had always been decisive. "No matter what happens to us, you have a family that loves you, and a full life ahead of you, a life that can bring you joy. Let me arrange a second dinner for you with Lord Grayden. He has approached me and inquired after you several times."

"Lord Grayden? But I spilled wine all over his father!"

He smiled wryly. "Sometimes men see spirit in a woman. And sometimes men don't like their fathers. Now, do we have an agreement?"

I thought over the things he had told me, the prospect of victory and glory, the possibility of punishment and death.

With a slow exhale, I breathed, "Yes."

Cannan escorted me back to the house with the promise that he would arrange something with Lord Grayden in the next few days. I assured him I had no plans, returned the cloak and bade him good-night, then dragged my feet up the stairs and to bed, thanking the Lord my mother was not waiting up for a better explanation than the one Cannan had provided.

By the following morning, I'd given almost more thought than I could stand to my talk with the captain. I'd racked my brain for a way to safely and discreetly involve myself in the revolt plot, but with no one keeping me updated and no concrete information about what needed to be done, it was impossible. As insignificant as it made me feel, I forced myself to let go of the notion and resign myself to the agreement I had made with my uncle. I needed to behave, stay out of the fray and think about how I could apologize to Grayden for ruining his father's fancy clothes.

I ate breakfast with my family, then Mother asked Dahnath and me to do some shopping. The younger girls needed materials to practice their sewing, and she thankfully had not heard a whisper of my latest misadventure.

We left shortly thereafter, each carrying a basket, though I doubted we would be buying enough supplies to fill them both. My beautiful, slender, auburn-haired sister was wearing a deep red cloak, while I'd swung across my shoulders a brown one that served its purpose. I could have dressed in the Queen's finery and still looked homely next to Dahnath.

Despite the chilly weather and perpetually gray skies, the Market District was quite busy, and Dahnath nodded politely to those she knew. But when she pushed her hood back and unpinned her wavy hair, fussing with it until it framed her face, I knew who she had seen.

It was mere moments before Lord Drael, tall and handsome with his dark blond hair and stubble, appeared at my sister's side, taking her hand and giving it a kiss.

"My lady, I didn't expect to find you here," he said, raising the color in her cheeks. "I'm a very lucky man."

I cleared my throat, drawing Drael's attention, then extended my hand. He stared at me for an amusing moment, then chuckled and took it, kissing it as he had Dahnath's.

"Good day, Lady Shaselle."

"Good day, my lord."

Dahnath scowled at me, and I took the basket from her hands. "I'll just finish our errand, shall I?"

I walked down the cobblestone street, past the bakery, the spice-grocers, the apothecary shops, the jewelers and the tailors until I reached the dry-goods shop, pushing through the crowd with little difficulty. I picked out what I found to be attractive from among the multitude of fabric choices, most of which would not have suited Dahnath's preferences, but she had decided it was more important to spend time with her betrothed. Thankfully, Mother had entrusted the money to me, and I approached the shop owner, giving him enough coins to cover the cost.

Not sure what to do next, I stepped back outside, spotting my sister up ahead, still flirting with Drael. Would I be expected to behave thus when I was betrothed? I hoped not; the thought made me shudder.

The baskets, both of which I had filled, were growing heavy. I held one in each hand and glanced around for a place I might sit until Dahnath was ready to go home. I was about to dodge across the street when my load lightened, one of the baskets having been taken away. Thinking a thief, I shouted and swung around, arm outstretched, and my nails scratched someone or something.

"Enough of that!" a man yelped, and the moment my eyes fell on him, I groaned.

"Saadi, what do you think you're doing?" I demanded.

"Well, I *thought* I was helping you. As it turns out, I'm bleeding."

"No, you're not!"

I stepped closer to inspect the tracks on his cheek where my nails had made contact, and gently lay my fingers on the scratches. He winced and took my hand, holding it away from his lightly freckled face. Acutely aware of his touch, I blushed. He was adorable, as much as I'd fought against admitting it. His pale blue eyes examined me for a moment, confused by my reaction, then he grinned.

"So…sewing?" he asked.

"For my sisters."

"Oh. How many?"

"Four. And a brother."

"Full house. Rava is my only sibling."

My mood dipped at mention of his sister. He put a hand gently on my back, guiding me to the side of a building and out of the way of traffic.

"We don't get along, if it helps," he added, aware of my feelings.

I laughed. "Do siblings ever get along?"

"I think so. At least, most siblings who argue will apologize and enjoy each other's company until the next fight comes along. I don't remember ever enjoying Rava."

"That's sad," I murmured.

He grinned again. "Well, would *you* enjoy her?"

"*I* don't know her, other than as an enemy. Maybe I'd like her if we'd grown up together. Why don't you get along with her?"

His expression sobered. "Rava is who she is. Being older than me and of more importance, she was raised differently and never felt the need to have much of a relationship with me. That's not to say she doesn't care about me—she does. I think she's even proud of me, in her own way." He touched the officer's insignia tacked to the shoulder of his black, asymmetrically cut uniform jacket. "I fought to achieve this rank, not an easy task, for men are not generally placed in command positions. We're too hotheaded, as a group. Still, she has no trouble stepping on and over me, which you can probably appreciate."

"Perhaps," I said, though his words confused me. Certain activities were not deemed appropriate for me since I was a woman, but for the most part, I did not resent my lot in life. But Saadi was strong, intelligent and extremely capable. In Hytanica, he would have been the pride of his family. How could he have been overlooked in Cokyri? Had Rava been the pride of his family instead?

"This place. It's so different from Cokyri," he continued, content to accept my simple answer.

"Not that different," I replied with a short laugh. "We eat and work and sleep."

"That's not what I mean." He rolled his eyes. "It's how people look at me. It's not the same at all."

"People hate you because you're Cokyrian. Did you expect to take pleasure in that?"

"That's not it, either." He thought for a moment. "It's strange, the level of fear in the eyes of your women. Belligerence I expect, from everyone, but the fear primarily radiates from the women." He shrugged, suddenly self-conscious. "But what do I know? Listen, I haven't even seen half of what there is to see in Hytanica. You could show me one day."

"You *seem* to be everywhere in this city," I scoffed. "There can't be much left for you to explore. Or have you just been following me around?"

"Well, you're the most interesting feature of the city I've come across."

He smirked, and I gave him a sideways glance. Was he admitting to stalking me? Then he chuckled.

"As long as I'm assigned to oversee the city, we're bound to run into each other. I would be lying, however, if I denied that I look forward to our encounters."

Heat again flooded my face. Saadi was making me uncomfortable. I was in danger of liking him too much.

"That reminds me," I said. "I owe you for a lock."

I glanced to see that Dahnath was still talking to Drael. He was holding her hands, preparing to depart. Knowing from the general length of their goodbyes that it would be at least five minutes more, I removed a coin from my pocket.

Saadi grinned. "I thought you had forgotten."

"Not at all." I pressed the coin into his hand. "But you have to go. My sister will be coming to find me at any moment. She can't see us together or she'll tell my mother and probably Cannan. We could both end up in dismal straits."

I expected him to ridicule me for being afraid of my mother, but he did not.

"What do you say, Shaselle? Two days from now I'll be off duty."

"You really want to see me?"

"Yes," he confirmed, pale blue eyes sparkling, his bronze hair sticking erratically up in front.

"All right then."

"Wonderful. I can meet you whenever, wherev—"

"On one condition."

His smile faded and his tone grew wary. "Which is?"

"I'll spend a day with you only if you can beat me in a horse race."

He laughed and shook his head. "Of course I can beat you."

"Then prove it. We'll each pick a mount and race—I'll need to borrow one from your Cokyrian stables. Take it or leave it. Either way, I have to go now. But I wouldn't be so cocky if I were you, boy."

He smiled, intrigued by my challenge. "I'll take it, but let's raise the stakes. Make it more worthwhile."

Curious, I motioned for him to go on.

"If I win, you agree to spend *two* days with me, when I'm off duty. If you win, you get to keep the horse you chose to ride."

I stared into his eyes for a long moment, until I was certain he wasn't toying with me. He knew as well as I did that I would choose one of my father's horses—one that had been stolen by his sister. He was giving me a chance to bring one of them home. My spirits soared, and I extended my hand. Saadi shook it, then shoved the basket at me, turning to stride away. Just in time, too, for Dahnath was approaching.

"A good chat?" I innocently asked her.

"You were terribly rude to Drael, you know."

I'd all but forgotten my sassy attitude toward her betrothed. The day had become too delightful, however, to risk landing in trouble at home, so I apologized.

"I *was* rude. I'm sorry. I was just having a little fun, but it was at his expense. I won't do it again."

Dahnath appraised me, then nodded. "Thank you, Shaselle. Let's go home."

Still worried she might tell Mother what I'd done, I let her present the fabrics once we were back in our parlor. Mother was pleased with the selections, and showed her appreciation by giving us leave to enjoy the rest of the day.

With no plans and no pressure, I jogged up the stairs to my bedroom, flopping gracelessly on the bed. I wondered what Cannan was doing right now, what Steldor and Galen were doing. Then my thoughts shifted to Saadi. What was he doing? Was he smoothing his hair? Was he fighting with his sister? Was he breaking up some brawl in the street? Or was he thinking of me?

Believing I had hit on the truth with the last possibility, I curled up on my side, permitting myself to daydream and doze. It was quite a pleasant way to pass the time, especially since I could see his freckled face behind my closed eyelids.

CHAPTER 21

IN SEARCH OF FAMILY

NARIAN WAS AGAIN PREPARING TO JOURNEY to Cokyri. There was much he needed to report to the High Priestess, including the news of the city's completion, but most notably the incident with Steldor and the Hytanican flag. I knew he was not looking forward to sharing that piece of information, but we didn't talk about it, for it had to be done. Nonetheless, he was tenser than usual, barking his final instructions to his soldiers in the strategy room. Though this was not the best time to raise an issue with him, I had something of greater importance than Steldor's behavior on my mind.

I caught his arm in the Hearing Hall before he could head to the Grand Entry.

"May I talk to you?" I asked, my voice hushed.

He sighed, impatient to be on his way. "Is something wrong?"

"No, not *wrong*. But it is important."

"Then walk with me. If I don't depart soon, I'll never reach Cokyri before dark."

He started toward the antechamber, motioning for me to follow. Left with no choice, I acquiesced, uncomfortable with the number of Cokyrians milling about, the number of people who could hear us.

"I'd prefer to talk in private, Narian."

He nodded and ushered me into the antechamber, which was fortuitously empty, then turned to face me.

"Very well. What is it that cannot wait?"

"I want you to talk to the High Priestess about Rava."

"Rava?" He seemed annoyed by my request, though it didn't strike me as out of line.

"Yes, I don't trust her. She's been creating problems since the start, and with the disrespect she displayed toward you, toward us, in carrying out Steldor's punishment... Something needs to be done."

"I see."

"You said the High Priestess was like a mother to you once," I pressed, trying to elicit something more from him. "She cares for you, regardless of your feelings for her. You can sway her."

"I'll do what I can."

His manner softened, and he walked toward me, brushed his fingers into my hair and kissed me sweetly on the lips.

"I have to go," he said, taking a step back. "I'll only be gone a few days this time. No longer than necessary."

He left the antechamber, and I did the same, but in the direction from which I had come, stepping back into the Hearing Hall.

"Grand Provost."

Rava's voice, clear and crisp, startled me. She stood to my left, in the doorway of her office, and I had the impression she had been watching for me.

"Come in for a moment."

The Cokyrian second-in-command retreated into her alcove, and I followed, closing the door as she went to stand behind her desk.

"How much power do you think he has?" she asked contemptuously, straightening her black tunic with a hard tug on the bottom.

"I don't understand." I tenaciously met her eyes, despite the dread creeping along my spine. It was obvious she had overheard my conversation with Narian.

"I understand the influence *you* have all too well. The commander will do exactly what you want, bend to your will. That alone should prove to you that strength is a woman's endowment, not a man's."

She was testing me, taunting me, and I resented her for it.

"Are you going to continue with cryptic comments or are you going to say what you mean?" I demanded, rallying to take the offensive.

"You may love Nantilam's little prince, but you're blind to the fact that he is an instrument. He has been from the beginning and he always will be, until she has no further use for him. Nantilam cares for him and would rather see him alive than dead, but she will not listen to him, or to words he bears from you. *I* have her ear. She will listen only to the most powerful woman in this godforsaken province, and that woman is me."

She was baiting me, successfully; I was on the verge of losing my temper. Knowing that would be a mistake, I let the silence between us lengthen, taking several slow and steady breaths. Then I gave her a small smile.

"The High Priestess made me Grand Provost because she wanted a woman in control who would understand the people. You do not understand my people, Rava. You keep them miserable because you fear them. And everything else aside, that makes *you* weak."

Though Rava glowered at me, I was done with her, and coolly left her office. I could almost feel the slow tick of time, counting down to Narian's return. He would prove one of us right and one of us wrong.

By midmorning, my mind felt dried up, brittle—I had not stepped out of my study once, busy with paperwork and tiny problems that Rava kept sending to me. She was in charge of the Cokyrian forces whenever Narian was gone, and it was manifest from the number of frivolous questions I'd been receiving from low-ranking Cokyrian soldiers that I had irked her during our brief conversation. Though this pleased me, I desperately needed something on the horizon if I were to survive this day.

Most often, this something would have been the prospect of Narian coming to me in the evening, but now I would have to fill that time in some other way. As my mind considered the possibilities, I thought back to Narian's hesitant inquiry about reconnecting with his Hytanican family. Perhaps there was something I could do to help. Perhaps it was time to begin building a bridge across the necessary waters.

I sent a message to Baron Koranis and Baroness Alantonya at their city home, soliciting an invitation to dinner. With Narian in Cokyri, I could, without his knowledge, get a sense of his family's feelings toward him; if there were no hope, he didn't need to be hurt. I received the reply I wanted later in the day—my sister, Temerson and I were invited to dine the following evening at the Baron's estate. I went directly to Miranna's quarters to tell her of the plans I had made.

"We'll be happy to accompany you," my sister effused. "I don't see Semari nearly as often as I used to, and I miss her so."

"Then I'm glad I was able to arrange this visit."

"But you didn't do it for me, Alera. I presume this has something to do with Narian?"

"Yes, it does. I thought I would see if there is any chance

of reuniting him with his family. He doesn't know I'm doing this, of course, but I believe he would be open to the idea."

"Are you sure this is something you ought to explore, Alera?" Her voice was skeptical, and she began to twirl her hair, a mannerism that took hold when she was nervous or worried. "Semari is already afraid her relation to Narian is limiting her choice of suitors. She and her family may well want to keep their distance from him."

I nodded, recognizing the truth in her statements.

She leaned toward me, a sparkle in her blue eyes. "They might feel differently, however, if they knew of *your* relationship with Narian."

"That's not yet possible." I laughed. "Koranis has never been one to keep his mouth closed. Can you imagine how fast the story would spread?"

"The juiciest stories spread the fastest!"

"Our people are still adjusting to the idea of a woman in power. They aren't ready to learn that the woman is in love with the enemy." I studied her, then a new thought came to me. "Mira, do *you* approve of my relationship with Narian?"

"Of course! I've known of your feelings for each other for two years now. He's a good man who was put in an untenable position. I don't know what any of us would have done had his decisions been ours to make, so I am not about to judge him. And I am bound as your sister to love him."

"Well then, perhaps you could share *your* opinions about Narian with Semari. Put in a good word for him."

Miranna smiled and gave me a quick hug. "I'll gladly help in any way I can, and I'll enlist Temerson, as well." As my eyes widened in concern, she cheerfully added, "I'll keep your secret, dear sister. I won't breathe a word about the fire that rages between Narian and you."

★ ★ ★

I spent the next day attempting to formulate some sort of strategy. While there was no guarantee Narian's family would welcome him back, his father would be the primary obstacle. Koranis had never been able to handle the fact that his son had been raised in Cokyri, and had disinherited Narian long ago. He would not feel the need to reconnect, although I hoped he would have some desire to do so.

I still had no clear idea of how I would proceed when we arrived that evening at the Baron's beautiful home. We were met by a servant and escorted to the Reception Hall, a sign that Koranis was approaching this visit quite formally, for this room was grand in scale and generally reserved for parties. As I crossed the threshold, I felt like I had stepped into a portrait, for everyone was in their finest garb and had been carefully positioned within the richly appointed space.

The Baron and Baroness stepped forward to greet us, Koranis attired in a gold-and-cream overcoat, with rings aplenty on his fingers. He was even heavier than I remembered him to be, his double chins having rolled into a third, and his pate was almost bald. Alantonya, her soft features still beautiful, wore a brilliant green gown with a striped and ruffled high-necked collar that regrettably brought a peacock to mind. As for their children, Semari struggled for breath in a tightly laced gown, her white-blond hair done up in a fancy bun; Charisa and Adalan, in jewel-toned dresses and simple gold tiaras, looked more like princesses than I ever had; and Zayle, freshly twelve and the heir to his father's fortune, displayed clothing that outshone the ostentatiousness of his father's, along with an attitude to match. This was likely to be a long evening.

Wine was served, and Koranis launched into a babble of small talk.

"We've been quite well, Your Highnesses. Zayle is learning of business and I'm rebuilding our country estate. Semari also has news, which I'm sure she would like to share herself."

"I'm betrothed," Semari announced with a blush, glancing between Miranna and me, her nervousness a sign that she was seeking our approval.

"To Lord Sharron," Koranis added, smiling indulgently at his eldest daughter. "The wedding will be in January."

Miranna and I exchanged glances, both of us valiantly holding on to our cheerful expressions. Lord Sharron had been an eligible bachelor for longer than either of us had been alive.

"A well-established family," I noted, not knowing what else to say. Koranis nodded proudly, though his smile seemed a bit feigned. With his status and wealth, Semari should have been able to marry a young, handsome, rising nobleman, not a lord who was past his prime. Was their connection to Narian really such an impediment?

"I look forward to arranging Zayle's marriage in the years to come," Koranis went on, clapping a hand on his son's shoulder. "My only son—he'll inherit the world, or at least a good part of this kingdom." He chuckled, then corrected himself. "Province."

It wasn't his slip of the tongue that bothered me; it was the way he referred to Zayle as his only son. How could he so maliciously deny the existence of his firstborn child? He had never tried to get to know Narian, didn't appreciate his intellect, his strength, his good heart. He didn't realize what he was giving up—what he'd already given up.

I glanced at Alantonya, who was staring into her goblet, and at Semari, who was still blushing, unconcerned about her father's slight to her older brother. The other three children showed no reaction, evidently used to this sort of talk. I was beginning to wish I had not come here.

A servant entered to announce that the meal was ready to be served, and we moved into the dining room.

"Grand Provost—how are affairs in the palace?" Koranis asked after we had begun to eat.

"Quite well. For the most part, the Hytanicans in the Bastion coexist peacefully with the Cokyrians as we work to improve conditions for our people. The news of the city's successful reconstruction has lifted everyone's spirits, and much is being accomplished toward restoring our economy, thanks in no small part to Narian."

All conversation ceased. Semari and her sisters pushed food around on their plates, the scraping sounds frazzling my nerves; Alantonya put her tableware down altogether; Zayle stared at his father as though waiting for him to set me straight; and Koranis looked shocked and outraged. If I had not been Grand Provost, I suspected he would have thrown me from the house.

Temerson came to my aid. "Narian has been invaluable to us. He is quite invested in the province."

"I'm sure he is," Koranis grumbled. "All the Cokyrians are."

Again that terrible silence. This was far worse than I had imagined, for the Baron was making it abundantly clear that he would never give Narian a chance. I didn't want the man I loved to be exposed to his father's attitude or wounded by it. Narian struggled with guilt the way it was—he didn't need Koranis heaping on more.

"Well, what a lovely meal!" Miranna chirped, her abrupt switch in topic enough to ease the tension. "Have you given any thought to the wedding feast?"

Alantonya began discussing wedding preparations with my sister and Semari, while the rest of us tried to show interest in the conversation, uncomfortable looking at each other. Thankfully, it was not long before we moved into the parlor, a quainter room that was more conducive to casual conversation.

My sister and Semari went to sit together on the settee, the younger pair of girls trailing along. Charisa and Adalan appeared relaxed for the first time all evening, their fear of receiving reprimands for any errors in etiquette banished. There was no need to be anxious around my kind sister. She would be the first to make a mistake, just to set the atmosphere.

Koranis was quick to snatch Temerson away to his study, where they would presumably smoke and have ale, which I knew my sister's husband would detest. He would much rather have stayed with Miranna, but to refuse would have been impolite. Zayle abandoned the women to follow his father, rather boldly, for he had not been invited to do so.

In the aftermath of the men's departure, Alantonya was standing alone in front of the window, staring out into the dark night. After a moment of debate over whom I should join, I walked over to her, wondering why she was keeping to herself.

"Queen Alera," she said, giving me a curtsey.

While I wished my people would use the title of Grand Provost, I understood that those who addressed me as Queen did so as an indication of utmost respect and loyalty. I nodded an acknowledgment, feeling strangely conspiratorial standing in the shadows.

"I must confess that you are worrying me, Baroness Alantonya. Are you unwell?"

"In health, no. The state of my heart, however, is a different matter."

This was such an enigmatic reply that I dropped all formality.

"Alantonya, if something is troubling you, please tell me."

I placed a hand on her arm, but she did not respond to my touch, simply staring once more out the window. I waited, not knowing how else to approach her.

"You're a good woman, Your Highness. You are honest,

steadfast and fair. At one time, I might have been able to make the same claims for myself, but I can no longer do so. For months, years now, I have been lying to my husband, and I am damned to hell for it."

I reeled from this declaration, so outlandish coming from the sedate and polite Baroness.

"I tell him I love him. I sleep beside him and act as a wife should. I raise our children to respect him when I do not. *Cannot*."

"Why is that?" I hoarsely whispered. A woman professing such things about her husband could be put to death under traditional Hytanican law.

"You know the reason." Her voice was sad, melancholy. "It's because you will understand that I am confessing this to you. With anyone else, I would continue the farce. But I believe you love him, too."

"Narian?"

"He is my *son*," she stressed, her passion hitting me like a punch to the stomach. "I carried him inside of me, I gave birth to him. When I close my eyes, I can still feel the heartbeat of that beautiful baby, my firstborn. Koranis wishes he had never returned to us. He lives as though our son is dead. I would have Narian commit his worst crimes a hundred times over, and yet love him. That is the promise you make when you bring children into this world—that you will love them forever, come what may. And I cannot abide Koranis for breaking that promise." She turned to me, a rare spark of anger in her eyes. "And he has the gall to poison the minds of our other children against the one I long to hold."

What was I to say? Could I risk agreeing with her? Alantonya had to stay with her husband, had to live out the years with him. The best course for her to take would be to bury her feelings and move on. But Narian, whether he was a part of her life or not, would always be in Hytanica, at my side, so close and yet out of her reach.

"I've spoken to Narian," I ventured, redirecting the discussion. "It does not concern him that Koranis has disowned him, for he has likewise rejected the Baron. But he still thinks of himself as *your* son. The only way he could be hurt now is if you renounced him."

Alantonya looked at me with the strangest expression, her blue eyes hopeful, but the rest of her face despondent.

"Don't tell him what I've said," she whispered, clasping my hands. "Tell him only that I love him."

I stared at her, thoroughly confused, and she elaborated.

"I cannot be his mother, Alera. Not until Koranis is in the ground, for I dare not disobey him." She reached out and touched my cheek in a motherly gesture. "But you have given me the will to try to outlive my husband."

Her eyes glistened for a moment, then she smoothed her hair, unwilling to succumb to her emotions.

"Let's sit, shall we?" she invited, motioning toward the younger women.

I nodded, and we went to join my sister and Semari, but Alantonya's words haunted me for the rest of the evening.

My mood was pensive as we returned to the Bastion in our carriage an hour later, for conversations I'd had with my betrothed over the past few months had resurfaced in my memory. He had endured so much—a harsh childhood, betrayal, fear, loneliness, devastation, hatred. Now he would be denied the family he craved. But he had me, and he would have my family, once they understood—my mother and Miranna already did. If I loved him, they would at least accept him. And he loved me. I had always known it, but the words had actually come from his mouth, despite how difficult it was for him to voice his feelings.

London was another man who had endured much. I couldn't help but think that, under different circumstances, he and Narian would have forged a friendship. But London was gone, presumably hiding somewhere in the mountains. Narian had suspected me of knowing my bodyguard's whereabouts, and though knowing would have required me to speak on the matter, I suddenly wanted assurance that he was all right. I feared for his well-being. I feared I would never see him again.

"Temerson," I blurted, for he had been one of the people in the dungeon on the night of the failed rebellion. Perhaps in the aftermath he knew what had become of the deputy captain.

He looked at me, brown eyes curious.

"I wondered if…I *hoped* you might have some information about London. I—I don't need to know *where* he is, just that he is safe."

"To the best of my knowledge, London fled following the failed attempt to retake our kingdom," he replied, although I was certain he knew more. "I'm sorry, but I haven't heard a whisper from or about him since."

I accepted this grudgingly. London had become my bodyguard when I was just over a year old. If I knew anything about him, it was that he did not run away.

Upon our arrival at the Bastion, I retired to my quarters to prepare for bed, thoughts of London continuing to plague me. Narian had not yet returned from Cokyri, and while I hoped the delay was due to his efforts to have Rava dismissed—perhaps he and the High Priestess were selecting a new second-in-command—I was left with no one to share my frustrations. Before Narian had come into my life, London had been a long-time confidant of mine, listening to my problems, soothing my worries and offering sage advice. But tonight, I had to simmer in silence over Koranis's attitude toward Narian and the ongoing headaches Rava caused me. I was beginning to feel like I was stuck in the mud, working hard but making little progress. And if I felt that way, it was likely the rest of Hytanica did, as well. I needed fresh hope, a bright light on the horizon. Both my people and I needed something about which to be excited.

CHAPTER 22

THE RACE

I DID CHORES FOR MY MOTHER UNTIL EARLY afternoon, on edge the entire time. I received several bemused looks from my family members, although I had no inkling of the reason, but nobody scolded me. Eventually, my mother laughed and threw up her hands.

"Shaselle, just go! You're making *me* nervous, bouncing all over the place!"

I grinned and dropped my sewing to run from the room, flying up the stairs. I wasn't meeting Saadi for a couple more hours, but I could hardly contain my excitement. Not only would I be seeing him, but I would be riding a horse for the first time in months.

Feeling I had permission to do what I pleased, I changed out of my skirt and put on a pair of dark brown breeches, tucking a cream-colored shirt into the waistband. Then a flash of common sense struck, and I picked up the skirt, pulling it over my trousers. I had no desire to draw questions, and what my mother didn't know couldn't create a problem for me.

Fully dressed, I stared at myself in the mirror, at my hazel eyes, my long, heavy brown hair, the lips that weren't terribly thin but weren't thick enough to be perfect. I was built like my mother, a bit stocky, although I was muscled and athletic—which admittedly girls were not expected to be. I sighed, trying to be objective about myself. I wasn't pretty, but neither was I ugly, just rather plain. But in the end, my appearance wouldn't matter. I had status enough to attract a good Hytanican man. Still, I hated the fact that *beautiful* was not a word Saadi would use to describe me.

I tied my hair in a braid, wrapped it around itself and pinned it at the back of my head. Today was about having fun, not romance. And I didn't need Saadi to see me as a beauty. I didn't *need* him at all. I picked up my cloak and glanced around the room, for there was a nagging in the back of my brain that told me I was forgetting something. When nothing jarred my memory, I left my room and bounded down the stairs in an unladylike fashion. Reaching the first floor, I headed to the front door, hoping no one would be paying any mind to me, but Mother called my name.

"Shaselle? Where are you going?"

"Just out for a walk," I said brightly, praying she wouldn't stop me.

"Dinner will be served in three hours. Be back in an hour and a half."

Though I hadn't a clue why she was being so accommodating, I darted out into the brisk, late-September air, knowing I wouldn't make her deadline. Better to seek forgiveness later, especially when she'd never let me leave if she knew what I was going to do. The barn door was open, and I entered, supposing I would find Steldor and Celdrid inside. My cousin had come earlier in the day to spend time with my brother, and with every one of his visits, Celdrid's spirits improved.

"How's your back?" I asked Steldor, deeply inhaling the sweet-smelling hay and, for once, not despising Briar's empty stall. I would be winning back one of my father's stolen horses today.

He glanced up from a saddle he and Celdrid had been examining and ran a hand through his dark hair.

"It looks like I got into a fight with a wildcat, but the pain is gone."

"I believe it was a *she*-cat," I teased, and he cracked a smile. I walked up to the saddle and ran a hand over it, not recognizing it. "And what's this?"

"It's mine!" Celdrid exclaimed, practically hopping from foot to foot. "Steldor brought it for me. He *made* it for me."

"Did you really?" I asked our cousin, leaning closer to admire the saddle's fine leatherwork, its handsome shape and style. It was the ideal size for my brother, and its deep reddish-gold color would be handsome with his mount.

Steldor shrugged in response. "I've had time on my hands."

"Time put to good use. It's gorgeous." Turning to my brother, I asked, "And when do you plan to try this out, young man?"

He hadn't ridden since Papa's death—he'd been avoiding every reminder of our father. We all wanted Celdrid to embrace his memories and not be afraid of them, but it would take time.

Instead of answering, Celdrid looked expectantly at Steldor.

"Not enough time now." Our cousin laughed. "You need to get cleaned up for dinner before long. But I'll meet you here tomorrow, and we'll go riding then. What do you say?"

Again, Celdrid's face lit up, and he nodded vigorously. I smiled just as brightly, happy for him and secretly relieved that they had not decided to ride today—I didn't want to consider what would happen if Saadi and I ran into them.

"Is there a reason you're bothering us, Shaselle?" Steldor teased.

"No. I was just going out for a walk."

His brow furrowed. "If you need to run an errand, I could go with you."

"I'll be fine," I said, bemused by his protectiveness.

For the second time he shrugged, then he waved me out of the barn, returning his attention to Celdrid and the saddle.

Leaving them behind, I walked to the Market District, feeling more like a bundle of nerves than a person. The city was busy, a sign of the improving economy, although it would quiet over the next couple of hours as merchants closed up shop for the day. The afternoon sun was finally breaking through the cloud cover, but I just wanted it to drop lower. Saadi and I had agreed to race at dusk, wanting to limit the number of potential witnesses.

I strolled north, in the direction of the military base from whence Saadi would come, then stepped into an alley to abandon my skirt, the shake in my hands making it difficult to unlace. I took a few deep breaths, trying to quell the jitters. This was a race I could win, *would* win. Then Saadi would give me my father's horse. That was all I wanted.

I hastened onto the thoroughfare, spotting Saadi by his distinctive gait. It was easy, yet confident. I blushed, feeling silly for admiring him from afar, but I couldn't make myself stop. He was tall, he was strong and those damn freckles constantly got the best of me. He picked up his pace, walking straight toward me, having seen me, as well.

"I've learned it's best to approach you from the front, for the sake of my well-being," he quipped upon reaching me.

"For the sake of your dignity, perhaps you should also forfeit the race," I suggested, and he chuckled, falling into step with me.

"Shaselle, I wouldn't be so arrogant if I were you. I may be a mere man, but I am not without skills."

"We'll see, won't we?"

I was enjoying our banter, feeling strangely giddy. I was happy, an emotion I had never again expected to experience. This was good, and right—and wrong. What would my mother, my uncle, Steldor, Galen and the rest of my family think if they knew with whom I was spending time? But that wasn't important now. I had a mission.

We went toward the military base, my anxiety ratcheting up the closer to our destination we came. The Cokyrians now controlled this area, and no Hytanicans were allowed to enter; but Saadi ignored the odd looks of the guards, who did not question him, confirming my suspicions about his status. He took me to the stables that my father had once controlled, and where I had unsuccessfully attempted my prank, and we walked up and down the line of stalls.

"Is this the one then?" Saadi asked, when I stopped to give Briar a pat.

I shook my head. While I would have loved to reclaim the mare, she was young and refined, without the power and stamina required for racing.

"My father's stallion—the black-and-white. That's the horse I want to ride."

I heard his low whistle from behind me. "That's a mighty spirited animal. Are you sure you can handle that much horse?"

"If I can't, you'll have an easy victory," I retorted, turning to face him.

Saadi considered me, one eyebrow raised, no doubt trying to assess my riding ability, not because I was a woman, but because I was a Hytanican woman. Then he stepped past me, motioning for me to follow.

"To the stallion barn," he said. His tone was patronizing, but I didn't care. I would have my father's prized stallion back.

Saadi's horse was a gelding, and we shared a laugh at the

problems we might have had if he'd happened to pick a mare. The animal was strong and long-legged, good for distance running, but Saadi had no idea what my father's King could do.

I pulled the hood of my cloak up over my head as we rode together through the city, hoping I would pass for a Cokyrian. No Hytanicans wanted to look too closely at the enemy; it was not good to attract *their* notice. We were stopped at the gates, to be quickly permitted passage, for every Cokyrian apparently knew Saadi. I felt slightly guilty, for there was a long line of Hytanicans, some trying to enter, others to depart, who could not bypass the rigorous security check that had been initiated under the High Priestess's regulations.

We continued to hold our mounts to a walk, the stone thoroughfare turning into a dirt highway that would lead us south to the only bridge that spanned the Recorah River. I was eager to begin the race, but understood the need to put a little more distance between us and the city before we did so.

This was the first time I had been outside the city's walls since the Cokyrian takeover, and I gazed ahead at the odd patchwork our lands had become. Some areas were alive with crops that had been sown by Hytanican villagers and were almost ready for the harvest; other parcels lay scorched and barren; still others were struggling to support life, weeds and an occasional wildflower rising above the ash. It was all so still—no field hands were about in the evening, nor were the Cokyrian guards who oversaw the planting. And given the paucity of trees, little birdsong could be heard. Eventually, my eyes were drawn to the looming shape of the Cokyrian Wall to the west, and sadness and grief assailed me. That wood and stone barrier, designed to keep us in, was a wrenching reminder of our fallen status.

Saadi, following my gaze, sought to distract me.

"To the river?" he suggested, pointing ahead down the road.

The Recorah River, which flowed south out of the Niñeyre Mountains before curving to the west, marked both our eastern and southern borders, and was the reason construction of the wall was necessitated only along the boundary we shared with the Kingdom of Sarterad.

"Won't there be patrols?"

He shook his head. "One of my duties is to regulate the patrols. I know exactly where they are. So—to the river?"

I nodded, and we lined our horses up as best we could, for our mounts had caught our excitement and were straining against their bits. We locked eyes and counted down together.

"Three, two, one—" I dug my heels into King's sides and he sprang almost violently forward.

My father had never liked me racing. It was dangerous—the horse could fall, I could drop the reins or lose my seat, and at a full gallop, my chances of survival would be slim. But he had always loved to do it, and so had I. There was such freedom in letting a horse have its head, such joyful abandonment in the feel of the animal's hooves striking the earth time after time, as fast and as hard as they could go. There was power and exhilaration in leaning forward, moving with the animal, feeling the wind on my cheeks, my hair whipping back. There was a oneness that could not be achieved in any other way, a single purpose represented by the finish line that loomed ahead.

King and I had the advantage at the start, and I turned my head to grin at Saadi before giving my full concentration to the task at hand. I would leave him far behind, but there was no point in testing fate. It wasn't long before my confidence and my lead were challenged—I caught sight of the gelding's front legs to my left, gaining ground as they arched and reached in beautiful rhythm. We bumped and battled, following the winding road, the horses breathing hard.

Then it was Saadi's turn to grin. He gave me a nod, urging his horse up the slight incline that lay before us, gradually inching ahead until he succeeded in passing me completely as we flew down the other side. Knowing the race would be won or lost on the remaining flat ground from here to the river, I lay low against King's neck, and the stallion pressed forward, sensing my urgency. *Race for Papa, King,* I thought. *You can win for Papa.*

The Recorah River spread before us, and both Saadi and I would have to slow soon to avoid surging into it. King's burst of speed was enough to put us neck-and-neck once more, but my frustration flared, for I doubted we could push ahead. At best, the race would be a tie. And a tie wasn't good enough, not when King needed to come home with me.

Then suddenly I was in front. I glanced over at Saadi in confusion, and saw him check his gelding, letting me win. King did not want to stop, but I pulled him down just before the river, swerving to let him canter, then trot, along its bank. Saadi came alongside me and we halted, dismounting at the same time. I leaned for a moment against my saddle, panting from my own exertion, then slid it off King's back. Without a word, Saadi likewise stripped his mount, and we freed the horses to go to the water for a drink. Muscles aching, I flopped down on the grass and stared up through the branches of a tree to the graying sky above.

A shadow passed over me, then Saadi lay down beside me.

"You won," he said.

"You let me."

There was a silence—he hadn't expected me to know. Then I heard the grass rustle as he shrugged. "You're right. I did."

Laughing at his candor, I sat up and looked at him. He was relaxing with his arms behind his head, his bronze hair damp and sticking to his forehead.

"Why did you let me win? You know that means I don't have to spend any more time with you."

He propped himself up on his elbows, perusing my face. "That doesn't bother me."

I frowned. Did he no longer desire my company?

"I never wanted to *force* you to spend time with me, Sha-selle. I wanted you to *want* to spend time with me."

"You're a poet," I joked, amused by his graceless word choice, and he grinned.

"Besides, a victory is a victory. You won and now have the best of everything—you get your father's horse, and you can be rid of me if you want."

With a mischievous glint in my eye, I put my hands on the ground on either side of his waist. "I would have won, anyway."

He chuckled, once more lying down flat. "You're shame-less."

I rolled back to my original position, and we both quieted, but there was an aspect of my victory that still bothered me.

"Tell me, why did it matter to you who won? I mean, even if you'd won, you still could have released me from the bar-gain. You could have said I didn't have to spend those two days with you."

"I could have," he acknowledged. "But after…after you told me about your father, I wanted you to have his horse back. Rava should have had more respect for his memory. She shouldn't have taken him—*them*—away."

Tears stung my eyes, and I swallowed several times to loosen my throat. What a stupid reaction.

"Thank you," I murmured, and I felt his hand close around mine, giving it a squeeze. I sighed contentedly, letting myself enjoy the moment. "What was *your* father like?"

"I don't know," he said offhandedly.

"What do you mean, you don't know?" As usual, my typical phrasing was somewhat coarse, driven by my curiosity, and I caught myself, adopting a more considerate tone. "Did he die when you were young?"

"No, he's still alive."

I turned my head to gape at him, greatly confused. "He left you?"

"No."

"Then *what?*"

I sat up again, close to exasperation; he just looked at me, bemused, my hand still in his.

"Fathers don't raise their children in Cokyri. They aren't trusted with such an important responsibility. I never knew mine."

This was not an answer I could have foreseen, and I shifted uneasily, trying to figure out how to proceed.

"I'm sorry," I said lamely.

He was quiet at first, his eyes fixed on the darkened sky as he pondered our different experiences.

"I never felt sorry about it. My mother was a good woman—she and her maidens took care of me. But like I told you before, I had to work harder than you can imagine to achieve my military rank, and only because I'm a man. I can do everything Rava can do. I always could, but no one would see it, not even her. A struggle like that makes you question things."

"So now you wish you'd known your father?"

Again, he reflected. "No. I wish I'd known *yours.*"

I looked away, once more fighting tears. I didn't understand how he could affect me so deeply.

"I'm not sure my father would have been to your liking," I finally said, meeting his eyes. "I found him brave for his willingness to fight, even when there was no more hope. You would probably have found him weak."

He sat up and gazed earnestly at me. "There is a way to accomplish things, but it's rarely to declare a war, private or otherwise."

"Sometimes the war is not of your making," I retorted. "You must fight, otherwise you're a lamb. And lambs are slaughtered, Saadi."

His brows drew together, and we stared at each other for much longer than we should have, and I knew I had rattled him. Then he shook his head.

"See those lights up there? They're called stars."

I laughed. "I can take a hint. We should go back."

We caught and saddled our mounts, then took our time returning to the city, neither of us really wanting the day to end. But as we reached the front gates, my anxiety rose, bringing queasiness along with it. My mother wouldn't know where I was, and I had definitely missed dinner. Presented with yet another set of broken promises, she wasn't likely to be forgiving.

We rode under the raised entry gates without interference from the Cokyrian guards, continuing along the thoroughfare in comfortable silence. When we reached the street that branched off into the western section of the city, I expected Saadi to continue north, but he did not. We dismounted and walked side by side, leading our horses, until my house came into view.

"You should leave," I said to him, hoping I didn't sound rude.

"Let me help you take King to your stable."

I hesitated, unsure of the idea, then motioned for him to follow me as I cut across the property to approach the barn from the rear. After putting King in his private stall at the back of the building, sectioned off from the mares, I lit a lantern and grabbed a bucket. While Saadi watched me from the open door of the building, I went to the well to fill it.

"You should really go now," I murmured upon my return, not wanting anyone to see us or the light.

He nodded and hung the lantern on its hook, but he did not leave. Instead, he took the bucket from me, placing it in King's stall, and I noticed he had tossed in some hay. Brushing off his hands, he approached me.

"Tell your family I returned the horse to your care, that our stable master found him too unruly and disruptive to serve us other than to sire an occasional foal."

"Yes, I will," I mumbled, grateful for the lie he had provided. I had been so focused on recovering the stallion that explaining his reappearance had not yet entered my mind. Then an image of Rava, standing outside the barn tapping the scroll against her palm, surfaced. What was to prevent her return?

"And your sister? What will you tell her?"

He smirked. "You seem to think Rava is in charge of everything. Well, she's not in charge of our stables. And our stable master will be content as long as we can still use the stallion for breeding. As for Rava, keep the horse out of sight and she'll likely never know he's back in your hands."

"But what if you're wrong and she does find out?"

"Then I'll tell her that I have been currying a friendship with you. That you have unwittingly become an informant. That the return of the stallion, while retaining Cokyrian breeding rights, furthered that goal."

I gaped at him, for his words flowed so easily, I wondered if there was truth behind them.

"And is that what this is really all about?"

I studied his blue eyes, almost afraid of what they might reveal. But they were remarkably sincere when he addressed the question.

"In a way, I suppose, for I am learning much from you." He smiled and reached out to push my hair back from my face. "But it is not the sort of information that would be of interest to Rava."

His hand caressed my cheek, and he slowly leaned toward me until his lips met mine. I moved my mouth against his, following his lead, and a tingle went down my spine. With my knees threatening to buckle, I put my hands on his chest for balance, feeling his heart beating beneath my palms. Then he was gone.

I stood dumbfounded, not knowing what to do, then traced my still-moist lips, the taste of him lingering. This was the first time I'd been kissed, and the experience, I could not deny, had been a good one. I no longer cared that Saadi was Cokyrian, for my feelings on the matter were clear. I'd kiss him again if given the chance.

I extinguished the lantern and all but skipped to the house, bursting happily through the front door. My mood was short-lived, however, for my mother stalked into the entryway, no smile within miles of her face.

"You've finally decided to turn up, have you?" she castigated. I could smell food wafting on the air, confirmation that my family had already eaten.

"I'm sorry, Mother, I meant to be back—"

"Oh, you *meant* to. I shouldn't have let you go out at all, Shaselle! How could I have been so foolish?"

She was unusually frazzled—I knew I hadn't been completely reliable of late, but her reaction was excessive. Then Steldor stepped out of the parlor, followed by Dahnath and my other curious, but hesitant, siblings, for they didn't know if they would be in trouble for listening. They had nothing to worry about. I was holding all of my mother's attention.

"Lania, this won't do any good now," Steldor said, walking over to lay a hand on my mother's arm. She shook him off.

"Don't you tell me what will and won't do any good, young man. She's *my* daughter and I will handle this how I see fit."

Raising his hands in surrender, Steldor stepped back, muttering something about grabbing his cloak. He briefly disappeared to return with the garment in question draped across his arm, then gave a small bow to my mother, whose glare remained steadfast. With a shake of his head, he stepped around me and through the door.

"Mother, I'm sorry, but I'm only a little late for dinner. I haven't done anything horribly wrong."

"Oh, really? Then what's your excuse? What was more important to you than being here for Lord Grayden's visit?"

I paled as recollection hit. This was what had generated the nagging feeling in the back of my brain. And this was the reason Steldor had still been at our house, for he would have stayed to dine with us.

"And just what are you wearing?" She scanned me and her pitch rose even higher. "Have you been riding?"

"No, I mean…yes, but I—"

"Am I to understand that engaging in an activity I have specifically forbidden was more important to you than eating dinner with your family and our guests?"

"No, that's not right, that's not what happened." I wanted to tell her about King, in the feeble hope it would partially excuse my behavior, but she wasn't in a frame of mind to listen.

"But you did nothing wrong. You only disobeyed my rules, brashly relied on us to entertain your suitor, cast us into the unforgivable position of lying to him about where you were and what you were doing, and risked our family's honor had we been unable to placate him as to the reason you decided not to show up!"

"Please, I beg of you to hear me out! I forgot he was going

to be here. Something unexpected came up—something important, and…"

Mother's expression was so dangerous that I trembled, wanting to disappear.

"I told you this morning that he was coming, Shaselle. Either you weren't listening to me, or you deliberately ignored the importance of this evening. Which was it?"

I sniffed, looking to Dahnath for help, but her face held no sympathy. Since Mother wasn't going to give me the chance to explain, I picked what I believed to be the more forgivable of the two options.

"I—I wasn't listening."

"If you were younger, I'd take a strap to you, girl, but as it is, you had better tell Lord Grayden you're sorry. He was generous to come back after the way you behaved during his first visit. I doubt he'll come thrice, but perhaps you can stop him from telling the entire kingdom what kind of lady you are."

Though I felt guilty, trapped and pitiful, I also felt a pang of indignation. "And what kind of lady am I, Mother?"

She shook her head. "Not much of one, Shaselle. Not much of one."

Mother turned around and pointed up the stairs, directing my other siblings, who were only too eager to comply, to go to their rooms. I didn't know if I should go, too, but when she snapped my name, I hurried after them.

I forcefully closed and locked my bedroom door, then leaned against it, fighting tears. My bed awaited, more inviting than the arms of any member of my family, and I curled on top of it, too miserable to change into my nightgown. There were days when no decision I made was a good one, and this day came close to topping them all.

But what if I hadn't forgotten that Grayden was invited to dinner? If I had been asked to choose between sharing a meal with him and racing against Saadi, what would I have done? The question was a lot easier to answer than it should have been, and though my response confirmed my wicked nature, it also made me feel better. Knowing that I would have intentionally slighted Grayden made accidentally slighting him more tolerable. While I certainly owed the young man an apology, perhaps I had also done him a favor.

I rolled off the bed and went to the washbasin, finally calm enough to go to bed. I didn't expect to sleep much, however. Not because I was in trouble with Mother, but because I wanted to relive the race over and over again. And Saadi's kiss over and over and over and...

CHAPTER 23

WISE DECISIONS

I WOKE WITH A FRESH IDEA ON THE FIRST morning of October and sent word to Cannan that he should meet me in the Royal Ballroom. The King and Queen had long ago been provided with an entrance into the ballroom through the Dignitary's Room that was just down the corridor from their traditional quarters, so I arrived in advance of the captain. I crossed the floor of the massive hall and stepped out onto the balcony, which extended over the East Courtyard, to wait for him.

Unlike in May, when I had tried to calm the Hytanican people in the wake of the posting of the High Priestess's rules, all was peaceful today, and I surveyed the grounds, for this was the only one of the original palace courtyards to have survived the Cokyrian takeover with little damage. Its paved central area remained intact, with multicolored stones forming concentric circles around a large two-tiered fountain, and I idly considered the social events my mother used to host in order to continue the etiquette training of the kingdom's young noblewomen. I sighed, thinking of how my life and the lives of all those in my circle had been affected by the war. Both Reveina and Kalem, long-standing acquaintances of mine, had been widowed when the Overlord had murdered our military officers. In Reveina's case, the loss of her husband was a partial blessing, for the Master at Arms had treated her poorly; but Kalem had been smitten with Tadark, and her sweet dreams of their life together and their future children had been destroyed. And there were so many fatherless daughters, their brothers and uncles now charged with the responsibility of finding them husbands. Such was the case with Galen, whose twin sisters, Niani and Nadeja, were of marriageable age. And Baelic, Steldor's uncle, had left behind five daughters, only the eldest of whom was betrothed.

Footsteps drew me from my thoughts, and I glanced over my shoulder to see Cannan approaching. He stepped up beside me, his hands clasped behind his back, and I wondered how even shoulders as broad as his could carry so much responsibility.

"You wished to see me, Queen Alera?"

"Yes, I did. I would like to know your thoughts on how our citizens are doing. I see the poor and desperate every day in my Hearing Hall, but you spend considerable time out among the people. How do you perceive their overall state?"

"The citizens are better than they've been, now that homes and shops have been rebuilt."

"They're better but..."

"All things are relative, Alera. The Cokyrians see the reconstruction as finished—most Hytanicans do not."

"I don't understand."

The captain exhaled heavily and placed his hands on the smooth wood of the railing.

"Conquerors remake the lands they claim in their own image. Structures are rebuilt but not necessarily restored. After all, the victors take the spoils. Just look around the Bastion,

Alera—the palace no longer exists for more than one reason. And sacred places are unlikely to be rebuilt, for no better reason than a show of power and dominance."

"The churches?" I inquired, hating to admit, even to myself, that Steldor had been right about a number of things.

"Power and dominance, Alera."

I carefully considered his words. Better meant improvement, which was not necessarily the same as good. After all, sixteen people dying in a harsh winter was better than twenty, but it was still too many.

"Then spirits have fallen already?"

"Spirits are difficult to maintain when merely being Hytanican casts you under suspicion. People are stopped and searched on the streets with impunity. Homes are searched any time of the day or night, and punishments for real or imaginary transgressions are harsh. Our people are not easily cowed—they fight back. Most incidents are not serious, just some throwing of stones or jeers. But yesterday a Cokyrian soldier was attacked in the street by a group of Hytanican men."

I bowed my head, my hands gripping the railing. At times like these it seemed to me that the arduous road that lay ahead was never ending. Was there really such a thing as abiding peace?

"We need to do something—something that will make a difference," I asserted, meeting Cannan's eyes. "Something that will show our people that we can adjust to this world, that we can move forward with our lives."

"What do you have in mind, Alera?"

"A festival."

I tried to sound decisive, but was truly seeking his opinion. The idea might be foolhardy, after all—assembling the people, providing them with ale, letting them celebrate and feel invincible. It could be a disaster. Or it could be exactly what they needed.

The captain showed no reaction, other than to direct his gaze out over the buildings and homes that made up our city. In the silence, I grew nervous—it was easy to be intimidated by Cannan. His unflappable demeanor, self-confidence and determined nature, coupled with his height, impressive build, and nearly black hair and eyes, were enough to make even the most dangerous beast recoil.

He turned to face me, and I was encouraged to see he was nodding. "A festival would be good for our people, Your Highness. A wise decision."

I smiled, my mind beginning to whir. Historically, our Harvest Festival consisted of a faire and a tournament and usually entailed months of planning. We didn't have months, but then, the Cokyrians wouldn't permit us to sponsor all of the customary events.

At that thought, I blurted, "Without a tournament, of course."

"Yes, it would be difficult to hold a tournament without weapons." A flicker of amusement showed in the captain's eyes. "But a faire would be possible."

We stood side by side for a few minutes more, both of us enjoying the view of the city. The sun was shining, and the landscape looked stunning to me, in no small part because of the work that had gone into the homes, businesses, churches and schools over the years. But more than that, Hytanica was rich in history and tradition, and I was responsible for guiding her future.

"Hytanica is a beautiful place, even in enemy hands," Cannan reflected, his thoughts tracking my own. "You do your kingdom justice." He briefly laid a hand over mine, then left me alone to determine how best to proceed.

In previous years, the Hytanican Harvest Festival had been
one of the largest and most talked about celebrations in the
Recorah River Valley. Vendors and traders from neighboring kingdoms would come with their distinctive products;
dressmakers would receive a rash of clothing orders and hire
young girls to help with the sewing; bath houses, places of
lodging, taverns and livery stables would stock up on supplies
for a large influx of visitors; and food would be planned and
prepared for the feasts.

Last year, there had been no festival, for our kingdom had
been under siege. No festival was expected this year, either,
and it would be a sign that we still had things to celebrate if
I reinstated it. Admittedly, planning would be rushed, for in
the past, criers and heralds would have already been sent out
to announce the event, which always took place during the
last few days of October, less than a month away. But it could
be done, especially since there would be no tournament, generally the most difficult part of the festival to coordinate.

I decided to seek assistance from my mother in pulling
things together, and I went to my parents' quarters, unexpectedly finding my father with her in their parlor.

"Alera, come in, come in," he greeted me, stepping forward
to usher me to an armchair. His hair was now more salt than
pepper, and his waistband was a little tighter, but he otherwise
exuded the same warmth and command I remembered from
when he had been King. "What a pleasant surprise this is," he
continued, sitting next to my mother on the sofa.

"Thank you, Father. Nice to see you, Mother."

"To what do we owe this visit?" my mother asked, and I
was struck by how young she looked today, so like Miranna,
with her blond hair down about her shoulders and her blue
eyes sparkling.

I quickly told them of my idea, encouraged by their receptive attitudes.

"Given how little time we have for preparations, I'm wondering, Mother, if you would be willing to organize a feast sponsored by the Bastion. It would be served out of doors, in the style of our annual Christmas Eve feast."

"Yes, of course, and I'll coordinate the banners and the decorations for the faire grounds and marketplace."

"What about you, Father? I know you've been occupied with repairs here in the Bastion. Do you have time to spare?"

"All three floors of the West Wing are nearly restored. The only real work that remains is in the East Wing, in the first-floor quarters that used to be occupied by the Palace Guards." He paused, then added with a chuckle, "I think the Cokyrians can undertake that work without the benefit of my expertise."

"Would you be willing to seek out minstrels and other entertainers to perform at the faire?"

"I'll send out a call at once. Good entertainment is something I've always been able to spot." He rubbed his hands together in anticipation, ready for a more enjoyable—and less Cokyrian involved—task.

"Thank you. If you would like, you can use the Hearing Hall in the mornings to hold auditions for performers."

"I will indeed. This is an inspired idea, Alera. A return of our Harvest Festival is long overdue."

He beamed at me, and I blushed at his compliment, gladdened by the enthusiasm my parents were displaying, for it was exactly the sort of reaction I hoped to inspire in all of Hytanica's citizens.

Over the next few days, I grappled with the decision of where to locate the faire. The military field was the best option, but I was hesitant about seeking permission from Rava to use it. In the end, I decided to wait for Narian's return—he would be in favor of the festival, and I wanted as little to do with his current second-in-command as possible.

On the third day of hasty preparations, I sat down at my desk to draft the proclamation that would announce the Harvest Festival. When I was finished, I sent it to the scribes who worked out of the library on the second floor. They would make several copies of the document and distribute it throughout the city and, with Narian's permission, to our neighboring kingdoms.

Pleased with my efforts, I straightened my desktop, then left the study, intending to join my family for dinner. Rava stepped out of Narian's office area at the same time and advanced on me, her expression even less friendly than usual. Without a word, she slammed her hand against my closed door, dangerously close to my face, pinning a copy of my proclamation in place.

"I have spoken to your scribes and have forbidden this from being issued."

I took a step back, then resolutely met her pale blue eyes. "You can forbid whatever you wish. But the proclamation *will* go forth."

Rava slowly and deliberately crumpled the parchment, then tossed it at my feet.

"If this is sent out, you will be sorry," she threatened, her lip curling in disgust. "I will not permit your people to rally."

"Is that how you see this? I don't plan to facilitate a rally, Rava. I plan to let the people of this kingdom *smile* for once."

"The people of this *province* should learn their place before they are allowed to smile."

"Then I'm thankful it is not your decision to make." I had taken enough of her condescension, her arrogance and her despotism. Her belief that she ruled this Bastion and this province needed to end. "That proclamation will be issued, or *you* will be the one who is sorry."

Her fingers locked around my wrist. "If you are lying about your intentions, *Grand Provost,*" she said in a near whisper, "I will see you dead."

I did not doubt the sincerity of her threat, but had too much at stake to back down. Despite my fear, I grabbed her wrist in the exact way she was gripping mine.

"If you thought you could get away with killing me, Rava, you would have done so by now."

I wasn't certain of my standing in the High Priestess's eyes, but I knew from her conversation with Narian that he, at least, was important to her. And she would lose him if Rava—or any Cokyrian for that matter—injured me.

Rava growled, a low and animalistic sound that shook me to the core, and shoved me into the door. Pain shot through my shoulder, but she had turned away, storming back toward her office at the other end of the hall. I watched her go, my wrist throbbing, Narian's cynical words coming back to me— *she is no diplomat, I'll grant you that.*

Narian returned the next afternoon, seeming well-rested, leading me to believe the trip had gone smoothly. We greeted each other formally, but I was eager for the day to pass so that we could talk in private—and without fear of being over-heard. Though Rava did not know it, she had unnerved me with her warning, and I wanted him to assure me that she would soon be gone.

As usual, he dropped into my bedroom through the window that night.

"Don't you ever worry you'll fall?" I asked from where I was sitting on the bed, reading. It was easily a twenty-five-foot drop from my window to the ground, and even farther from the roof where he began his descent.

"No," he said, taking off his sword belt and laying it on the side table before sitting next to me. "There's no room for fear once you're committed to a course of action."

I gaped at him, for he made it sound like fear could be extinguished much like the flame of a candle.

"But think how high up you are! You *never* consider that you might slip or lose your balance?"

"No," he repeated with a laugh. "But I'm starting to think you fear clumsiness on my part."

"It's your neck," I said, scooting closer to him. "Although I would hate to see it broken."

He put his arm around me and I snuggled against his chest, realizing how much I had missed the sound of his heartbeat and the cadence of his breathing.

"How did things go in Cokyri?" I asked.

"Better than I anticipated. The High Priestess took the news of Steldor's recent actions quite well. She thought the punishment was appropriate."

"The punishment, yes, but surely not the method by which Rava carried it out?"

He was so quiet that I sat up, inferring something was wrong. He straightened and ran a hand through his thick golden hair.

"Alera, the High Priestess is not our ally on this issue."

"What do you mean? How can she overlook Rava's blatant insubordination?"

Once more he sat quietly, and understanding came to me.

"You didn't talk to her about Rava."

"No, I didn't," he flatly admitted.

I frowned, feeling slighted and betrayed.

"I'm sorry, Alera, but not because I didn't discuss Rava with the High Priestess. I'm sorry because I didn't take the time to clarify my thoughts on the subject before I left."

"What *thoughts?*" I demanded, Rava's threat against my life fueling my anger.

"If you'll calm down, I'll explain."

I scrambled out of bed, too agitated to stay still, and began to pace.

"We're in the midst of a very delicate political battle, Alera, and everyone plays their part. You are the province's figure-head, the voice of the people. The High Priestess presides over us all, and she placates me—not out of trust or respect, but because I am powerful. She doesn't know that I've sworn never to use those powers again, and therefore sees Rava as her means of keeping me in check. Rava is her ally, her hand-picked shield maiden, her confidante. The last thing she'll do is remove her ally when she sees me as a risk."

He paused, assessing me, trying to determine if I under-stood the true nature of our situation. I stopped pacing and met his gaze, not wanting to believe he was right, and he tried once more.

"If I speak against Rava, the ice on which we stand will crack. The High Priestess will suspect me, she'll suspect you and it doesn't matter if we've done anything or not—we'll be gone, and we'll no longer have a hold on Hytanica."

For the first time, I fully appreciated the danger of our po-sition, and I swayed on my feet. I had foolishly trusted the High Priestess, believed that I was important, that she was on our side, that Narian and I could restore this city, that my people would be treated fairly. Rava had seemed an unim-portant player—now she seemed a puppet master with Nar-ian and me on strings.

I stumbled to the bed and sank down upon it, my eyes burning.

"While you were gone, I began planning for the return of our Harvest Festival. Rava doesn't want the event held. She told me to call it off."

"I know," he wryly acknowledged. "She made me aware of your activities and her decision when I arrived."

"And?"

"She won't yield. She's already sent word to the High Priestess."

I nodded, then asked, my voice barely audible, "And what do *you* say?"

"I say…" He reached for my hands, determination building in his intense blue eyes. "I say we proceed with the festival until and unless the High Priestess comes here herself and brings it to a halt. Political fires aren't interesting without kindling."

I smiled, and he took me into his arms, lightly kissing me.

"At least we don't have anything to worry about tonight," I murmured as we lay down next to each other.

"I always worry."

"Really? I wouldn't have thought of you as the worrying kind."

"I worry when I cannot act," he mused, drawing me close, and I felt life and strength flowing into me, warming me from head to toe. "I can handle heaven and hell, but not limbo."

"I thought you had no religion in Cokyri. How do you know about heaven and hell?"

"We don't practice religion, but we have education. I probably know more about your faith than you do."

I placed a hand on his chest and pushed myself up to look at him in mock umbrage. "Then tell me how our wedding will proceed."

"*That* I don't know," he said with a grin. "I suspect Hytanica's marital traditions and rites would fill a volume more than double the rest of our history texts put together."

"You're ridiculous!" I lightly smothered him with a pillow, then nestled upon his chest, content and ready for sleep.

At some point in the night, I woke and looked over to see Narian staring at the ceiling.

"What are you doing?" I asked, stifling a yawn.

"Thinking."

"Do you want to tell me what you're thinking about?"

"Candidates for my new second-in-command. I have a feeling your Harvest Festival is going to bring matters to the breaking point between us and Rava. If things go our way and the High Priestess removes her, I intend to be the one to name her replacement."

"And this cannot wait until morning?" I asked, even though I knew how he would respond.

"I believe in being prepared." I nodded and closed my eyes. Anticipating, planning, developing strategies and counter strategies, was another ingrained aspect of Narian's nature. As I drifted back to sleep, I wondered for how many contingencies he was prepared that I knew nothing about.

CHAPTER 24

FRIEND AND FOE

MY DAYS OF PUNISHMENT WERE MISERABLE, IN large part because of the glares and sideways glances I received that were meant to make me feel guilty. Since I already did, I undertook the extra chores I was given without complaint, not wanting to prove myself even more irresponsible.

I tried several times to speak with Mother, wanting to make her understand that I had not missed dinner with Grayden on purpose, hoping she would realize how important it was to bring King home. But she would have none of it. In the end, the only way left to redeem myself was to apologize to the young man.

Dressed in my finest day clothes, I set off toward the wealthy residential area that lay east of the thoroughfare, opting to go on foot despite the distance. While I could have taken a buggy, the Cokyrians seemed to enjoy seizing—*stealing*—every reasonably well-bred Hytanican horse they came upon, and all of my father's horses were better than well-bred. I didn't want to chance losing my mare, my brother's gelding or Alcander.

It was a sunny afternoon, and the breeze felt fresh upon my cheeks, giving my spirits a lift. Were it not for the Cokyrian soldiers on the streets, I could have let myself believe that we were returning to simpler, more pleasant times. In years past, October in Hytanica would have been a time of rising excitement, for the harvest would have been well underway, and city dwellers and country folk alike would have been stocking the larders for winter. And young men would have been honing their skills for the annual tournament, while young women would have watched and admired them from afar. Would Lord Grayden have competed this year? At eighteen, he would have been eligible for the first time. Uncle Cannan had said he'd excelled in military school, and the tournament was the place to demonstrate one's skills. Or perhaps, being good with horses, he would have entered the races. Had I been a boy, nothing could have prevented me from doing so, just as Papa had done when he was my age.

When Lord Landru's two-story manor house loomed before me, I scanned its newly placed stone, wondering where within its walls the rebels had hidden their weapons. I slowed my steps as I started up the path toward the front entrance, feeling like I was about to walk on smoldering embers. Had the fire burned down enough that it couldn't harm me? Or would I be scorched? Reaching the front door, I took a deep breath, aware of the importance of what I was about to do and fearful that I would not succeed. Then I rapped firmly upon the dark wood. This was not the time to practice timidity.

Grayden opened the door himself and our eyes met. For a moment, neither of us moved, equally flustered—he was stunned to find me on his stoop, while I had expected a servant to answer my knock.

"May I come in, my lord?" I inquired, sounding more nervous than I would have liked.

"As you wish."

He leaned back against the door frame and gestured for

me to enter, his manner not entirely hospitable. I stepped inside and glanced around the spacious foyer, then cleared my throat, ready to begin a short, but well-rehearsed, statement of contrition.

"I owe you an apology, Lord Grayden. I'm sorry for failing to attend the dinner to which you were invited at my family's home. While I do not deserve your kind regard, I hope you will be gracious enough to forgive me."

"That depends on what you were doing instead."

"Excuse me?" I squeaked, for this was an unexpected reaction. My mind spun, trying to decide what to do. Did I need to apologize better? Or should I just leave?

He laughed, and I felt even more flustered. "Your mother and sisters kept changing their stories. Makes me think they didn't know what you were doing. I'd like the mystery solved."

Taken aback, I surveyed him, noting his dark brown hair that made his skin appear all the more fair, his perfectly proportioned nose, his gorgeous green eyes and his inviting smile. He wanted me to be honest. I decided to risk it, for nothing worse could come of his knowing the truth.

"I forgot you were coming."

He straightened and rubbed the back of his neck with one hand. "At least I know you're not a liar."

"Not usually," I blurted, and he laughed once more.

"Well then, I accept your apology."

"That's very considerate of you." I hesitated then gave him another curtsey. "Good day to you, my lord."

His eyebrows rose in surprise. "You're leaving so soon?"

"Yes," I replied, a grin playing at the corners of my mouth. "You see, I haven't been invited to stay."

Before he could respond, I slipped past him and out the door, pleased at his befuddled expression. All in all, things had gone well—I had accomplished my appointed task; at the same time, I was certain I could cross another suitor off the list. After all, even the best impressions Lord Grayden had of me left much to be desired. But I didn't feel as happy about that outcome as I had expected. Strangely, the young man held more appeal for me now than he had before. I sighed, for my nature did indeed appear to be a fickle one.

My mother was eager to hear every single word of my exchange with Lord Grayden, although I couldn't see that there was much to tell.

"I apologized for forgetting we had invited him to dinner," I announced, baiting her. "*He* forgave me."

"We were the ones embarrassed by your behavior, Shaselle, not Lord Grayden," she chided, and what I had thought to be solid ground shifted beneath my feet.

She said no more, but set me again to chores, although fewer frowns came my way. Perhaps this would soon be over. I ate with the rest of my family, then retreated to my bedroom, desperate for some breathing space. Not that there was any to be found for me inside this house, where the bits of freedom that were doled out were dominated by boredom. I had felt much the same during my schooling days, when tutors would come and sequester me with lessons for hours on end. My blessed relief back then had been riding with my father after he came home from the military base, where he served as the cavalry officer. Now there was no relief in sight.

Hearing my mother's footsteps in the first-floor corridor, I groaned. It was too early to go to sleep, yet I didn't want to be downstairs. I idly considered opening a book, but what I craved was a touch of excitement. I sat up, then went to my wardrobe and dressed in breeches, boots and a woolen shirt, shrugging my cloak over it all. Despite the amount of trouble I would be in if I were caught, I returned to the window and pushed it open, once more escaping by scuttling down the oak tree.

I headed out on foot, lurking in the shadows of houses and cutting through alleys between the shops in the Market District, not wanting to draw the notice of the enemy soldiers who patrolled twenty-four hours a day. A destination had entered my mind, a potentially foolish destination, a definitely dangerous destination. I didn't know why, but the risk appealed to me.

The barracks on the military base came into view, and I strode toward them, hoping my bravado would enable me to pass for Cokyrian. But the closer I came to the buildings, the more idiotic my idea seemed. I didn't want to end up in the enemy's hands. I didn't want to be brought to Rava. I stopped to turn around, but it was too late.

"You there! What are you doing?" A sentry was approaching, her strides swift and purposeful. "Identify yourself!"

She held a lantern close to me, and I squinted in the light, my heart thrumming loudly. On the chance that I could still pull off the charade, I attempted to mimic a Cokyrian accent. The inflection was subtle, but not terribly different from our own, and I hoped the guard would be none the wiser.

"I was sent to deliver a message."

"And what message is that?" Her voice was skeptical and she laid a hand on the hilt of the sword at her hip.

"The message is not for you."

The sentry laughed. "Get out of here, girl. I have no interest in arresting you. I'll consider this an amusing part of my night duty as long as you don't cause any trouble."

"The message is from Rava," I tried again, my natural stubbornness overcoming my fear. "For her brother."

"Messages should be taken to the main building," she pronounced, no longer confident that she should send me away.

"Rava instructed me to deliver it to no one but Saadi. She said he would be in the officer's barracks."

The woman deliberated, looking dubiously at me, although she ultimately decided in my favor.

"Then I'll take you to him. We'll see what he has to say about this."

The sentry grabbed my arm and led me toward the building. There were two guards at its entrance, and she instructed one of them to fetch Saadi.

Despite the coolness of the weather, I could feel myself sweating. If Saadi refused to come, I would be locked up and likely taken to Rava in the morning. But if he did come, how did I know he would be happy to see me? He might not approve of the game I was playing. Nausea roiled my stomach, and I glanced at the Cokyrians on each side of me, trying to decide if I should beat a hasty retreat. Too afraid of the consequences if I failed to get away, I waited, praying the fates would smile upon me.

It wasn't long before footfalls reached my ears, and the door to the barracks swung open. Saadi stood there in breeches and a loose, unlaced shirt, strapping on his weapons, obviously having been awakened. Would he be angry that I had disturbed his sleep?

"Well?" the guard who discovered me prompted.

"I recognize her," Saadi answered, staring directly at the woman. "She works for my sister as an errand girl."

I briefly closed my eyes in relief. Saadi waved the guard back to her post and issued an order to the man behind him to retrieve his cloak. When it was thrust into his hands, he escorted me back across the base, not speaking until we were out of earshot of those on patrol.

"So, Rava has a message for me?"

I shoved him unthinkingly, teasingly, and he laughed, jumping away.

"*You* wanted to see me, remember?" I pointed out. "But you never picked a time or place!"

"So you decided to do it for me. Fair enough, but I'm dying to know what you have in mind to do."

"I don't have anything in mind."

We had reached the thoroughfare, and he chuckled. "You braved Cokyrian soldiers and the stronghold of the military base, but don't have a thing in mind for us to do?"

"That's right," I admitted, irritated that he was laughing at me. "Would you grow up please?"

"Shaselle, there's nothing 'grown-up' about what we're doing. I assume you snuck away from home to see me, and I have a five o'clock call in the morning."

I came to a halt and turned to face him, my eyes issuing a challenge. "If you want to go back, feel free. Tell those soldiers that Rava just wanted to make sure her baby brother went to bed on time."

He grinned, enjoying my feisty responses, and smoothed his bronze hair forward, a habit I still found annoying. It also served to make my heart flutter.

"Trust me, I've survived many a night without sleep." He came closer, putting his hands on my hips, and I spontaneously leaned in to kiss him. He drew me close, his mouth more hungry than it had been in the barn, and a tingle ran from my lips to my toes. Then I pulled away, smiling mischievously, loving how reckless my actions were.

He took my hand, kissing each of my fingers before tugging me down the street.

"Come on, Shaselle."

"Where are we going?"

Saadi didn't answer, but led me in the direction of the Market District. As a Cokyrian soldier on horseback trotted by, he pulled me into the shadows of a storefront, placing a finger upon his lips.

"I've thought of something for us to do," he whispered. "Since you came so unprepared."

Once more he took my hand, and I went with him blindly, happily, until we reached the shop from which I'd stolen fruit and wine when I'd run away from home.

"What are you—?"

He gave the door a strong kick, and I winced at the crack of the wood in the stillness.

"Saadi!" I hissed, glancing around, expecting the mounted Cokyrian to come galloping back.

He ignored me, pushing the door open.

"Come on now. No errand girl of Rava's would be such a coward!"

He stepped inside and I followed, peering through the darkness, watching him pry the lid off a crate and pull forth a bottle of wine. He tossed it to me, and I gamely caught it. After grabbing another, he darted back into the open, snatching hold of my wrist to make sure he didn't lose me.

We hurried down the street, halting where the road intersected the thoroughfare, and Saadi clamped the cork of the wine bottle between his teeth, tugging it free. He spat it on the ground, raised the bottle in mock cheers and took a long swig. After wiping his mouth with the back of his hand, he passed the bottle to me. I hesitated, not wanting to seem fainthearted, but knowing this was not how I should be behaving. His eyebrows rose, and I grabbed the bottle, not about to let him make fun of me. I put it to my lips and gulped, feeling the wine burn down my throat, and he clapped, applauding me and flashing the most adorable grin I had ever seen.

It didn't take long to finish off the first bottle, and Saadi attempted to open the second, but couldn't seem to get a good grip with his teeth. Giggling, I took the bottle and tried chewing through the cork; he snatched it back, trying in vain to drink its contents without removing the cork at all. I shoved him and he stumbled, dropping the bottle, the cork finally popping loose, and we laughed uncontrollably, falling into each other's arms while the wine flowed onto the street. Sobering somewhat, Saadi gripped my shoulders and held me away from him.

"Shaselle!" he cried, eliciting another spasm of giggles from me. "You've spilled the wine."

"No, no, no. You're the one who spilled the wine."

I tossed my hair back, my upper body weirdly following the motion, and would probably have hit the cobblestone street had he not caught my arm.

"Don't worry—I have something." He dropped his hands to his belt and untied his water flask, presenting it to me like it was the legendary Holy Grail, and I stared stupidly at him.

"Do you know what this is?" he crowed, his words slurring together.

"That's your water, silly!" I leaned back against him, craning my neck in an attempt to see his face. His balance was fortunately better than mine, and he managed to keep us both upright.

"Do you really think I would keep water in here?" he asked.

I gasped and lunged for his great discovery. He stepped away, laughing.

"Come and get it!"

I did my best, zigzagging after him down the street, while he dodged and stole swigs from the flask.

"You're going to drink it all!" I shouted, then pointed helplessly at him, trying to find the words to tell him we were no longer alone. He took another step backward, right into the horse of the Cokyrian soldier we had avoided earlier, bouncing off to land gracelessly upon the ground on his rear end.

He stared up at the woman, making no attempt to stand.

"Your horse is very solid," he slurred. "Congratulations on having such a fine mount."

"Saadi, what are you doing?" she muttered, banishing my initial fear that we would be taken to Rava. I should have remembered how well known he was among the Cokyrians.

"Ah!" he exclaimed. "A friend of mine!" He brandished an arm toward me, struggling to his feet. "She's a friend of mine, too. That...that girl over there. She's helping me take care of important business."

"I can see that," the woman said, humoring her young comrade. "I'll leave you to get on with it. But, Saadi, let me remind you that you're to report to Rava first thing in the morning."

He nodded, giving a small salute. "Yes, I plan to do that very thing."

The soldier sighed wistfully. "Oh, how I wish I could be there." She nudged her horse forward, adding, "Enjoy the rest of your night."

She headed up the street, continuing her patrol, and Saadi turned to me.

"See how I handled that?" he proudly said. "She didn't have a clue."

The fuzziness pushing at the corners of my mind prevented me from pointing out how wrong he was, so I nodded and snickered instead. We continued down the street, somehow avoiding other unwelcome encounters, meandering toward the western residential section where I lived. I tugged at his arm when my house came into view, shushing him loudly.

"My mother's in there," I hissed.

"Isn't she asleep?"

I hit him on the arm with a breathy giggle. "She is!"

"Then let's go!"

"Go where?"

"To your home. I want to see it."

I took his hand and dug my heels into the ground to keep him from moving forward. "No. Saadi, no!"

"Just show me quick and then I'll leave. I promise."

His blue eyes glistened with curiosity, robbing me of both the desire and strength to resist, and I relented. He followed me onto the property and we crept along the side of the house until we came to the sturdy oak that had twice enabled me to escape.

"That's my bedroom window," I whispered, pointing straight up, and he redirected my finger. "I sleep there."

Saadi wasn't surprised by this revelation. I went over to the tree, needing a boost from him to get into it. Given his height, he had no difficulty pulling up behind me, which proved to be a good idea. I would surely have lost my balance swinging my leg through the window had he not steadied me.

"We made it." He chortled, pulling himself inside. "I believe that's cause for celebration."

He handed me his flask, and I poured wine into my mouth, feeling some of it dribble down my chin. I fell upon the bed, holding the drink out to him, and he drained it, landing beside me when he tipped his head too far back.

"Do you want to know something, Shaselle?"

"If you want me to know something." I giggled. He was very funny.

He took a breath, then proclaimed, "Lady Shaselle of Hytanica, I am in love with you."

I burst into laughter, pulling my legs up to ease my aching stomach muscles. He rolled onto his side to look at me, propping his head up with his hand.

"I'm serious," he insisted, grinning foolishly at me.

"You're drunk."

"True, but even drunks can be in love."

"But that's just stupid!"

"Being in love with you is stupid?"

"Well, yes!"

"Why?" he demanded.

I mirrored his position, then met his shining eyes. "Because you're Cokyrian! And no matter what, Cokyrians have to pay."

"How's that?"

"You're going to die," I declared, poking him in the chest. "You know that dagger I had? It wasn't my papa's! There are weapons to kill all you Cokyrians right here in my house—in everybody's houses." I made a sweeping motion with my arm, falling once more onto my back. "That's what you get for putting us in charge of the recon...recontract...rebuilding."

Saadi pushed himself upright, no longer smiling, and I reviewed my words. What had I said? Panic shot through me, for I had confessed our great secret. He stumbled to his feet, and I tried to follow him, becoming entangled in the bedcovers.

"No, wait," I called, for he was headed for the window. "Saadi, come back!"

Freeing myself, I reached for him, wrapping my arms around his waist before he could climb out. He twisted and tried to push me away, but I clung to his arm, refusing to let him shake me off.

"Shaselle, let go!" he ordered.

"Saadi, you can't tell anyone! You have to promise!"

"I promise I won't get you in trouble," he mumbled. Satisfied, I released him, and he ducked through the window and out onto the tree branch.

It took me a moment to realize he hadn't made the promise I'd asked for. In my altered state, I couldn't wrap my mind around what he might do with the information, but the fact that he knew something he shouldn't cut through the fog in my head like a beacon.

"Saadi!" I cried. "If you really love me, swear you won't tell!"

He twisted around to say something, but lost his balance in the process. The crack of tree branches accompanied his fall, then his body hit the ground with a sickening thud. I sucked in air and held my breath, listening for him to rise, then leaned out the window.

"Saadi?" I whispered, my chest squeezing my heart. I jumped when his disembodied voice responded, for I could not see him in the dark.

"I promise, Shaselle. I won't tell anyone."

Relief flowed through me, then I realized how strained he sounded.

"Are you hurt?"

"No, I'm fine."

He didn't sound fine. "I'm coming down."

"No, don't. Just stay there. If I fell, it's definitely too dangerous for you to be climbing."

"Are you sure you're not hurt?" I looked out once more, unnerved that I could not see for myself.

"Just a little bruised. Now go to bed and sleep off the wine."

"Saadi? It's been a really good night. Thank you."

"I know. Just don't worry and go to bed."

"But Saadi? Is it okay if I love you, too?"

"It's definitely okay. But see how you feel when you're sober."

I closed the window and moved back to my bed, lying down without changing into my nightgown, for the room was spinning. I shut my eyes, which did little to stop the sensation, and let myself spiral down into a black sleep.

★ ★ ★

The first thing I did in the morning was retch on the floor beside my bed. My head throbbed, my entire body ached and my mouth was cottony. The smell of my vomit caused another wave of nausea, and I fought it back with all my strength, easing myself down on the bed and throwing an arm over my eyes.

The events of the previous night were unclear, like bits of a strange dream; with the pounding in my temples, I wasn't inclined to push too hard to remember. But despite my haze, I had an uneasy feeling that something important had happened, something I needed to recall. I groaned, pressing my palms against my forehead, trying to keep it from cracking open. As memories surfaced, I lumbered to my feet, gasping from the pain the movement wrought. I couldn't have. I shouldn't have. Yet I had told the enemy about the weapons. Stepping around the mess I'd made on the floor, I stumbled through my bedroom door, my sickness suddenly irrelevant.

I rushed down the stairs, the adrenaline that was pumping through my system helping to calm my headache. No one was about. That was good. I rushed out the front door and into the barn.

It was still early—perhaps early enough to catch Cannan at his manor house. I grabbed a bridle from the tack room and hastily fastened it on Alcander, our steadiest mount, then scrambled onto his back, not bothering with a saddle. I had to tell someone what I'd done; perhaps there was time to fix things, some way to make sure Saadi didn't break his promise. I didn't want to think about what that might be, but Hytanica was more important than any Cokyrian, no matter how cute and freckled he was.

Traffic on the streets was thick and maddening as people rose to do chores and shopkeepers prepared for the day's business. Even though my uncle's residence was not far from ours, the ride felt interminable. When I at last arrived, I urged my horse past the hitching post and right up the walk. Before I even slid from the gelding's back, Cannan stepped over the threshold, and I wondered if my mounted appearance at the door had set the servants buzzing.

The captain ushered me inside and down the corridor to his office, not a place miscreants wanted to find themselves. Steldor and Galen had received a good many lectures here; I had received a few as well, on those occasions when I had tagged along with them and gotten into trouble for my devotion.

Cannan closed the door and turned to me, my unconventional arrival having put him on full alert.

"What is it?"

"I'm so sorry," I fumbled, trying not to cry. "I'm so sorry, Uncle."

He didn't have patience for my apologies. *"What is it?"*

"I... I..." Staring into his dark and forceful eyes, the coward in me took control.

"I was followed home last night. By a Cokyrian. I'm sorry, but I revisited the weapons stash, and...he saw me. He knows."

Cannan's jaw tightened. "Do you know who it was?"

"His name is... I—I'm not sure of his name, but it's the officer you talked to after I was arrested."

"Stay here," Cannan ordered, then he stormed out the door.

I huddled in my uncle's office for a few more minutes, then thought I would find a place to lie down. Regrettably, my aunt, Baroness Faramay, was sitting in the sunroom off the foyer. She was surprised to see me, and immediately asked that I join her, which was the last thing I wanted to do. Following the death of Steldor's younger brother in his infancy, she had suffered a breakdown from which she had never recovered. In the aftermath, she had become simpering, needy and dull;

she also clung to my cousin beyond reason. If there was one woman in this world my own mother could not stand, it was Faramay. If there was one person who could make my illness worse, it was Faramay.

Thankfully, the baroness noticed my pallor after a short conversation, and left to request some soup from the cook. I took the opportunity to steal out the back door into the garden and vomit in some lovely flowers, for the churning in my stomach was even worse than when I'd awoken. When Faramay came to find me, she put me to bed in the guest room, suspecting I had the same illness her son sometimes caught. I couldn't hide a smirk at her assessment, but she didn't seem to notice. She decided she would sit with me and read, and though I was unremittingly fretful, her taste in literature was enough to put me to sleep.

I roused to the sound of my uncle's voice. "Faramay, would you leave us?"

Blearily I opened my eyes to find that the sun had shifted position and now shone through the western window, lighting up Cannan's shape in the doorway. Faramay stepped by him into the hall, and he softly closed the door, moving to take up the chair his wife had vacated.

"We were lucky," he said simply, and I waited in confusion for him to elaborate. "The soldier you mentioned—Saadi—died last night. Apparently before he told anyone what he saw."

I stopped breathing altogether, staring at Cannan, feeling my heart shatter. If I could have willed it, my body would have shattered as well, into a thousand painful shards.

"How?" I croaked, hoping Cannan would attribute the tightness of my voice to my sleep.

"Internal bleeding—I would guess a run-in with someone who did not enjoy his company."

"Oh," I whispered, casting my gaze downward. I wanted to

close my eyes, to black out this horrible world, but I couldn't. I couldn't stop staring…at my hands, at the bedspread, at the floor, all so normal. And yet, here was my uncle, telling me Saadi was dead. And not knowing, not having any idea what had happened, what had *truly* happened. This could not be real.

"Shaselle," Cannan murmured, and I thought for one terrifying moment that he had read my thoughts. I raised my head, wide-eyed and unblinking. "Forget what you know. Never look at the weapons again. While nothing disastrous came of this incident, it should prove to you that it is not your place to be involved."

The chair groaned as he came to his feet. "Faramay tells me you're unwell. I've sent word to your mother. Get some rest."

Then he was gone and I was alone. I rolled onto my side, my hands cold and shaking. The sun was dropping lower and lower, and I was terrified of the darkness that would soon descend. The darkness that would claim me, because it matched the void inside of me. I felt corpselike, then slowly became aware of a warm trickle on my face, the only warmth I could feel. Tears.

CHAPTER 25

AN INQUEST

I DIDN'T KNOW WHAT HAD IGNITED OUR PASSION, but with my hands in Narian's hair and our mouths moving together, I was rapidly losing my ability to think. It was afternoon, and we were in my study, the door closed but not locked, and anyone, Cokyrian or Hytanican, could walk in at any moment.

Narian lifted me and set me on my desk, knocking a few papers to the floor, and I wrapped my legs around his waist. I laughed through our kiss until he was forced to come up for air.

"What?" he asked, cheeks flushed, his visage happy and dazed.

"What are we doing?"

"I don't know, but I'm enjoying it," he said, caressing my neck with his lips.

Despite how difficult he was making it for me to form words, I stuttered out a halfhearted objection. "Narian, you realize…we're going to be caught."

He was breathing heavily and took a moment to answer,

too busy concentrating on the hollow of my throat. "Some-how...I can't bring myself...to care."

Still grasping his hair, I pulled his head back, kissing him once more fully on the lips. "That's a new attitude you've adopted."

He laughed. "The High Priestess and Rava appear to know we're in love, so even if we're discovered, it won't be much of a shock to the *powers that be*."

Despite his words, he practically leaped away from me when the door opened. I crossed my legs, giving him a sideways glare for leaving me sitting rather inappropriately on the edge of my desk, and he rubbed the back of his neck in sheepish apology.

Of course it was Rava crossing the threshold, and she took in our postures before slamming the door, her expression particularly unpleasant.

"So *this* is how the two of you handle the affairs of the province," she growled.

"What is it, Rava?" Narian asked, crossing his arms.

The Cokyrian second-in-command was pacing across the front of my study, unusually agitated. "I assume you heard about the murder last night."

Despite her rude entrance and the awkward circumstances in which we found ourselves, she had our attention. I slipped off my desk to stand beside Narian.

"What murder?" he inquired, and I held my breath in anticipation of her answer. For Rava to be this upset, the victim had to be someone of significance within the Cokyrian forces.

"The murder of my brother."

My hand went to my mouth in shock, while Narian's eyes grayed with both sadness and concern. Saadi's reputation among the Hytanicans was better than most. What could have happened in the night to bring about such a disastrous consequence?

"Rava, I'm so sorry," I murmured, sympathy washing over me. Even Rava could feel loss.

"And you should be!" she rumbled, bestial in her ferocity. "Hytanicans are responsible for this. Saadi was ambushed and killed by your people. He never even had a chance to draw his sword."

"Tell me what you know," Narian calmly requested, not appreciating her attack against me, but understanding her anger.

"He was found this morning. Broken, bloody, bruised. He was assaulted during the night."

"And the responsible parties—they're in custody?"

"Of course not!"

Rava was tense, enraged, and I thought back to when Miranna had been abducted. The ache, the fear, the grief… Just a couple of days ago Rava had threatened my life, but now I fervently wished her peace.

"We must hunt them down," she went on. "We must find whoever did this and make them pay. And if we cannot find them, then every Hytanican in this godforsaken city must pay."

"Rava, I'm sorry for your loss," Narian said, trying to pacify her. "And I will see that everything that can be done is done. But have we any proof that Saadi didn't die from some sort of accident?"

"No," she admitted, straightening her spine and glaring at her commander, as though she'd predicted that he would not act. "Not by your standards. But I know. I know in my gut how my brother died."

Narian glanced at me, his eyes troubled. His second-in-command was not in her right mind.

"I will handle this," he told her.

Rava snatched a vase from atop my mantelpiece and hurled it to the floor. It exploded, spraying glass everywhere, and I muffled a shriek.

"You will handle it like a coward," she sneered. "You will investigate, and you will determine nothing, and you will keep the foul nature of this deed a secret. If this were *my* Hytanica, the murder of one of my own would not be overlooked. Cokyri is the controlling force in this province, and these Hytanican curs need to be reminded of that, once and for all."

Narian walked forward, kicking glass across the rug with the toe of his boot, halting when he stood face-to-face with her.

"This is not *your* Hytanica, Rava. I understand that Saadi was your brother and that you are grieving. Take time to do so. I will determine the cause of his death and what action should be taken."

The silence echoed with pain, then Rava nodded. "Very well, Commander. I will see to Saadi's burial. But he will not be given to the earth on Hytanican soil."

She turned on her heel and departed, leaving Narian and I to stare at one another, fully aware of the volatility of the situation. Whatever had happened to Saadi, there was no way this would resolve well.

"I'll look into it," Narian murmured, then he followed Rava out the door.

Though as Grand Provost, Saadi's death could easily have been my business, it became clear in one short evening that this was a Cokyrian affair. Rava's brother had been a high-ranking soldier—unusual for a man, to be sure, in their culture—and there were many hushed conversations about him in the Bastion. Cokyrian soldiers glowered at any Hytanican who drew near, including me, and I stayed out of the matter both due to a desire to show respect and to keep tension from escalating. If I had not known the investigation was in Narian's hands, I would have been afraid. The only positive aspect was that the matter was mostly a political issue, and so I went ahead with my plans for the Harvest Festival.

When I had concluded my duties for the day, I retired to my bedroom, anxiously awaiting Narian and whatever word he would bring on the alleged murder. I all but threw my book aside when he came through my window.

"Didn't like what the author had to say?" he said by way of greeting.

I motioned him over, impatient, and he removed his weapons belt before sitting on the bed across from me.

"I went with Rava to examine her brother's body."

Though this notion gave me chills, I didn't address it. "And?"

"No sword or dagger wounds. No wounds from any sort of weapon. He was either beaten brutally with fists or he fell from a significant height. Or he could have fallen from his horse and been dragged or kicked. From the bruises and the bones that were broken, the physicians think that he most likely fell, but they can't be certain."

This was a strange comfort to me, and I felt sick knowing that any attribute of Saadi's death could lift my spirits.

"Then we have to assume it was an accident," I forced myself to say.

"It looks that way, but Rava won't easily accept that explanation."

I frowned, imagining Narian's attempts to deal with her, and what Rava would be feeling—no closure, no reason, no justice. It was terrible.

"Is there anything we can do for her?" I asked.

Narian shrugged. "Tomorrow I'm going to interview everyone who was on duty when Saadi died, to see if I can trace his movements. Other than that, I don't think she wants anything from us, other than permission to transport his body to Cokyri. I am no friend of hers and neither are you. When the High Priestess is informed, she will offer Rava solace, and compensation for her brother's sacrifice."

"And until then?" The dim, flickering light of the lantern created an eerie atmosphere and seemed to finish my question: *Can we trust her?*

"Honestly?" Narian said, staring into my eyes and unintentionally increasing my foreboding. "I don't want to think about it."

"Well, then, is there anything I can do for you?"

His brow furrowed. "What do you mean?"

"From what I knew of Saadi, he was not only respected, but well-liked. And you would have known him better than I. You must feel his loss yourself."

"He was a good man." Narian stretched out on his back, and I tucked pillows underneath his head. "Saadi made it possible for me to believe that our goals were attainable, that Hytanicans and Cokyrians could come to understand one another and to cooperate with each other. His death, especially under suspicious circumstances, leaves me feeling defeated."

He put his arm around me, and I curled up at his side, and I could almost feel him becoming more introspective.

"In some ways, Alera," he quietly revealed, "I had more in common with Saadi than I did with any other Cokyrian stationed here."

"You know, we Hytanicans have a name for someone like Saadi. We would call him a friend."

"Interesting," Narian said, and I knew I had given him even more to think about.

"Are you tired?" I asked, aware that he could not sleep on his back.

"Not particularly."

"Good. Then I don't have to move."

He gave a soft laugh and kissed the top of my head.

"I will make any sacrifice for you," he murmured, letting me drift into sleep.

As usual, Narian was gone by the time I woke the next morning. I rose and dressed, then went to meet Cannan in his office, generally my first meeting of the day. As I descended the Grand Staircase, I was surprised to find him talking to Narian in the Grand Entry.

"Come," he said, as soon as his gaze fell on me. "We're needed in the Hearing Hall."

Without giving me a chance to reply, he led Narian and me through the antechamber and into the hall, where numerous Cokyrian soldiers milled. My eyes immediately went to the head of the room where Rava sat in one of the hearing chairs.

"Good of you to join us, Commander," she contemptuously greeted Narian as we walked forward. "I have gathered all the soldiers who were on duty or who had contact with my brother on the night of his death. It's starting to look like our Hytanican pranksters may have had something to do with his so-called accident."

My blood turned cold at her comment, and I felt Cannan stiffen beside me. Pranks were one thing, but there was no way Galen and Steldor would have beaten a Cokyrian officer to death—at least not without significant provocation.

"We shall see, Rava, but I will talk to the witnesses myself. You are, of course, welcome to stay, but I will be conducting this proceeding. Keep your thoughts to yourself and do not interrupt, or I will order you from the hall. Do you understand?"

"Yes, Commander."

"Alera, Cannan, since this may implicate certain Hytanican citizens, you may wish to stay, as well."

We nodded and I moved to sit in the other hearing chair, Cannan standing nearby. I knew from the daily reports that Saadi had provided to me that the Cokyrians generally had reliable proof before imposing their brand of swift, sure and often horrific punishment. Still, I didn't want any determinations in this case to turn on Rava's judgments.

As Narian questioned everyone from the guards stationed at the officer's barracks to those patrolling the streets of the Market District, one thing became quite apparent—Saadi had spent a good part of the night in the company of a young Hytanican woman. While no one had a name or a very good description, the possibility existed that this girl may have led Saadi into a trap and to his death.

Cannan sat quietly, calmly, while fear and anxiety made me feel alternately hot and cold. I knew Shaselle and Saadi were acquainted, for he had brought her to us when she had been caught with an illegal dagger. Could she be the girl in question? Could she have had some involvement in Saadi's death? While I did not want to believe it, this investigation was turning into a nightmare.

Having gathered as much information as he could from the Cokyrian soldiers, Narian dismissed them, then he turned to Rava.

"I will see if I can find this Hytanican girl, but you are to stay out of it. We need to know the truth before any conclusions can be drawn as to whether Saadi's death was accidental or some sort of ambush. But until we know the truth, no action is to be taken against any Hytanican. Is that clear?"

Rava defiantly met his eyes, but did not respond.

"Is that clear, Rava?" he more forcefully asked.

"Yes, Commander, I will await your determination."

"Good. You may leave."

We watched her walk toward her office at the opposite

end of the Hearing Hall, and then Narian turned to Cannan and me.

"We need to talk—your office, Alera."

The three of us silently entered my study, Narian closing the door. Then he asked the question that was lurking in all of our minds.

"Could your niece be involved in this, Cannan?"

"Involved? I don't think so. I know of no relationship between them. But even if she were with Saadi that evening, I don't think she could have played a part in his death. Shaselle doesn't have it within her to deliberately hurt someone."

"What about Steldor and Galen? Could they have been involved?"

The captain shook his head. "No, of that I'm certain."

"Very well," Narian replied, surprisingly willing to accept Cannan's answer, and I wondered what was transpiring between them beneath the surface. It felt as though they were realigning themselves, almost *allying* themselves. "I'll need to talk to Shaselle. But not here, not in the Bastion."

The captain hesitated for a moment, seeming to take Narian's measure.

"Let me talk to her," he finally said. "I give you my word that I will report to you whatever I learn."

"Even if it implicates her or some other member of your family?"

"Even then. I will bring you the truth."

The two men locked eyes and Narian nodded, choosing to trust the captain. Despite the dreadful circumstances in which we found ourselves, this was good progress.

CHAPTER 26

BLACK BILE

AFTER A TIME, I COULDN'T CRY ANYMORE, BUT still I lay in my bed. Cannan had brought me home, thinking my mother would be better able to tend to me, but my ailment was not one she could heal. I lay still, staring at my window, trying not to move, trying not to blink. Sometimes I would hold my arms close to my body and pretend I was frozen; sometimes I felt so cold that I was certain I was. Then my mother or Dahnath would step into the room and try to talk to me. But I had no voice. Not knowing what was wrong with me, they kept the younger children away, afraid I had fallen seriously ill.

I *was* ill. I was sick in my heart, in my gut, in my conscience. Maybe if I'd climbed down after Saadi, I could have gotten help for him. Maybe if I'd refused to bring him to my house, he never would have professed to love me, and I never would have told him about the weapons. Maybe if I'd said no to the wine, he would have neglected to drink as well, and he would not have lost his balance. Maybe if I'd listened to instinct, I would have stayed away from him altogether, and he would still be alive, and he would not even know who I was. Yes, that would have been best.

More than anything, I was terrified. I was terrified that someone would discover my secret, that the soldier we'd encountered on the street would remember I had been with Saadi that night and identify me to Rava. I was terrified of my own mortality, of the idea that I had been more inebriated than Saadi when we'd been climbing the tree. I was terrified that if I kept this to myself, I would be damned to hell, and I was terrified over my lie to Cannan about what had happened—Saadi had not brought this on himself. I had invited him to his death.

Strangest of all was that Saadi was gone. There was no warning when it came to death, there was no going back, there was no chance for one last conversation.

He had told me he was fine. At that thought, dry sobs racked me, making my throat ache. This was the worst kind of grief—my eyes had no more tears to shed, my body had no more energy to cry, and yet the urge to do so persisted. Why had he said he was fine? To protect me? He had dragged his broken body as far from my property as he could, probably to keep anyone from connecting me with what had happened. He must have known he was dying; he'd certainly known he was grievously injured. Yet he hadn't told me. Was it because he'd loved me?

I hadn't been in love with him. I knew that. But I could have been. I truly believed I would have been, eventually. A course that would have led to misery in the end, for Cannan never would have sanctioned a marriage between us. I would have been left heartbroken, and would always have yearned for him, wondering what type of life we might have had, Saadi and me together. The same sort of pain I was feeling now.

But at least he would have been alive. If one of us was to die, it should have been me.

These thoughts spun round and round in my head, sometimes in a different order, but always the same. I knew nothing but the torture of my own mind.

The door opened, but I did not look. I never looked. My mother came around the bed and pulled up a chair to sit beside me, blocking my view of the window.

"Shaselle," she said, reaching out a hand to push back my unkempt hair. "Shaselle."

I stared at her with no alertness in my eyes.

"Love, please talk to me. Please say something."

I clenched my teeth, feeling hot tears burning the corners of my eyes.

"I need to see the window," I choked out, and it was enough to send those tears streaming down into my pillow.

My mother leaned closer to soothe me, moisture glistening on her own cheeks. "Don't cry. No, don't cry, darling. Just tell me what's wrong."

Clutching the underside of the pillow, I turned my face into it. How could I tell her? She stroked the back of my head, not minding my dirty tresses, eventually moving her hand down to rub my back.

"Shaselle, you know you're safe here. Please tell me, are you ill?" She hesitated then pressed, "Did something happen?"

Her voice told me that she was afraid of the answer she might receive. I knew in that moment that I could never tell her what was wrong. It would hurt her. I couldn't let her know that I'd been spending time with a Cokyrian, and I certainly couldn't let her know that I was responsible for his death. And I couldn't tell her of the weapons. I'd broken my vow of silence once, and was not about to do so again.

I shook my head back and forth, my face still buried in the

pillow, wondering if it would be possible to suffocate myself. She sighed, then stood and departed. After an hour or so, she returned with a bowl of soup, which she left on the side table. I didn't touch it.

Night fell, the best and worst time to be alone. The best because at long last, the city and my household slumbered— no one was thinking of me, no one was suspecting me, no one tried to talk to me about what had occurred. The worst time because the darkness of the world melded with the darkness of my nightmares, and I felt I was losing my mind, myself, my very soul.

I dozed in and out of awareness until the sun rose once more, the day crisp and clear. As I studied the bit of sky I could see through the window, sounds from the hallway infiltrated my gloom—the shuffling of footsteps, my mother's voice and that of a man, the creak of the door as it opened.

My visitors entered and stepped around to my side of the bed, three in number. I had only heard one man, but there were two. I shouldn't have been surprised—Galen had brought Bhadran, physician to the royal family, known to be the best doctor in the kingdom, no doubt at Cannan's instruction.

My mother and Galen stood together in the background while Bhadran took the chair next to the bed that she had vacated. I watched him despondently. Why did everyone insist on blocking the window? I needed to see the window.

"Good morning, Shaselle," Bhadran greeted me. "Will you permit me to examine you?"

I didn't bother answering. Doing so would have expended energy I did not have, and his question was posed out of politeness. He would examine me regardless of my response. After a moment, he lifted my wrist, feeling for my pulse.

"Well, you're alive," he joked, then he spoke to my mother and Galen. "A good, strong heartbeat."

My mother pressed her palms together in an attitude of prayer, apparently having entertained the possibility that I was dying.

"No fever," Bhadran next pronounced, removing his hand from my forehead. He lifted the blankets, checking the skin of my arms, legs, abdomen and back. "No rashes or injuries, either."

His voice had grown puzzled, and he considered me with a crease in his brow.

"Shaselle, do you remember being around anyone of late who's been ill?"

I shook my head, knowing the silent reply could be interpreted more than one way, but feeling too dreary to care.

"Has she been vomiting?" the doctor asked my mother.

"She did once, a few days ago. Not since then. But she hasn't eaten much, either."

"I see." Bhadran pondered me for a second time, and then stood. "I cannot name her ailment definitively since she exhibits so few symptoms. However, the indifference, the sadness and lethargy, the lack of appetite…they would seem to suggest Melancholia. It afflicts young women in particular come the fall of the year. That is, cases are rare in the spring and summer. Has your daughter shown a tendency toward Melancholia in the past?"

"No," my mother whispered, her eyes wide and glistening. "But it's…it's the first fall since Baelic's death."

There was a pause. "I'm sorry for your loss, Lady Lania. I should have remembered that your husband was Cannan's brother."

The doctor turned again to me, and Galen placed a comforting arm around Mother's waist.

"What can be done to treat her?" the young man asked.

"Bloodletting would only aggravate the problem, I'm afraid.

Her humors are unbalanced—she needs more warmth and moisture. Soup, baths, lotions, hot water bottles in her bed, a fire in the hearth day and night. There is no medicinal cure I can offer. The black bile must simply run its course."

My mother gasped, trying not to cry. "She will recover... she will survive, won't she?"

"She will if she wants to."

"I don't have Melancholia," I whispered, my voice hoarse. How dare this doctor make my mother worry I might die.

"Then what do you believe you have?" Bhadran inquired, surprised I had spoken.

I did not have a disease, mental or physical. I was tired, and I was sad, and I was coping.

"You should leave now. I don't need a doctor."

The gathered adults looked at one another uncertainly, then Bhadran opened his mouth to say something else to me.

"Please!" I repeated, more insistently.

He handled my strange behavior well, stepping backward and raising his hands in a gesture of surrender.

"Think about what I said," he murmured to my mother, then he left the room.

"Shaselle," my mother breathed. "What is going on with you?"

Galen took her arm, whispered something to her and led her to the door. I heard it close, and thought perhaps I was alone again, but boots scraped against the wooden floor. Galen came to sit in the chair beside my bed, observing me with his soft brown eyes, his demeanor an odd mixture of concern and a reprimand. Feeling uncomfortable, I started to roll away from him, away from the window, but he grasped my shoulder, holding me in place.

"Shaselle, stop. Just stop, please."

I complied, though I wasn't sure why I was obeying him.

"Cannan sent me when Lania asked for a doctor. He had me bring Bhadran, but doesn't believe you're sick. He thought you might talk to me. I don't know if you want to or not, but for starters you don't have to *explain* anything to me. I know you feel responsible for what that Cokyrian found out, and that's something you couldn't tell your mother. But Shaselle, everyone is worried about you. And *no one* blames you."

"I blame me," I whimpered.

"For what? Cannan says he followed you, spied on you and died by an accident. Where is any of that your fault? Is it because you feel you shouldn't have been looking at the weapons?" Galen hesitated, then gently pressed, "Or is it because that's not how it happened at all?"

I wasn't going to cry again. But he was so close, so close to figuring it out. I couldn't let him, and yet I wanted him to know.

"Don't tell," I sobbed. "You mustn't tell anyone, Galen."

"I won't tell anyone unless absolutely necessary," he promised, leaning close to kiss me on the cheek. "And I certainly won't tell your mother."

"I told him about the weapons," I confessed, my voice embarrassingly high-pitched. "He didn't follow me—I was with him, by choice. He was in the house with me, and I told him, then I tried to stop him from leaving, and...and he fell."

"He fell? Shaselle, was he here...in your room?"

I nodded, the words coming more easily now that I was through the worst of my admissions.

"We climbed in through my window, and we drank some wine, and when he tried to leave, he fell."

Galen said nothing, but his expression shifted as quickly as the waters of the Recorah River, through shock, disappointment, sympathy, dismay.

"Shaselle, I... My God."

"It was a mistake!" I wailed, writhing like someone demon possessed and shocking him to his feet. "Can't God forgive a mistake? Why can't he... God..."

I collapsed, limp and lifeless on the bed, certain the only thing keeping me alive was the anguish festering in my gut. Then Galen sat on the bed beside me and pulled me into his embrace.

"It's not your fault," he said again and again, holding me close. "It's not your fault."

I lay quivering against him, thankful to be in his arms, though some part of me felt that even his comfort was more than I deserved.

"There was nothing you could have done to help him, Shaselle. If you had called for Cokyrian aid, you would have put yourself in danger. Even he knew that. This is hard to accept, harder to accept than blame, in fact, but sometimes things just happen."

I wanted to believe him. But even if I could not, at least I was no longer alone, dragged down by a whirlpool of guilt. My head had broken the water's surface, and I could breathe.

After a while I quieted, and Galen released me, but he did not leave.

"I have to tell Cannan what you've told me," he said, stroking my hair. "Narian is investigating the officer's death, and we cannot let him come to the wrong conclusion."

I gazed at him, fear clutching at my heart.

"Don't worry. Cannan won't let anything happen to you, and Narian is reasonable—he will recognize it as an accident."

I nodded stiffly and closed my eyes. Galen was probably right; and if he wasn't, I'd receive the punishment my conscience told me I deserved.

After Galen left, I ate the soup my mother brought, then I rose from bed for the first time in a week. I went to my wardrobe, feeling woozy and frail, but I was resolved. I abandoned my nightdress, put on breeches and a shirt, pulled back my disgusting hair, then crawled shakily out onto the limb. My boots scraped against the oak tree during my descent, for I clung especially tightly to the branches and trunk. At last reaching the ground, I surveyed the place where Saadi's body had been broken.

When I could stand it no longer, I wiped my eyes and nose on my sleeve and headed for the barn, using the back door to access King's private stall. The proud, vibrant animal had been fed and was restless, ready for exercise. I snatched a bit of hay from the aisle floor and held out my palm so he would let me rub his soft neck. I would always remember Papa when I looked at him. Now he would also be a way for me to remember Saadi.

I left King and went outside to sit against the front wall of the barn, sheltered by the roof's overhang. It was there that my mother found me. Though she was surprised to discover I was out of bed, she was also relieved that I had seemingly come back to life. No matter how acutely I hurt, I was on the mend.

CHAPTER 27

NO DIPLOMAT

I WOKE ON MY BACK WITH NARIAN'S ARM draped across my waist, aware that we had slept later than usual. What time was it? Late enough that the sun was fighting through the gaps in my drapes; late enough that someone was pounding on my parlor door.

I jolted upright, startling Narian into wakefulness. He was on his feet before he had gotten his bearings, and he looked amusingly disoriented until he realized where he was, that he had overslept and that someone wanted to see me.

He snatched up his weapons belt and flew to the window, giving me a nod before vanishing through the opening, crawling upward using the rope he'd left hanging. He would go over the roof and return to his own quarters to avoid being caught in mine. Once he had departed, I threw on a robe, then crossed the parlor, unsettled that whoever was in the corridor was still pounding. In my experience, unexpected visitors tended to herald trouble, and my thoughts immediately went to the investigation of Saadi's death. I opened the door and my eyes fell on Cannan.

"Get dressed, quickly," he said with no overture. "We're needed in the Central Courtyard."

Too alarmed to press him for an explanation, I hastily complied.

We met Narian at the top of the Grand Staircase, and I exchanged a nervous glance with him during our descent to the first floor, for angry shouts once more penetrated the Bastion walls. The captain led us through the double oak doors and into the Central Courtyard, where a shockingly large crowd was gathered beyond the gates. We hurried down the white walk, my attention gradually shifting to a group of people standing on top of the courtyard wall—Rava and a dozen Cokyrian soldiers.

Rava swaggered back and forth before the crowd, half of her soldiers threatening the people below with whips and drawn swords, warning against attempts to set up a ladder or otherwise try to reach them. But four women under Rava's command stood still, each holding a cloaked and hooded charge in front of them.

I covered my mouth in horror, not knowing what Rava was doing, but well aware of her propensity to be cruel. My eyes flashed to the guard towers at the corners of the courtyard wall, and my stomach lurched, for the ladders had been pulled into the towers. Rava turned her head as the people called out to me, her smile disquieting, for it was not friendly or welcoming. Then she was done with me, shifting her gaze to the citizenry.

"Three nights ago saw the death of a Cokyrian soldier at Hytanican hands," she proclaimed to grumblings among the crowd, a few gasps and a few unsympathetic shouts. "He was my brother and I have no doubt that he suffered greatly in passing. Those who should by rights answer for his murder have been too cowardly to come forward. They may never answer for their crime, but to my mind, a dog is a dog. I will show all of you miserable whelps what your brave and daring fellows accomplished."

"Rava," Narian shouted. "Release those people and report to me at once."

"Not today, Commander," she sneered. "When you fail to carry out your duties, they fall on me. When you are too weak to do what must be done, then the task becomes mine."

She turned from him to glower down at the crowd, and Narian left my side, heading back toward the Bastion. Swallowing the lump of fear in my throat, I watched as Rava stepped up to put a hand on the shoulder of the first bound Hytanican. The man jerked, and the crowd quieted, strained faces fixed as one on her.

"Your religious book in this *kingdom*," she proclaimed, "decrees 'an eye for an eye.'" She let her words reverberate in the chill air, her hand gripping the cloak of her prey. "My brother will see no more."

She yanked off the man's hood, and screams and shouts erupted from the audience. My stomach wrenched and Cannan grasped my arm to steady me, his jaw tight, for where the man's eyes had been there were now bloody, gaping holes.

Rava, enjoying the reaction she had elicited, strutted to the side of the second captive.

"Your *wise* Bible says 'a tooth for a tooth.' My brother will never again savor food or conversation."

I knew what would come when she ripped back the hood of the second man, but could not stop myself from looking. To yet more shrieks, the man moaned, his empty mouth hanging open, thick red blood oozing from his gums.

Desperately, I cast about, searching for Narian, wanting him to put an end to this by whatever means necessary. It wasn't until Rava approached the third prisoner that I saw him drop down from the roof of the Bastion onto the court-yard wall where it met the building. While others struggled against Rava's faithful servants in an effort to raise ladders, Narian was coming from behind.

The third prisoner cringed when Rava laid a hand on his shoulder, and even from where I stood, I could see him trembling.

"'A hand for a hand,' your church preaches. My brother will never hold sword nor flower again." She pulled back this captive's hood, then loosed the tie of the cloak about his shoulders, letting it fall to the ground. Grabbing his wrists, she raised his arms to show red-stained bandages covering stumps where his hands had been, and I fought down a surge of vomit.

"Most significantly," Rava preached, with a smirk that sent a shiver through me, "your religion demands a life for a life. My brother's life is over."

With a quick tug, Rava uncloaked the last captive, the smallest of the four, revealing not another man but a young woman. Now frantic, the crowd protested loudly, and I prayed Narian would hurry. But there was no way he could be fast enough—her people were loyal, hindering his approach, and he would not use his powers, whether they knew it or not. The last thing he wanted to be was like the Overlord.

Rava stepped behind the girl, who was quivering and crying, and put her hands on either side of her victim's head, preparing to snap her neck.

"Rava," Cannan abruptly called, stepping forward. "Let her go and I will tell you who is responsible for your brother's death."

"You have already lied, claiming it was an accident. Why should I believe you now?" Her voice was a snarl, and she did not remove her hands from the quaking girl.

"I know everything that involves my men. And I wanted

to protect my son, but now I see that he will have to protect himself."

Narian was moving past the last Cokyrian soldier who stood between him and Rava—the loyalty of her underlings extended to getting in his way, but not to a clash of arms, for such an offense was punishable by death. I held my breath, praying Rava would be too distracted by Cannan to notice Narian's approach.

"So you will admit your son played a part in my brother's death?"

Before Cannan could answer, Narian drew his long, thin sword and extended it to touch the soft skin of Rava's neck, and the girl crumpled to the stone of the walkway, sobbing. I was so relieved that I almost broke into sobs myself, and was thankful when Cannan supported me with an arm around my waist.

On our side of the gate, within the courtyard, ladders were now being successfully placed, and other Cokyrians climbed up at Narian's command, taking the offenders into custody and helping the Hytanicans to the ground.

"Send for a doctor and find their families," Narian ordered, then he fixed his steely eyes on Rava.

Frighteningly nonchalant in the face of a sword at her throat, Rava said, "Is there a problem, Commander? I merely did what you couldn't. We now know the truth about my brother's death." Her voice became low and menacing. "You should thank me."

"What we know is that Cannan will gamble his innocent son's life to prevent the murder of others."

Removing his sword from her throat, Narian thrust her toward his soldiers.

"Take her," he snarled, and they snatched her arms, securing them behind her back with shackles. "To the dungeon."

As his troops obeyed, Narian dropped his sword upon the stone wall, then walked along it to the gate, a number of gratified shouts greeting his actions. He jumped to the ground, landing on bended knee, too agitated to notice the startling support he was receiving from the Hytanicans. Without a word, he marched back into the Bastion, leaving me and the rest of our party to follow.

I gained respect for the Cokyrian officers in the Bastion when not one of them spoke up in Rava's defense after she and her accomplices were thrown in the dungeon. Even they recognized the brutality of what she had done. This like-minded attitude was a great help to Narian as he went about the task of making amends with the Hytanican people, who seemed to be holding back their outrage as they waited to learn of Rava's punishment. It was strange—Narian's stand against one of his own had created an uneasy truce between him and the Hytanican people.

The High Priestess had seized the royal treasures at the time of the takeover, granting Narian and me a certain sum of money to use in encouraging cooperation and lifting morale. To a large extent, this money was funding the upcoming festival, but we removed an additional sum to divide between the families Rava had wronged. Men with no hands and no eyes could not work, and a man with no teeth could not eat as he once had. It was our duty to comfort these people in the only way we could—with words and funds. I wrote condolences to each family, which were sent with the money in my name and Narian's—Narian's to help bridge the gap between Cokyrian and Hytanican, and mine to make sure the payments would not be rejected.

Two of Narian's officers were assigned to deliver the packages, and though they saw the necessity of taking this action,

I was thankful when Cannan offered to accompany them. The people needed a show of unity in compassion and regret.

The next day, my thoughts returned to the Harvest Festival. Following what had happened, would a celebration seem disrespectful? And Rava's concern that the event would give the people an opportunity to join forces was no longer dismissible. They were agitated, and certainly some among them would be seeking to avenge those who had been maimed. I didn't want more deaths to result.

I brought my fears to Narian, catching him in the Grand Entry, and was not surprised to learn he had also been considering the issue.

"Despite the risk, I don't think it would be wise to cancel the festival," he said, and would have left it at that had I not pursued a justification. "The Hytanicans are on edge, but there are still several days until the event. Word of the compensation we provided will spread, tempers will cool and excitement over the festival will set in. If we shut down the celebration, the people will feel twice wronged, and I'll again be the most hated individual in the province. I'm the one they will blame."

Narian was accustomed—as accustomed as one could be—to being disliked, but he didn't want to lose the small bit of progress we had made toward redeeming his character. I wondered if this was in part because our marriage hung in the balance.

We were interrupted by sounds of a trumpet fanfare, and turned to stare at the door in confusion. There was no royalty outside, no one to be announced. Cannan stepped out of his office, drawn by the commotion, and we all three hit on the reason at the same time.

"The High Priestess!"

"Why is she here?" I asked, my heart beating erratically. But there was no time for Narian to reply, for the doors swung wide and the Cokyrian leader entered, surrounded by five shield maidens and an entourage of heralds.

The High Priestess waved off the criers and trumpeters—I could not imagine they were to her liking. It was Hytanican custom to make a show of a ruler's arrival or departure; Cokyrians preferred stealth in all matters.

"Narian. Alera. Cannan." She walked forward, removing the black riding gloves she was wearing. "How gracious of you to meet me."

She scanned the quickly amassing crowd, all of whom bowed, and I knew she had already noted an absence. "Where is Rava?"

"Not here, for the moment," Narian said smoothly.

I glanced at him, not sure that lying to the High Priestess was prudent, realizing a second too late that her highly observant eyes would catch my movement.

"There is something you aren't telling me, Narian."

"Yes, but this is not the time or place to discuss it."

The High Priestess's sharp green eyes narrowed. "This is the time, but we will move to a more appropriate location." She gestured to the antechamber doors. "Alera, you will come, as well."

Narian led us through the antechamber and across the Hearing Hall, Cannan remaining behind. But instead of taking us to his office in the Cokyrian command center, Narian escorted us to my study, thereby minimizing the possibility that someone might overhear. Before entering, Nantilam took a moment to instruct the shield maidens who had accompanied her to prepare accommodations, then she crossed the threshold, closing the door behind her. She looked suspiciously between Narian and me, and I went behind my desk, consciously mimicking what Cannan always did. I also wanted to put distance between myself and Nantilam, for her eyes seemed to pierce my flesh. Narian, on the other hand, went to stand directly in front of her.

"We weren't expecting you," he admonished boldly. Having grown up a member of a royal family, I winced, knowing if anyone had addressed my father, the King, in such a manner, great offense would have been taken, followed by great retribution.

"That much is apparent," Nantilam responded, her words clipped. "I ask you once more, where is Rava?"

"In the dungeon."

"*What?*" Nantilam was shocked—of all the answers she might have postulated, this was the most outlandish. She dropped her riding gloves on the seat of an armchair before the fireplace, then crossed her arms, her icy expression suggesting that Narian and I might trade places with Rava if we did not have a good rationale.

"Narian, I grant you many privileges as the commander of my army, but imprisoning the shield maiden I have placed as your second is *not* among them."

She was patronizing him, and he glared at her. "Unless I gravely misjudge you, Rava was never granted the privilege of arbitrarily torturing and murdering Hytanican citizens."

Nantilam scrutinized him, trying to determine if his judgment of Rava's actions was skewed by his loyalty to me.

"My party was intercepted by a messenger during our journey to the province," she said testily. "She brought news of Saadi's death. I don't know what transgression Rava committed which, in your eyes, makes her deserving of punishment, but this is not how she should be treated during her time of grief."

"Then you had best remove her to Cokyri. I won't release her here."

The High Priestess was not amused by Narian's response,

and she approached him, her lips compressed into a thin line. Laying a hand against the side of his head, she grasped a handful of his hair.

"That is for me to decide," she said, her voice dangerously soft.

Narian pushed her hand away, and she raised a displeased eyebrow. Feeling like an intruder, I racked my brain for a way to leave, for the sake of my own comfort.

"Your party was intercepted?" I asked, reminding Nantilam of my presence. "Then you were traveling here for some other reason?"

"Yes," she said, shifting her focus to me, her tone rounding into the rich, controlled cadence of a ruler. "Rava sent word to me about the festival you are hosting."

Now I wished I had not spoken. I looked to Narian for help, but he offered none, perhaps could offer none. Still, the issue needed to be addressed at some point, and she didn't sound angry.

"Yes, I am reinstating, on a smaller scale, Hytanica's annual Harvest Festival."

"Rava wished me to put a stop to it, but I see no need to do so. I believe, along with you, that it will lift the people's spirits. But I share Rava's concerns about rebellion, and have come so that my presence may discourage such foolishness."

"Your presence is most welcome," I said, relieved that she did not intend to interfere with my plans. "I'm glad you thought to come."

"Thank you, Alera," she said, bestowing a slight smile on me as though making a point to Narian about his rudeness. She turned on her heel to go, picking up her gloves as she did so. Just before she stepped into the Hearing Hall, she spoke once more to her commander.

"Narian, you will release Rava at once and escort her to my rooms."

"I won't," he said, a simple, firm refusal.

A simple, firm refusal that merited a significant reaction. The High Priestess closed the door again and stood facing it for a long moment, then she turned toward us, her quiet anger heating the room.

"You will, Narian."

"You haven't even asked after Rava's crimes. I will not release her, and if I see her free within the Bastion, I will *personally* return her to the dungeon."

"Tell me, then, what she's done. Justify your defiance if you can."

I foresaw this battle between them growing lengthy, for neither of them was disposed on principle to give ground.

"I'll tell you of her crimes," I said, perhaps imprudently, but instinctively knowing that it would be best if I gave answer.

The High Priestess's brows drew together in irritation— I was not the person from whom she wanted to hear. But when neither she nor Narian spoke, I took the opportunity and forged ahead.

"Release Rava, and I guarantee she will not last long on the streets of this city. Whether you see it as punishment or protection, your shield maiden belongs in that dungeon cell. What she did to my people in retaliation for her brother's death was neither fair nor justified. It was cruel, inhuman, archaic vengeance that has no place in a civilized land. Saadi's death was never proven to be anything but an accident, yet she seized four innocent Hytanicans, mutilating three—the fourth she would have killed if Narian had not stopped her. At best, her presence here has been endured. Now she is hated openly. I believe that the *only* course of action, not merely the best course, is to remove her from Hytanica."

There was utter silence, the benevolence toward me that I had seen in the High Priestess's green eyes replaced by outrage, perhaps due to my outspokenness, perhaps due to Rava's brutal actions. Nantilam had a heart, and it was the cause of her defense of Rava; but it was also what had prompted her to end her brother's life. Like me, she did not crave or abide violence, although she would not hesitate to use force if she viewed it as necessary.

"Narian, are you confident in your ability to oversee the festivities?" she queried, her gaze never leaving my face.

"Yes," he answered, though he was no more certain than I.

"Then I shall depart, with Rava, in the morning. We will take Saadi's body to Cokyri for burial. I shall leave one of my shield maidens behind, Narian, to take up position as your second-in-command during Rava's absence. At the close of the festival, you will come to Cokyri and report. Understood?"

"Understood. But I think it would be better if you let me appoint a new second-in-command from among the officers who currently work with me. They have the advantage of familiarity with the province."

I knew from Narian's words that he had a person in mind, and that the officer would be someone he trusted, not just someone the High Priestess trusted.

"We can discuss that on the morrow," she decreed, showing no reaction. "I bid the two of you good-night."

She exited, leaving Narian and I to wonder how we had escaped her wrath. Nantilam was a woman of great pride, but from what I had learned about her over the past few years, she chose her battles carefully, and she made certain to win them.

"She is not happy," Narian declared, in answer to my unspoken question, his words perhaps the largest understatement I had ever heard.

CHAPTER 28

WELL AS WELL

I WAS IN A BATTLE AGAINST MYSELF. I ENVISIONED a warrior in my head, a warrior fighting a snake, both wearing my face. One side of me wanted to be strong, to let go of Saadi and my regret, and the other side maintained that everything that had happened was my fault. Both sides were united, however, by grief. My family was overly solicitous toward me, believing me to be recovering from an illness, trying to please me and keep me happy. While I appreciated their efforts, they unwittingly added to my guilt.

Cannan had come to see me in the aftermath of Rava's brutal actions, wanting to assure me that Narian had decreed Saadi's death to be an accident. Rava alone was responsible for what happened after that, he told me, for no one could have made her accept the commander's conclusion. Her interest had not been in finding the truth, only in revenge. I wanted to believe him, but could not banish the ache in my heart.

The extent of Cannan's desire to pull me back into the world became known a few days later when Steldor paid us a visit, this time bringing word that he was to escort me to Lord

Landru's estate for a casual lunch with Grayden. My mother was shocked, but pleased.

"Lord Grayden wants to see her again?"

"Indeed," Steldor replied with a furtive smirk for me. "In two hours' time. The young man was quite insistent."

"How is that possible?" I asked, trying not to sound disappointed.

Mother frowned at me, and I dropped the subject, for Grayden was still a sore point between us.

"Dahnath, take your sister upstairs and assist her to prepare. A casual lunch, you said?"

Steldor nodded, and Dahnath took my arm, leading me up the steps past Celdrid, who was bounding down in long sleeves, carrying his boots.

Mother caught him with an arm around his chest at the foot of the stairs. "Coat!"

"Mama, this shirt is *warm*. We're going to be riding anyway!"

"Ah, even soldiers need coats," Steldor said, winking at my mother. "Soldiers also put their boots on *before* leaving the house."

Celdrid grinned, then ran back up the stairs past Dahnath and me, for my sister was insisting that we proceed at a ladylike pace.

I didn't even have the energy to run Dahnath in circles as she sorted through my wardrobe, trying her best to elicit opinions from me on the gown I would wear and how I wanted to style my hair. Usually, I would have enjoyed driving her crazy. In the end, I settled on a green gown that complemented my hazel eyes. I didn't want my garb to be dubbed "distinctive" on the chance that Lord Landru would be in attendance at the luncheon.

Steldor and my brother returned from their ride just be-

fore Dahnath was done with me, giving him time to clean up
before readying a buggy. He came to the door to fetch me,
bowing and kissing my hand, succeeding in the impossible—
he was making me feel beautiful. It came to me then why he
had been the one to reach Celdrid through his sorrow. Steldor
had Papa's charm, and now he was using it on me.

He let me sit on the front bench seat with him, which was
not strictly proper, and we drove through the western residential section, across the thoroughfare and into the eastern
section of manor houses. During the drive, I caught Steldor
looking at me once or twice, which confirmed that Galen
had shared my confession with his best friend as well as with
Cannan. This didn't really bother me, for they often seemed
to be a single person. But I made an effort to talk with him
to allay his worry, knowing full well that I was wasting energy I should be saving for Grayden.

Steldor brought the buggy to a halt in front of Lord Landru's home, and I thought of the earlier visit I had made to
this estate to apologize to the young man. Despite that and
everything else, he *still* wanted to see me. This was incom-
prehensible, and worry nipped at me as to what the luncheon
would entail.

After handing the reins off to a servant, Steldor lifted me
down from the buggy and we approached the front door.
He gave me a reassuring smile just before he knocked, having picked up on my rising anxiety. Grayden answered, and I
wondered if it were a habit of his to stand in for their butler.

"Lady Shaselle," the slender young man said, bowing at the
waist, and I curtseyed politely in return.

Steldor had been assigned the task of chaperone, and he thus
followed when Grayden took my hand and led me through
the impressive house to the sunroom, where a small table was
adorned with a cloth and plates. Grayden pulled my chair out

for me, waiting for me to sit before he moved to his own place. There was a third chair for Steldor, but he showed more interest in the comfortable settee by the window.

"I'm not overly concerned about your conduct," Steldor said when Grayden inquired if he would be joining us for lunch. "I have every confidence in Shaselle's ability to scream if you upset her."

Grayden was not sure how to take this, but I couldn't quite stifle a laugh at my cousin's humor. Steldor picked up a book from the side table and settled down on the settee, prepared to ignore us and his vital duty for the next hour or two—or however long this would take.

Servants entered with soup and bread, no doubt delicious, but neither Grayden nor I had much of an appetite. We didn't speak, either. This, ironically, Steldor found interesting. His eyes flicked to me several times during the meal, and he made no effort to hide his mirth.

Finally, my suitor managed to ask, "How have you been?"

"Well."

The awful silence recommenced, and I started counting the seconds, hoping Steldor would interrupt and take me home. He didn't; he was enjoying our plight.

"How h-have *you* been?" I stuttered.

"Oh, I've been well, as well."

I laughed. "'Well, as well.' How very…articulate."

I paled, for he could consider my comment an insult. I needed to win him over in a hurry if I were to salvage our time together.

Grayden chuckled, rescuing me from embarrassment. "I thought I heard your uncle say that you have been ill. Is that true?"

And here I thought the situation could not get any more awkward.

"My uncle is an honest man," I said, trying to dodge the topic.

"Of course! I certainly didn't mean to imply otherwise."

"And I didn't mean to imply that you meant to imply... anything."

We stared at each other, and I could see that Grayden was on the verge of laughing. I probably would have laughed myself, but the spatter of freckles across his nose forced me to look down at my napkin. My eyes welled at the powerful recollections sweeping through me, and at the images of handsome, strong, charismatic Saadi that rose unbidden in my mind.

"Are you all right?" Grayden asked.

I raised my gaze to his and forced my tone to brighten. "Yes, I'm sorry, just a speck of dust in my eye."

"I understand. Perhaps some fresh air would help." He was unexpectedly astute, but at least was not asking any more questions. He glanced at Steldor, who motioned us from the room with but one piece of advice for me.

"You'll have to scream more loudly from out there."

Grayden escorted me into the corridor and through a back door that I anticipated would open upon a garden. But what I saw instead was my version of Eden—a row of paddocks beside a large stable, all filled with beautiful horses.

"I'm afraid it's not exactly fresh air," Grayden jested, walking to lean against the nearest fence, leaving me to follow.

"It's fresh enough."

I gaped at the well-bred animals, not even aware of Grayden's eyes on me.

"Your uncle told me of your love for horses, Shaselle," he said, startling me out of my trance.

"Do the Cokyrians know about them?" I inquired, hoping to discourage him from a reprimand like the one Taether had seen fit to provide.

"They've taken a few, but we were able to hide our best."

"How very fortunate."

My eyes roved over each and every one of the horses, approximating their age and probable stage in training, assessing their form and temperament and noting their reproductive potential. Eventually it dawned on me that silence had fallen. I turned toward Grayden to offer some excuse, but to my surprise, he was gazing at me with affection and sympathy in his green eyes. He smiled and produced a small box, which he extended to me.

"What's this?" I asked, thoroughly confused.

He shrugged. "A token of friendship. I would be honored if you would accept it."

Curiously, I took the box from his hand. Anticipating jewelry, I prepared for a show of fake enthusiasm. Such a gift would be a sweet gesture, and undoubtedly beautiful, but I was not one for baubles.

The box did contain jewelry, but not of the type I supposed. On a lovely chain of gold hung a small, golden horse, head high, legs outstretched in a gallop. I looked at Grayden, stupefied, although I didn't need to feign my pleasure.

"As I said, your uncle told me of your love for horses," he explained almost shyly. "That it was a love you shared with your father."

"But I...I don't understand. What are you...?"

Seeing how flustered I was, he reached out and took my hand.

"I'm not asking for anything, Shaselle. I just... I think you're used to being seen as a problem. Maybe it's presumptuous of me to say that, but your family apologized for so many things about you that I can't help drawing the conclusion."

Not sure how to react, I opted to remain silent.

"I think you're only a problem for those people who are trying to turn you into something you're not."

"A lady?" I wryly suggested, regaining my sense of humor. I leaned back on the fence, certain he would agree.

"No," he said, and there was conviction in his voice. "They need to stop trying to turn a free spirit into a traditional wife."

I couldn't move, couldn't speak. Could he truly believe what he was saying? Men played games to placate women. But I knew of no man other than my father who would enjoy seeing a horse pendant around the neck of the woman he was courting.

"I do have a question for you," Grayden said, leaning against the fence next to me. He hesitated, obviously uncertain about where our relationship stood. "The Harvest Festival is approaching. If you have no other plans to attend, would you consider accompanying me?"

My eyes again filled with tears. There was no good reason—why should I be breaking down now, when Grayden was being so understanding, so tolerant of my eccentricities?

"Come," he said softly. "I'll take you back to your cousin."

I let him escort me into the house, feeling like an ungrateful fool. I hadn't even thanked him for his gift, and I desperately wanted to do so. But I couldn't conjure the words to convey how I was feeling, and so I murmured farewell at the door.

Just as he had before, Steldor glanced at me over and over again on our journey home, until I finally addressed his conduct.

"Really, Steldor, I know I'm in a fine dress, but I can't possibly look that different."

Since I had opened the conversation, he said what was on his mind. "Are you all right? You didn't seem…yourself…when we left Lord Landru's, although I never heard you scream."

For once, I didn't feel like I was lying when I said, "I'm all right, I truly am. In fact, I'm better than I've been in a long time."

"Well, judging from your conversation, you and Grayden are made for each other." I gave him a shove on the shoulder, and he laughed. "I don't suppose you noticed all the horses? I hear Grayden is very good with them. Although he might lack Baelic's way with people, I think he may have your father's way with horses."

"I did notice," I said with a smile, thinking it had turned into quite a beautiful day.

When we arrived at my house, Steldor escorted me to the front entry and came inside to bid a cheery "Good day" to my family. With a wink for me, he departed, closing the door to leave me in my mother's care.

"How was lunch?" she asked, watching me bound up the stairs.

"The soup was excellent," I called over my shoulder, knowing she wasn't inquiring about the food, but not yet ready to talk about Grayden. I hurried to my bedroom, forestalling further questions.

The moment I entered, my eyes went to the window across from me, and I sighed, my happiness seeming to leave my body along with my breath. I would never forget; this room would never let me forget. My only hope was that the nightmares would stop, someday, somehow. Perhaps the way to ensure they did was to replace them with dreams, good dreams of someone else. Moving to my writing desk, I took a piece of parchment, a quill and ink, and began to write.

My dear Lord Grayden, I have given your kind invitation thought, and would be honored to accompany you to the Harvest Festival. Perhaps we shall even make it into an adventure. Looking forward to seeing you again, Lady Shaselle.

CHAPTER 29

FATHER FIGURES

NARIAN HAD BEEN RIGHT—WHEN THE FESTIVAL opened, the people were thrilled. For the first time in over a year, children ran freely up and down the streets, laughing and playing; couples young and old wandered the military training field without fear; and the Market District was abuzz with vendors and shoppers. Cokyrian guards circled and supervised, but relaxed as the day went on—nothing worse than the occasional scuffle broke out, and even enemy soldiers could not resist the entertainment, food and overall excitement generated by the event.

I was out among the crowd at dawn, participating in games; perusing fabric, jewelry, spices, fragrances, books and treats for sale; and greeting everyone I saw. The celebration was going well, even better than I had dared to hope, for more foreign traders had elected to participate than I had foreseen.

At noon, I met my mother, father, Miranna and Temerson for lunch. There was no formal dinner scheduled for this first day of the festivities, but the following evening would offer a free meal for all, which I had dubbed the Commander's Banquet. Narian had made some inroads with the people, and I wanted to continue to show him as a benevolent and caring liaison.

Joining us for lunch were Cannan and his wife, as well as Narian's Hytanican family, with the exception of the younger girls. Semari and her betrothed, who was at least double her age, sat beside my sister, while Koranis, Alantonya and their son Zayle were across from my parents. I scanned the area for Narian, whom I had thought would accompany me, but to my consternation, he did not approach until the meal had concluded. Although I had made the decision to invite Baron Koranis and his family with Narian in mind, I now considered that they might have kept him away.

Whatever the case, he came to my side when our group began to formally tour the festival grounds. Though we had all participated individually in the event during the morning, it was important that we appear together to show accord and remind everyone of Cokyri's sponsorship of the event.

My fear about the reason Narian had missed lunch was soon confirmed, for he maintained a considerable distance from Koranis. Both gradually became bookends to our company, which made sense for neither—my father, who was Koranis's best friend, walked in the center of our assemblage next to my mother and me. There was nothing that could be done about the situation, so I concentrated on the people who lined up to greet us. I waved and nodded to them, accepting the garlands of flowers that were thrust into my hands to wish me good fortune and happiness. Children would occasionally extend a single flower, and I would pass them a treat from a sack of candy carried by one of my Cokyrian guards.

A little girl, perhaps five years of age and bursting with enthusiasm, broke away from her mother and ran toward me, stopping a couple of feet short, suddenly aware that she was in the midst of strangers. She was holding a purple flower, her dark hair held back by a woven headband, her large blue eyes round with alarm.

"It's all right," I said to her, believing she intended to give the flower to me. "Don't be afraid."

She looked at me curiously, then took a tentative step—not toward me, but toward Narian. He watched her draw closer, his expression uncertain, as though he were trying to determine the girl's motivations. When she stood before him, he knelt down to accept the flower, while the crowd held its collective breath, and I wondered if they thought he would harm her.

"You're brave like my papa," she said, and the people chuckled. The girl blushed, not used to such attention.

A smile flicked across Narian's face. "And you're beautiful like the woman I love."

He touched her cheek, and the girl giggled, then ran back to her mother. A sprinkling of applause broke out, which Narian acknowledged with a nod. When I caught his eye, I beamed at him, suddenly envisioning our future. He would be the father of my children someday, and a wonderful father he would be.

When the first day of the festival had concluded, I retired early, my feet aching and my body exhausted. Narian had left us after our tour of the grounds, and I had not seen him since, although I hoped he would come to me now. He did, but even as he dropped through my window, he seemed distracted, far away inside his own head. I tried to engage him in conversation, but found it to be mostly one-sided, for I could not hold his interest. Though there was no smooth way to launch into the necessary topic, I did so anyway, doubtful that he was even listening.

"Are you upset that your family was with us today?" I asked.

"You invited them?" Judging by the tone of his voice, I had landed upon the correct issue.

"Yes. It made sense to do so."

"I suppose," he replied, but I knew the answer did not reflect his actual thoughts.

"They're old friends of my family, Narian. And I thought perhaps you would…enjoy seeing them again."

"Alera, *they* don't want *my* company."

"Your mother does."

His eyes at last met mine.

"I spoke to her about you. She would give up her husband to regain her son."

"I doubt that's true," he said with a short laugh.

"It *is*," I insisted, reaching out to run a hand through his hair. I might have changed her words a little, but I understood her intent. "She told me so herself. Believe it."

Narian stared at me, a flicker of hope on his face that quickly faded into his stoic facade.

"Even if what you say is true," he said at last, "in order to have a relationship with her, with my siblings, I need to have one with Koranis."

"You're right," I admitted, for my dinner at the Baron's home had proven that to be the case.

He sat on the bed beside me and drew one knee close to his chest. "Koranis doesn't want to be anywhere near me, and to be honest, I have no interest in a relationship with him. I have no respect for him." Narian read the sympathy in my eyes. "It's all right, Alera. I don't need a family."

"Maybe you don't need one," I said with a shrug, playing with the fabric of the quilt that lay between us. "But you deserve one."

I thought for a moment I had hit a nerve, but instead he made a joke out of it.

"Just think—if I'd *had* Koranis as my father, I might have turned into him by now. I'd be brutish and pretentious, but at least my boastful garb would distract you from those flaws. Oh, and this hair you love? It would be gone."

I laughed at the ounce of truth in his statement, then fell silent, for some reason feeling sadder about his situation than he was. He reclined upon the pillows, considering me.

"You know, in Cokyri, fathers don't raise their children. I think maybe it's better that way."

"How can you think that?" I asked, troubled by the decided tenor of his voice, and he sat up again, not having expected this reaction from me.

"Your father controlled you and forced you to marry Steldor. How can you disagree with me after living through that?"

"Because…" I faltered. "Because I love my father for all the *good* things he's done. Because he made me laugh when I was a child. That's what I think about when I see him. Not his mistakes."

"I couldn't forgive him like you do."

"Could you forgive me? I mean, if I did something awful."

Narian did not immediately respond, unsettling me, but it was in his nature to weigh all things.

"I don't know," he slowly answered. "But I would still love you."

He looked at me, an epiphany in his eyes, finally understanding my connection to my family. Then his expression changed, and I knew he was going to raise a difficult issue.

"Explain this then. If that is how families are supposed to function, and you would forgive your father anything, and clearly my mother would forgive me anything, then Koranis fails because he won't accept me. The women, you and my mother, are loving, but the man fails."

"Yes, but not *all* men fail."

"Prove it. Your father sold you into marriage, and the only

father figures I've known have respectively made my life hell and rejected me."

He lay back once more, watching me, and though he had caught me off guard, I was determined to make my point.

"Cannan is a just and fair man."

"Whose son is *Steldor*."

"Who has faults, yes—"

"As all men do."

Frustrated, I threw my hands in the air. "Are you going to keep interrupting me?"

"No," he said apologetically. "Go on."

"What about you? Am I, the woman who is in love with you, supposed to believe you're a terrible person when I know better?"

"I would be a terrible father," he said, shifting onto his side. *"What?"*

"Come, Alera, you have to admit it."

"I don't have to admit anything, especially when I think you're wrong."

"On what grounds?"

I was so exasperated I wanted to tear my hair out. And his bemused visage only made it worse.

"Because I saw you with that little girl this afternoon! You were perfect with her. And if you can be perfect with a stranger's child, how could you be any different with our own?"

"It's different *raising* a child than talking with one," he contended. "I never had a father, Alera. No one taught me how to be one."

"And did anyone teach you how to love me?"

This stopped him short. "No."

"Well, you're pretty good at it. So be quiet, and accept that our children are going to love you."

Narian's eyebrows rose, and I started laughing. Taking my

hand, he pulled me toward him and I lay down beside him, mirroring his position.

"I'm sorry for yelling at you," I murmured, giving him a light kiss.

"You never know where a conversation is going to take you," he said, gazing into my dark eyes. "I'm rather glad you did."

We lay contentedly together, occasionally kissing, my fingers twined in his hair. I loved the feel of it, its texture, its color, and I brushed it back along the nape of his neck.

"You're tickling me," he said with a smile. "Are you trying to keep me awake?"

"No." I laughed, pushing up on my elbow to look down at him. "It's just—"

I stopped, staring at the birthmark on his neck, the *mark of the Bleeding Moon,* as it had been called in the legend, and my hand began to shake.

"What is it, Alera?" he asked, alarmed.

"Nothing. It's just…" I struggled to form a cohesive thought, for in all my dreams of a life with him, of having children with him, this question had never before occurred to me.

"Just what?" He sat up, placing a hand on his neck where I had been playing with his hair.

"When we have a child, what will happen? I mean, the High Priestess told me, when she was our prisoner in the cave, that the powers of the Empress of Cokyri were supposed to pass to her firstborn daughter upon the child's birth, but that they were split between her and her brother when she was born a twin. The possibility of the powers reuniting and passing into the High Priestess's firstborn daughter gave us our negotiating leverage with the Overlord."

"Yes, but what does that have to do with anything?"

"Well, you have powers, too. I'm wondering…"

A shadow fell over his face. "You're wondering if my powers are unique to me. Or might a child of ours inherit them."

"Yes, or if…" I took a deep breath. "Could they pass from your body and into the child upon birth, like the magic of the Empress of Cokyri?"

From the expression on Narian's face, it was plain this was the first time he had ever considered the question.

"I don't know, Alera. The source of my power derives from an ancient legend and the circumstances surrounding my birth." He touched my face, then added, "Perhaps it's time we took another look at the origin of the legend—and we should find out if anything else was ever written about the powers I was destined to have."

I sighed. "I wish London were here. He uncovered the scrolls that foretold your birth, hidden somewhere in Cokyri. He would know what else was written."

Narian nodded, but said nothing more, and I tried to imagine what he must be feeling. Were his powers a blessing or a curse? Would he want them to pass to a child of his? And if a child held them, what manner of life would he or she lead? Then I asked myself the same questions, and an overriding answer became startlingly clear.

"It would be good to know, Narian. But it doesn't matter. I want children with you, and I do not fear the powers you hold, nor would I fear them in the hands of our own child."

He nodded, then settled on his back. I snuggled against him, lost in thought. At some point, I would fall asleep; it did not appear that he intended to do the same.

The second day of the festival showcased a wide variety of performers—tumblers, jugglers, singers and musicians; dancers and play actors; men who handled whips and fire; magicians and mummers. The list was never-ending, and we enjoyed it all from our seats in the royal box atop the hillside overlooking the military training field.

Two stages facing us had been erected in the bowl-shaped field for use by the performers, and bleachers had been built during the night on the north side of the hill. Other spectators sat on the ground, the slope itself providing a form of tiered seating. The laughs, jeers and applause that rang out from the audience on all sides felt like manna from heaven—only it fed my soul, not my stomach. My sister, father and Semari were almost bouncing up and down in an enthusiastic show of appreciation, while my mother, Alantonya and I less flamboyantly indicated our delight. Koranis and Temerson were quite vocal, tossing out taunts and cheers with the rest of the crowd. The only people we had invited who had not yet joined us were Cannan and Faramay. When I inquired after the captain, no one had information on his whereabouts, and I did my best to dismiss my concern.

"Perhaps he's ill," I suggested.

"The man hasn't been ill in all the years I've known him." My father chortled. "He's never missed a day of service. And if he had taken sick, he would have made sure it was on a day when he was off-duty!"

Other than Narian, who seemed lost inside his head, we all laughed at the joke, then went back to observing the festivities.

Another hour passed, along with lunch, which was served to us within the royal box. I received a few odd glances from my father for conversing freely with Narian throughout the meal, but he didn't address it, perhaps because of the looks my mother was sending *his* way.

Once servants had removed our plates and dishes, Temerson stood and stretched.

"I think I'll step out, if you don't mind, love," he said to

Miranna, who nodded, then he turned to my father and Koranis. "Would anyone care to join me?"

They both agreed, and all were soon departing through the door behind us. I chuckled at their odd behavior, and Semari came to sit by Miranna, taking up Temerson's seat. It was then that I noticed Alantonya had been left a bit stranded. She didn't seem to mind, but I nonetheless pointed this out to Narian. Though he looked almost like he was swallowing medicine, he rose to his feet and walked to his mother, ignoring Semari's stare.

"Do you mind?" he asked Alantonya, gesturing to the vacant chair beside her.

"No," she said, surprised. "No, not at all."

With one final glance at me, to which I responded with an encouraging nod, he took a seat.

"Are you enjoying the festivities?" he asked the Baroness, beginning some small talk, but their voices gradually dropped lower, their conversation more private. Though I could not hear their words, their postures relaxed. Then Alantonya reached out to place her hand over her son's where it rested on the arm of his chair, and he smiled.

CHAPTER 30

GOOD MEN

I SPENT THE FIRST DAY OF THE FESTIVAL HAND-in-hand with Grayden. Mother had been more than willing to bless my attendance with the young man, even though with Dahnath accompanying Drael, it left her hands full with the other children. We explored the market, and dodged Lord Taether when I spotted him coming toward me down the street. I told Grayden of my misadventure with this suitor of mine, and he laughed, recalling the subsequent dinner during which I had spilled wine on his father.

"Of all the potential marriage partners I've been introduced to, I haven't had a single experience as memorable as *either* of yours." He paused a moment to ponder, a twinkle in his green eyes. "But then, it has to be acknowledged that *you* are the common factor in these peculiar occurrences."

"I don't know what you mean to suggest," I replied, fingering the golden horse that hung from the chain around my neck, the horse that seemed to give me permission to be a free spirit. Grayden noticed what I was doing, and he smiled.

When evening fell, we left the faire to attend dinner at Grayden's home with his family. He had three younger siblings, a mother from whom he had inherited his slight build, and a father who had not forgotten nor forgiven my conduct toward him. He tossed frowns in my direction throughout the meal and asked about the well-being of my mother and siblings, unconcerned with my own.

"Your father dislikes me, doesn't he?" I whispered to Grayden in the parlor, noticing that I was offered tea, but not wine.

"He has a tendency to hold grudges," Grayden muttered back. "I should know—he's been holding one against me for nineteen years."

I stifled a laugh with my hand, earning yet another glower from Lord Landru.

The second day of the Harvest Festival was a literal carnival, with entertainers at every turn. I hesitantly approached the military training field, the site of my father's murder, afraid I would hear the echo of the Overlord's voice and relive the images of that macabre scene. Grayden held my hand, but to my relief, the happy babble of the crowd, the flash of bright colors, the smells of food, wine and ale, and the raucous laughter transformed the landscape, and I put another fear behind me. He and I settled on the hillside to boo, hiss, clap and cheer, and in the midst of it all, he put his arm around me. I didn't recoil. I didn't even mind.

Evening fell, and the delicious aromas of the Commander's Banquet drifted on the air, arousing appetites and calling everyone to the feast. Torches were lit, and a group of musicians assembled to play, ensuring the festive mood would continue throughout the meal. I stood in line with Grayden, awaiting a share of the generous spread. Meat of every sort—boar, venison, pheasant, peacock, lamb—sizzled on spits, with hot soups, crisp vegetables and several varieties of bread for accompaniment. Fruits, sweet breads and candies were heaped on a table for dessert. Wine, ale and mead flowed freely. No one would have reason to go to bed hungry this night.

Those who had been first in line finished eating before the last comers were served, and soon a circle of young women rose to stamp their feet in rhythm with the music. As Grayden and I settled on a bench with our plates, shouts rose to encourage them, and an area for dancing was cleared. By the time we had eaten our fill, several couples had taken to the floor, and Grayden pulled me to my feet and into their midst.

I was warm from the glass of ale I'd enjoyed, and the light from the torches wavered with the breeze, casting strange shadows and overloading my senses. We finished two dances, and I would have taken a break had the musicians not begun to play a lament. Grayden drew me close, swaying side to side, but even with the slower pace, I couldn't seem to catch my breath.

"Would you like to know something, Shaselle?"

"Just don't tell me I have food in my teeth."

"No, silly," he said with a grin. "It's just that I've never been happier than I am now. And I was wondering…that is, I was thinking…" He took a deep breath and blurted, "I'd like to ask your uncle for permission to court you."

"I thought we *were* courting. Or is that a secret?" I felt euphoric from his closeness, my head swimming, my heart light. So naturally, I had to tease him.

"I just want to do things the right way." He hesitated, gazing into my eyes, before softly adding, "But if we are courting, then I believe certain liberties may be taken."

He touched his lips to mine in a kiss so sweet that it threatened to halt my breath altogether.

"What do you say, Shaselle?" he murmured, raising his hands to my face, his touch tender. "May I speak with your uncle?"

I scanned his dark hair, sparkling green eyes and upturned

nose, thoughts of other suitors I had met, of Saadi, of my mother's and Cannan's plans for my future tumbling over each other. In the fallout from everything that had happened, I had never expected to feel truly happy, wasn't certain I deserved it. But this was the course my life was supposed to take, and if the fates were willing to include happiness along with it, I wasn't going to pass it by.

"Yes," I said with a wistful smile. "I think courting is an intriguing possibility."

He threaded his fingers through mine and led me aside, an exuberant grin affixed in place. Then the world exploded. Fires lit the sky and loud blasts rent the air from several directions. Mothers ran with their children, their screams and cries tearing at my ears. Metal flashed and clashed as sword-wielding Cokyrian soldiers engaged Hytanican men armed with broken bottles, farm hoes, meat cleavers and other make-shift weapons, on occasion brandishing a sword wrenched from the enemy. Grayden held my hand tightly, crushing my fingers together and pulling me out of the fray of blood and pain and death. He turned to say something to me, but I never heard a word—not due to the bedlam surrounding us, but because of the ringing in my ears as I sank to my knees, the world going black.

Sometime later I awoke in the front parlor of Grayden's home, a cold cloth on my forehead, having no idea how I had come to be here. I looked around to see his mother ministering to him, for he was likewise laid out on a sofa, barely stirring.

"What happened?" I croaked, and she came to my side, offering me a cool drink.

"You're fine," she soothed. "Both of you are fine. Just lie still."

"But…how did I come to be here?"

"You and my son passed out. No one knows how or why, but a lot of people lost consciousness. The Cokyrian commander summoned physicians to treat everyone, then my Lord Landru found you and brought you both here."

"I need to go home. My mother must be frantic." I struggled to sit upright, then fell back, my head pounding, nausea sweeping through me that was so debilitating I would have gladly traded it for a hangover.

"Shaselle, are you all right?" It was Grayden, his voice weak and confused. His mother replaced the damp cloth on my brow, then went to offer him something to drink.

"I think I will be," I managed in response.

I heard voices in the foyer, then Lord Landru strode into the parlor.

"She's there, Cannan," he said, and my uncle approached, his atypical worry lines relaxing when he realized I was conscious.

"How are you, Shaselle?"

"Never better."

He laughed in pure relief. "I'm going to let you rest here for a while yet. Then I'll return and take you home. But you're going to be just fine."

"What went wrong, Uncle? Everyone was so happy, and then…it was chaos."

"I know. There was a disturbance—Hytanican caused, I'm afraid. But the Cokyrians were only too eager to respond. Feebly armed Hytanicans in various stages of inebriation were no match for sober, well-armed and well-trained Cokyrian soldiers. It would have been a bloodbath had it not been for Commander Narian." Cannan shook his head, as if trying to figure something out. "I'm not sure what he did, but he must have been anticipating trouble. He released some type of poison—no, not a poison. But some type of airborne sub-

stance that knocked everybody off their feet. Shut the fighting down at once."

He placed a hand on my cheek, brushing away a few wisps
of my hair.

"You no doubt feel poorly right now, but I've been told
the effects wear off in a few hours. You'll be back to normal
after that."

"Captain, sir?" It was Grayden.

My uncle gazed over at him in surprise. "Yes?"

"This may not be the ideal time to ask, but, would you
please permit me to court Shaselle?"

There was stunned silence in the room, then loud laughter.

"I'd be a fool to deny you a chance with my niece. Assuming Shaselle favors the idea."

"I do, Uncle," I assured him, easily slipping back toward
sleep, images of Grayden and Saadi drifting through my head.
Then a remembrance of Queen Alera and Commander Narian
came to the forefront—how deferential he had been with her
when I had been caught with that dagger, how she had looked
at him. And I knew two things with absolute certainty. She
was in love with him, and he had to be a good man.

Refusing to be intimidated by what had happened the previous evening, I ventured forth to spend the final day of the
Harvest Festival with Grayden. My mother tried her best to
keep me home, but the weather was splendid, and the worst
everyone had feared had already occurred. Besides, there were
to be horse races, even if no tournament was to take place;
even she realized that, short of tying me down, she would not
be able to keep me from attending.

Grayden and I sat again on the hillside, sizing up the horses
and the riders, choosing our favorites, wagering between us.
The crowd was abundant, but more subdued, in part because

no alcohol was being served—Commander Narian had decided to shut down certain aspects of the celebration rather than closing down the entire event. For once, I agreed with him.

After the races had ended, the faire wound down, and Grayden tugged me toward a stand where the vendor's wares were rapidly depleting.

"Come!" he exclaimed. "I want to get you something—a remembrance."

I laughed, for he was pulling me toward a display of headpieces made of woven flowers and ribbons, but he was not to be deterred. He worked toward the front of the stand, extracted a coin from his money pouch and flipped it at the woman in charge.

"I'd like your best one for the girl I'm courting," he proclaimed, and I suspected the real truth was that he wanted to say the words.

"They are all finely made, young sir. Which one is best is a matter of the color you desire."

Grayden studied me, trying to choose. I struck a pose to help.

"Green," he decided. "For she has the loveliest hazel eyes."

His words shocked me into silence, and a strange notion flashed in my brain. He had said my eyes were lovely. Could he possibly think I was beautiful?

"Shaselle?" he faltered, probably afraid he had offended me. "Would you prefer a different color?"

"Not at all! I adore green!"

His grin resurfaced and he nestled the chosen crown into my hair, which fell in a simple braid down my back. I beamed at him, the world seeming brighter, less tainted and revitalized, for somehow my uncle Cannan had come through—he had found me a young man that Papa would have been proud to know. When Grayden continued to gaze at me, adoration in his eyes, my cheeks pinked, then he abruptly turned me to face away from him, his hands resting on my shoulders.

"Your cousin is over there. Would you like to share the news?"

Sure enough, Steldor and Galen were making a show of themselves, bantering back and forth as they flirted with the young women that surrounded them. Steldor was paying more attention to the ladies than Galen, of course, who would occasionally raise the hand that held his betrothal band to fend them off.

I nodded, eager to share my happiness, and Grayden clasped my hand to take me to them. As we drew nearer, it became clear that Steldor, wearing an emerald-green doublet, black trousers and shiny boots that buckled all the way up the shafts, was in top form. He was bidding farewell to a particularly beautiful young woman with voluminous black hair, kissing her hand in his classic style. She curtseyed to him, then flourished her hand in the air and took her leave. I had never seen her before, but noticed that he watched her until she had disappeared into the crowd. Had he found a marriage prospect or a fresh amusement? I didn't care, for it was irrefutable that he had found something.

"Shaselle!" he crowed, giving Galen a shove on the shoulder to draw his notice. "Enjoying yourself?"

"Yes!" I exclaimed, ready to make my announcement. "Grayden and I—"

"Say, have you seen Cannan?" Galen interrupted, focusing on Steldor rather than on me. "Sorry," he added, his contrition not entirely believable.

"He was looking for us, wasn't he?" Steldor grew more somber, and I marveled at how self-absorbed the two of them could be. Addressing us, he asked, "Have either of you seen the captain?"

"No, not tonight," I replied, too elated to be annoyed.

"Could be important." Galen nudged Steldor, a touch of urgency in his voice, and I glanced back and forth between them, perplexed at their manner.

"Probably is."

"We should find him."

"Come on." Steldor threw an arm around Galen, and the two of them strode off together. I watched them in awe, for they seemed to have forgotten I existed.

"Excuse me," I said to Grayden, curiosity burning. "But I must speak with my cousin. He'll see me safely home."

"Are you sure you don't want me to—"

"No, no, I'll be fine." I flashed a smile, then gave him a quick kiss on the cheek before hastening after the frustrating duo, determined to make them listen. I tagged along for ten minutes before they acknowledged my presence, but even then they didn't slow their pace, for Steldor had caught sight of his father up ahead. Cannan came to meet them.

"Two hours I've been searching for you boys. Having fun?" The captain was irked, but that didn't forestall Galen.

"Yes, sir," he declared, with an impudent grin.

Cannan almost rolled his eyes, then he dropped his volume. "The manor house, half an hour. Understood?"

Steldor and Galen nodded, then Cannan's eyes fell on me.

"Shaselle, you should go back to the faire," he decreed, a warning underlying his tone.

I knew I should obey, and I certainly knew Cannan wasn't likely to give me permission to remain with Steldor and Galen. Still, something was up, and I wanted to be a part of it. I stayed put, peering sheepishly up at him.

"Shaselle," he prompted.

"I'd like to come," I murmured, fearful of his reaction. "I'll stay out of the way and won't cause any trouble."

The captain crossed his arms. "No, there is too much at risk."

"Uncle, please! I may be able to help. Perhaps messages need to be delivered. You might all be under surveillance, but no one would be watching me."

"She already knows where we're meeting," Steldor pointed out, an argument that had not yet come to me.

"So there's not much point in trying to keep her away," Galen finished, looking at me with understanding in his eyes. He had heard my confession about Saadi and probably wanted to show that he still trusted me.

Cannan glared at his son by blood and his son by familiarity and responsibility. To my astonishment, he relented.

"She can come, but one of you takes her when we split up. I don't want her getting lost."

I bounced on the balls of my feet, exhilarated by the captain's decision, then froze when his stern eyes fell on me. He did not see this as cause for celebration.

"Half an hour," he grumbled in reminder, walking away.

I went with Steldor, and we surreptitiously departed the festival grounds, heading up the hillside and stopping a few times to talk with folks. I worried we would be late, but my cousin was not bothered.

"Trust me, stealth is much more important here than punctuality," he told me with a smirk.

When the crowd began to thin, my heartbeat calmed, for we were making better progress. We passed through the Market District only to be slowed once more when we reached the thoroughfare.

"We *are* late by now," I harassed.

"My father will either assume we're dead or that I'm up to my usual tricks. If I'm not worried, you shouldn't be."

His eyes glinted wickedly, suggesting he enjoyed needling his father, perhaps even to the same extent he enjoyed his popularity.

I shrugged, keeping my silence the rest of the trek to Cannan's manor house, where Steldor had grown up. He rapped four times on the door and we were ushered inside by Galen, who locked the door before heading through the kitchen and down a flight of stairs into a cellar. Only a single torch was lit in the small, clammy space, making it difficult to distinguish the faces of the men who had gathered.

"Delayed?" Cannan asked with a touch of sarcasm.

"Come now, Father. I had baggage," Steldor shot back, and I shoved him, not appreciating his gibe.

"Everyone's here," Galen said from beside me. "Doors are barred. What's the word?"

My eyes had adjusted to the dim lighting during the brief exchange, and I glanced about me, recognizing the rest of the men: King Adrik, Baron Koranis, Lord Temerson and, most shocking of all, London. No one in the city had heard word of the deputy captain since the failed rebellion.

The former Elite Guard was first to answer. "The High Priestess is back in Cokyri."

"And Narian will leave to report to her on the outcome of the festival tomorrow morning," Temerson added, apparently the rebel party's ears within the Bastion.

"Give him a day of travel, and he, too, will be out of our way," London asserted.

"Then our course is clear." Cannan's voice was strong, decisive. "No more waiting. The plan goes into action two evenings hence."

A strange mixture of excitement and panic hit me at my

uncle's words, but the demeanors of those around me did not change. They had been involved in this for a long time.

"It's not safe for me to remain in the city for long." London was speaking again. "I can't risk being seen and will need to ride hard for Cokyri. I'll do my best to keep Narian and the High Priestess occupied."

Cannan nodded, and London took the steps to the main floor two at a time, his shadow falling upon us like an ominous portent when he opened the door, the darkness feeling more oppressive upon its close.

"All right," the captain said, reclaiming our attention. "Word has been spread to our accomplices within the city, London has armed the villagers and all are waiting for our signal."

Koranis stooped to hoist up a canvas bag, which he dropped on the rickety table before us.

"The rockets," he said, pulling a long, slender tube from the bag. "The King of Sarterad had to send all the way to Alidovia for these—they only arrived yesterday. Prop them up facing skyward, light the wick at the bottom and we have our signal."

He tossed the strange tube he held to Steldor, then removed two more from the bag for Galen and Temerson.

"Set them off as planned, in the designated areas of the city, and be ready," Cannan ordered.

"I'll certainly have to be," said a new voice—one with an accent. We all leaped backward to face the cellar stairs, where we could hear methodical footsteps descending. Knives had appeared in the hands of the men around me; they were small, but they would be effective.

The Cokyrian commander emerged into the torchlight, calm and unarmed.

"Oh, good Lord," King Adrik breathed, but everyone else stood silently, rigidly, their eyes assessing the enemy.

Addressing the captain, Narian declared, "This stops now."

Cannan clenched his jaw and I slipped behind Steldor, hoping he would shield me. But if we were arrested, not even he could protect me. Maybe if I hid...but there was nowhere to conceal myself. I certainly had a knack for stumbling into the most compromising and dangerous of situations. I hadn't been involved in this at all, but was sure to be sentenced for it now. Taking a breath, I forced myself to step into the open. After all, I had wanted to be here. And if I had to die, I stood in good company.

"What is it you think you know?" Steldor demanded, but Narian ignored him, speaking only to Cannan.

"You have the ability to be the voice of reason here. Don't let these men walk to their deaths."

"Should I have them die by execution instead?" the captain ground out, but Narian did not flinch, continuing to stare at him, steely conviction in his eyes.

"I'm alone, Cannan. I've been following your movements and the movements of your men since Shaselle was caught with that dagger, and I haven't said a word to the High Priestess, to my comrades, not even to Alera. I'm giving you a chance to walk away, to *live*. Don't be a fool—take it."

Cannan tucked his knife into the shaft of his boot, then cast his eyes over Steldor, Galen, Adrik and Koranis. All resolutely met his gaze.

"I don't see fear in this room, Narian," he said, shaking his head. "Do what you must, as will we."

"Then you're asking to die!" For a moment there was a pleading note in Narian's voice, an indication of how torn he was about his position. He didn't want to put these men to death. "If I arrest you, you will be executed. If I let you go forward, you will fail."

"The only way we could fail," Steldor interjected in a low

voice, "is by accepting what you have handed our people. We owe this to them."

"You owe them your leadership, not the sacrifice of your lives. The High Priestess will not relinquish this province, in that she is unyielding. She and the Overlord fought too long and too hard for it. *Don't do this.*"

My uncle approached the Cokyrian commander with an almost sympathetic expression. His dark eyes had lost none of their determination, but he meant to reach the young man with his words.

"Who are you, Narian?" The question was strange, but Narian seemed to understand its significance. "From the moment you set foot in Hytanica, you have tried to play both sides. You've spent far too long being a Cokyrian with Hytanican blood, and it ends now, for better or worse. There is no more in between, so do what you must. Either have us arrested, or allow us to go forward."

Narian met Cannan's gaze, not discomfited by the taller man's proximity. In truth, he had nothing at all to fear from us, what with the powers he possessed. But I wished I could see something in his eyes, some indication of what he would do from here.

"Very well, Captain. I will do as you say—what I must."

Showing us his back, Narian ascended the stairs, disappearing through the cellar door. Steldor immediately made to follow, but Cannan grasped his shirt.

"Let me go," my cousin snapped, but his father stepped closer, until their faces were just inches apart.

"Don't be reckless," the captain muttered. "He will kill you if you challenge him."

Steldor gave in, and his father released his grip.

"Then what do we do?" Galen asked.

"Nothing has changed." Cannan looked around at the men

who would follow his orders, to the grave and beyond. "We will do exactly what we have planned. Until and unless Narian stops us, we proceed."

"But...but isn't that dangerous?" King Adrik queried.

"This has always been dangerous. But I'm willing to take a chance on Narian."

The silence in the aftermath of the captain's statement reinforced my sense that, at a single wave of the Cokyrian commander's hand, we would all be buried alive.

ALERA

CHAPTER 31

INCONGRUITIES

A CREEPING SENSATION AT THE BASE OF MY SPINE woke me in the middle of the night. I had gone to bed alone, for Narian had not come to me, but I was no longer certain I was the only person in the room. Unnerved, I slowly opened my eyes to see him next to me on his back, hands behind his head, fully awake and staring at the ceiling.

"What are you doing?" I whispered, and he shrugged.

"I'm…thinking."

"Yes, I can see that much." I plucked at the bedclothes, then tried again. "What time is it? It must be close to morning—have you slept at all?"

Again, that shrug.

"I'll take that as a *no*." I laughed, trying to lighten his mood.

I draped my arm across his chest, pressing myself against him, and he lowered one arm to embrace me. I was concerned about him—the previous evening he'd left the royal box shortly before the feast and had not returned to eat with us, unlike the other men. Perhaps he had wanted to avoid all contact with Koranis, or avoid problems for Alantonya if the Baron saw her with their firstborn. It wasn't until the feast had concluded, and the drinking and dancing had begun, that he had returned. And at that point, he had, without explanation, taken me back to the Bastion, insisting that I stay there. I had done as he had requested, despite the fire and explosions that had occurred a few hours later, and I had not attended the faire on this, its final day, again in accordance with his wishes. He had handled the disturbance of the night before but did not trust that there would be no further breaches of the peace. Now he was avoiding sleep, and he would be leaving early in the morning for Cokyri.

"You need rest, Narian," I murmured, fighting off drowsiness. "Are you thinking about your family?"

"Alera, you are my family. You're all the family I need." He hesitated, then changed the subject. "Can...can I ask you for a favor?"

"Of course," I answered, sitting up, for whatever was on his mind was more serious than I had thought.

"Come to Cokyri with me."

I peered at him, unable to see his face clearly in the darkness. "What? Why?"

"I want you to see it. The mountains. When all is said and done, I don't know how often I'll be returning there. I just... want you to see it."

"All right," I said, baffled by the unusual nature of the request and by his explanation, for he regularly went to Cokyri. But if it was important to him—and obviously it was—I would go.

We left the Bastion a few hours later, neither one of us having fallen back to sleep, Narian having spent a good part of the morning in discussion with his new second-in-command, who would be in charge while we were gone. Despite his total lack of rest, Narian showed fewer signs of tiredness than I did.

Horses were brought to the courtyard gates for our use,

and we departed with an entourage of guards. Cannan bid us farewell, bowing to me and giving Narian a respectful nod of his head which my betrothed solemnly returned. As we rode down the thoroughfare, people stopped to watch, a few spitting in the street at the Cokyrian guards who were with us, a few calling to me. I could imagine how strange I looked to the citizenry, dressed in the breeches and cloak I always wore when riding. But comfort came first on a long trip such as this.

We passed through the city gates, then turned east, which I found troubling, for the only bridge across the Recorah River lay to our south. When we drew near the shimmering surface of the water, I was taken aback to find that I was wrong—the Cokyrians had reconstructed the bridge that had burned during the original war, making it easier to reach their homeland, which lay in the mountains to our northeast. While this made sense from their standpoint, it was another reminder that we no longer determined our own fate. From the bridge, we would either continue east across the Cokyrian Desert or turn north directly into the mountain range. Recalling my own trek through the forest and into the Niñeyre Mountains when we had fled the palace, neither route seemed appealing. One would be hot and dusty; the other would be steep and full of pitfalls.

After crossing the bridge, we turned north, following the river and avoiding the desert. Narian had chosen a mountain route. When we neared the thick tangle of the Kilwin Forest, we stopped to rest and water our horses, and to eat and drink ourselves. I was tired and sore, but dared not complain, not wanting the Cokyrian soldiers to think I was weak.

We resumed the journey at full strength, moving uphill, following a trail that the enemy had cleared to make the trek to and from Cokyri an easier one. Nonetheless, the ride was strenuous, uncomfortable and meandering, for the trail wound its way through rock outcroppings and thick stands of trees. In the late afternoon, we reached a plateau, where the river flowed beneath the rock on which we stood, and I realized this was where the enemy had crossed the river to invade our kingdom and attack us from the north.

Members of our guard had spread out and were surveying the area, though for what I did not know. It was hard to imagine encountering danger here, and I wondered if this were just another sign of the thorough nature of the Cokyrians. They never took anything for granted, and being on alert seemed inherent in their makeup.

"Narian," I called, approaching him where he had dismounted. "How much farther is it to Cokyri?"

"Another half day's ride. Cokyri sits in the shelter of those peaks." He pointed to show me where we were going. "We'll make camp here tonight and proceed in the morning." He didn't elaborate, but I knew this decision was made to accommodate me. The journey could be made in a single day if one traveled fast and hard.

I watched while he pitched a tent for me, realizing everyone else would throw a bedroll down on the cold earth. A fire had already been started, and some of our guards had snared a few rabbits in preparation for a stew.

I sighed, nervous about what the next day might bring.

"Does the High Priestess know I'm traveling with you?" I asked as Narian held the tent flap open for me.

"No, she doesn't," he replied, unperturbed. "Would you like to wash? I can heat some water if you'd like."

He was trying to change the subject, but I wasn't ready to let him do so.

"Do you think that's wise? Not to inform the High Priestess?"

"I think it's appropriate. After all, she didn't give us advance notice of her visit to Hytanica. And she will have no choice but to deal with the unexpected."

I frowned, wondering if there were something hidden within his last statement.

"Water?" he again asked, and I nodded, too tired to press him further.

It was dark by the time the stew was ready, and Narian and I ate around the campfire with our guards, most of whom were women. Conversation was scant, but genial, and it seemed strange to so casually interact with Narian's soldiers. I realized then that, with the exception of Narian, I had never really thought of the Cokyrians as people, with lives and loves and the same types of worries, big and small, that I had. And it was apparent that they missed their homeland. If given a choice, I wondered how many of the conquerors would forsake the conquered land without delay.

We rose early the next morning and headed deep into traditional Cokyrian territory. I was stiff following our night's sleep, a testament to the roughness of the terrain and the sumptuousness in which I usually slept. We trotted our horses along a forested ridge, and I concentrated on standing slightly in the stirrups, trying to limit the bumps and jars that were inherent in the gait. But I forgot my discomfort when the trees thinned and the walled fortress of the enemy empire came into view. I had always imagined Cokyri as dark and lifeless and had grown up believing the people to be uncivilized, unfeeling. But the city that loomed in the distance was awe-inspiring, built ingeniously into the dark gray stone of the mountains surrounding it. Magnificent spires could be seen beyond the wall that protected it, with one building in particular drawing the eye, for it shone white and gold in the afternoon sun.

I looked at Narian, for he had stopped his horse and was

gazing upon the city he loved. He had grown up here, lived here for most of his eighteen years—it was what he remembered of his childhood, and it was beautiful despite the horrors it had wrought for him.

"It's breathtaking," I murmured, and he nodded, a smile playing at the corners of his mouth, then he motioned our entourage forward.

The route we took avoided a steep descent in favor of a long, gradual one—we went in what seemed like circles for almost two hours before the gates of the Cokyrian stronghold were before us. The sentries immediately permitted us entry, greeting Narian with extreme deference. If he were hated in Hytanica, the admiration he received in Cokyri more than made up for it. Word of his return spread quickly, and men, women and children ran out to the streets to get a glimpse of the young commander who had at long last conquered Hytanica. I was grateful that few glances were spared for me, for I wasn't certain I could bear the disdain they would likely show if my identity were known. Besides, my senses were reeling with information, for the residences and business establishments that we passed were astonishingly different from their counterparts in my homeland. All of the streets were paved, and everything was clean, almost pristine. Most of the buildings had sheltered and columned front entries and wide arching windows. Some structures spanned an entire block and had enclosed yards where children ran and played. Were they schools? Or some type of communal living arrangement? And most of the buildings had etchings around their front doors—symbols and words that I did not understand.

It wasn't long before we approached the brilliant white-and-gold building that I had glimpsed from afar, and I was pleased to discover it was our destination. We pulled the horses to a halt before the iron gates of its walled courtyard and Narian dismounted, giving me a reassuring look as he came to hold my horse so I could do the same. Then he ushered me into the inner sanctum, and I would have stopped and stared had he not been beside me. Up close, the beauty of the palatial structure defied description. It stood three stories tall, with separate wings that stretched thousands of feet to my left and right. The columns and steps of its front entry were made of white marble, and intricate, elegant patterns plated with gold were chiseled into its stone walls. The arches of its expansive windows were embedded with jewels that were almost too dazzling for the eyes to behold, and flowers and wreaths left by the people for the ruler they adored were strewn all along the walk and the base of the building.

"The Temple of the High Priestess," Narian confirmed as we strolled up the wide path. "Welcome."

I swallowed several times, trying to remove the lump from my throat. Never had I envisioned myself in this country, let alone being welcomed into its ruler's temple. A part of me was instinctively afraid, for this was, after all, *Cokyri*. But I was with Narian, and he would never let me come to harm.

We approached the double front doors, which were drawn open by servants, and stepped across the threshold. The splendor that had marked the outside of the temple was nothing compared to what greeted me on the inside. The floor of the expansive foyer was marble, and a chandelier as large as the old dais in the Hytanican Throne Room hung from its domed ceiling. Ahead lay a double marble staircase with golden banisters, the walls to each side painted with lavish murals. I had been raised a princess, and even I was overwhelmed.

The servants who had permitted us entry took our cloaks, then a young woman stepped forward.

"Come with me," she invited. "You will want to wash and change following your travels."

I glanced nervously at Narian, but he smiled.

"Go ahead, Alera. Let them pamper you. We'll be reunited shortly."

I nodded and went with the servant into a room with benches lining its walls and a sunken tub in the middle of the floor. A scented bath was prepared for me, and it wasn't until I had settled into the warm water that I realized how tense and aching my muscles really were. I lay my head back, letting the servant brush and clean my hair, knowing that if I relaxed totally, I would fall asleep.

Deciding it would be best if I didn't let my skin shrivel, I asked for a towel and gave up the luxury I was enjoying. As I dried off, the servant presented me with a soft, white blouse that closed asymmetrically in front, loose-fitting leggings and soft-soled shoes. I slipped the garments on, realizing that my traveling clothes had been removed, then was returned to the foyer where Narian awaited me. He, too, had bathed and was dressed similarly to me, although his clothing was black.

"What now?" I asked, unsettled by the echo of our voices.

"Duty," he replied somewhat cryptically, but at my quizzical expression, he added, "Dinner with the High Priestess."

"You're remarkably calm, considering the manner in which she left Hytanica."

"I feel better having you here with me. Your presence will have caught her off guard and might keep her from yelling."

I laughed and walked with him down the hall, our footfalls resounding as chillingly as our voices. "So that's why you wanted me to come with you."

"Maybe." He smirked, leading me to a door on the left side of the staircase. Without knocking, he put his back against it, pushing it open and dragging me through.

The room in which we now stood had a long table with straight-backed oak chairs and yet more marble flooring. A series of golden chandeliers blazed gloriously above the table, casting shimmering light upon its polished wood surface, which was set for two at its far end. The High Priestess, dressed in a black tunic and leggings with intricate gold and scarlet stitching, stood in front of a wide window that granted an expansive view of the mountain range. Seeing me, she snapped her fingers at a servant who was just coming through a door to her right. The man glanced at me and abruptly turned around, no doubt going to retrieve another place setting.

Narian took a great breath, then twined his fingers in mine to lead me across the room, ready to make our relationship known. The High Priestess took note of our clasped hands, but though she was undoubtedly displeased, she chose to disregard Narian's display of affection.

"Alera," she greeted me. "What a pleasant surprise."

The servant returned to add a plate, wineglass and cutlery to the tabletop, positioning it opposite the place setting that had been laid out for Narian, then scurried from the room.

"Let us sit," the High Priestess invited.

Narian and I took our seats, Nantilam between us at the head of the table, an arrangement that was deliberate on her part. Platters of food were brought, and as the meal was served, I began to feel that we were under inspection, for her cool green eyes seemed to take in everything. Narian shot me several apologetic glances that I was certain did not pass the High Priestess's scrutiny.

"Narian—tell me of your journey," Nantilam at last inquired, and I was glad she was not addressing me, for I was intimidated by her presence. She was like a mythical goddess, beautiful, regal, forceful and perfectly composed. I sat a little taller, wishing I had the grace of my mother, for I felt that I was representing all of Hytanica, and that it could be done better.

"It was uneventful," Narian replied. "Ordinary. Much the same as I hope yours was a few days ago."

"Yes, my journey was easy," the High Priestess replied. "Of course, I had much to occupy my mind and Rava to keep me company."

"How is Rava?" I ventured.

"Well. She is staying here in the temple and will resume her shield maiden duties when she is ready."

I nodded, and the silence was filled with the scrape of tableware on plates. Nantilam, I noticed, was watching Narian almost shamelessly, and I began to count the seconds, for each one that passed brought us closer to the end of this awkward meal.

Narian abruptly set down his fork and leaned back in his chair to address her. "The festival went well."

"I'm glad to hear that. No disruptions, disturbances?"

"A few minor matters, but nothing serious."

I tensed, for he was keeping information from her, for what reason I did not know.

"Good. Then finish your meal."

"I'm afraid being under scrutiny has cost me my appetite."

It was a bold assertion, and the hardening of the High Priestess's eyes confirmed that it was less respectful than she generally tolerated. She sat silently, locking her gaze on his, neither of them showing the slightest inclination to yield. Perhaps he was more like her than he cared to admit.

"I assumed things had gone well when I saw Alera with you," she resumed, her voice sharp. "You surely would not have taken the Grand Provost from her province in a time of unrest. You intended to address this, Narian, did you not?"

I didn't understand the subtext of their exchange, but the look they were sharing was distrustful and unfriendly.

"I wanted to show Alera the mountains," Narian told her,

and though I was confused, I knew his word choice was deliberate. "Affairs in Hytanica are as they should be."

The tension remained high throughout the rest of the meal, and I was more than a little relieved when the High Priestess called dinner to an end. A servant was instructed to escort me to the room that had been prepared for me, and Narian walked beside me toward the door.

"Narian, a word," Nantilam called before he could escape into the hall.

"I've had a long day of traveling," Narian responded, formal and polite. "I'd prefer to talk in the morning."

The High Priestess was offended by his attitude, but with me present, she kept her temper in check.

"Very well," she said, but her words were clipped. "Then I will see you *early* in the morning."

Narian nodded and we left the dining room in the company of a servant. We climbed the marble staircase, then the woman led me down a different wing from the one into which Narian turned. I wanted desperately to talk to him, but it seemed we were being kept apart.

I entered the room where I was to spend the night and crossed to the wardrobe, my feet sinking into the thick rug laid upon the wooden floor. Opening the door, I discovered my things had been unpacked and hung inside. I glanced toward the large four-poster bed with its golden comforter, noticing that a nightgown had been laid across it for my use. The Cokyrians certainly knew how to treat their guests.

Feeling a bit unsettled, I sat down upon the bed, tired, but not so tired that my mind would quiet. I wondered if Narian would come to visit me, knowing he might have been honest with the High Priestess about his state of exhaustion, for he hadn't slept well in several days. I sighed, doubtful that I would find rest, despite the lavishness of my surroundings.

This temple was where Miranna had been imprisoned for months. Somewhere in this city, perhaps even as part of the temple, was the Overlord's Hall. Out of morbid fascination, and a desire to know, to *understand* what my sister had endured, I wanted to see these places. Maybe then I would be in a better position to help her.

About a half hour later, there was a knock on my door and I stiffened, my heart hammering. Who could want to see me?

"Come in!"

Narian slipped through the door, closing it quietly behind him, and I laughed at myself. I was not used to him entering my room in a conventional fashion.

"I never knew your home—all of Cokyri—was so beautiful," I confessed when he was sitting beside me. "We're not told about these things when we learn about history."

"It is beautiful," he agreed, almost wistfully, and I wondered what he was thinking.

"You really grew up here, in this temple?"

He was nodding, absentmindedly rubbing his wrist, and I simply watched him for a moment.

"And you love it," I surmised.

"I suppose I do. It feels like home. But I don't miss it when I'm with you."

He kissed me, then leaned back against the pillows, pulling me along with him.

"Narian," I murmured, lifting my head to look at him. He was so handsome, so perfect with his halo of golden hair and his intense blue eyes that I ached for him to kiss me and touch me. But there were things I wanted to ask him. "What was causing the friction between you and the High Priestess?"

An ironic smile lit his features. "Call it a familial disagreement. She doesn't understand my change of heart—that I don't care anymore if she sees us together. Ever since the Overlord's death, she's been trying to win me back, you might say. She knows I'm not happy with her. But she doesn't realize that she's already lost me—this place may feel like home to me forever, but it will never again *be* home. This part of my life is over. My loyalty has turned."

"You've never said that before," I pointed out, feeling like there was something important he was not telling me. "That your loyalty is to Hytanica."

"I only recently came to realize it myself. But that is where my loyalty lies."

He was resolute, decided—and he was making me uneasy. What had the High Priestess said at dinner? *The Grand Provost wouldn't leave her province in unrest.* I hadn't, had I?

"Narian—" I started, sitting up, but he interrupted me.

"Your loyalty has always been to Hytanica, and I don't want there to be anything standing between us. So I've made up my mind, Alera. It's a good thing."

I nodded, trying to shrug off my disquiet, for he was, of course, right. I stood up and tugged on his arm, trying to get him to move.

He laughed. "I told you I was tired, remember?"

"Yes, but as long as we're here, I'd like you to show me something."

"What might that be?" He came to his feet, and I dragged him toward the door.

"I want to see where Miranna was confined." I clutched nervously at my blouse, unsure how he would react, for I had not been able to think of a tactful way to raise the topic.

He stopped, forcing me to face him. "Alera, do you really want to see that?"

"You told me she was well cared for here," I bristled, my tone slightly accusatory. "If that's true, then you have nothing to hide from me."

Narian released me. "I didn't lie to you. The High Priest-ess made certain Miranna was well accommodated. But she was still a prisoner. I just want to be sure that you are ready to see this."

"I'm ready."

Relenting, he led me out of the room, and we walked side by side through several corridors and down a flight of stairs. Had he not known his way, I would have been lost in the lab-yrinth. After a few more twists and turns, I found myself in a narrow hallway that was shrouded in darkness.

"This area of the temple isn't used much," he explained, and though I had felt certain that I wanted to see this just a short time ago, my spine now tingled with the eeriness of what we were doing. I would be exploring my sister's cell as a guest in her prison.

To my surprise, Narian had only to push a small lever on the bottom of a torch on the wall to ignite it—the Cokyrians had invented a way to trigger a spark within the apparatus. He opened the door nearest to us, showing me a room that was simply but comfortably furnished. There were no thick rugs on the floor here, and it was smaller than the guest room in which I was staying, but it contained a bed and a desk and had an adjoining bath chamber.

"This is it," Narian announced, letting me pass by him to enter the room.

I stood in the center of the floor, allowing myself to get a feel for the space. Only the window was unusual, for it was set high in the wall and covered by iron bars. Had I not known that my sister had been locked away within these walls, the room would probably not have made me uncomfortable. Part of me wanted to look more closely at the details that Miranna had likely spent months memorizing, but the dominant part drove me back into the hall.

"Let's go," I said to Narian, my throat tight.

He led me back through the maze, not speaking until we had climbed the flight of stairs to the floor where our rooms were located.

"Would you like to return to the guest room?" he asked, halting beside me on the landing.

Feeling better now that we had emerged from the past, I shook my head. "I'd like to see your quarters."

"What? Why?"

I laughed at his expression. "Why? Because this is where you were raised! This is where you were a boy. If you don't want to show me, I'll understand, but it would tell me more about you and help me to know you even better."

He scratched the back of his head. "Well…let's go, then."

"It's all right if you don't want to show me," I said again, detecting some hesitation on his part.

"No, it's fine. Really, I don't mind."

Bemused, I trailed after him into the opposite wing of the second floor from where my room was located.

When we reached his door, he went inside, leaving it open for me to follow. I stepped across the threshold and closed out the hall, then surveyed what lay before me: a lavish main room much like mine in Hytanica, with a fireplace; a rich, comfortable sofa upon which Narian settled; several armchairs; a carved wooden table scattered with papers; and two bookshelves stocked with volumes. Heavy drapes covered one wall, and when I crossed the thick rug that blanketed the floor to push the fabric aside, I learned the reason—they hid a set of large windows. I turned around and saw that an expansive mural covered the wall above and to the sides of the door. It combined horses, a sunrise and sunset, stars in a deep blue sky, noblewomen and men, creatures of myth and a Cokyrian flag into a single stunning piece of artwork. Intricate tapestries were common in Hytanica, but I had never seen anything approaching the beauty of this painting before.

Narian was content to let me explore, so I approached the table, skimming the papers atop it, which ranged from correspondence and scrawled notes to maps and battle strategies. Spying his bedroom beyond, which was open to the main room but secluded by a wall, I glanced at him for approval, and went inside upon his nod. His bed was built into a corner, on a raised platform, permitting access from only one side by what appeared to be a climbing net. Practical for a military man—and fun for a child.

He followed me, stopping in the archway to watch me explore his private space.

"May I?" I asked, crossing to his wardrobe, for I was curious about the style of his attire here in Cokyri, and he again motioned me ahead.

I glanced between Narian and the clothing inside the wardrobe several times, trying to understand the disparity. The Narian I knew dressed practically, ever a soldier, thinking of comfort and of blending into his surroundings. Yet he possessed a collection of rich clothing, the fabrics similar to what I would have expected to find in Steldor's or my father's wardrobe, not in his. Mounted on the inside of one of the doors were dress swords, and on the other, shelves that held jewels far more valuable than anything we had in Hytanica.

"Narian, this is…" I started, then shook my head in wonder.

"Ridiculous, I know." He crossed to his bed and leaned against the netting.

"No!" I exclaimed. "It's *unbelievably* beautiful."

I pointed to an exquisite ruby ring and flashed him a smile. "*This* could have been my betrothal ring."

His bath chamber across the main room was all that remained, so I backtracked and entered it. The extravagance to which I was accustomed within the Hytanican palace did not range so far as to include the depth and size of his bath, nor the unusual mosaic tiles set into the floor. But what struck me the most were the shelves filled with ointments and bandages, and the long table against the wall that was similar to what one would find in a physician's examination room. He had in many ways grown up a prince, but this chamber was more telling of his past than all the finery in his wardrobe.

When I returned to the parlor, I felt strangely cold. Narian had once more taken up his place on the sofa, and I went to sit at his feet, wanting to be closer to the fire. He swung around and put one leg on each side of me, then started to massage my back. After a few minutes, he slipped down behind me to wrap his arms around my waist, and I leaned against him. He was warm and safe and all that I wanted. At times I felt that there was no world outside of him, and it was the best feeling I ever had. This was one of those times.

"Were you ever happy here?" I softly inquired.

"Yes," he answered after a moment of thought. "I was— here in the temple."

Though I had not handled seeing Miranna's room very well, I again had a surge of curiosity about the Overlord's Hall, which Narian had subtly referenced. But I did not ask him to take me there—seeing it would not help me, and it would not help him. He needed to forget that place.

"Then tell me something about your childhood. Something pleasant."

I closed my eyes, feeling the vibration of his chest as he began to speak.

"I remember when that mural on my wall was painted. I was perhaps six or seven. The High Priestess commissioned an artist, and gave her freedom to paint something colorful and unique, something that would amuse me. I was permitted to watch, but at that age…"

"Watching wasn't enough," I guessed, and he laughed.

"The artist was on a ladder, and she had her palette with her, but she'd left the majority of her paints on the floor. I was into them before she could say a word, and I spread paint *everywhere*. In my hair, on my clothes, the floors, the wall where she was trying to create her masterpiece, everywhere." He was reminiscing now instead of just telling me a story, seeing it unfold in his mind. "I'd forgotten, honestly forgotten, that I'd been told not to touch the paints. Nan was furious—we were supposed to go to a banquet that night and I'd—"

"Nan?" I asked, and he tensed for a moment.

"That's what I used to call the High Priestess, when I was young."

Smiling at the idea, I nestled against him and said, "Go on."

He continued the story, and I listened contentedly, eventually falling asleep in his embrace.

SHASELLE

CHAPTER 32

GAINS AND LOSSES

IT BEGAN NOT WITH A SIGNAL, BUT WITH A FIRE in the dead of night. Temerson had been sent to the edge of the military base to light his rocket, but first he had set the barracks aflame. Screams from Cokyrian soldiers trapped within echoed through the streets of the city, awakening men and women and children. Then three beacons soared silently into the air, all from different directions. They exploded in the sky, raining down sparks and ash, calling Hytanica to arms.

It wasn't long before I heard shouts, followed by pounding, and the very foundation of our home shuddered. I raced out of doors and to the side of the house where my father's office was located, coming to an abrupt halt at the scene before me. Men had broken through the foundation and were tossing weapons to each other, paying no mind to me. When the cache was empty, they marched off, some destination in mind. I scanned the neighborhood, watching other groups of men joining ranks, having broken into more stores of weapons, and I knew this was happening all over the city.

I stood still, debating what I should do. The question itself should have been an easy one—my mother needed me, my

siblings needed me and it was my responsibility to help keep
them safe. But excitement was now in my blood. If I returned
home, I would end up waiting hour after hour with them for
news, which really wouldn't do anyone any good. Surely I
could be of more use out here, gathering information, seeing
the course of the battle for myself. Yes, that would be best.

My energy and senses heightened, I headed down the street
toward Uncle Cannan's house, hoping I would find Steldor
or Galen there. While I knew they would keep me out of the
fighting, I hoped that they would give me a weapon; then I
would find a safe vantage point from which to watch, for I
wanted to see my father's death avenged, wanted to enjoy the
sight of our men routing the enemy once and for all.

But as I drew within a square block of my destination, I
came upon a troop of Cokyrian soldiers, likewise in well-
ordered ranks, sweeping the neighborhood for rebels. I ducked
down and hastily crawled under the front porch of one of the
houses, praying they had not seen me and wouldn't discover
me. What I was doing was not safe; what I was doing could
get me killed.

The noise level within the city continued to rise, until the
din made my head throb—it was impossible to close out the
pounding of feet; the shouts and screams; the clank of weaponry; the screeching of terrified animals; and the roar of fires
and crack of burning wood. Gathering my courage, I emerged
from my hiding place and headed toward the military base,
feeling a morbid desire to see the destruction and chaos for
myself. I didn't get far before nausea and fear overcame me.
Men were engaged in combat up and down the streets, their
movements jarringly erratic in the flickering lights of the fires
and torches. Blood sprayed off swords and daggers as they
sickeningly pierced flesh, muscle and bone; and gasps of pain
accompanied by the horrid, gurgling sound of blood-filled

breathing assaulted my senses. I staggered to the side of the street, crumpling against a building, my hands covering my ears as I fought to retain my sanity. This was not at all how I had pictured our glorious revenge. This was unimaginable horror.

Then explosions rocked the buildings around me—Cokyrian powder, capable of killing many in a single blast. No longer wanting to be a part of this, I ran down the street in terror. Flames sprang to life, and I caught glimpses of men fighting and dying, any sense of an organized battle eradicated. The screaming and shouting was constant, like an avalanche of heart-wrenching sound. The smell of smoke and blood was overwhelming. The heat on my face brought beads of sweat to my forehead, and when I wiped them away, layers of dirt smeared with the moisture. This did not look or feel like my city anymore. This was a nightmare. This was like going back in time, back to the military training field, back to my father's death.

His brother. The hand outstretched—

My feet pounded against the earth. I didn't have time to think of Papa now. I needed to reach home—I should not have left when I saw the flares soaring through the night sky. It had been an idiotic, dangerous notion to try to determine what was happening.

Homes crackled and collapsed as I flew past them—fire spread quickly in this dry and windy weather, destroying what it had taken months to rebuild—and my house could easily be among them. A man stumbled out of an alley clutching his gut, blood running between his fingers, and I leaped aside. I squeezed my eyes shut and tried to keep moving, not wanting to see, but my foot caught on rubble and I fell, hitting the stone of the street and scraping my hands and chin. Pain shot through my head and neck, then shrieks of misery rent the air and someone kicked me.

I rolled over to be met with an image so gruesome it could not be real, yet I knew it was. A Cokyrian soldier was on fire, moving frenetically in a dance of agony, her screams fighting to be heard against the deafening noise that surrounded me. Quaking, I buried my head beneath my arms, praying for her to die. When the shrieks were no more, I scrambled to my feet, my hand coming into contact with warm metal. I snatched up the dagger and started running again, one word pounding in my head. *Home. Home. Home.*

Adrenaline was feeding my body, protecting me from exhaustion. I'd sprinted across what must have been half the city and felt no need to slow or stop. The western residential district lay ahead, and I dashed down the street, praying no one would intercept me. I didn't want to die by the sword. I didn't want to die at all.

My home was up ahead, but I could hardly see it through the smoky miasma. I rushed up the walk, my mind whirring, for the front door was hanging off its hinges. Then a man in a Cokyrian uniform dragged my brother, kicking and screaming, onto our front stoop.

"No!" I screeched, and the Cokyrian soldier looked up just as I barreled into him, my dagger pointed at his stomach. Both the soldier and I hit the ground, and I felt warm, sticky wetness seeping over my hands. The man gasped and stiffened, then moved no more.

I thrust his body away from me, leaving the dagger buried between his ribs, and came to my feet, my entire body atremble. Celdrid was on his hands and knees, crawling back toward the door, sobbing, then someone wrapped an arm around his chest and picked him up. I leaped forward to save him a second time, but the man snatched my arm, saying my name. It was Steldor. The strength almost left my legs as relief hit me—he was alive, and he would protect us.

My cousin hurried us inside, where my mother was coming to her feet, blood trickling from her temple.

"Where are the others?" Steldor demanded as Celdrid struggled in his arms, confused and afraid.

"Thank God!" Mother cried, taking her son into her embrace. "The children are in the cellar. I sent them there."

"The three of you, join them," Steldor ordered. "You'll be safer there than anywhere else. Hurry."

Just before he pushed us ahead of him toward the stairway off the kitchen, I got a good look at him. His shirt was torn and bloodied, his boots grimy, his hair soaked with sweat. He'd put away his sword in order to help us, but I could see blood on its hilt—he had been fighting for his life.

"Where is everyone else?" I asked as Steldor all but forced us down the cellar steps. "Do you know if they're all right?"

"No, it's impossible to keep track of anyone."

We reached the earthen floor of the cellar, and Mother passed Celdrid to Dahnath. The other girls were huddled together in the corner, wrapped tightly in a blanket. I gazed up at my cousin, and a noise caught his attention. He laid the fingers of his left hand against his lips, his right hand grasping the hilt of his sword. Then Grayden appeared on the stairs.

"Shaselle!" he called, rushing to join us.

"She's all right," Steldor told him. "Stay with them. Put boxes, bottles, anything that will hinder descent on the stairway, and move everyone into the wine cellar. Barricade that door, and do not come out until I return for you."

"And will you return?" Grayden asked, coming down the last few steps.

"Yes."

With that promise, Steldor flew up the staircase, disappearing from view with the closing of the door, shutting out the light and noise from above.

Mother, Grayden and I used whatever we could lay our hands on to block passage, while Dahnath herded Celdrid and the younger girls into the wine cellar, trying to stay their crying. We soon followed, closing and barring the door, then carrying crates and shelves to provide a further barricade, hoping no one would be able to break through. Having done what we could, Mother and I joined Dahnath and the huddled children, sitting close together, not daring to speak. Ganya curled up against me, her small frame shuddering, and I held her, sharing the warmth of my body with her.

I could hear everyone's breathing, so much louder now than the noises from outside. Muffled shouts still reached us, the occasional sound of an explosion and of fighting. Grayden stayed on his feet, gripping his sword tightly, prepared to fight for us if necessary. I stared at him, my eyes gradually losing focus, the exhaustion I had been ignoring setting in. Through the terror, the panic and the uncertainty of this battle, sleep called to me, and I gave myself over to it.

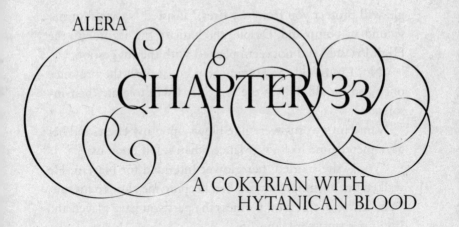

CHAPTER 33

A COKYRIAN WITH HYTANICAN BLOOD

THE AIR WAS THICK. SOMETHING WAS BURNING. Something was on fire. Then I was pulled to my feet, roughly and urgently. As my eyes oriented, I remembered where I was—in Narian's quarters—and he was dragging me toward the door.

"What's going on?" I rasped, coughing, but he didn't answer. Instead, he tugged me down the corridor toward the staircase. I gazed through the large windows, where everything was red and hazy with smoke, then the wind blew, parting some of the gray billows, and I could see buildings in flame. Panic seized me, my heart hammering so forcefully I thought it would explode.

"Narian!" I cried, but still he did not respond. With no choice but to follow, I stumbled along behind him as we descended the stairs to the main floor. We hurried into the foyer, and he pulled me toward a set of large doors on our left. We went inside to find the High Priestess pacing in front of a regal, imposing throne set with diamonds, emeralds, sapphires and rubies. Six shield maidens surrounded her, Rava among them.

"Your Highness, we must stay here. The stone of the temple will protect you from the fires," insisted Narian's former second-in-command. Despite the logic of the argument, the High Priestess did not seem pleased with the suggestion.

"No, I must ride to Hytanica and deal with the province once and for all. This is the last time I will tolerate their insolence."

Nantilam's words were like blows upon my chest, and her gaze pierced me like a war lance when it fell upon us.

"You!" she snarled, her glower intended for Narian. He walked unflinchingly toward her, keeping me close to his side. "You knew of this plot! Confess the part you have played and I will perhaps spare your life."

Narian put a hand on my shoulder, telling me to stay where I was, then took a few steps closer to the woman who had been like a mother to him. I stood frozen, waiting along with her to hear his answer. What was going on? What had Narian done?

"I am not a part of this," he declared.

Nantilam quickly closed the remaining distance between them. She was infuriated, her green eyes flaring as vividly as the flames outside.

"But you know more than you have told me." Her voice was low, dangerous, rumbling with anger.

"I know that the Hytanicans's first rebellion was meant to distract us, and that those captured willingly sacrificed their lives. I know that right now, the men you wanted to execute are waging one last fight to reclaim their kingdom."

My head was spinning, both at the news and at my own idiocy. How could I have failed to see this? How could I not have known it would happen? I had chosen to be blind, even when Narian had all but begged me to come to Cokyri with him. I hadn't *wanted* to see it. But the clues had been there. Now people were dying in Hytanica. Someone, probably London, had set the fires here in Cokyri to hinder the arrival of messengers from the province with word of the revolt and to forestall the High Priestess from sending reinforcements. We were trapped and helpless, able only to imagine the battle taking place on the other side of the river.

"I knew something was amiss," the High Priestess simmered. "I knew it the moment I saw Alera with you. You're a traitor, Narian."

He shook his head, his expression hard. "I am no traitor. I did everything you asked of me. I conquered Hytanica for you and the Overlord, I administered the province as you wanted for months, and I did not plot against you." Narian's voice dropped to a fierce whisper. "I am not to blame for what is happening today—for giving the Hytanicans a *fair* chance at retaking what is rightfully theirs. My only sin is that I did not try to stop them."

Nantilam scrutinized him for what seemed an eternity.

"I listened to you," she vehemently said at last. "I loved you, and I trusted you, and I fought not to lose you after my brother's death."

"You never trusted me," Narian contradicted, interrupting whatever else she had intended to say. "And with good reason. You believe the only way to repay a betrayal is with a betrayal. You betrayed me in the worst way imaginable. You lied to me my entire life, trained me and used me as a weapon, never telling me the real reason I was of value to you." His blue eyes flashed, their sapphire brilliance rivaling the ever-changing emerald sparks in hers. "But I will no longer be manipulated for your causes, and I will *not* become another warlord. You can consider yourself repaid."

The High Priestess's rage built to a frightening level, her body almost shaking with the effort to retain control. Her shield maidens watched in fear from where they stood near her throne, while I locked my knees to force myself to stay in place. Then she backhanded Narian across the face, forcefully enough that he stumbled.

"You will regret what you have done, Narian," she swore as he brought a hand to his cheek. "The Hytanicans will not succeed. You will pay for protecting their leaders from execution and for your willingness to step aside."

"They may very well succeed. Don't pretend otherwise. This is no longer a game of tug of war, *Your Highness*. It is a game of chess. And as you well know, Cannan and London have always been masterful strategists."

"London?"

"Yes, he is alive and well. I suspect he is responsible for the chaos that surrounds us."

At the mention of London, my eyes snapped to Narian, and my heart ached to hear more. But something in Nantilam's visage changed, and she turned away to take up her throne.

"So you have lent no assistance to the Hytanicans—you have not armed them, have not repositioned our troops to aid their strike, have not left our soldiers without strong leadership?"

"No, I have not. Our forces are in place, and I took all the usual precautions before traveling here as you ordered."

"Then it may indeed be interesting to see what the Hytanicans can do. Cannan as a commander long rivaled my brother, and London...well, a man such as London is rare. If he and I had not been enemies, I would have chosen him to father my own child."

My heart lurched at this revelation, but Narian showed no reaction, continuing to stand stiffly before her. The High Priestess met his eyes, evaluating him for another long moment.

"I have wondered always what kind of man you would become, Narian. You can believe what you will, but to me you were never just a tool to be forged, an instrument of unique purpose and, therefore, worth. You came to me as a babe in arms, and I treated you as my son to the extent my brother would permit. Now I see that you are also a rare man."

Nantilam shifted her commanding eyes to me.

"And you, Alera, are no doubt part of the reason. Had you been born Cokyrian, you would probably be at my side, one of my trusted shield maidens, for you have more than enough courage and ingenuity to merit such an honor. Again, something I did not expect to find in Hytanica."

"Then let's come to it," Narian snapped. "Be the wise and fair ruler I grew up believing you to be. If Cannan and his men should succeed in routing our troops, then accept that outcome and recognize Hytanica as a free land. Negotiate a peace treaty with Alera. Ask for whatever crops and goods Cokyri needs, but *trade* for them."

"You cannot rewrite history, Narian," she reproached. "Hytanica asked to be conquered the day its king attacked us. I was charged with that crusade before I was even crowned."

"You cannot rewrite history, but you don't have to be controlled by it, either," he argued, and Nantilam's eyes narrowed dangerously. "In the end, the Overlord's crusade had little to do with history. He wanted to dominate Hytanica for domination's sake. That was never your purpose—you fought to preserve your people's pride and their heritage, you took the actions you believed necessary to ensure your empire's growth and prosperity. Reaffirm your goals now—recognize that what is best for Cokyri is enduring peace with Hytanica."

"And are you giving me advice as the commander of my military, or are you issuing a threat?"

"I am offering advice," Narian replied, with a deferential bow, then his tone and posture subtly became more intimidating. "Although I will stand against you if I am forced to make that choice."

The High Priestess came to her feet, and for the first time, I saw indecision on her face. If Narian fought against her, any battle with Hytanica would be long and brutal, with no guarantee of victory. The Overlord's powers had not passed to her, would not in all probability reemerge until Nantilam gave birth to a daughter, so for the time being, Narian held the upper hand.

Nantilam glared at him for a long time, battling her anger, her pride, her instincts. Then she nodded.

"I will speak to Alera. Alone."

After the room had been cleared, the High Priestess beckoned for me to approach. I complied, but did not show deference, for ruler did not bow to ruler. But neither did I speak, for hers was the first move to make. I waited, strangely calm, for I respected her, but was no longer afraid of her.

"A treaty with Hytanica is possible," she declared, walking toward me. "But it is not as simple a matter as Narian makes it sound."

I remained silent, waiting for her to set the direction of the conversation, for while I felt I could hold my own with her, I also knew she was far more experienced than I.

"Our countries have pushed each other to the brink of destruction," she continued, walking to gaze out a window at the conflagration, and I followed. "We have both lost much, but for enduring peace, we must each gain a victory."

She assessed me, her eyes calculating. "I did not misjudge you, back when you were living in exile in that cave. We can work together, but Hytanica must make certain concessions."

"Then state your demands."

"You already know we desire crops, tools, seed, planting and irrigation knowledge. I am willing to trade for those things—jewels, precious metals and advancements we have that you have yet to discover. I have other concerns, however. The first is perhaps the most significant. Will your kingdom recognize you as its ruler or will it clamor for a King?"

Her question took me aback, but I knew better than to be insulted. She was well aware of the history of my kingdom and was well informed as to the unsettled state of provincial rule.

"Yes, they will," I asserted, making steady eye contact. "Over the past six months, the citizens have been adjusting to me in that role. I have dealt with their concerns, eased their pain, guided the rebuilding of our city, reestablished foreign trade and reinstated some of our traditions, such as the Harvest Festival. And I *am* their Queen, duly crowned and with the right by blood to the throne. I can also assure you that no one will be crowned King, for Narian is the man to whom I will bind myself. But just as it is here in Cokyri, I will not head the military."

"And the men—Cannan, London, Steldor, the others— you can control them?"

"No," I answered honestly. "Nor would I want to. But they will not go behind my back. Neither will they flout me. We learned to work with one another and trust each other when we were in exile. I will always seek their *advice,* but I will be the one making the decisions.

"Very well, then. Peace may well be possible."

She strode across the room to take up position on her throne, leaving me to once more follow. Having spent much time observing my father during his reign as King, I knew she was posturing. What I didn't know was the reason she felt it was necessary.

Nantilam rested her forearms on the arms of the throne, watching me, and I forced myself to wait her out. At last she spoke, picking up an earlier thread in our rather one-sided conversation.

"While peace is possible, Alera, each side must have its victory. Trade is an even proposition, and your kingdom is regaining its freedom. As Cokyri's ruler, there are two things that I must have."

"And what would those things be?" For the first time I felt apprehensive, and Cannan's long ago words about the ability of the Cokyrians to manipulate surfaced in my mind.

"First, the trails we have laid through the mountains and forest will remain in place, making transportation of what we need less laborious. The same is true of the bridge to the east that my engineers constructed across the Recorah River. Second, Cokyrian citizens and official envoys must be permitted to enter and depart Hytanica without search or suspicion. We are to be treated in the same manner as you treat citizens of the Kingdoms of Emotana, Sarterad and Gourhan."

I hesitated, weighing this demand carefully. This was an issue of trust. In the end, I decided to trust my own military leaders to maintain vigilance

"Agreed, although the same terms should apply to any Hytanican who wants to visit Cokyri."

The High Priestess's eyes narrowed, but her voice remained unruffled when she next spoke.

"Very well. That leaves us with one final issue to discuss, Alera, and it is perhaps the most important one. Narian must stay in Cokyri."

I stared at her, the blood pounding in my ears, appalled and angry, for this demand went too far. Narian was his own man, was Hytanican by birth and choice, and he and I were to marry.

"Narian is not a bargaining point," I indignantly declared. "He will not be part of any treaty as though he is a possession."

"He will not be mentioned specifically in the treaty, but nonetheless, this issue is not negotiable. Narian has power that I intend to control. For me to do that, he must be here. When the time comes, I will choose an appropriate partner for him, and she will bear his child. I know the origins of Narian's power, but not if it will run in his blood. And I will not risk that it will. Any child of his will be Cokyrian."

I was dumbfounded, furious, aghast, indignant—more emotions than I would have thought possible to register in the blink of an eye.

"Narian will never acquiesce to such terms."

"If there is to be lasting peace between our countries, then he must agree." Nantilam leaned forward, her expression shrewd, and I knew everything Cannan had ever said about her was true. "It is up to you to convince him."

"I will not, nor could I."

"This is the test of a ruler, Alera. Will you sacrifice one for the good of all? Will you give up your own happiness for the good of your kingdom?"

"If my countrymen have been victorious this day, no treaty between us will be necessary," I boldly asserted. "We will be free of our own accord."

"A very short respite." Her eyes hardened, and the cordial tone in her voice disappeared, to be replaced by menace. "I will not hesitate to attack. We have always had superior numbers and weaponry. And the next time you are overrun, I will not be so foolish as to leave any of your military leaders alive. Your people will be enslaved, so dominated that no Hytanican will ever again look a Cokyrian in the eye."

I struggled not to break eye contact with her, even though her powerful aura diminished me. "Narian and I will not let that happen," I stated, as firmly as I could. "He will take away any chance you might have for victory, and by the time

Cokyri's defeat is secured, I will be twice the ruler and twice the woman you are."

"I think not," she said, with an artful tone that I did not like. "Did you really think I would give Narian the option of opposing me?"

"What do you mean?"

"He will have trusted his mother, taken me at my word, and he will have consumed the refreshment he was offered."

"What have you done?" I gasped, horrified at what I was hearing.

"He will be in pain by now, having drunk the poison I provided. And I am the only one who can save him. So you see, it is your choice, how you lose him. You can give him over to me, or you can let him die."

I staggered away from her, unable to think, unable to believe she could have done something so monstrous. "Why? Why would you do this? *How* could you do this?"

"Because *I* am able to sacrifice one for the good of all."

"Where is he?"

"In his quarters. He will be suffering by now, but he won't show it. He knows well how to disguise pain. When the chills and sweats begin, he will think he is sick. At that point, he will have about three hours. I suggest you keep that in mind."

I spun on my heel and fled the throne room, fate itself dogging my footsteps, then continued up the stairs and on to Narian's room. I did not know what I would say or do, or how I could thwart the chain of events the High Priestess had put in motion. I only knew that I could not let him die.

CHAPTER 34

TO HAVE TRULY LIVED

FIERCE HAMMERING AWAKENED ME. AT FIRST I thought it was the throbbing of my head, which ached as if I had the plague. But when I peeled my eyes open, I saw Grayden on his feet, facing the door, his sword at the ready.

I scrambled up, not sure how to help him, then grabbed a bottle of wine, knowing it could be used to hit someone, and that after it broke, the edges would be sharp. It was the best I had.

Men were groaning as they strained to push the door inward. Our barricade worked well for a while, then the crates tumbled down in a rush of noise and dust, and my heart leaped to my throat.

"Move, move!" Grayden whispered urgently to Mother and the younger children, while Dahnath came to stand beside me, likewise snatching up a bottle. We waited, blinking in the blinding light that shone through the doorway, not knowing whether the shape before us was friend or foe.

"Hello?" the man called, and I dropped my bottle, letting it shatter at my feet.

"Galen!" I cried, flying past Grayden. Dahnath set down

her wine bottle, and Mother came away from the far wall, all of us eager—and terrified—to find out what was going on.

"Come on," Galen said, reaching for my hand. He lifted me over the mess, then turned to assist the rest of my family, leaving Drael and a man I did not know to guide me up the stairway.

When I reached the top, I stood still, surveying my home, shocked at its condition. It had been ransacked—our belongings scattered and broken. Chairs and other furnishings were splintered, and glass from the windows crunched underneath my feet. At least it was still standing; I doubted everyone could say the same.

"Galen, is it…is it over?" I asked, for he had come to my side. Grayden and my family gathered round, Dahnath tucked firmly into the arms of her betrothed, wanting to hear his answer.

"We outnumbered the Cokyrians after Temerson took a third of their army in the barracks fire. We locked down the city gates, and the villagers prevented reinforcements from entering. But most important, Narian chose to stay out of it." He grinned and wiped some of the grime off his face. "Yes, it's over. It's done, thanks to Cannan and London and all those who fought. We once more stand as a free Hytanica."

Despite the death and destruction that lay all around us, relief coursed through my veins. As smiles appeared, Galen broke out laughing—a tired, incredulous, elated and absolutely beautiful sound. Then he led us toward the front door.

Mother held Celdrid, pressing his face against her shoulder as we stepped outside. I kept Ganya close to me, for neither of the younger children needed to see the carnage that lay beyond. The first body I saw was that of the Cokyrian soldier whose life I had taken, and Galen quickly shoved it out of the way. His action, however, was pointless—hundreds more bodies lay in the streets.

"Steldor, is he all right?" I tentatively asked, for my cousin had promised to return for us.

"Yes, he's fine. He sent me to find you. He couldn't come himself because he's busy dealing with the Cokyrians who surrendered or were taken captive."

"Casualties?" Grayden asked, his hand on my back, speaking for us all.

"Steldor is having a count made. Cokyrian deaths will be higher than our own."

I frowned, for Steldor seemed to have taken charge of a lot of things. Things that I would have expected to be handled by the Captain of the Guard.

"Is Steldor working with Uncle Cannan?" I ventured.

Galen hesitated, and the hair on the back of my neck prickled. Something was wrong.

"Some of our men are still missing."

"*Our* men?" I choked, though the answer was manifest from the words Galen had used.

He nodded nonetheless.

"Who?" I pressed.

Sadness washed over Galen's face. "Some are friends of Steldor's and mine. But there are others, too…the captain."

He said it so distantly, referring to my uncle by title instead of by name so he would not have to feel the same dread and grief that was knotting my stomach. I took a deep breath, trying to forestall panic. We didn't know Cannan's fate, which meant he could still be alive. He and London had been the masterminds behind the rebellion. Maybe he was with the deputy captain now, maybe they were dealing with Narian or the High Priestess, perhaps already negotiating terms.

While I could come up with a number of explanations for

my uncle's absence, a fundamental truth tore at my heart—no matter what else the captain might be doing, he would be searching for Steldor and Galen just as they were searching for him. And he would check on the rest of us. Yet he was unaccounted for—no presence, but no body, either.

At Galen's troublesome news, my mother and Dahnath, accompanied by Drael, took the other children back inside our damaged home. I knew they would begin to clear the rubble, for taking care of things was how Mother dealt with worry and sorrow. Grayden and I went with Galen, walking the streets, where other Hytanicans were assisting the wounded or helping to tally the dead. Every so often, people would dash by us, and Galen and Grayden would tense to defend us. A few Cokyrians still tried to flee, but were run down by Hytanicans and subdued. Fear gripped me whenever this happened, and I tried to focus on the tops of buildings, where dozens of blue-and-gold Hytanican flags proudly flew, with no danger that they would be removed and burned.

We turned onto the thoroughfare and walked north toward the palace, and my spirits lifted. Despite the destruction and death, this was a glorious day for Hytanica. I started to say something to this effect to Galen, but he halted, his face ashen, and the words died on my lips. His hand fell on my shoulder, and I looked at him in confusion, then followed his gaze farther up the road. My eyes fell on Steldor, who was kneeling on the unforgiving stone of the street, a few other men milling around him, and my confusion grew. Shouldn't Galen be pleased to find his best friend?

I couldn't see what Steldor was doing, but after a moment he stood, and the men who were with him lifted a flat litter bearing a body. My eyes took in the height and build of the man lying unnaturally still, the nearly black hair, the officer's insignia on the black leather jerkin, the blood—and my breath caught in my throat.

I tried to run to Steldor, denials raging in my head, but Galen pulled me against his chest. I stared uncomprehendingly at the litter, the image burning itself into my brain, while tears stung my eyes. Cannan's arms were folded over his chest, his sword tucked beneath his hands. It was really the only evidence any of us needed. As sobs shook me, Galen passed me into the arms of my suitor and advanced upon his best friend, his motion unnaturally stiff. Steldor turned his head at the sound of the approaching footsteps, his dark eyes dry but looking helpless, hopeless and alone.

Cannan had been Galen's father the same way he had been Steldor's, and the young men stood side by side, watching the Hytanican soldiers carry the litter toward the palace, not moving until it was out of sight. Both of them seemed lost, not knowing what to do or say, then they wrapped their arms around one another in a fierce embrace, befitting the brothers that they were. They held each other for a long time, almost as unmoving as their deceased father.

I fell back against Grayden, losing what little strength remained to me, and he hugged me, eventually leading me back to my house. Though I was only eighteen, I felt I had stumbled upon one of life's few truisms: with every step forward came a step backward, with every gain came a loss and with every joy came tears. In the end, the best for which one could hope was to leave the world in better straits than existed on the day of your birth; to have truly *lived*. And oh, how Cannan, the Captain of the Guard, had lived.

CHAPTER 35

FAREWELL

NARIAN WAS WALKING RESTLESSLY AROUND HIS parlor when I entered, and my worry increased tenfold. Was he moving about because he was in pain? I glanced around the room, noticing an empty wineglass and a half-eaten bowl of soup.

"You're out of breath, Alera," he said with a smile. "I hope that means your conversation with Nantilam went well."

I hesitated, unsure how to begin, unsure how to tell him what she was demanding, what she had done to him. Unsure how to tell him she had meted out one last betrayal.

"How are you feeling?" I blurted, and he laughed.

"I'm fine, but you don't seem to be. Come and talk to me."

He took my hand and led me to the sofa, pulling me down to sit beside him. He winced as he did so, an indication he was experiencing some discomfort. I brushed his hair off his forehead, subtly checking for a fever, then told him of the High Priestess's desires.

"The terms of the actual treaty are not a problem, Narian, but Nantilam won't enter into it unless you agree to make

Cokyri your home. She wants to control your power, now and in the future, even to the point of progeny."

"Alera," he calmly said, taking both my hands in his. "Those decisions are not hers to make. Besides, she's a little late."

"I don't understand."

He looked at me, bemused, then rolled up his right shirtsleeve, revealing an intricate tattoo encircling his forearm just below the elbow—the Cokyrian symbol that a man was voluntarily bound to a woman. I stared at it; I stared at him; and I burst into tears. His eyebrows rose in surprise, but he nonetheless took me into his arms.

"That's not the reaction I expected," he drolly commented, "but it's convinced me something is wrong."

"How…are…you…feeling?" I managed between sobs.

"You've already asked me that, and I'm fine."

When I finally had my weeping under control, words tumbled from my mouth.

"Even if the revolt has been successful, the High Priestess won't enter into a treaty unless you stay in Cokyri. Otherwise, she'll attack Hytanica again, and this time she will kill all of our military leaders and enslave my people. And she wants you to bind yourself to a woman of her choosing because if your powers pass to a child, she wants the child to be Cokyrian."

"That's all well and good, but this time, she won't be able to have things her way. There's no need for you to worry about this. We are strong enough to take her on, Alera."

"But we're not." I glanced once more toward the food he had been given, and a flicker of understanding appeared in his eyes. "We have no choice, Narian, because she's poisoned your food and drink and only she can heal you. And I don't know what to do, only that I cannot let you die!"

"Shhh," he soothed, holding me close, and I couldn't understand how he could be so calm. Not when panic rose higher inside me with each passing moment.

When I had quieted, resting with my head cradled against his chest, he tried to sort through the things I had said.

"So Nantilam, in her wisdom, has linked Hytanica's freedom to my willingness to stay in Cokyri, and she has effectively taken me out of the fighting by poisoning my food?"

I shuddered, then nodded.

"If I stay here, she is willing to sign a treaty, but if I'm not, she will never relinquish Hytanica and I won't be around to prevent it."

"Yes," I murmured.

"So she is tearing us apart, dictating the rest of my life and we have to go along with it or she will destroy Hytanica?"

"Yes. And we're running out of time."

He shook his head in awe. "I have to hand it to her, Alera. She's ruthless in pursuing what she wants."

"This is serious, Narian." I found his attitude almost irritating. He obviously understood the direness of his situation, yet was acting like it was only a game.

"I know it's serious, but there is only one choice as far as I'm concerned. I don't want to live without you, Alera. I won't live without you."

I sat up and searched the depths of his blue eyes. "What do you mean?"

He leaned forward and kissed me tenderly, and my pulse raced. Then I put my hands on his chest and pushed myself away.

"Tell me, Narian."

"All right. There are three things I believe with all my heart. Hytanica can withstand a Cokyrian assault, I can no longer let Nantilam control my life and I will die before I let you go."

His eyes met mine and he unlaced my blouse, slowly pushing it off my shoulders. This time I did not resist him.

"What I want," he softly finished, "is to spend these last hours holding the woman I love, the woman to whom I am bound."

"But how are you feeling?"

"Trust me, Alera, I'm not feeling any pain right now."

Tears trickled from the corners of my eyes as I opened his shirt and ran my fingers over the muscles of his chest. He stood, leading me to the rug in front of the hearth, where he drew me down to kneel beside him. His touch was warm, gentle, as he almost reverently removed my clothing, then he stripped off his shirt and breeches, his skin and his golden hair glistening in the light cast by the fire. As my pulse and breathing quickened, he caressed me, first with his eyes, then with his hands and mouth.

"I love you, Alera," he whispered against my skin, and I gave in to him completely, sinking into the feelings he stirred in me, knowing I stirred the same feelings in him. In all my dreams of what this moment would be like, I had never imagined the soaring bliss that came from giving yourself to another person without reservation, without fear, without pressure. A person you loved and trusted with all your heart and who returned those feelings a hundredfold.

The chills and sweats began about an hour later, but Narian was unyielding in his decision not to seek Nantilam's aid.

"But I fear for you, Alera, when I'm gone. I need to ensure your safe return to Hytanica."

"What are you saying?"

"We should leave this place while I still have some time. Let me at least get you close to home. I doubt the High Priestess will even try to stop us, since she knows I don't have long to live."

I nodded, his words igniting a spark of hope. "Maybe we can make it to Hytanica before you are too ill to ride—perhaps our alchemists will recognize the poison and be able to provide an antidote."

"You can hope if you like, but I doubt Hytanica will be familiar with a Cokyrian compound. Still, we should go."

I raced to my room to gather my personal items while Narian sent word for our horses to be brought to the front gate, saddled and prepared for riding. Another half hour passed before we were mounted and ready to leave, Narian wrapped in a blanket over his cloak, for his symptoms were worsening. The High Priestess stood in the background, watching us go, knowing Narian would soon be dead. I didn't understand how her heart could be so cold, especially toward someone she professed to love.

The air in the city was gray, colored with bits of ash, and it stung my nostrils and burned my lungs. Narian didn't need this aggravation on top of the pain and fever he was suffering, but there was little that could be done about it. We both tried to cover our mouths and noses with our cloaks, and we rode as quickly as the congested and rubble-strewn streets would allow. I was glad all the Cokyrians we passed were distracted and unaware that I was Hytanican. I doubted that I would get far if they realized who I was.

When we at last broke free of the city, the air cleared and our journey became easier, for in this direction, we were going mostly downhill. Narian briefly revived, the freshening breeze clearing his head and lungs, for which I was thankful. I wasn't familiar enough with the countryside to have found my way without him.

By the time we neared the spot where we had camped when traveling to Cokyri, the spot where the Recorah River flowed under a rock outcropping, Narian was slumping forward against his horse's neck. His fever was raging, and he was slipping in and out of awareness, sometimes haunted by hallucinations. I brought our horses to a halt, glad we had made it this far, but knowing he would make it no farther. This would at least be a good place for him to die, right on the boundary between the two lands he loved.

I dismounted, then went to assist him. He was barely conscious and almost fell from his horse, and the sorrow that tore at the core of my being was almost unbearable. I lay a blanket over a bed of leaves and made him as comfortable as possible on top of it, then gathered kindling for a fire. When I had done all I could for him, I sat down beside him, occasionally adding wood to the flames to chase away the chill and keep any wild animals at bay. But mainly I kept vigil, wondering how much time he still had.

As the night wore on, my mind began to drift, remembering other death watches, other times when people I cared about had been injured or ill—London, Steldor, even Narian once before. Those men had survived their ordeals due to the magic the High Priestess possessed. It was ironic and so unfair that she was the person who had now put Narian in jeopardy.

Eventually, Narian's breathing became slower and shallower, and I consoled myself with the thought that he wasn't in pain, as small a blessing as that was. Tears trailed down my cheeks, for I wanted more time with him, wanted a life and a family with him, wanted to grow old with him. The High Priestess had no right to play God with our lives like this, and I hated her for it. With a sigh, I whisked the moisture off my cheeks, then studied Narian's handsome features, creating a portrait in my mind. I traced his cheekbones and jaw, lingering over his lips. Impulsively, I leaned down to kiss him and his eyelids flicked open.

"I will always love you, Alera," he murmured, momentarily regaining clarity.

"And I will always love you." I curled up beside him, my arm across his chest, willing him to stay with me for as long as possible. I continually fought against drowsiness, but exhaustion and grief eventually got the best of me, and I drifted off to sleep.

Someone was shaking my shoulder and I slowly came awake to see London crouched down beside me. I bolted upright, then reached out to touch his face, certain I was seeing a ghost.

"Alera, it's all right. I'm here to bring you safely home."

I nodded, then shifted onto my knees, my voice urgent. "The High Priestess has poisoned Narian. She doesn't want him to fight against her if she sends reinforcements to Hytanica."

London placed a hand upon Narian's chest, feeling for a heartbeat, for the rise and fall of breathing, for warmth.

"He's still alive," he told me. "How long ago was he poisoned?"

"About ten hours now. He can't have much time left. According to what the High Priestess told me about the poison, he should already be dead."

"Listen to me. He may still have some of Nantilam's healing power inside of him."

"From when the Overlord tried to kill him?"

London nodded and hope surged within me. It had been the residual effect of Nantilam's healing abilities that had enabled the deputy captain to withstand the Overlord's torture.

"That's probably why his dying is prolonged," London continued. "With any luck, she may have miscalculated what it will take to kill him. But we need to help him fight, Alera."

"How?"

London retrieved his water flask and bedroll from his horse, handing them to me.

"Get as much water as possible into him, to dilute the toxin in his bloodstream, and we'll cover him with all the blankets and cloaks we have. He's fevered, so let's help his body sweat out some of the poison."

I began to cover Narian while London added wood to the fire. Then he removed his own cloak and tossed it to me.

"I'm going to gather some herbs that might help. I've learned a few things about Cokyrian compounds over the years, knowledge that I'm guessing the High Priestess would like to take away from me about now. You stay here and care for him as you have been doing. And, Alera, keep talking to him. He is strong and will fight to hear the sound of your voice—fight to come back to you."

"I think the High Priestess is in love with you, London."

"Just proves folly knows no limit."

I nodded, and London disappeared into the night in search of the herbs he had mentioned. After adding the deputy captain's cloak to the layers that covered Narian, I lifted his head, encouraging him to drink, talking to him about the future and the life we would have together.

London returned within fifteen minutes, then added the important parts of the plants to a second water flask, tipping the liquid into Narian's mouth.

"Any sign of improvement?" he asked.

I shook my head.

"Then we wait."

I examined London in the light of the fire. To my relief, he looked the same as always, ever young, his silver bangs partially obscuring his indigo eyes.

"Where have you been?" I asked.

"In Cokyri." He smirked. "Creating a diversion." He

paused, staring into the flames, then continued. "Prior to that I was in the mountains, helping Cannan and the rest in whatever fashion I could. Mostly trying to keep my head on my shoulders." He shrugged and ran a hand through his unruly hair. "I was a wanted man, you know, although not wanted in the way I would like to have been."

Had I been in better spirits, I would have laughed at his wry humor, but as it was I moved to his side to give him a kiss on the cheek.

"Thank you for coming. Thank you for finding us."

He nodded and put his arm around my shoulder. "Get some sleep, Alera. I'll wake you if things get worse."

I stayed where I was for several minutes, glad for his comfort, then lay down next to Narian, talking softly to him, wanting to be near him if he slipped away.

Morning broke, and I felt Narian stir. I sat up and stared at him, then at London, who was cooking some broth over the fire.

"He's going to make it," London said. "I told you he was strong."

Narian's eyes opened and his gaze fell on me. "Now this is a welcome sight," he rasped, and I kissed him. He looked over at London, then remarked, "And you're a surprising sight."

I helped Narian into a sitting position and London brought him the broth.

"I'll leave you two to talk," he said. "But we'll ride out in two hours' time. We need to keep moving in case the High Priestess sends guards to verify Narian's death. I don't want to be sipping tea when she fails to find a body. And we need to see who is in control of Hytanica this day."

CHAPTER 36

TRIBUTE

WHEN DUSK FELL, MY FAMILY, ALONG WITH WHAT appeared to be all the citizens of Hytanica, gathered at the military training field, where the Captain of the Guard's body had been placed on a litter above a stack of firewood, ready to be burned, his soul already committed to God by our priests. Soldiers had stood guard around the site all day, and people had been coming in a steady stream to pay their respects. Many of them had left tokens of esteem at the base of the pyre—weapons of various types, coins, embroidered hand-kerchiefs, trophies won in battle or at tournaments, military medals and insignia. Even small children came forward, lay-ing flowers, notes, toys and other items that had some special meaning to them among the other gifts. It made me both sad and proud when Celdrid walked forward and added his sword to the growing mound of mementos, the one that had origi-nally been given to Steldor by our father, to be passed on by Steldor to my brother. It was perhaps Celdrid's most coveted possession. He looked to Steldor as he came back to stand by us, and our cousin gave him a salute.

When all the individuals who wanted to do so had paid

homage to the captain, everyone stood in silence, the stillness of the large crowd itself a potent tribute. Grief could be a powerful, uniting force. Off to the side, separated from the masses, stood Steldor and Galen, their faces stoic, both wearing their military uniforms and holding lighted torches in preparation for setting the wood ablaze.

King Adrik finally broke the silence, stepping forward as the appropriate representative of the royal family to say a few words. Queen Alera had not yet returned from Cokyri, another source of worry for the subdued throng.

The former King cleared his throat and then began to speak, his deep voice easily carrying across the field.

"We come together to honor a man of duty and devotion, strength and compassion, courage and wisdom. A man who put kingdom and family before all else, but who included within his family every citizen in need. A man of unwavering allegiance who steadfastly served his King and Queen for over thirty years. A man whose legacy will live on in his son and in every life he touched. A man I was proud to name my Captain of the Guard and to call my friend. And who, while serving the kingdom he loved, made the ultimate sacrifice. Let us celebrate his life this night, and may his funeral pyre burn as a bright beacon of hope in the darkness, letting the entire Recorah River Valley know that Hytanica is free once more."

Cheers went up from the crowd, then Steldor and Galen stepped forward and touched their torches to the pitch-soaked firewood. With a roar, flames shot into the air, befitting the man who had lived with an equally fiery passion.

Mother took the younger children home after a half hour, for the November evening was cold. King Adrik and Queen Elissia took charge of Faramay, whose grief was too deep, too immobilizing, even for tears, and I was glad that Steldor would not have to be strong for his mother this night. He and Galen needed a chance to feel their own grief before being asked to comfort the rest of us.

Grayden and I, along with Dahnath, Drael and countless others, stayed to keep vigil, sitting on the hillside until the funeral blaze consumed itself, settling into cinders. In the early hours of the morning, a light, almost magical snow began to fall, and the moon's glow as it reflected off the ground brightened the scenery, making everything seem new.

My uncle's death had again set my family reeling. While we were accustomed to picking up pieces, sorting through rubble and holding on to memories, the brothers who had died had been the pillars of our family, strong leaders in Hytanica's military, and shining examples of all that was good and honorable within our kingdom. But this time, beneath the grieving, there was hope—hope that glowed like the remaining embers. This land was again our own, the Province Wall would be torn down, and we citizens would once more walk through the city gates without fear or suspicion.

I shivered, and Grayden put his arm around me, snuggling me close to him, and a melancholy smile played across my face. My uncle had promised he would find a husband for me who would meet my father's standards. And at what did the Captain of the Guard fail?

ALERA

CHAPTER 37

THE CAPTAIN
AND THE QUEEN

EVENING FELL AS WE REACHED THE OMINOUSLY closed gates of our city. Narian, London and I waited to see if anyone was on duty and, if someone were, whether the person would be Hytanican or Cokyrian. Impatient for an answer after our harrowing journey, London rode up to the gates and removed his sword, running the blade along the iron bars, creating quite a clatter, only to spin his horse around and repeat the action.

Narian and I looked at each other, uncertain what to do, then shifted our attention to the top of the wall where the scurrying of boots up a ladder signaled someone's approach. London brought his mount back beside mine and I gripped my reins, mouth dry. Soon we would know which side had been victorious.

A man appeared in the watchtower, staring down at us. Without a word, he turned to gaze at his comrades on the other side.

"The Queen!" he shouted, giving us our answer as to who was in charge. "The Queen has returned!"

The gates groaned as they were raised, and London, Narian and I rode forward to survey the aftermath of the battle. A low-lying haze, no doubt from scores of fires, clung to houses that were once more in shambles, the doors of pubs, shops and other businesses hung loosely on their hinges, and the thoroughfare was awash in reddish-brown dirt and ash. But despite the physical chaos, the city was quiet, seemingly abandoned, and I wondered if the battle had been so ferocious that few had survived. Fear seized my heart, robbing me of the strength to even urge my mare onward, but she followed instinctively behind the other horses.

It was when we approached the northern end of the city, nearer to the Bastion, that faces began to appear. From within the homes and shops that were still standing, my people stepped onto the street. They came from alleys and stumbled from piles of hay that had become makeshift beds, eager to see me. And almost every person I saw wore a tired but triumphant smile.

To my relief, no one tried to interfere with us as we rode— I had actually been worried about Narian's safety. We approached the Bastion—the palace once again, I supposed, feeling a buoyancy in my chest—and dismounted, leaving our horses untended outside the open courtyard gates. From what I could see, the home of my ancestors had not been harmed during the rebellion, our soldiers no doubt having protected it. All was, however, unnervingly still.

London left us, and I assisted Narian, who was still weak from his ordeal, up the courtyard path and through the front doors without encountering any servants or soldiers. We stopped in the Grand Entry to rest and let our eyes adjust to the heavy darkness, for no torches were lit, nor could the moonlight penetrate the stone. Though this was my home, the lack of light, the lack of noise and the lack of movement made it feel foreign, and I shivered.

With Narian leaning heavily on the banister, we walked up

the Grand Staircase, and I wished I had thought to bring the last of our food supplies from our saddlebags, for his stamina was waning. Upon reaching the second floor, we proceeded into the Royal Ballroom, crossing its expanse to step out onto the balcony, which afforded us the best view of the entire kingdom. But even from this vantage point, there was little sign of life. My eyes took in only one flickering light, no doubt generated by a single fire, its location suggesting the military training field. I couldn't help but think it was a funeral pyre.

With nothing to be done until morning, Narian and I went to my quarters. He sank onto the sofa in my parlor while I started a fire in the hearth, for the room was bone-jarringly cold. Satisfied with the strength of the blaze, I went to sit beside him, and we soon gave in to our exhaustion, letting sleep claim us.

The sound of voices and footsteps drew me to wakefulness in the early hours of the morning. I left my quarters, deciding to let Narian sleep, for this was a tonic he desperately needed, and hurried through the corridors to peer over the railing of the Grand Staircase. Below me in the entry hall, maids, cooks and other servants were arriving for work, accompanied by Hytanican guards. They were talking excitedly among themselves, oblivious to me. I continued to watch, embracing the utter simplicity of the scene as I debated whether I should proceed to the first floor or return to my parlor to check on Narian.

"Alera! You've returned!"

Miranna was hastening toward me, followed by Temerson and my parents. Though I had thought the palace completely vacant the previous night, my family had returned at some point to sleep in their quarters on the third floor. I hugged them one by one, exchanging happy greetings, then asked that they accompany me onto the ballroom's balcony, knowing our citizens would be gathering.

Despite the brightness of the sun, I shivered in the brisk November air, for I had not taken a cloak with me when I had left my parlor. As if by magic, one fell about my shoulders, and I knew without looking that Narian had joined us. His mere presence bolstered my courage and brought my thoughts into focus. I scanned the throng of eager Hytanicans, some of whom were gathered inside the Central Courtyard with more outside its walls, then raised my hands to quiet them. Taking a deep breath, I began to speak.

"Spread the word. Tell your families and friends. Let it be known across the Recorah River Valley that I am proud to be Queen of this *Kingdom* of Hytanica!"

Cheers exploded, rising and falling in waves, and I let myself enjoy the sights and sounds of victory for several minutes. Then I once more raised my hands to quell the crowd.

"Be it known that Commander Narian stands with me as a loyal citizen of Hytanica. Without him, I would not have been able to travel to Cokyri and safely return. And without him, I would not have been able to begin negotiations for lasting peace with the High Priestess. I believe a trade treaty that is fair for both of our countries will soon be signed. Regardless, we stand here now and forevermore as a people free of Cokyrian rule."

Jubilant shouts greeted these words, and I took Narian's hand in mine, raising it high into the air. The people did not know that we were in love. They did not know that we were bound to each other according to Cokyrian custom and would soon be joined in marriage under Hytanican law. But this was a step forward, and that was enough for now.

Out of the corner of my eye, I saw my mother appear at Narian's other side to likewise take his hand and hold it aloft in a show of support. When the rest of my family followed her lead, my father next to my mother, Miranna and Temerson at my side, tears spilled down my cheeks. I met Narian's mystified blue eyes and smiled, then gazed out at our people, a member of a united royal family, the man I loved among us.

When the noise had subsided, I addressed the sorrow that hid beneath the joy, for it was essential to pay tribute to those who had fought bravely and tirelessly, but had not lived to see this day.

"We all know the terrible price that was paid for our freedom. Remember those who died in the war. Honor them in your hearts, and join with me in honoring them with a memorial on the palace grounds. Let those who gave their lives for this kingdom never be forgotten." I paused, permitting a moment of silence for our lost loved ones, then finished, "Embrace your families. Return to your homes. And know that you go in peace."

This received perhaps the greatest response of anything I had said, and to the tumultuous cries of my tired but elated people, Narian and I reentered the palace.

"Father," I said before my family could disperse, "will you send for Steldor on my behalf? Ask him to come to the Queen's Drawing Room."

I did not want to meet my former husband in my study, which had been his office as King. Too many memories for both of us lurked within its walls. But I needed to lay the past to rest as soon as possible, and I needed to try to resolve matters between him and Narian.

My father nodded, but did not depart, and I looked questioningly at him.

"Alera, you have only just returned, and I don't know what, if any, news met you on your journey."

"Very little." I considered him, then my eyes grew wide

with fear. Perhaps I had been right about the nature of the single fire I had seen burning in the night. "Is Steldor…?"

"Steldor is alive and well. But Cannan. He… The captain died in the fighting."

My father's words were enough to knock the air from my lungs. With tears blurring my eyes, I glanced at the faces around me, needing someone to catch me lest I fall. Miranna took me into her arms while Narian stood helplessly by. I knew he would offer me comfort later, but our relationship was not yet known to all members of the present company, and this was not the time to declare it.

"I'm sorry, Alera," the former King continued, then he cleared his throat, suppressing his own emotions, for Cannan had been his friend as well as his faithful Captain of the Guard. "I'll send for Steldor."

He went down the steps of the Grand Staircase to the first floor, exiting through the front doors. Taking a mighty breath, I followed after him, leaving Narian and the rest of my family behind, intending to proceed to the Queen's Drawing Room. But I halted at the bottom of the flight of stairs, feeling an irresistible draw to the captain's office, for I wanted to believe I would stroll through its doors and find him there. Though I had heard my father's words, they had not yet penetrated my mind and my heart. How could Cannan be gone? I walked through the antechamber, answering the call.

The door to the captain's office was open, the room vacant but for the memories it held, and I staggered forward to sink into a chair. I closed my eyes, filled with a dreadful, yearning sorrow. Cannan had been such a powerful presence in the palace—in our lives—for so many years that it felt as though the heart of our kingdom had been taken from us. He had been Captain of the Guard for thirty years, and had not failed once in his duties; he had saved more lives than he had ever taken in war; and he had raised Steldor to be the man he was today—a bold, brave, sacrificing man. The son was his father in many, many ways.

I was startled out of my thoughts by a knock, and turned to see Steldor standing in the doorway. He glanced around the office, his expression composed, and yet it held a deep and immutable sorrow.

"I was told I would find you here," he said.

"How are you?" I asked, nervously twining my hands.

"As good as can be expected, I suppose."

"And Galen?"

"He has Tiersia."

I nodded, averting my gaze. I knew his answer had been an honest one, and had not been meant to hurt me, but sadness filled me. I wanted him to have someone—he deserved to have someone. Only that someone could not be me.

"Let's go to my drawing room," I suggested, for Cannan's office was not a place that would allow us to talk about the future, and that was what we needed to do. Steldor stepped aside, allowing me to exit first. He spent one last moment absorbing the look and feel of his father's office, then respectfully closed the door.

When we reached the Queen's Drawing Room at the front of the palace, we walked over to the bay window that granted a view of the Eastern Courtyard to talk, much as we had when he had told me of his plan to annul our marriage. But this time, I was the one who needed to speak. I slipped my hand into his, and he glanced at me in mild surprise.

"I'm sorry about your father's passing. I know how close you were to him. His strength and guidance will be missed by all. Despite our kingdom's glory, Hytanica is less without him."

Steldor did not respond, but gazed stoically out the window. Then he nodded twice and took a deep breath, reining in his emotions. Even now, with me, he was proud, not knowing that I wanted to hold him and let him cry, and that if he did, I would not, even for an instant, find him weak. He ran a hand through his dark hair and turned to face me, silently begging me to change the subject, and I obliged.

"And how is the rest of your family?"

"Amid our losses, there is also some good news. Shaselle has a suitor."

"Do you approve of her choice? After all, you are the man of the family now."

"There's no accounting for taste." He smirked, seeming thankful for my attempt at normalcy. "Actually, Lord Grayden is a good man—a man who met my father's approval and, I believe, would have met Baelic's. When the time is right, I expect a betrothal." Again a smile played across his features. "Now I just have to worry about the other three girls in the family."

I laughed, lacing my fingers through his when I felt he might pull away. I did not know how he would react to my coming proposal—and whether he would admit it or not, he needed some comfort now.

"Steldor," I said, my tone and demeanor once more serious, "when I see Galen, I will reinstate him as Sergeant at Arms."

"An excellent decision."

I nodded, then continued. "But our military needs to be reformed. It needs a strong and passionate leader, someone who will do Cannan and all of his work justice. I cannot think of anyone more suited to taking over the position of Captain of the Guard than you."

He did not immediately reply, but his eyes went to our hands, and he raised mine to his lips as he had so often done before.

"I don't know what to do, Alera," he said, and the wistful

tone of his voice confused me. "This is not what you want to hear, but to me, it doesn't seem there was a time before I loved you. And though I try to keep my distance from you... even now, you keep giving me reasons to love you more."

I had nothing to say, no notion of how to react. He hesitated, then stepped forward, pressing his mouth against mine in a sweet, gentle kiss.

"Now," he whispered, "you need to forget my words, and go to the man *you* love. As for me, I will be your Captain of the Guard and try to live up to my father's legacy. And that is all I will be."

He let go of my hand, then strode out the door, the warmth of his touch lingering longer than it should have.

Steldor moved into his father's office, but did not change a thing, I suspected both because of nostalgia and because he was so like Cannan. He immediately took control of the city, pulling together a semblance of the City Guard and the Palace Guard, which he then put under Galen's control. Men were also assigned to oversee the reconstruction work, a task that I prayed would be necessary for the last time. Perhaps most important, he permitted the citizenry—men, women and children alike—to tear down the Cokyrian wall, a highly symbolic act and an important step toward healing the wounds left by the war.

It was from Steldor that I received the final list of Hytanican casualties, all I needed to begin building the memorial I had in mind. It seemed only natural to entrust its supervision to my father, the former King, and to Temerson, who had lost his own father during the war. They would see to the removal of the scorched and bloodstained white stone path through the Central Courtyard, and would arrange to have stones from the Cokyrian wall laid in its place. The names of every man, woman and child who had fallen during the battles to try to protect our kingdom, and the subsequent ones to reclaim her, would be etched into the new path. In this way, anyone who walked from the courtyard gates to the front doors of the palace would be reminded of the sacrifices that had been made to preserve our way of life.

Narian, who was unsure of his place within the Hytanican hierarchy, was no longer using the strategy room as an office. In truth, he was, as much as possible, staying out of Steldor's way, not out of fear, but out of deference to Cannan. Since veneration for the legendary captain was one thing the two young men had in common, and since Cannan had clearly come to respect my betrothed, I hoped in time that Steldor and Narian would make peace with each other. While I had already decided upon the position Narian should assume, for he was ideally suited to it, I didn't want to push it on Steldor. I wanted him to come to his own conclusion that the former Cokyrian commander could offer much to Hytanica as head of its reinstated military school.

In the meantime, Narian was assisting me in preparing for peace talks with the High Priestess. Based on his advice, I had charged two imprisoned Cokyrian officers with delivering a message to Nantilam and sent them back to their homeland. It was reasonable to expect that a treaty conference could take place within the next month.

It was about a week later that I left my parlor to find my long-absent bodyguard leaning with his back against the wall, as though there were nothing unusual about his presence in the corridor outside my door.

"London!" I exclaimed. "I didn't expect to find you back on duty."

"I hope you're not disappointed, but I figured I might be

welcome here again," he said with a laugh. "I assume I'm no longer a war criminal."

"Quite the contrary—you are a war hero. But I haven't seen you since you escorted Narian and me back to the city. Where have you been all this time?"

"I had to take care of some other business." He shifted his weight and glanced downward, unable to conceal a grin. "There was another woman who deserved to know I was all right."

I immediately glanced to the third finger of his right hand, where rested a golden betrothal ring, and my smile lifted along with my heart.

"Tanda is a fortunate woman to have you."

In atypical form, London confessed his feelings toward her. "After so many years, I never thought I would be so blessed as to have her once more by my side."

Was this the effect Tanda had on my bodyguard, even dating back to the beginning of their courtship? Was her love the key to making him less guarded, more open, more relaxed? And did my love have the same effect on Narian?

Seeing London like this, happier than he had been in years, led me to a decision. I wasn't sure whether or not it was wise, but there had to be closure for Narian and his family.

After he had escorted me to my study, London departed to carry out his other duties, and it dawned on me that Steldor was now his commanding officer. While the notion seemed odd, I suspected that the new Captain of the Guard would rely on the more experienced man as an advisor, for London was the only Elite Guard who had survived the Cokyrian effort to decimate our military leaders.

While I had several tasks ahead of me this day, I took care of what I viewed as the most important first. Moving to sit behind my desk, I wrote a note to Koranis, Alantonya and their children to invite them to dine with my family at the palace. Narian had let go of his reservations with the High Priestess; it was time I did the same with my family.

Shortly before the dinner hour was at hand, I went to meet Narian in the quarters that had been mine as Crown Princess, where he had again taken up residence. London, who had rejoined me, knocked upon the door, and Narian bade me to enter. When I stepped into the parlor, however, he was not there. I crossed the floor and entered my former bedroom, the brisk breeze that greeted me telling me the balcony doors were open.

Narian was outside, leaning on the railing and gazing out over the city and the rolling hills beyond. I walked up behind him and placed my hands on his shoulders, resting my head upon his back.

"Will you miss the mountains?" I asked, and he twisted to face me, lightly holding me around the waist, my hands upon his chest.

"I can still see them, Alera, just from a different perspective. And I imagine I will eventually return for a visit."

I nodded and gave him a light kiss. "I want to show you something."

He looked curiously at me, and I removed my betrothal ring from the chain around my neck, placing it on my finger.

"I am no longer going to hide that we are in love."

He smiled and took me into his embrace, then we went to the King's Dining Hall on the second floor together. We entered at the perfect moment, holding hands, for everyone else had already arrived. All conversation stopped, but we calmly took chairs next to each other, ignoring the astounded expressions on the faces around us. With our attitudes unassailable, our guests glanced curiously at one another, hardly daring to ask.

It was my effervescent sister who finally spoke. "When is the wedding?"

At her candid question, our guests burst into animated conversation, and I leaned close to kiss Narian—entirely inappropriately—full on the lips.

Much was unknown to me in that moment—when the treaty with the High Priestess would be signed, when the citizenry would accept Narian, when our wedding would take place, what life would bring to me from here—but for once I was not hiding, from anyone or anything. Instead, I was staring into deep blue eyes filled with love, acceptance and hope. Deep blue eyes that would be mine to gaze into forever.

★ ★ ★ ★ ★

 ACKNOWLEDGMENTS

I would like to thank my family: Mom, Cara, Kendra and all my non-biological siblings, for supporting me always. Without you I would be a mess.

Fully earned thanks go to my agent, Kevan Lyon; my wonderful editor, Natashya Wilson; the ever-enthusiastic Lisa Wray, PR pro extraordinaire; Taryn Fagerness for building bridges to so many new readers in foreign countries; and everyone on the Harlequin TEEN team. My love and gratitude goes to you all.

I owe my followers on Twitter and my Facebook fan club many hugs and kisses for their loyalty and encouraging words. Readers are some of the best people in the world, and I'm honored that you all have given me a chance.

Peace, love and coffee until next time,
Cayla

QUESTIONS FOR DISCUSSION

1. In *Sacrifice,* Alera has turned from a queen in hiding (*Allegiance*) to Grand Provost, a leader who must be a bridge between two vastly different cultures. What kinds of decisions have you had to make for a greater good that were perhaps not what you would choose just for yourself? What do you think of Alera's choices?

2. London and Cannan both encourage Alera to take charge sooner. Why do you think Alera did not fully take charge at first, and how did she handle being a leader who had to work within Cokyrian control?

3. Shaselle offers a new point of view and perspective in the Legacy trilogy. How did her experience contrast and complement Alera's? Do you agree with the author's choice to tell this final story from two different points of view?

4. Even when conquered, Hytanica remains at heart a patriarchal society. Cokyri is matriarchal. How did the two different cultures clash in the story? What kinds of com-

promises on both sides might have helped the situation? What would be your ideal type of society to live in?

5. Was Saadi's death a shock to you? What do you think would have happened with his and Shaselle's relationship if he hadn't died? How would it have affected her relationship with Grayden? How did his death affect Shaselle's character?

6. What do you think future relations between Hytanica and Cokyri will be like? Do you believe the treaty that Alera and the High Priestess negotiate at the end will stand? Why or why not?

7. Although Hytanica regains independence, the government has changed from a ruling king to Alera as queen. What effect do you think this new leadership will have on Hytanica as a country? How might it affect the next generation of Hytanicans? Do you believe Alera will remain in power? Why or why not?

8. Alera and Shaselle's world is a fantasy kingdom and different from the modern world. But some elements are universal to every society. What similarities do you see between daily modern life and life in Hytanica? What goals and priorities are universal to any society? What makes us able to believe in and empathize with a fictional world?

Be sure to read the first two books in

THE LEGACY TRILOGY

"I recommend you get this book in your hands as soon as possible."
—*Teen Trend* magazine on *Legacy*

On the eve of her seventeenth birthday, Princess Alera of Hytanica faces an engagement to a man she cannot love. But she could never have imagined falling for her kingdom's sworn enemy. Amid court intrigue and looming war, Alera must fight the longings of her heart and take the crown she is destined to wear. But as magic, prophecy and danger swirl together, it will take more than courage to lead a kingdom.

Available wherever books are sold!

THE GODDESS TEST NOVELS

Available wherever books are sold!

A modern saga inspired by the Persephone myth.

Kate Winters's life hasn't been easy. She's battling with the upcoming death of her mother, and only a mysterious stranger called Henry is giving her hope. But he must be crazy, right? Because there is no way the god of the Underworld—Hades himself—is going to choose Kate to take the seven tests that might make her an immortal...and his wife. And even if she passes the tests, is there any hope for happiness with a war brewing between the gods?

Also available:
The Goddess Hunt, a digital-only novella.

www.HarlequinTEEN.com

HTGT2011TR6

The Clann

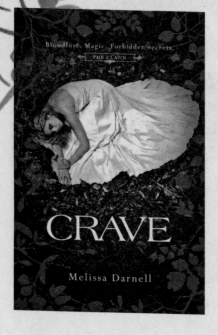

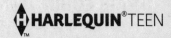